Dear Readers,

This series is especially meaningful to me because I was born at the beginning of World War Two, and remember bits and pieces of it quite well.

My father was away in the Army from almost the beginning, so my mother and I lived with my grandparents and my aunt, who was only sixteen when I was born to a twenty-year-old mother. A particularly vivid memory of that time is going to my grandad's allotment with him and pinching pea pods, which he pretended not to notice me eating. People were told to 'dig for victory' and he certainly did. My mother said we never went short of vegetables.

Like many other children with fathers serving overseas, I was photographed many times to keep him in touch. My favourite photo of myself is one taken in Falinge Park (aged four) with my mother. It's been used as my author photo in this book. I hope you like it. My husband says I still greet the world with that expression on my face!

My grandad was my surrogate father and he was a wonderful man, spending a lot of time with me. Every day we would cut the Rupert cartoon out of the newspaper and stick it into a scrapbook with paste made by him from flour and water. He taught me to read as we did this and of course, we were making a 'book'. It's no wonder I became a storyteller.

I took my first tottering steps into my Auntie Connie's arms and it's one of our family's joys that she's still alive and will turn ninety in 2015. She's much loved and we shall be having a big family party to celebrate!

I was four when the war ended, and I had never 'met' my father, or talked to him in any way, because he was posted to the Middle East, serving there for four years. All I'd seen were photos of a soldier. He saw me as a baby just before he left, but of course, I don't remember that.

When he was demobbed at the end of 1945, he arrived home in Rochdale late at night, so they woke me up to meet him. All I knew was that they'd brought a big loud soldier into my room and I didn't want to wake up, so I greeted him by sticking out my tongue. He never let me forget that!

My father had been a slender young man when he left, but was a big man when he returned, having grown into his six-foot prime. His size came as a big shock to my mother. And he was used to managing people, having reached the rank of Warrant Officer in the Army Medical Corps, so had a fairly powerful aura.

I still have a letter from my father to my mother in which he talks about his dreams for peacetime and for his beloved daughter's future. They wrote to one another every day of those four years, but when he came back they burned all but a few significant letters. I do wish they hadn't!

Researching the background to this series of stories was utterly fascinating. I remembered the war and the coming of peace with a child's eyes, but now I know a lot more about it with an adult's understanding.

People born decades later have told me that the years after the war were depressing. I think they're wrong. I've searched my memories and checked with my husband, who is a year older than me and also remembers those times clearly.

We both remember people being happy to be done with war, enjoying themselves in simple ways such as playing cards with friends or going to Saturday dances at various clubs – where I learned ballroom dancing as a child.

Best of all I was able to ask my aunt about the post-war

years because she was there, serving as a Wren for the final years. She says people were so glad to have the war and killing over that it was a happy time. They had something to look forward to and their sacrifices hadn't been in vain.

I hope my stories do justice to the era.

Anna Jacobs

ANNA
JACOBS

A Time to Remember

Rivenshaw: Book One

HODDER

First published in Great Britain in 2015
by Hodder & Stoughton
An Hachette UK company

First published in paperback in Great Britain in 2015

2

A CIP catalogue record for this title is available from the British Library

Paperback ISBN 978 1 444 78770 2
eBook ISBN 978 1 444 78769 6

Typeset in Plantin Light by Palimpsest Book Production Limited,
Falkirk, Stirlingshire

Printed and bound by Clays Ltd, St Ives plc

Hodder & Stoughton policy is to use papers that are natural, renewable and
recyclable products and made from wood grown in sustainable forests.
The logging and manufacturing processes are expected to conform to
the environmental regulations of the country of origin.

Hodder & Stoughton Ltd
Carmelite House
50 Victoria Embankment
London EC4Y 0DZ

www.hodder.co.uk

PART ONE

1941

I

Judith read the letter again, tears of pride welling in her eyes. She gave her eldest daughter a big hug. 'You're a clever girl, Kitty. I'm so very proud of you. To think of a daughter of mine going to Rivenshaw Girls' Grammar.'

The girl hugged her back, then pulled away, her smile fading. 'It's nice to know I could pass, Mum, but we both know Dad won't let me go to a posh private school.' She sniffed hard and when that didn't work, smeared away a tear with a damp, crumpled handkerchief.

'Your father isn't here much now he's in the Army. I'll make sure you do go.' Judith gave her daughter another hug. 'No one turns down the Esherwood Bequest.'

'But it'll cost a lot more than Baker Street Senior School, so how will you manage? There's the uniform to buy and other things too, like hockey sticks. And before the war, the girls went away on a *trip* every year.'

It might have been the moon, to hear Kitty speak of travelling anywhere. Judith felt guilty that she'd never had the money to take her children away from Rivenshaw, not even into Manchester. But things were going to change now. Oh, yes! Kitty wasn't going to miss this opportunity.

She tapped the letter. 'It says here that not only will your school fees be paid by the bequest but they'll buy your uniform and books. I don't see how your dad can complain about that.'

'He'll find something to moan about. He always does. Anyway, only posh people go to the Girls' Grammar. I wouldn't fit in.'

'That's changed. There are other girls sent there by the local authority these days. I was reading about it in the paper. The grammar school isn't just for fee-paying students now; it's for everyone who deserves a good education.'

Kitty gave a bitter laugh. 'Dad doesn't care about that. He wants me out earning as soon as possible so he can take my wages for his boozing.'

It upset Judith that her children's lives were being increasingly affected by Doug's failings as a father and earner. He'd changed greatly from the man she'd married, never had a kind word for anyone these days.

She knew what Kitty was doing – preparing for disappointment, that's what. Well, this time Judith wasn't going to let her daughter lose her big chance. 'You'll fit in anywhere if you're polite, friendly and work hard. I'll manage whatever you need apart from uniform and books.'

She saw Kitty's disbelieving look. They had been very poor before her husband joined the Army after a drunken spree. There had been days when she'd gone without food, apart from a slice of bread, so that her children could eat.

Now she got part of her husband's Army pay every week as well as what she earned, which made a big difference. There was talk of making women take up the jobs men had left. She didn't need much convincing; she needed the money too much.

Other women wept at their husbands going away; she'd been hard put not to dance for joy.

Kitty shook her head, not so easily convinced. 'There'll be bus fares, as well. It's right out at the other side of town.'

Judith sighed. The hard times before the war had marked

her eldest, made poor Kitty grow up too quickly. At eleven, the child should be thinking of skipping ropes, not worrying about money. 'I'm working at the mill now and I'm managing to put a bit aside, so we'll have enough money for the extras and the fares. We'll get by.'

Kitty snorted. 'When Dad comes back, he'll take your money and buy rounds of drinks for his friends at the pub.'

'Not if I hide the money. Things are going to change in this family, love.'

'Dad hasn't changed and he won't. When he comes home on leave, he still hits you.'

Judith hated the children to see that. She hesitated, nibbling her thumb, as she always did when thinking hard. 'Look, for the time being, we won't tell him about you getting the scholarship.'

'He'll find out.'

'Even if he does, he won't be here to stop you going to grammar school. It's a wonderful chance for you.'

Kitty looked at her sadly. 'You always look on the bright side, Mum. How do you manage that?'

Judith didn't tell her eldest child how hard it was to smile sometimes. Doug hadn't been like this when he was younger, or she'd not have married him. He'd been a bit rough, but fun. The fun stopped when she fell pregnant. And now, at thirty-two, she sometimes forgot the good times. They'd never really returned, after all.

Yet out of her increasingly unhappy marriage had come her three children, who were the joy of her life. They were such good children and deserved a chance for a better life. She'd do anything for them.

She turned as Ben and Gillian came rushing in, hungry after playing out with their friends. 'Come and hear how clever your sister is.'

When she'd finished telling them about the scholarship,

she untied her apron. 'Now, let's go and tell your grandpa. It'll make his day.'

She kept an eye on Ben, who could be a bit jealous of his older sister, but he was looking at Kitty as if he'd never seen her before. Judith took the opportunity to whisper to him: 'See what happens when you work hard at school. You and Gillian are just as clever as our Kitty. You could get a scholarship too, if you tried hard, Ben love.'

He frowned but for once didn't pull away when she hugged him. He was growing fast, her lad was. At nine, he was the tallest in his class. She reckoned he was going to be a big man like his father. She prayed he wouldn't have Doug's violent streak, though.

As they walked along the street, she wished her mother were still alive to hear the news. She'd have burst with pride.

On his next leave Doug was even more grumpy than usual. He complained that Judith was out at work when he arrived. As if she had any choice!

While she was making tea for the family, he complained about the new sergeant and living conditions at the camp, then asked her for money.

'I've not got anything to spare.'

'If you're out at work you must have. You should give some of your money to me now. It's criminal the way they take money out of my wages to send to you lot when you don't need it.'

In spite of her struggles, he got her purse out of her handbag and took all the coins it contained.

'What about the children? I have to feed them.'

'You've food in the pantry. They'll be all right.'

Fortunately, she'd hidden most of her money, but she resented losing even that small amount.

When the children came in from playing – they'd been

wise enough to stay outside – he complained about their noise. He hit Ben within the first half-hour, then smacked little Gillian's cheek when she tripped over and made him splash hot tea over his hand.

Kitty was still at her friend's house down the street. After she came home, she ate her meal quickly then said she had homework to do and escaped into the front room. This was furnished only with an old table and rickety chairs Judith had bought second-hand for the children to do homework on.

Kitty didn't come back into the kitchen till her dad went to the pub, then they all listened to the radio. It was an old set someone had given them and very crackly, but it was wonderful to be able to listen to what was going on in the world.

Judith was tired after a hard day's work, but she stayed up after the children had gone to bed, in case Doug was still in a bad mood when he came home. She didn't want to face him in bed anyway, or it might lead to something else.

She couldn't afford to have another child, not with what she was planning. Though actually, her husband hadn't seemed to want her in that way for months. And thank goodness for small mercies.

Just after closing time the front door banged open and Doug stormed into the kitchen. 'Why didn't you tell me about our Kitty getting that scholarship?' he yelled, clutching a chair back to steady himself.

'I was going to, only you went straight out to the pub.'

'Think I'm a fool? You didn't tell me because you were hoping I wouldn't find out.'

'Yes, I was. Because I knew you'd not be pleased and proud like any other father.'

'I'm not pleased. I won't have a daughter of mine going to a fancy school and looking down her nose at me.'

Judith folded her arms. 'If you'd stop getting drunk and fighting, she'd have no reason to look down her nose at you. You used to be a good worker till the booze got you. Anyway, she's going to the grammar school, and that's that.'

He gave her a slow, superior smile. 'No, she isn't. The lads at the pub were telling me what to do. I can write to the Esherwood Trust and refuse my permission. She won't be allowed to take up the scholarship without it. The father is the one who has the say about things like that. *Head of the household* still means something, you know.'

Judith stared at him in shock. This was even worse than she'd feared. Was what he said correct? 'What sort of man are you, trying to deny your daughter this chance?'

'A working man and proud of it. I know where me and my family belong, and that's with our own sort. So don't try to go against me or you'll regret it. *My* daughter isn't going to a posh school. She's going out to work as soon as the damned government will let her, then she can pay me back for what she's cost me to bring up. Now, stop nagging and make me a cup of cocoa.'

Judith did as he'd ordered, though normally she'd have told him to make it himself, even if he did thump her. As he relaxed in front of the fire, she tackled him again. 'Doug, please won't you reconsider and—'

'*Please won't you reconsider*!' he mimicked in a silly high voice. 'You read too many books, you do, then spout fancy words at me. No, I bloody well won't reconsider. I'm the master in this house and don't you forget it.'

'Some master you are, taking your bad temper out on the children. Fancy hitting a seven-year-old child like our Gillian and then spoiling Kitty's big chance.'

Upon which he thumped his wife as well, knocking her to the floor and yelling, 'Shut up, you nagging bitch! Shut— bloody— up! It's a waste of time educating girls. They'll only marry and have children. Look at what all that reading did to you. Made you a know-it-all, that's what. You're not fit to be a wife, you aren't. You don't do anything to please a man. You even dress like a dowdy old hag.'

She stayed on the floor as he stared at her. Then he cursed and went up to bed.

She spent the night on the sofa, and glad to.

She wasn't going to spend her life being knocked around. She couldn't do anything yet about leaving him, though, not till she had some money saved. She'd ask to work full-time at the factory from now on. Kitty could keep an eye on Gillian after school and on Saturdays.

Judith wished she had brothers and sisters, cousins, someone to turn to, but her father wasn't much use, and the last cousin of her own age was in the Army. His wife was living down south with her family. It was really hard sometimes to manage on her own with three children.

The next day was a Saturday and Judith didn't have to go to work, though she would have to once she started full-time.

She got ready to go shopping. Doug was still in bed and didn't stir when she crept into the bedroom for clean clothes. He was lying on the bed, fully dressed. Lazy devil!

She made no attempt to hide the bruise on her face, as she had done in the past, and as she got out her shopping bag, the children stared at her in puzzlement.

'Shall I fetch your make-up, Mam?' Kitty asked.

'No, thank you. My face is fine as it is.'

'But it shows where Dad hit you.'

'Then it'll just have to show, won't it?'

'When I'm a man, I'll hit him for thumping you,' Ben muttered.

'Thanks, love, but I don't want you hitting anybody,' she

said quietly. 'Don't grow up like him, Ben love, or you'll break my heart.'

He nodded and put one arm round Gillian's shoulders. She'd noticed before that he tried to protect his little sister whenever their father was home.

'Why don't you children walk over to see Grandad?'

They nodded. They knew why she was saying that. To get them out of the house.

Head held high, Judith walked a little way with the children, to the far end of the group of terraced houses people called Lower Parklea.

Unless it was raining, they always took the long way round to their grandad's, going along the edge of Parson's Mead. It was a small park but everyone enjoyed having some greenery and open space nearby, and they were grateful to the Eshers, who'd given the park to the town nearly a hundred years ago.

As she went into Timmins Corner Store, Judith could feel people staring at her. She intended to show the world what Doug was like from now on, so she'd come here to buy a pound of potatoes she didn't need and would take her time about it too.

When Mrs Timmins stared at her face, Judith said, 'Doug's home.'

'You usually try to cover the bruises up.'

She could feel her face going hot. Had it been that obvious? Of course it had. She'd been fooling herself. 'Well, I'm not bothering to hide it any more. Gillian has a bad bruise on one arm, too.'

'Eh, love. He didn't hit that little lass as well?'

She nodded.

'What some women have to put up with!' Mrs Timmins paused, holding the scale of potatoes above Judith's sacking bag. 'My husband says your Doug's upset about Kitty winning the scholarship. He was grumbling about it in the pub last night. You'd think he'd be proud.'

'He says he's not letting her go to the grammar school.'

'Eh, that's mean, that is.'

Judith tried to blink away her tears, but some escaped. As she fumbled in one pocket after another for her missing handkerchief, Mrs Timmins came out from behind the counter and pushed one into her hand.

'Here. Use this, love.'

'Thanks. I'll wash it and give it back.'

'No, keep it. I've got plenty.' She changed the subject. 'What are you going to do about sheltering from bombs?'

'Doug says we can hide under the stairs.'

'You can come into our shelter, if it gets bad round here like it has in London.'

'Thank you. We've been lucky here. Most of the bombers head for Manchester.'

As Judith walked home, she felt even more determined to follow her plan. Her girls weren't going to grow up being beaten, and her son wasn't going into a lowly job, either. She'd do whatever she had to do and *make* it happen.

Doug was out when she got back and he didn't come home till the pubs closed that night. Judith didn't care where he'd been, as long as he wasn't at home.

He announced his arrival by yelling, 'What did you tell Mrs Timmins, you bitch?'

'I didn't tell her anything.' Judith pointed to the bruise on her face. 'This spoke for me. Anyway, people already know what you're like. I haven't been able to hide all the bruises you've given me over the years.'

He breathed deeply, but didn't hit her again. 'I'm going to bed.' He turned to say, 'I don't want you in my bed any more, you know. Who'd want to screw a scraggy old bitch like you when there are other women eager to please a soldier? Yes, eager and willing. Women as aren't so scraggy where it counts.' He touched his chest suggestively then went upstairs.

She tried not to let her shock at this boast show. She got her blanket, put out the light and curled up on the old sofa.

But in the dark, tears flowed. She'd guessed Doug was finding his pleasure elsewhere when he stopped taking her in bed. Now it was out in the open, that settled it. When he came home, she'd sleep down here.

And as soon as the war was over, she was leaving him. They said in the papers the fighting would last a year or two more. That'd give her time to save up and make plans.

Next morning, Doug lay in bed till eleven o'clock then got up and raided the pantry. He ate the whole of the family's meat ration and most of the bread.

'The children will have to go without meat for days if you take it all,' she protested. 'Take my share but leave theirs, for pity's sake.'

'I'm the man of the house and I'm a soldier. I *need* good red meat to keep up my strength so that I can defend my country.' He cleared his plate with a challenging expression, cramming the meat into his mouth and chewing it noisily.

Pig! she thought but kept her lips firmly pressed together. She sighed with relief as he went out. He didn't say where he was going and she didn't care. She'd have to beg some bones from the butcher's and make up a broth with potatoes and barley, but it wouldn't be the same without meat.

When Doug came home he looked round for his kitbag, which she usually left ready by the door. 'Haven't you packed for me yet?'

'I don't pack bags for people who thump me.'

He glared at her so fiercely, fists bunching, that she thought he was going to hit her again.

'You're no use for anything, you aren't. Where are my clean clothes?'

'I didn't have time to do any washing. I was too busy comforting the children for being thumped and bathing my own face. Besides, they do the washing for you at the camp. Why should I do it?'

He raised his fist again, and she turned the other cheek towards him. 'Go on! Black my other eye. Let everyone in the street know what you're like.'

He didn't take her up on this invitation, but he did give her a shove that sent her staggering across the room to sprawl on the hearthrug. 'You're not worth the effort. But I won't forget to write to the Education Department about our Kitty. She's *not* going to that fancy school.'

Judith got up and stood by the fireplace, wishing there were a fire to give her comfort, but it was warm enough to go without, so she was letting the coal rations pile up for the winter. Arms folded, she let him rant on as he packed his own bag. She watched in disgust as he crammed the dirty, sweaty clothes in with the few clean ones.

He'd never been this bad before. What had got into him? Was it those friends of his from the pub? Word was they were into black market stuff and kept flashing their money. Was he jealous? Or was it his new mates in the Army? She had a sudden thought: some soldiers pinched Army stuff to sell on the black market. She hoped Doug wasn't doing that, but he certainly seemed to have enough money to buy booze.

She didn't dare ask him, hardly dared move until she'd seen him leave the house.

She didn't go as far as wishing him dead, but if he did get killed, she'd not grieve, she admitted to herself.

2

On the Monday, Judith sent word to work that she had a family emergency and would be late in. Packing and labelling boxes of uniforms and mopping the floor could be done by anyone. Before she went out, she put her sheets to soak, because they smelled of Doug's sweat. He hadn't washed himself properly this weekend, not once, just scrubbed his hands and face and had a shave.

She got out her best clothes. She was going to ask the vicar for help.

When she explained her dilemma about her daughter's scholarship, Mr Saunders shook his head, looking grave.

'The man is the head of the household, Mrs Crossley.'

'Even if he's a drunkard who's spoiling his daughter's best chance in life? Not to mention doing this to me.' She pointed to her cheek.

'My good woman, you mustn't speak so harshly of your husband. Whatever his faults – and who among us is without them? – it is for the man to make such decisions and for you to respect them. When you got married, you promised to love, honour and obey your husband. Do that now and remember that the man always knows best.'

'Doug doesn't know best and he doesn't care two hoots about the children.' She paused and looked at Mr Saunders pleadingly. 'Won't you at least speak to him next time he comes home? For Kitty's sake?'

'I cannot go against God's natural law.'

'Then you're as bad as he is.'

As she stormed out of the little room where the vicar saw the poorer members of his congregation, she vowed that would be the last time she came into this church, much as she enjoyed the beauty of the building and the choir's singing.

She was so upset she couldn't hold back the tears, so went through the back alleys to Parson's Mead. There was a bench she could sit on near the top of the sloping piece of land. It was out of sight of the street, under some trees. It used to look across an expanse of grass to the flowerbeds in the centre, but of course the grass and flowers had all been dug up, so that people could plant vegetables for the war effort.

Old Mr Jennings was in charge of the allotments they'd created for people in nearby terraces. She hadn't asked for one because she simply didn't have the time to tend it. She did chat to the old man sometimes and admire his garden.

Mr Jennings had even got her and the children running out with a shovel if a passing horse left some dung behind. They had a rule in the street that if the droppings were deposited outside your house, they belonged to you. They took the dung to him in a rusty old bucket and in return he gave them vegetables now and then.

She made it to the bench without meeting anyone, thank goodness. Only when she was sitting half-hidden in the dappled shade did she let the tears spill out. It was all so unfair! She began to weep, something she didn't do in front of the kids. As her sobs died down, she fumbled for her handkerchief but then remembered that she'd given it to Gillian this morning.

Someone said quietly, 'Here, take this.'

For the second time that week she used a borrowed hand-kerchief as she struggled to control her emotions.

'May I sit down?'

She nodded and looked at him for the first time. He was in uniform, an officer. His face looked vaguely familiar but she couldn't quite place him.

'You're Mrs Crossley, aren't you? I've seen you in church. It was your daughter who was awarded the Esherwood Bequest this year. My father was telling me about it.'

The penny dropped. 'You're young Mr Esher.'

'Not that young now.' He held out one hand. 'Maynard Esher at your service, Mayne to my friends. The War Office has requisitioned our house, so my family is living in the Dower House.' He gestured towards the narrowest and highest part of Parson's Mead. 'Since I'm no longer allowed in the grounds of Esherwood, I walk round the Mead sometimes. I like to sit on this bench, too.'

As if she didn't know that the War Department had taken over Esherwood and the family had had to move out. People in Lower Parklea kept an eye on all the posh folk who lived round the upper end of Parson's Mead. 'I'm Judith Crossley.'

He held out his hand and she shook it, conscious of how damp hers was, how red her face must be, how the bruise must show.

'Did you fall and hurt yourself?'

She shook her head, her hand going up instinctively to cover the bruise. 'My husband was . . . angry.'

'*What*? He hit you?'

For a moment the bitterness spilled out. 'It doesn't matter. I'm used to it.'

'You shouldn't have to get used to being beaten.'

'He's gone back to the Army camp now. He won't be home for weeks.' She felt a bit embarrassed because Mr Esher looked very smart and even in her best clothes, she didn't. Hers were nearly threadbare. At least he hadn't met her in her working clothes, with her headscarf and overall, ready to go to the mill.

That reminded her of Kitty. If she didn't find some way to help her wonderful, clever daughter, Kitty would be sentenced to a similar life to hers, working hard at boring jobs for low pay. Another tear escaped.

'Tell me what's upsetting you. You know what they say. A trouble shared . . . '

His expression was so kind, it all tumbled out: about the scholarship, how Doug was going to write a letter to the education people, forbidding his daughter to take up the Bequest.

'I went to see the vicar, to ask his help. He says he can't interfere between husband and wife, and I should do as Doug tells me,' she finished. 'I don't know where to turn next for help.'

Mayne looked furious. 'It's the sort of thing Saunders would say! I only go to his church to please my mother. I can't stand the man. He bullies his own wife, treats her like his personal slave. Hmm. I wonder . . . Let me think.'

She waited. Was it possible he could help them? Everyone knew his family weren't as rich as they used to be, but maybe they still had some influence.

'I have an idea, Mrs Crossley. Would you allow me to help?'

She didn't hesitate. 'Yes. I'd be very grateful.'

'I can't guarantee anything, mind.'

She shrugged and waited. Who could guarantee anything in this life?

'I'm going to tell my father about this and ask him to speak to the lawyer who handles the Bequest.'

'Why would your father care?'

'When he hears that someone is trying to prevent an intelligent child from taking up this year's Esherwood Bequest, my father will throw a fit. He's a scholar and values two things in life more than anything else: documenting the history of this part of Lancashire, and providing a good education for intelligent children. Father is inordinately proud of what our family has done for the town.'

'You must be missing living in your lovely home.'

'We're not the only family who's been turned out. The government's requisitioned a lot of big houses. We'll probably have to sell Esherwood after the war. Or if we manage to hang on to it for a while, we'll have to sell when my father dies.'

That surprised her. 'Why would you sell it?'

'Death duties have hit the family hard this century. My father lost two older brothers in the Great War, one after the other. The family has to pay death duties on Esherwood each time it changes hands.'

'Then how can your family afford to give people the scholarships?'

'There's a trust fund for that and the money is not allowed to be used for anything else.'

'I see.' She repeated the word *inordinately* in her head. She'd look it up when she got home. She liked learning new words.

'What is she like, this Kitty of yours?' he asked.

'Tall for her age, with dark hair and green eyes. She'll be pretty when she grows into her face. At the moment it's too old for her body.'

'In other words, she looks like her mother.'

'People say that. But she's much cleverer than me.'

'She had to get her brains from someone and your husband doesn't sound very clever.'

That made Judith think. She knew she wasn't stupid but

as to clever . . . no one had ever suggested that before. 'I . . . do like to learn. I'm so grateful for the public library. I'd better get back to work now.'

'I meant it about helping you.' He glanced at his wrist-watch. 'No time like the present. Could you come and see my father this afternoon, if necessary?'

'Oh. I've already asked for time off this morning. I can't afford to lose a whole day's pay. They dock us for each hour or part of hour away from the job, you see.'

'What time do you finish work?'

'Six o'clock, seven sometimes.'

'Then if Father wants to see you, I'll come to fetch you about seven-thirty. Would that be all right? It'll give you time to prepare tea for your family.'

A bitter laugh escaped her. 'There's only bread and jam. Doug ate all the meat.' She clapped a hand to her mouth. She hadn't meant to tell anyone that.

Mr Esher shook his head as if annoyed but didn't comment. 'Where do you live?'

'Leigh Street, number seven. It's that short street, three streets back from the park.' She watched him stride off up the narrow path between the beds of vegetables. He was a fine-looking man, but it was his kindness she valued most. He'd made her feel better today even if he couldn't change what Doug was doing.

But what if his father could get Kitty her chance? It was worth a try, anyway.

Of course, Mr Esher had walked off towards the posh end of Parson's Mead. She watched till he'd disappeared from sight, admiring his tall, upright figure, then turned in the opposite direction and headed down the gentle slope towards the poorer terraces.

Here, ten narrow streets were crowded together near the longest side of Parson's Mead, which was shaped like a pyramid with the point cut off. Only the Eshers lived at the narrow end.

She and her family didn't live in one of the better terraces that actually overlooked the park. The rents of those were higher, far beyond their reach.

She'd struggled for years to pay the rent on this house near the park, and even Doug wanted to stay here. She and the children could walk round the corner whenever they could snatch a minute and get out into the lovely open space where the air always seemed fresher. You could even walk across Parson's Mead at night, because it wasn't fenced off like the big park on the other side of Rivenshaw, whose huge iron gates were locked at dusk every day. A few times, when she was upset, she'd gone out and walked in the moonlight, leaving Doug and the children sleeping.

It always lifted her spirits to be among greenery. Before the war, if the weather was fine, there had been groups of children throwing balls, playing cricket or football on the grass. Now, most of the grass had gone and vegetables were being grown all over the meadow. *Dig for Victory*, the posters said and people were doing just that.

But children would play there again after the war ended, when Britain and its allies had beaten Hitler and Mussolini – and anyone else who was wicked enough to try to take over the world and kill people.

You had to believe that.

Mayne arrived home just as his mother was going out. Since this leave was unexpected, she gave him a quick kiss, a rare caress from her, and went back into the house, calling for his father to come and see the lovely surprise she'd found on the doorstep.

His father shouted down from his study that he'd join them in ten minutes and for once kept his word.

As they sat over tea and biscuits, Mayne first assured his mother that he was well, then told them about his meeting with Mrs Crossley in Parson's Mead.

His mother merely grimaced, but his father's reaction was as he'd predicted. 'I won't *allow* the fellow to do that. It's outrageous, stopping an intelligent child from getting an education.'

'Can you stop Crossley?'

'Oh, I think our lawyer will find a way.'

'Could we make the arrangements this afternoon, do you think? I've only got forty-eight hours' leave, so I'd like to sort something out before I go back to camp.' It wasn't often his father and he were in agreement about something.

'I'll telephone Lionel's rooms. I'm sure he'll fit us in. He manages the trust, after all.'

'You've still got the phone, then?' Mayne teased his mother while his father made the call. Last time he'd come home, there had been some problem about the phone bill not being paid and it had been temporarily cut off.

'Oh, that was just a mix-up. I thought your father had paid it and he thought I had.'

Mayne smiled. His father could get very vague when he was lost in his studies of Tudor Lancashire, a passion Mayne didn't share and which seemed to cost a lot of money for rare research books. His father talked about publishing his research one day but had never made any attempt to do so that Mayne knew of.

His father came back smiling. 'Lionel can see us in half an hour.'

Fifteen minutes later the two men walked briskly into town and entered the rooms of Lloyd and Graveston. They were shown straight into Lionel Lloyd's office.

Mayne watched in amusement as the two older men exclaimed about the effrontery of Doug Crossley.

'But can you stop him?' he asked, when they had calmed down a little.

'Oh, I think so,' Lionel said. 'Give my clerk all the details you have and leave it with me. I have a few connections in his regiment.'

'You see? We Eshers still have the standing in the community to do such things,' his father said as they walked back. 'Never forget that.'

Mayne didn't respond. What good was their so-called standing going to be if he had to sell his home when his father died? Anyway, he mixed with all sorts of people in the Army and had learned to value personal qualities more than accidents of birth. Times were changing rapidly.

When they got home, there was a telegram summoning Mayne back to his regiment urgently.

With a sigh he got ready to leave, wishing he could tell Mrs Crossley that he'd set matters in train for her daughter to take up the scholarship. He'd have liked to bring a smile to her face.

The poor woman would be quite pretty without that dreadful bruise, and without the careworn expression. Why had she married such a brute?

When someone knocked on the front door that evening, Judith opened it and was surprised to find old Mr Esher lifting his hat to her, not his son.

'Could you spare me a moment, Mrs Crossley?'

'Of course. Do come in.' She'd been going to set out their simple tea, but this might be important. She didn't let herself hope for too much, but gestured to Mr Esher to come into the part-furnished front room. They never sat in here normally, but the kitchen was in a mess.

'I'm sorry, Mr Esher. We haven't got a proper parlour so I hope you don't mind sitting here. It's where the children do their homework.' Ben had started coming in here more often and seemed to be working harder since his sister had been offered the scholarship.

'That, Mrs Crossley, is a much better use for this room than filling it with furniture that is rarely sat upon and ornaments that need dusting. Do sit down. This isn't a social call.'

She gestured to a chair but he waited till she'd seated herself before taking it.

'My son told me about your problem with the scholarship.'

She sighed. What could she say?

'I came to tell you that my lawyer is taking the matter in hand. He's going to contact your husband's commanding officer, whom he knows from school, and see what can be done. I'll let you know as soon as we hear. I expect to be successful in ensuring that your daughter takes up the girls' scholarship this year. The Esher name still means something, you know, and soldiers don't disobey their commanding officers.'

'Thank you, Mr Esher. I can't tell you how grateful I am.'

Judith was thoughtful as she closed the front door behind him. Old Mr Esher wasn't at all like his son; he was rather distant in manner as if he knew he was superior and could afford to be kind. His son hadn't been at all like that. However, she'd put up with any amount of patronising behaviour if it helped Kitty.

Mr Esher came back a few days later, again in the evening.

'Your husband has been informed by his commanding officer that if he doesn't allow your daughter to go to the girls' grammar school, my lawyer will take the matter before the magistrate and obtain an order requiring him to give his permission.'

'And Doug's agreed to that?'

'Your husband has signed a letter giving permission. It was witnessed by his captain and will be sent to the trust.

So there is now no reason why your daughter should not obtain a proper education.'

Tears filled Judith's eyes. 'I can't tell you how grateful I am for your help.' Doug would be furious but she didn't care if he beat her up every day for a week, because Kitty was going to grammar school.

Mr Esher turned to leave, then snapped his fingers. 'I nearly forgot. My wife says that given the shortage of new clothes, because of rationing, the school has set up a second-hand clothing exchange. She will be happy to accompany you there to acquire the necessary garments and shoes for your daughter.' He looked round and added, 'The trust will, of course, pay for the uniform.'

'That's very kind of your wife. And we're grateful to the trust. Very.'

He nodded as if this was only his due. 'The school is a rather rambling building and it's easy to get lost, especially now that part of it is being used for other purposes. But since my wife is on the Board of Governors, she knows exactly what will be needed.'

'I'd welcome Mrs Esher's help. You and your family have been very kind.'

'It's our duty to help you. Education is as important for girls as for boys. The hand that rocks the cradle and all that, you know.'

He stood up. 'Now, if you could come up to the Dower House at nine o'clock tomorrow morning, my wife will take you to the school in the car they always send for her. Oh, and I've spoken to the factory manager, who will be happy to allow you the time off as long as you go straight back to work afterwards.'

When he'd gone, Judith sat down in the front room because her legs felt suddenly wobbly. She'd given up hope of getting Kitty into the grammar school. And now . . .

'Thank you, Maynard Esher,' she said aloud. Her daughter was going to Rivenshaw Grammar School for Girls, she really was. Judith stood up and twirled round a few times in sheer happiness.

Wait till she told Kitty. She ran to the front door and saw the children waiting a short way along the street. She beckoned to them to come in.

A week later, when Judith received a postcard from her husband, she cried for sheer relief. It was the sort of card the Army gave out to men going overseas for them to send home. Doug had never once written her a proper letter since he joined the Army, only sent the occasional postcard like this one, to indicate a change in his circumstances or a new posting. He'd been promoted to lance-corporal at one stage, then demoted for brawling. Typical!

Doug had filled in the gaps on the printed card with ticks and crosses, and had scrawled a message in the space provided at the bottom.

I won't forget what you done. You're wasting your time. As soon as this war is over and I'm out of the Army, she's leaving that school.

Judith felt sick to the stomach at this spite. And she knew that underneath his words was a very serious threat to her.

She reread the line that said: *Destination – Middle East.* That cheered her up all right. He'd be gone for a long time, several months at least, even a year if she was lucky. And maybe the edge would have gone off his anger by then.

No, it wouldn't. He was good at holding grudges.

But at least she and the children would be safe for a while. And by the time he came back to England, she'd have worked out a way to continue defying him about Kitty's education. She might even ask the Eshers' advice about that, too. She'd do anything to keep her girl at grammar school, Ben and Gillian too when their time came.

Kitty had such a bright, lively mind. She was a pleasure to have around when her father wasn't home. She could make everyone laugh or get them singing the old songs. Maybe now they could even afford a better radio. The old one wasn't working properly. It made such a difference to their daily lives, a radio did.

Judith looked at herself in the mirror as she mopped her eyes. Dare she leave her husband? It was considered a shocking thing for a woman to do. People would think the worst of her.

But her children would be safe.

PART TWO
1945

3

Judith watched the final events of the war in Europe unfold, reading newspapers avidly, mostly yesterday's papers that she borrowed from Mrs Needham next door. Her neighbour's son was serving in the Army and though Mrs Needham was a capable woman, she had lost one son already and her fear for her other one seemed to hang around her like a cloud.

Judith listened to the radio whenever she could, feeling both joy about the end of the war and fear about what would happen to her family then. Unlike Mrs Needham, she wanted the Army to keep her man away.

She'd been given nearly four years' grace, with Doug stationed in the Middle East the whole time, so she'd stayed in this house. Now she had to get ready to leave before he returned, even though she hated the thought of leaving her home, which was now a lot more comfortable than it had been when he had been around.

In spite of the rationing and restrictions of the war years, and her own need to save money, she'd picked up a few pieces of decent furniture second-hand and made the house into a real home.

No one had broken anything in a fit of rage, and the children were old enough to appreciate what she'd done.

Lots of things were changing. Britain had had the 'dim out' in operation since September last year, and now they didn't have to black out all lights at night, just make sure nothing indoors could be seen clearly from outside. When the more relaxed rules were put in place, Judith had immediately put up the curtains someone had given her, which she'd mended carefully. The front room looked so nice now.

As long ago as last December, lighting on buses and trains had been allowed again. Not that Judith ever travelled anywhere on them, because feet were cheaper than bus fares. But still, it was a sign of normal life returning and as she walked home from work, she liked to see a bus go past her all lit up with the passengers chatting to one another.

So normal, so blessedly normal.

The winter had been bitterly cold, but somehow hope kept you going, hope that this would be the last winter of the war.

It took longer than people expected for peace to be declared, however, and it came in a series of steps, which reminded Judith of the lines of standing dominoes the children had made when they were little. One domino would fall and knock down the next, and the next, till they had all tumbled one after the other. It seemed as if events were leading them towards peace in the same way.

It wasn't until late April that the blackout was totally abolished and everyone went outside after dark to look at the lights showing down the streets.

Gillian clutched her mother's hand, even at eleven, whispering, 'It feels strange, doesn't it, to have the lights on fully? Are you sure it's safe, Mum?'

'Perfectly safe, my darling. This is how it used to be.'

One of the smaller children from a few houses away got very upset by the lights, and began screaming for them to be turned off quickly. It was a while before he could be comforted and reassured.

The day after the blackout ceased, the Americans met up

with Russia, dividing Germany in two. That seemed a very important step to Judith. Peace had to be close now, really close!

Everywhere you went there was speculation as to exactly when peace would be declared and people at work ran little sweepstakes about which day and hour the official announcement would be made.

'I'm getting out my bunting,' one of Judith's fellow workers said. 'I've had it packed away carefully, ready to pull out when the war ended. And if they don't make an announcement soon, that bunting's going up, whatever anyone says. We all know the war's over.'

'Not quite,' the man next to her said. 'Hitler's still alive, isn't he? It won't be over for me till that monster is dead.'

'And they're still fighting in the Far East,' a woman chimed in. 'Don't forget about that.'

At the end of April, three important things happened, though people didn't hear about them straight away. When she did hear the news, Judith could see the rest of the line of dominoes falling, falling . . .

Benito Mussolini was executed in Milan by Italian partisans.

Some people deplored the lawless way this had happened; others cheered.

On the first of May it was announced that Hitler and Eva Braun had committed suicide the previous day.

'Is it true?' Mrs Timmins at the shop asked in her breathless, childish voice. 'Can it really be true that the monster is dead?'

'It must be,' old Mr Sharp said. 'It's an official announcement. I say good riddance to him and his fancy woman. He's saved our side the job of executing him, at least.' He shook hands with Judith and then with Mrs Timmins, before going off to see what people were saying in the town centre.

On the evening of May 2nd, BBC radio programmes were interrupted for the announcement that the German forces in Italy had surrendered to the Allies.

'It won't be long!' Ben crowed. 'We've beaten them, Mum. I knew we would.'

And that means it won't be long till your father comes home, Judith thought. She caught Kitty's worried glance and knew her elder daughter was thinking the same thing.

But it was as if Judith was frozen and could only wait for the war to end before it would feel right to leave this house. She told herself she should start making preparations, but by the time she got home from work each evening, she was so tired it was all she could do to feed the children, do any bits of washing or cleaning, then fall into her own bed.

That night, just as she was about to switch off the radio and go to bed, there was a sudden announcement: all German troops in Denmark had surrendered.

Doors opened down the street, lights streamed out and people shouted the news to one another.

Ben came pounding down the stairs in the pyjamas that were getting too short for him to ask what was going on.

When Judith told him, he put on his raincoat and went out to join his pals.

She didn't go out with him, but stood for a moment at the door with the tea towel clutched to her chest. No more fighting, no more killing, she thought. Surely the governments of both the Allies and the enemy countries would have learned from this dreadful time and would never, ever let another war start?

And yet word of a formal end to the war still didn't come. Why not? everyone asked. Surely nothing could go wrong at this late stage?

On Monday May 7th there was such tension at the

factory that it was hard to get any work done. Some people hadn't even come to work, sure this would be the day peace was declared. Every time a supervisor came round, they looked up, hoping to hear the news that the war was over.

The manager kept the radio on in his office and people looked towards its windows at regular intervals. But he was still sitting there, waiting. They were all waiting.

Was nothing ever going to happen?

By afternoon, even the manager had stopped trying to work. He came out of his office and stood on the stepladder he used to make announcements and yelled, 'Stop work, everyone, and listen!'

Everyone fell silent and turned to him.

'No, it's not the news you're waiting for, but we all know it's coming and we can't settle. So I might as well save electricity and you might as well go home and wait there with your families to hear what Churchill says.'

'What about our wages?' one woman with a large family called. 'I can't afford to miss work.'

'To honour this important occasion, your wages will be paid for the whole afternoon.'

This offer was greeted by loud cheers, then people set to work to tidy up for the night. With a bit of luck they'd not be here tomorrow, because surely a holiday would be declared?

At home, Judith fidgeted around, unable to settle down to anything, even Daphne du Maurier's *Rebecca*, the library book she'd been reading avidly last night. The hours crawled past and she kept the radio on, listening to the news several times. But no announcement was made.

Her children ran in and out of the house, even serious Kitty caught up in the excitement.

Down the street the neighbour was stringing up her bunting.

'I'm not waiting any more,' she yelled when a couple of neighbours called to ask if she had heard something. 'We all know it's peace so I'm starting celebrating now. As soon as the pubs are open, I'm going for a glass of stout.'

Smiling, Judith went back into the house to listen to the radio.

At six o'clock the calm, upper-class voice told them Mr Churchill would not be broadcasting that night.

Disappointed, Judith tried to play board games with the children, but none of them could settle, and they certainly didn't feel sleepy, so she let Ben join his friends as long as they stayed on the street, sent Gillian up to bed and let Kitty sit reading her library book.

Then, just by chance, she switched on the radio to see if there was any music to listen to as she did some darning. She heard news of a coming announcement and tossed Ben's sock aside.

Guessing this was it, she called her son in from the street, yelled to her neighbour that they were going to make an announcement on the radio after all, and shouted for Gillian to come down and listen.

Once they were all settled, she made the children quieten down. 'This is a time you'll remember all your lives,' she insisted as the final domino fell delicately into place.

The voice on the radio told the people of Britain that the war in Europe was over and General Alfred Jodl would sign the official surrender of Nazi Germany the following day, which would be celebrated as VE Day. May 9th would also be a public holiday.

'Is the war really over?' eleven-year-old Gillian asked in a hushed voice. 'Is it really, really over?'

Judith felt sad that her youngest didn't remember the days before the war clearly. 'Yes, love, it's over.'

'Not quite. Don't you know what VE stands for?' Ben asked with the scornful superiority of his thirteen years, backed by two years at the Boys' Grammar School. '*Victory – in – Europe*. So no, the war isn't completely over. They're still fighting in the Far East.'

'But that's right at the other side of the world,' Gillian insisted. 'It doesn't affect us here.'

'It affects some of our Forces. It may even affect Dad in the Middle East.'

There was silence. Kitty looked at her mother, as if to ask whether they should say something to Ben, but Judith shook her head. He seemed to have an idea that his father would be a happier person to live with once he came out of the Army.

She didn't think so. It wasn't the Army that had upset Doug, but life itself, which hadn't, he claimed, done well by him. She always thought there was something festering inside him, something dark and angry.

She dismissed that image. She didn't want to talk about Doug tonight, or even think about him, let alone have an argument with her son about his father. She wanted to rejoice, needed to. Time enough to worry about the future later. It'd be a good while before her husband came home, after all. Months, she hoped.

She'd be out of here well before that. She'd start looking for somewhere else to live tomorrow. She'd miss Leigh Street and her kind neighbour, though.

And then what? If she found somewhere else for them to live in Rivenshaw, Doug would still be able to get at them. And when he found that two of his children were now at grammar school, he'd go mad. She hadn't told him about Ben and she didn't think his pub friends were the sort to write to him.

Ben hadn't won the boys' Esherwood Bequest for his school

year, but the local council's education department also sent a few clever children to the grammar school these days and he'd won one of those much-coveted places. She'd had to buy his uniform for him, but she'd managed.

Was there any way of keeping Doug away from them if she took the children and left him? She couldn't think of one.

She went to bed with mixed feelings. The war was over in Europe and would surely soon be over in the Middle and Far East.

But her personal war might just be beginning.

The children got up early the next morning, too excited to lie in bed, delighted not to have to attend school for two whole days.

Gillian giggled as she brought the milk in from the front doorstep and called Ben to come to the front door. A couple of the neighbours were setting out for work as usual.

'Serves them right for going to bed so early,' Ben crowed. 'How could they have missed the announcement with people making so much noise?'

'They told me once they sleep with earplugs in so they don't get disturbed,' Judith said.

'But there was a repeat broadcast this morning. Don't they listen to their wireless?'

'Well, they start work so early they're always in a rush to get out of the house. Don't mock them. It isn't polite. Why don't you run after them and tell them what's happened?'

He shrugged. 'They're just going round the corner. Someone else will tell them.'

She didn't insist.

Later she nipped along to the corner shop. A neighbour had popped into the house to tell her it was opening briefly for an hour that morning at ten o'clock. There would be queues, probably even longer than usual, but she wanted to get something special for tonight's meal and for the street party the next day.

It was definitely a time to remember, this first day of official peace. Everything must be just right today.

Mrs James from three doors away was in the queue ahead of her and looked as if she'd been crying. 'Are you all right?' Judith asked, even though she could guess what was wrong.

'As right as I can be, dear, thanks for asking. It's a comfort, really, that my sons didn't die in vain.'

Judith couldn't think of anything to say. The James boys had been such lively young men, and for both of them to be killed had made her feel sick. Petey Needham was dead too, with his cheerful smile and unruly hair. Thank goodness her Ben had been too young to fight.

It took her a while to walk the two hundred yards home with her shopping, because neighbours kept stopping her, wanting to talk about arrangements for the street party, some wanting a fancy dress parade even. They were determined to celebrate in style. It was silly really. There weren't enough people living in Leigh Street to have a parade and the same people wanted the party only for their own street.

By the time she got home, Gillian and Ben were outside with their friends. Gillian was in a group of giggling girls playing skipping games and Ben was lounging at the corner with three other youths. Goodness, his friend Joe had a faint moustache on his upper lip. Those lads were all growing up so fast!

Inside the house, Kitty was just finishing clearing up the kitchen on her own.

Judith felt annoyed. 'The others should have helped you with that before they went out.'

Kitty shrugged. 'Ben only helps now when you tell him to. He says this is women's work.'

'Just let me hear him say that and I'll give him what for! We all dirty the dishes, so we all take turns at clearing up. My dad always used to do the washing up for Mum at weekends.'

Kitty put some saucers away. 'It doesn't matter. I didn't want to spoil their happiness. Mum . . . are you glad the war's over?'

'Yes, of course I am.'

Kitty gave her one of those adult glances they sometimes shared. 'But . . . ?'

'But I'm worrying about your father.' She didn't have to explain.

'He'll make me leave school.'

'I've been studying the newspapers, the way the points system will work for demobbing people. I think it'll be a while before he gets sent back.' She took a deep breath. 'What would you say if I left him before then and found us somewhere else to live?'

Kitty dropped the plate she was holding, but luckily it fell on the rag rug, so didn't smash. She bent to pick it up, not saying anything.

'Well?'

'I'd be glad if you left him. It's been so nice here without him. I've never forgotten how he used to hit us, all of us, not just you. And you know what, Mum? My friend at school's parents separated a couple of years ago and she says both her father and mother are happier since they did it. They used to shout at each other all the time before he left, though her father never hit her mother.'

'Do you talk about your father hitting me?'

Kitty patted her shoulder. 'Only to my best friends at school. But everyone round here knows about it anyway.'

'Yes, I suppose so. When I look back, I don't know why I put up with it all those years.'

'He's so big, he seems to fill the house when he's here. You couldn't have stopped him. The only way is for us to leave. I've been wondering why it's taken you so long to decide, only you never want to talk about it.'

'You shouldn't have to worry about things like that at your age.'

'I haven't had much choice, have I? He hit me, too. And he wanted to destroy my chance of a good education. I hate him.'

'So do I.'

It felt as if she and her elder daughter were two women chatting, not mother and daughter. 'I'm glad I've got you.'

Kitty came and put an arm round her shoulders in a woman's gesture of support. 'I'm glad I've got you, too. Why have you waited so long, though?'

Judith tried to explain. 'It's still considered a shameful thing to leave your husband. I find it hard to go against what most people think is right and . . . it puts a stigma on the children as well as the woman. I don't want that for you. And well, we had this house. I like living in this street.'

'We've got a stigma already, with a man like him for a father. Have you talked to Grandad about this?'

'Yes.'

'And?'

'He didn't like the idea of a separation, said I should stay. He believes marriage is for ever, just as the marriage service says. He reminded me of that: "Till death do us part" and "for better for worse". So I haven't spoken about it to him again.'

'I'm disappointed in him.'

'Don't be. I never told him how bad it was.'

'You should have done. And he can't have missed the bruises.'

Kitty picked up a pile of small plates, but didn't move to put them away. 'How will we find somewhere else to live? I've been worrying about that. There's a terrible housing shortage because of the war. People have come here from Manchester to live. I've read in the newspapers that it's bad all over the country.'

'I don't think it's as bad in Rivenshaw as it is in some places. We're not a big industrial centre and we've only had a few bombs drop here, so fewer houses have been lost than in the big industrial cities.'

'There was that bomb that hit Park Gardens. One house in that street was completely destroyed.'

'Yes. That poor family. At least it'd have been quick and they'd not have known what happened.'

They stood close together for a few moments, silent, thinking.

Kitty spoke first. 'Even if we find another house, Dad will still come after us.'

Judith felt tears gather in her eyes. 'It'll be me he comes after.'

'It might be best to go to another town. I could get a job to help out. I'm fifteen now, so I can leave school.'

Judith put her hands on her daughter's shoulders and held her at arm's length. 'The one thing I'm certain of is that I don't want you leaving the grammar school. You're doing so well. They're even talking about you going on to university or teacher training college.'

A sigh was her only answer. Just as she didn't like to talk about Doug, Kitty didn't like to talk about university. They were alike in that, not wanting to tempt Providence by counting on anything till it was safe in their hands.

'How will you know when he's coming back?' Kitty asked. 'He hasn't written to you, not really, and he's been stationed in the Middle East for four years.'

'I've had postcards and official letters, so they'll probably make him send one of those.'

'Postcards with ticks and crosses on them! And he must have been forced to fill those in every single time by the officer in charge. He hates reading and writing, and he isn't very good at it, either. I've seen the way he squints at the page. I reckon he ought to wear glasses. He might not mind Ben going to grammar school as much as me, though.'

She began fiddling with the edge of her apron. 'So, when are you going to tell the others we're leaving?'

'Tonight. Or maybe tomorrow morning. We'll see.'

'Why can't we stay here and Dad leave? There are four of us and only one of him.'

'His name is on the rent book. Anyway, we should make a clean break and give him nothing to complain about. I'll only take the furniture I bought myself, even if I have to sleep on the floor in the new place. After the public holiday, I'll start looking for a house to rent. I really will.'

That earned Judith another big hug from her daughter.

People got together to set up for the street party, carrying out tables and chairs, covering them with an assortment of tablecloths, chatting and laughing.

'It's easy for us, with only eight children in our street,' Mrs Needham said. 'I wouldn't let them set places at the tables only for children. "What we have we all share," I told them. Well, the little ones won't understand what it's about and that lad at the end house will eat himself sick, given half a chance.'

So unlike in some other streets, the adults from Leigh Street sat down with their children at the tables, crammed together on chairs and makeshift benches made from planks. Bunting was flying from several houses, secret stores of food that had been kept for a special occasion had been raided and there were cakes as well as sandwiches. And if these weren't the lavishly iced cakes from before the war, who cared? Their sweetness was a rare treat these days.

After the meal, the adults sat and chatted, some already making plans for the coming peace. Everyone was sure they'd win the war in Japan. Well, they'd beaten Hitler and Mussolini, hadn't they?

Judith didn't say anything about leaving. Not yet.

At last people started calling their children to come to bed. The tables and chairs were taken back inside.

The party was over, Judith thought as she lay down in bed. It'd make a lovely memory of her time in Leigh Street.

She and the children must now find a new home.

4

Helen Bretherton hefted her suitcase in her good hand and let her two bundles of oddments stuffed into pillowcases dangle awkwardly from the other. She had always been tall and strong, but there was a limit to what one person could carry easily and, anyway, her left arm had been badly injured in a farm accident.

She wasn't supposed to lift things with it yet, so shouldn't be carrying the bundles at all, but she'd needed to take all her possessions with her when she left the Land Army.

She moved across to the sign saying *TAXIS*. Taking a taxi wouldn't be an extravagance today; it'd be a necessity. She was utterly exhausted after a much-interrupted journey.

She smiled as she looked round. Even though it was mid-May, it was quite cool and threatening rain, but what did she care about the weather? It had been three years since she'd seen Rivenshaw, when she visited her mother's aunt.

The town centre lay around the old Market Square, which was more or less square, like its name. The station in front of which she was standing took up the whole of one side, and shops standing cheek by jowl with pubs lined the other three sides. Vehicles could only get out of the square at the two corners opposite the station, but pedestrians could slip out through various narrow alleys between shops and pubs.

Sadly, there was a gap and nothing but bare earth studded

with fragments of brick where the Red Lion pub should have been. The walls of the shops on either side of the gap looked to have been patched up with a motley collection of modern bricks and big wooden props. Parts of their front-ages had been mended too. It must have been a bomb, perhaps one of those originally meant for Manchester but offloaded here instead. She hoped no one had been killed.

She looked down at her hands, the nails short but not looking grubby now, after her stay in hospital. What a place to spend VE Day, in a hospital! Still it'd got her out of the farm work she hated. It wasn't just the mess and the dirt, but the poor living conditions and the long hours – forty-eight hours a week in winter and fifty in summer, plus extra unpaid hours if the farmer could find an excuse to get more out of his Land Girls.

For that they'd paid her a miserable £1–16–00 a week until last year when they'd raised it to £2–85–00, which had made the farmer complain loudly that they'd bankrupt him.

It was necessary war work, because people had to eat, so she'd done her bit without complaining, but she'd never expected to spend three long, tedious years in the Women's Land Army, or to end up with a damaged arm. Some of those farm tools were wickedly sharp.

'God bless you all!' Churchill had said in his broadcast on VE Day, after the war in Europe had ended. They'd listened to him in the hospital. He'd been praising the people of Britain for their huge war effort, and they deserved that praise. But oh, she never wanted to go near a farm again for as long as she lived.

Not all the men would come back to their old farm jobs. Some had been killed, others wouldn't be demobbed for ages. It'd take time to fill their places, so most of the other women hadn't been allowed to leave their Land Army jobs yet. It was just as vital for food to be grown in peacetime, and in a month or two the harvest would need to be gathered in, every precious seed and leaf of it.

Food was scarce in Britain, but it was even more scarce in the former enemy countries, from what she'd heard on the radio. People were already grumbling at the thought of having to share their scarce supplies with them. But you couldn't leave people to starve, could you? Think of the children, she always told those who complained. Children weren't enemies.

Helen felt lucky to have escaped from the Land Army early. It was almost worth the accident that had sliced open her arm. The long, deep cut had affected one of her bigger muscles and they'd had to operate on her. It would take months to recover, the doctor told her afterwards, and there might always be some weakness in that arm.

She had to be careful not to strain it by heavy lifting, especially during the first few weeks, and above all she mustn't let the cut get infected. 'Farm work is too risky with this type of injury,' the doctor had said and written her a note to that effect.

She'd managed not to cheer when they decided to demob her early and send her home to convalesce. Oh, the lies she'd told to get away, because they insisted she had to have someone to look after her.

She'd said she was going to live with her Auntie Ethel, but actually, she had no close relatives left now. The home she'd grown up in had been rented, so the landlord had let it out to other people after her father died in late '43. She'd have been allowed to go to his funeral, but they didn't tell her about it until too late for her to get back to Lancashire.

A neighbour had put the remaining furniture and family possessions into storage in someone's half-ruined workshop on the outskirts of Manchester. She'd have to pay a modest sum to get them back, but it'd be worth it because such items were in short supply. Well, everything was in short supply. She was sick and tired of mending her clothes. She enjoyed sewing, but not darning and fiddling around with old clothes suitable only for the ragbag.

Luckily she really did have a place to go to, even if no one was waiting for her there. Last year she'd been informed by a lawyer that poor Auntie Ethel had been killed by a bomb blast. Just imagine that, in sleepy little Rivenshaw of all places!

Helen would have liked to go to the funeral, but she hadn't been allowed to leave the Wiltshire farm where she was working to go up to Lancashire, because a great-aunt wasn't considered a close enough relative by her area supervisor.

Auntie Ethel had left everything to her great-niece, not because they bore one another any great love, but because Helen was the only family member left bearing the name Bretherton.

If it hadn't been for the bomb, Auntie Ethel would probably still be alive. She had been a tough old bird, who boasted that she didn't have time to be sick and was going to live to be a hundred, as her grandmother had.

Helen sighed. So many lives had been cut short in the war. It wasn't just people in the armed forces dying for their country, but civilians at home being killed by bombs.

She thought her mother might still be alive, but didn't know where Elsie was, or whether she still called herself Mrs Bretherton. She didn't want to know, either, and only thought of her as Elsie, not Mother. Such a foolish woman! And immoral. She'd left her husband and daughter for another man fifteen years ago, but she hadn't married him, had she?

She'd never tried to contact her daughter since then, not even a letter at Christmas or on Helen's birthday.

Life gave to you with one hand and took away with the other, Helen thought sadly, turning up her coat collar and wishing a taxi would arrive. It was cold for May. She moved about to keep warm, her thoughts jumping here and there.

She'd have been married by now if Wilfred hadn't been killed in 1942, his plane shot down over Germany. The Air Force hadn't informed her of his death, because a fiancée didn't count as family, but his mother had written to break the sad news.

Helen found it difficult to remember Wilfred clearly now, unless she got out her photos, something she avoided doing because that always made her feel sad. She did remember clearly how wonderful it had felt to be in love, how happy they'd been together. You never forgot that.

She turned her thoughts firmly to something more cheerful. The group of Land Girls in the village had discussed what would happen after the war and everyone had agreed that there wouldn't be enough spare men to go around. They'd joked about bringing back polygamy, and letting men have two wives, because they all had spinster relatives who hadn't found husbands after the Great War.

The joke wasn't all that funny, though, because Helen might live and die a spinster now. She wasn't good-looking, too thin-faced with mousy brown hair, and too tall for most men's taste. The thought of never marrying made her sad, because she loved children. She wouldn't even be an auntie, since she was an only child.

At last a taxi drew up and an older man got out and walked into the station. She told the driver where she wanted to go, then left him to stow her luggage in the boot.

As she leaned back in the vehicle, she wondered whether she should visit her great-aunt's lawyer first. No, she was exhausted and all she wanted was to go straight to the house and sleep for a million years. She didn't want to hang around waiting to see a lawyer, then hang around waiting for another taxi. Anyway, she didn't know the new lawyer. A Mr Gilliot had now taken over the legal practice. She could go and see him tomorrow or the day after.

The previous lawyer, Mr Lloyd, had given her some information about the 'accident'. One of the few bombs to fall on Rivenshaw had apparently struck the house next to her great-aunt's. Number 8 Park Gardens had been totally demolished and its occupants killed instantly, but Miss Bretherton's house, Number 10, had only received damage to one side of the upper storey.

The old lady would still be alive, but unfortunately she had always refused point-blank to 'cower in the cellar like a rat' and had been sleeping in her usual bedroom. She'd died two days later without regaining consciousness, apparently.

Mr Lloyd had informed her that the house was still structurally sound, and could be made fully habitable again once the war was over. He had paid some men to board over the damaged windows. In the meantime he was getting older and not in the best of health, so was moving to live with his son in Scotland, and a Mr Henry Gilliot would be taking over the practice from now on.

His successor had been slow to reply to Helen's queries, but a letter came eventually, apologising for the delay. Mr Gilliot was a newcomer to the town, who had been unfit for active service. He hadn't been aware of all the facts of her case till he had time to look into it. He told her he was doing the work of two men at the moment, since another legal practice had closed down at the same time, due to the sudden death of its elderly owner.

He hadn't checked out her great-aunt's house personally, but his senior clerk had sent someone, who said it was securely locked up and the windows in the bombed rooms were still boarded up.

He was also pleased to inform Miss Bretherton that she had inherited other items besides the house, and the more

valuable ones, like her aunt's jewellery, were in safe keeping
in the cellar strongroom at the practice. Obviously, he couldn't
send her the original, detailed list, as it was the only copy,
and given the manpower shortages, he couldn't spare anyone
to type it out again.

He ended his letter: 'Although the house can be repaired,
that isn't likely to happen until the building industry starts
up again after the war, and a house for one person won't
have a high priority. That shouldn't inconvenience you too
much, as I've heard women won't be released from their
admirable work with the Land Army for a good while.'

Only she had been released. And she did need somewhere
to live. There must be some parts of the house still habitable,
surely. She was banking on that.

Her living conditions at the farm had been distinctly primi-
tive and surely the house couldn't be any worse. The farm
billet had been in an old shed, weatherproof but smelling
disgusting at times, when the nearby cesspit overflowed. She
shuddered at the memory.

A stab of pain made her look down at the bandaged arm,
which was aching now. She was quite prepared to live
roughly in order to get a home of her own, but she couldn't
do much physical work yet to make things better. She didn't
want to damage her arm permanently. She thought she'd
got away with carrying things, but she wasn't going to push
her luck.

The taxi pulled up at Number 10 Park Gardens, the even
numbers of which ran along this side of the park, while the
odd numbers were along the other side. Each row of large,
detached villas was separated from Parson's Mead only by
the narrow road, so it was almost as if you lived in the
country.

It was strange to see an empty block where Number 8
had stood. She remembered the old house next door having

a beautiful garden. Now it was a wasteland of rubble with a few shrubs and one lopsided tree at the rear.

Her aunt's house looked weather-worn but Helen couldn't see any damage at the front. Her spirits lifted and tears of sheer happiness welled in her eyes. She was here at last, had a home of her own.

That meant so much. She would be able to do what she wanted when she wanted, get back her books and the other possessions that had been stored after her parents' deaths. She wouldn't even have to look for a job, because there was enough money to live on if she was careful.

By the time she'd got out of the vehicle, her luggage was standing on the footpath. The driver didn't offer to help her into the house with it, even though he couldn't have failed to notice the bandaged arm, so she only gave him a small tip.

As he drove away, she tried to push the gate open, but it was stiff, hanging off its hinges. She managed to lug the suitcase and bundles through the half-open gate onto the path, one by one, using her good arm. You didn't leave things lying around in times of great scarcity. She'd learned that the hard way. People might not steal from friends and neighbours, but strangers were considered a fair target by the more unscrupulous folk.

She tried the front door but it was locked. Well, she'd expected that, didn't know why she felt so disappointed.

She raised her head to sniff the air, which seemed to be getting damper by the minute. The sky was filled with dark clouds. She must try to get into the house before it began to rain.

She tucked her bandaged arm between the buttons of her coat, because she hadn't thought to keep her sling to hand. It seemed to help a little and she walked slowly along the overgrown path that ran round the side of the house.

When she turned into the back garden, she stopped in surprise. Someone had dug out a vegetable patch and plants were growing in neat little rows. Early lettuce and spring onions, she noted, with some radishes, which might or might not be ready to pick. There were no signs of winter crops, so she assumed the garden had only recently been created.

Who could have done this? The house should have been empty.

She looked round but could see no sign of anyone. Perhaps one of the neighbours was making use of this garden to grow extra food. That'd be very wise. She didn't mind, though she hoped they'd share some of their produce as a thank you.

She went to try the back door, which led into the kitchen, she remembered. Unfortunately, that door was also locked. Surely Auntie Ethel would have hidden a spare key somewhere? Most people did. Helen felt above the lintel, but found nothing there except dirt and a busy little spider that ran across the back of her hand till she shook it off.

She swung round, intending to look for another hiding place, and gasped in shock when she almost bumped into a man standing quite close to her. Instinctively she jerked away, banging her bad arm on the downpipe from the roof. She let out an involuntary yelp of agony and clutched the arm, feeling sick with pain for a few moments.

It wasn't till the pain ebbed away that she realised he had his arm round her, supporting her. If he hadn't, she might have fallen over because of the waves of pain and dizziness.

As soon as he saw she was recovering, he let go and stepped back, which was a relief.

'I'm sorry. I did not mean to startle you.' He pulled a rough wooden bench forward. 'Sit down, please, miss.'

As she hesitated, he added, 'I will not hurt you.'

His English was excellent but he had a slight accent, not

strong enough for her to tell what his nationality was but enough to show he wasn't British.

For a moment all hung in the balance, then she gave in to the pain and tiredness, and eased herself down on the bench. Her arm was still throbbing from the bump and she shoved it back between her coat buttons, trying to keep it still.

He stepped back and pulled forward an overturned bucket with a rusty bottom, sitting on that a couple of yards away from her, watching her warily the whole time. He looked like a wild animal that was ready to flee at the slightest sign of aggression, but not like someone poised to attack her.

Her tension eased a little. He was taller than her and probably stronger, but there was something about his face that said he wasn't a violent man. At least, that was how it seemed to her. He didn't speak, seemed to be waiting for her to say something, so she obliged, 'Who are you?'

'A refugee.'

'Are you waiting in England to go back to your own country?'

'No! I came here to escape and I won't let them send me back to live under Russian rule. If you try to report me to the authorities, I will vanish and they won't find me. I have done this many times before on my way to England.'

'Why do you want to stay here?'

'It is supposed to be a free country. It is more free than my own, anyway.' He sighed. 'But even here, they have rules about foreigners, I find.'

'You speak English well.'

'I learn languages easily. This has saved my life a few times. I have taken much care to practise English when I could, because I have wanted to come here from many years ago. My grandfather came here to visit and told me many tales about your country.'

'What about your family?'

He shrugged. 'There is no one to go back to, no home left, nothing for me there.'

She'd spoken to prisoners of war sometimes when they were working on the farm, and had heard similar sad tales. 'Were you working here as a prisoner of war?'

'No.' He looked at her very solemnly. 'I will tell you the truth, miss, because you have a kind face and did not shout for help at the sight of me. When the war started, my grandfather told me to run away. He said I would have more chance of surviving if I left the village.'

She nodded to encourage him to continue.

'Month by month, year by year, I managed to travel across Europe and then, lately, to Ireland. I stayed in one place for a time, then I stayed in another. I moved forward, or I moved back if there was danger. I was lucky. Many people were friendly and helped me stay alive.

'But I did not want to stay in Europe. I got to Ireland in the end by ship. Then I came across to Fleetwood with some fishermen, even before the war ended. I could see that it would end soon. I had to pay them, so I don't have much money left.'

He stared down at the ground. 'I am not a thief, and I'm very sorry, but I was desperate. When I saw that no one lived in this house, I got inside and took some food, just a little. Then I stayed, only for a few days, I thought. But it's been longer. This is a very nice house.'

He waved one hand towards the plants. 'I found seeds and planted a garden for when the people return, in payment for my stealing. Everywhere in England they plant vegetables but it is not always well done. I have worked on farms and I know how to do it properly.'

Words seemed to flow from him, as if he'd been starved for company.

'I won't tell anyone about you,' she said. 'Can you get me into the house?'

'You wish to break in too? You have no home to go to?'

'I'm the owner of this house. It used to belong to my aunt and now that she's dead, it's mine. But I don't have a key yet. I should have gone to see the lawyer first, but I was very tired and wanted to come straight home.'

She looked down at her arm. 'I've been in hospital. The journey north was difficult and long. There were a lot of interruptions.'

'You look pale. Come. Let me help you inside.' He stood up and held out his hand to pull her up.

She took it without hesitation, too weary to think beyond the fact that she simply couldn't manage alone.

He pulled a big key out of his pocket and opened the back door, locking it again as soon as they were inside.

It was dark there, with blinds drawn across all the windows.

She stayed near the door, wondering whether she was being stupid trusting him. What if he wasn't as harmless as he seemed?

Her heart started to pound as he moved towards her.

5

As the days passed and planning for peace got under way, Judith began hunting for a house to rent. She would have taken anything, but she only heard about three houses becoming available, and each time was told the place had been taken even before the previous occupants had moved out.

She heard about another place before it was advertised and went to knock on the landlord's door early in the morning before work. The man who answered it frowned at her.

'It's Mrs Crossley, isn't it?'

'Yes, and you're Mr Dewhurst.' Her heart sank. He wasn't known for his kindness, would make a terrible landlord. But she'd take that risk to get somewhere where she and the children could live in peace.

'I believe you have a house to rent.'

'I thought your husband was already renting a house in Lower Parklea.'

She didn't know how to answer that one, hadn't intended to give away what she was doing.

He stared at her, eyes narrowed. 'Well? Why can't you answer me?'

She could think of nothing but the bald truth. 'I need a house because I'm separating from my husband.'

'You rotten bitch! He's away overseas, putting his life on

the line in his country's service, and you're doing the dirty on him.'

'I'm not doing the dirty on anyone. I just . . . didn't get on with him before and when he comes back, we'll both be happier apart.'

'Does *he* know that?'

'Not yet. How could he? He's never written to me, not once.'

'Well, he's had better things to do. I'll tell you straight: you're not going to be leaving him to come and live in *my* house. I'll save it for a decent family, thank you very much.' He slammed the door in her face.

She felt depressed all day. How was she going to get away from Doug if she couldn't find another house? Would people immediately think the worst of her if she tried?

Worried sick that her husband might come back unexpectedly, she continued to study the official announcements about how demobilisation was to be managed, as well as reading the local newspaper carefully each day before work, looking for somewhere to live. Anywhere.

It was difficult to figure out when Doug would be demobbed, even approximately. Most servicemen and servicewomen were to be released from the armed forces according to their 'age-and-service number', which was calculated from their age and the months they had served in uniform. That said where they were in the queue, but not how long they would have to wait to be demobbed.

Doug had served a long time overseas. Information about forces serving in the Middle and Far East seemed scarce. The Army couldn't send men home one at a time when they came due to leave, could it? You couldn't just hop on a train from Iraq or Cairo. Surely the authorities at least waited till they had enough men to fill a plane or troopship? She hoped so, was counting on that.

Would she have any warning of his return? The Army would expect Doug to tell her. But the other people from Rivenshaw who were serving overseas hadn't come back yet, so she thought she had a little time yet.

The next night Judith discussed the problem with Kitty after the other children had gone to bed, even Ben seeming exhausted.

She spoke quietly, not wanting to tell the younger children yet. 'After what happened today, I didn't want to tell the others I'm trying to find another house. They might tell other people.'

'Gillian might, but I don't think Ben would.'

'I don't know where to turn next.'

'Why don't you ask your friend Irene to keep her ears open for one coming vacant?' Kitty suggested. 'She hears things from her customers.'

'I suppose I could. But I'm afraid I'll just get the same reception from another landlord as I got from Mr Dewhurst, and it might lose business for her, if she's known to be a friend of mine.'

'This is 1945, not 1845, Mum. People are changing. Women aren't slaves to men. You have to keep trying.'

Judith was so desperate, she did go to see her friend, who ran a hairdressing salon in the front room of her house. Kitty was right. If anyone was going to hear about somewhere to rent in times like these, it would be a popular hairdresser. What's more, Irene's husband worked at the local newspaper, where people and gossip passed through the office all the time.

Irene was so lucky. Her husband was a lovely, kind fellow, who had failed his Army medical because of a weak heart due to having had rheumatic fever as a child. That hadn't stopped him from serving in the Home Guard, as well as continuing in his daytime job of typesetting the local newspaper, the *Argus*.

He'd had to work longer hours than usual, but he'd been safe. Well, as safe as anyone could be with bombs liable to fall from the sky and kill by blind chance.

Irene was always glad to have a visitor and as she had no customers due for another half-hour, she offered Judith a cup of tea.

'You look worried,' she said as they waited in the kitchen for the tea to brew.

'I am. Worried sick. Now the war's over, Doug will be coming home. Irene . . . I'm going to leave him.'

'I never thought you'd get up the nerve to do it.'

'What do you mean?'

'I'd have left him years ago if he'd been *my* husband. He's a brute, an absolute brute. And he's not the only one. The tales I hear in the salon. You wouldn't believe what some men who're well thought of do to those at home. Not that your Doug is well thought of.'

She stopped speaking briefly to pour two cups of tea. 'Your husband was friendly with some very shady characters before the war. Did you know one of them got put in prison last year for thieving and black marketing?'

'Yes, I did hear about that. Doug was overseas, though, and anyway, he wouldn't get involved in thieving.'

'Wouldn't he? Well, I suppose you know him best.' Irene took a sip of tea, looking thoughtful. 'Good tea, that. Best I've had from the grocer for ages. Look, I think you should leave Rivenshaw and not tell anyone where you go. Let's face it, that's the only way you'll be truly safe.'

'I don't want to do that, except as a last resort. Kitty's at the grammar school and she's doing really well. They're even talking of her going to university. It's for the children's future that I'm doing this.'

'I'm talking of saving your life, Judith love. He'll easily find out where you are, you know he will. It's a small town. Better your Kitty and Ben don't finish their education than lose their mother.'

Judith shook her head stubbornly. 'I'll be careful, I promise you. I've got a little time yet. Can you keep your eyes open for me? You hear all the news first here.'

'You've got somewhere to live. Let *him* find another place. You have three children to think of. Tell Doug to get out.'

'He wouldn't do it. Anyway, his name's on the rent book.' She picked up her teacup again with a hand that trembled slightly as she told Irene about the terrible things Mr Dewhurst had said to her.

'What does *he* know? He's a nasty sod as well. You should hear how he treats his own wife. You're too sensitive, love. You'll have to grow a thicker skin if you're to manage on your own. Who's your landlord now?'

'Old Mr Esher still, I think, but of course his new lawyer and an agent deal with the rent.'

'Then speak to the lawyer. He'll tell you what to do. Or go to Mr Esher and ask his help. He got the lawyer to help you with Kitty's schooling, didn't he? So he knows already what Doug's like. Tell him how promising she is, but she won't be able to continue her education at all unless some way is found to keep you all safe.'

'I suppose I could try that. But I don't like to bother him again. He's having a bit of trouble with his wife, from what I hear. She's become very short-tempered. I heard her shouting as I walked past their house.'

'Well, you have to try. But I will let you know if I hear anything.'

Judith gave her a hug and leaned against her for a minute before pulling back and standing on her own feet, comforted.

'What about your job,' Irene said thoughtfully. 'Won't it

end when the men come back from war? How will you live if you're not earning anything?'

'I don't know. I've asked to be kept on at the factory, even though I hate the work. They use us unskilled workers as general dogsbodies.' She looked down at her roughened hands and grimaced. 'The manager says they can't tell me if I'll have a job till they see who comes back. They want to give the ex-soldiers their jobs back before they settle anything. I'll go out charring, if I have to. People always want house cleaners.'

But her friend didn't hear about any houses to rent and Judith felt increasingly helpless as the days passed.

Her fallback plan had been to go and live with her father, but he was seeing a woman he'd met while fire-watching. He seemed very taken with her. If he was thinking of marriage, that might stop him helping his daughter.

She needed to provide the children with a proper home, where they could do their homework and feel safe. She didn't want to risk a magistrate or judge taking the children away from her because they were living in a slum, and giving them back to their father. She'd heard about that happening to one woman.

It was the stuff of nightmares and she was sleeping badly, racking her brain to think of a solution.

It was dark in the kitchen, with the old-fashioned wooden shutters tightly closed across every window. Helen didn't know her way round this part of the house. She'd not been in the kitchen the few times she and her family had taken tea with Auntie Ethel.

She felt nervous and prepared herself mentally to hit the refugee if he so much as laid a finger on her, then run out of the house screaming. How stupid she'd been to come in here alone with a stranger! What had she been thinking of?

But he didn't come near her, just moved away, whispering from across the room, 'Stay there till I fold the shutters back. You might trip over something.'

When he'd done this, he stayed where he was near the window, not looking at all threatening now she could see his face again.

She stared round eagerly. This had been the elderly maid's territory. She wondered suddenly what had happened to Mavis. Had she been hurt by the bomb too?

It was a big, square room, with an old-fashioned stove, the sort that burned coal or wood and probably heated the water, as well as providing heat for cooking. Her grandmother had had one of those, but Helen had never cooked on one.

'Isn't there a gas cooker?' she asked.

'No, just a single gas burner. It is very old-fashioned for a house in a town, but very nice downstairs. A comfortable house. Not so nice upstairs, though.'

'What's wrong with the upstairs?'

'When the bomb destroyed the house next door, it also knocked holes in the side walls of this house, and it broke most of the window glass there. Someone put wood across the gaps but did it badly and there have been leaks. Even the bedrooms which were not hit by the bomb are too damp to live in.'

'Oh, no! Then I'll have nowhere to live.' She frowned at him. 'Where have you been sleeping, then?'

'In here on the floor.' He gestured round the kitchen.

'I can't see any bedding.'

'I hide it every morning in case someone comes to the house. I go out every day, looking for work that will give me food.' He sighed. 'Not much to be found. Farmers are best but it is a long walk to get to them and my shoes are worn. I manage to find some little job now and then.' He looked down thoughtfully at his hands. 'I am very good with these. I can work with wood, too.'

'You must be good at gardening. Those vegetables look to be flourishing.'

'Yes, I can do quite a few things. I learned a bit here, another bit there. You never know when something will be useful, so I always pay attention.'

He looked sad, not frightening, and she felt sorry for him. She hadn't enjoyed farm work but she'd been safe and fed. He'd been travelling across a war-ravaged Europe on his own. What must that have been like? How clever he must be to have coped and stayed free! 'It's been hard for you, hasn't it? When did you start travelling across Europe?'

'Soon after the beginning of the war.'

'How old were you then?'

'Sixteen. I did not want to fight for Hitler, or go to one of the so-called work camps. I was sorry my grandfather was too old to leave with me. He said he would die soon and I must live.'

'So you're about twenty-one now?' Younger than her in years but his eyes were old and sad. He must have seen a lot of terrible things to get that look.

He shrugged. 'Twenty-two. I feel much older.'

'I'm twenty-four. I feel older sometimes, too. My fiancé was killed in '42.'

'That is sad for you. I hope you had some happy times with him before that.'

She smiled at the thought of Wilfred. 'Yes, I did. He was a happy sort of person. Nice to be with. Everyone liked him.'

'I have never had a woman friend. Too dangerous.' He straightened his shoulders. 'But I am lucky. My grandfather was right to send me away. I am alive. Many are dead.' He turned to look outside.

She wondered what he was looking at, then saw it was starting to rain.

'I will leave your house now, miss, and I thank you for the shelter. If you look after the garden, you will have some food soon. I'm sorry I had to take food from the pantry. There are still many jars left.'

She felt so weary that for a moment she couldn't think clearly, then she realised he was holding out the key to the back door. She grabbed his hand and the key. 'No. Don't go. Please.'

He stayed where he was, not even trying to pull his hand away, as if he welcomed the warmth of a human touch. He was waiting for her to speak, only she didn't know what to say, or what she wanted, really, only that she didn't think she could manage alone.

'I have a job for you,' she said in the end. 'Just for a while. I can't pay you in money, but I'll give you shelter and buy you food.'

'Job?'

She watched him swallow hard and, after one jerk, remain still, as if he didn't dare believe what she was saying. She took away her right hand, leaving the key in his. She gestured to her injured left arm, holding it against her body. 'I can't manage on my own. I thought I could but I can't. My arm hurts. I need a bed, food, help. For a few weeks, at least.'

'You trust me?'

'Yes.'

'You won't tell the authorities I'm here?'

'No. I promise I won't. I really do need help. All my family are dead, I think.' Well, her mother was as good as dead. Something important occurred to Helen suddenly. 'You haven't told me your name yet.'

'Could you call me John? That is a nice English name.'

'It doesn't suit you. You aren't English.'

'I try to be.'

'Don't. People will get annoyed if you tell lies about yourself. You don't even look English with those high cheekbones and dark eyes. What is your real name?'

'It means John. It's Jan.'

He pronounced it 'Yan' so she repeated it that way, but she remembered it was spelled with a J. 'And your surname, Jan?'

'I shall never use that again. My father collaborated with the Germans from the beginning, dirtied our name. I shall choose another one. What is your surname?

'Bretherton.'

'Then I shall start my name with B too. Borkowski. I knew a kind man called that once.'

She was too tired to argue. And anyway, if he was telling the truth, he had a good reason to change his surname. 'Very well, Jan Borkowski. I'm pleased to meet you.'

'And I am pleased to meet you, too, Helen Bretherton, and to work for you.'

'Good. We'll manage as best we can for a day or two.' She let herself sag then, felt as if her body was boneless and limp. 'I can't do anything more today, Jan. I need to lie down. Is there a bedroom I can use, even if it is damp?'

'Why not use the front room downstairs? It has a big sofa. That will make a good bed. And the room isn't damp. I can find blankets for you. There is a cupboard of blankets and sheets upstairs. I will light a fire here to air them.' He smiled. 'We can have a fire here now if you are the owner. I did not dare light one before.'

'That's good.'

He pulled a wooden rocking chair forward and put a cushion on the seat. 'Sit on this, Miss Bretherton. It will be more comfortable for you if I light the fire first. It is a damp, chilly day.'

She changed chairs and leaned back, rocking gently, feeling as if she could rest at last. 'Call me Helen, and I'll call you Jan. "Miss Bretherton" sounds too much like my aunt.'

'Helen, then. I like that name.'

'Look Jan, I haven't eaten properly since yesterday. There was nothing to eat on the train. If I give you some money, can you buy a loaf, food?'

'You have a ration book?'

She nodded. 'Of course. Oh. I suppose you don't have one.'

'No. You will need to register the ration book at a shop.'

'I don't think I can walk very far today.'

'Is there a neighbour who knows you?'

'Miss Peters next door at number twelve may remember me. If she's still alive.'

'She is very alive. I have spoken to her a few times. She is kind. She gives me a piece of bread sometimes. She said she wouldn't tell anyone I was here if I promised not to do any damage. Shall I fetch her?'

He was back in a few minutes accompanied by a scrawny old lady who looked a lot older than the last time Helen had seen her.

Miss Peters stood in the kitchen doorway staring at Helen, then walked across the room. 'You have more of a look of your aunt now you're older. When Ethel died, the lawyer told me you'd inherited the house and asked me to keep an eye on it.' She turned to look at Jan. 'I've been keeping an eye on this man. Do you want him to leave? I can send him away now you're back. He hasn't done any harm, though.'

'He's going to stay and help me.' Helen gestured to her arm. 'I was injured and I can't use this arm much yet. I've hired him for a week or two.'

'I saw you arrive in a taxi. You looked very tired. You

should have made the driver carry your luggage into the house.'

'I wasn't thinking clearly. Besides, I didn't have a key to the house. Jan let me inside. I'll be glad to have his help for a while.'

'War makes for strange partnerships,' Miss Peters said. 'He's made a garden.'

'Yes, I saw it.'

'Thieves don't make gardens.'

'I take your point.'

'The ration book?' Jan prompted, looking at Helen.

'I need to register my ration book to get some food, Miss Peters, but I can't get to the shops today. I've been in hospital and the train kept getting delayed, so I've overdone things. I feel exhausted.'

Again, that sharp-eyed scrutiny. 'You look pale.'

'I thought . . . well, you know me, so perhaps the shop-keepers will take your word for it that I really am Helen Bretherton. Can you spare the time to go to the shops with Jan, so that he can buy me some food?'

The old lady stood thinking this over, then nodded. 'Yes. I'll bring you a slice of bread first to keep you going. Best I can do for the moment. Jan and I may be gone a while, though. There are always queues.' She turned to him. 'You can carry my bag back from the shops for me as well, young fellow. I'm not as spry as I used to be.'

'I will be happy to help you.'

Miss Peters turned back to Helen. 'I'll tell them he's a displaced person and your family knows his, or they'll be suspicious about what he's doing here. You'd better register him at the police station as soon as you're well enough to walk into town.'

'Register with the police!' Jan looked at her anxiously.

'You'll have to risk it if you're to stay in England, young man.'

'But if they send me back, the Russians will put me in a work camp and I will never get out again. They will work me to death. I am afraid to register.'

'We're all registered somewhere these days. Ration books, identity cards, everyone's keeping an eye on everyone else. And this is England. There are no Russian camps here.'

After a pause, he nodded acceptance. 'You think this will work, to say I know Helen's family?'

'It stands as good a chance as anything if she'll back up your story.' She eyed Helen, who nodded.

'Very well, then. Time for you to take a risk, Jan, if you want to settle in England. Now, I'll go and get Helen something to eat.'

Miss Peters brought a slice of grey-brown bread with a scrape of anonymous reddish jam on it. 'I'm looking forward to eating crusty white bread again one day,' she said with a sigh.

They left Helen to eat and rest, and set off for the shops.

What a strange pair they made, she thought. The tiny old woman and the tall, emaciated young man towering over her.

She ate the bread, hungry for more, but there wasn't any so she drank a glass of water. Then she snuggled down in the chair, enjoying the warmth of the fire. She'd just have a little rest before exploring the rest of the house.

6

Mayne Esher saluted his commanding officer for the final time and made his way out of the regimental headquarters. They'd asked him to stay on in the Army, even though the special project he'd been working on for the past year had finished, but he had refused . . . gently, politely, but very firmly.

He'd never let people know how unsuited he felt to the role of soldier. Well, he hoped he hadn't shown it.

First he'd have a few days' rest at home, then he had some ideas about what he'd do with himself in Civvy Street. Making these plans had kept him sane at difficult times, and he had some friends who were going to work with him. Well, they were hoping to work with him if things went well.

He couldn't make a start on the detailed planning until he'd discussed his ideas with his parents. Without their cooperation, his first civilian business project wouldn't get off the ground.

He knew his mother would expect him to live with them at the Dower House, but he didn't want to do that. He'd grown too used to his independence. He'd stay for a few days, but he'd try to find somewhere of his own to live as soon as possible. He didn't want her to look after him, because she inevitably treated him like the child he'd once been.

The war had changed him, as it had changed most people,

whether they went into the armed forces or not. He called his present mood 'battle weary' in his own mind, even though for the past year he'd not been involved in any actual fighting, thank goodness, but had been seconded to a special planning section of the War Office. He'd been working with some very clever people, men and women, and had appreciated that.

It hadn't been as easy a job as some people believed. In the past few months he'd lived in the depths of the country, working long hours on a secret project, under the constant strain of knowing how crucial this project was.

He'd been shocked at how badly treated the old house he was living in had been. No one seemed to care about maintenance, let alone repairing any damage – and there was damage. He hadn't seen his own home, but guessed he'd find Esherwood in a similarly poor condition too once the war was over.

He had to be formally demobbed from the Army via the regiment, hence this faffing around in London, handing in bits of equipment and filling in forms. Now that peace had come to Europe, the old rules and regulations were being pulled out of drawers, and things were being done by the book.

He was luckier than most of the chaps he'd been working with. He had a small private income that his parents hadn't been able to touch, and had guarded his legacy carefully. His father had asked about it once, obviously in need of money, but Mayne had told him he needed it all and they should sell another of the family paintings if they were short of cash. The Eshers either had ugly ancestors or had hired bad painters. Or both. He'd not miss most of the paintings.

Mayne didn't need the money he'd built up from his legacy yet, but he would. He wasn't like his father or his mother where money was concerned. He'd had no trouble living on his Army pay for the past five years, so had left the quarterly payments from the legacy in the bank, to gain interest. Once posted to the country, he'd even saved money from his captain's pay, and added that to his cache.

Well, he wasn't a heavy boozer, so his mess bills were low, and he'd lost his taste for womanising. Lost his taste for a lot of things. He could only hope his former enjoyment of the small things in life would return. Not that women were small things, exactly, but after a betrayal by the woman he'd expected to marry, who'd gone off to marry a much richer man early in the war, he'd stayed clear of long-term relationships.

He supposed he ought to consider getting married now, if only to have children and continue the family name. His mother had already told him several times that it was his duty and had offered to introduce him to some 'nice, well-bred gels, people of our class'. How she did harp on about 'our class'! He'd fought and worked with men from all backgrounds, didn't feel it was right to look down on anyone.

But he wasn't rushing into anything. He worried that any children he had might become the cannon fodder for another war when they grew up, so he'd wait and see if the country really had made a lasting peace.

The Great War of 1914–18 was supposed to have ended the possibility of more major wars and look at what had happened when Hitler took over Germany: an even more widespread world war.

Now, people in the know had some concerns about Russia and there was some speculation about whether World War Three was waiting in the wings.

No, he'd not think of marrying yet, he'd decided. For the moment, he'd do nothing except set himself up to earn a decent living. Focus on that. Be *practical*.

When he left the regimental headquarters, he was delighted to find his former assistant waiting for him at the gate.

The sight of him cheered Mayne up enormously. 'Nice to see you, Travers.'

'Nice to see you . . . sir.'

The pause and cheeky look made him realise his error. 'Sorry. It's Victor and Mayne from now on, of course it is. Look, do you have time for a farewell drink before you catch your train?'

'All the time in the world.' Victor picked up his kitbag and fell in beside him as they began to stroll along the street.

'It feels good, doesn't it? To have peace again in Britain, I mean. Even with all the shortages.'

'To tell you the truth, Mayne old fellow, I'll feel a lot better once we've sorted out the Japs. Most civilians in England seem to consider the war over now, but it won't be till we get our chaps out of those damned prisoner of war camps and set the Far East in order again. The fighting could go on for quite a while.'

'I've heard rumours that the Yanks are testing some new secret weapon.'

'I've heard them too, but nothing specific. Powerful, is it?'

'More powerful than anything we've seen yet, by a long chalk, apparently.'

Victor sighed. 'If it's that powerful, it'll hit the civilians just as much as the military. It's always stuck in my gullet how many civilians were killed on both sides.'

'Yes. Even in peaceful little Rivenshaw, we had a few bombs kill people. Anyway, enough speculation, let's go into this pub. They have good beer and it won't be *Officers Only* now, and if it is, we're both wearing civvies and you have an educated accent, so they'll never know you were only a sergeant, and a reluctant one at that.'

When they were seated, Mayne asked, 'Why didn't you become an officer, Victor? You would never talk about it. Or should I shut up? Only, you're an educated man. They had to twist your arm to get you to become a corporal, even. I always wondered.'

'I can talk about it now. I didn't want to order other men to be killed. I'm not exactly a pacifist, and I did my bit, but I wasn't happy to give that sort of order and live with it on my conscience for the rest of my life.'

'Yet you got a medal for bravery.'

Victor grinned. 'They made a mistake.'

'No, they didn't, you ass. I heard how many lives you saved by risking your own.'

Victor shrugged. 'It was my life to risk. I agreed to minor promotions in the end because I got into training and felt I could look after the lads better than most, train them well, help *save* their lives. And I did. Then I got transferred to the project and that was all right too.'

He smiled, the most relaxed smile Mayne had ever seen on his face. 'I can face peace with a clean conscience now. Some of the chaps have dreadful nightmares.'

Mayne didn't want to think about the dark side of the war's impact, so concentrated on Victor. 'It was a lucky day for the rest of us when you were transferred to the special project. You never said anything about how you felt about the move.'

Victor grinned. 'When I was in the Army? I'm not that stupid.'

'I didn't expect you to be demobbed this quickly.'

An even broader grin. 'It's surprising how quickly they can get rid of you when you bravely try to hide a limp.'

And Mayne found himself doing something he hadn't done for ages – roaring with laughter. That felt so good.

'I'll always remember these post-war days,' Victor said. 'The feeling of sheer relief that it's over, the hopes and plans, the joy at the prospect of being reunited with our families.'

'I know how much you're looking forward to spending time with your daughter.'

Victor smiled, then sighed. 'And to resting. The whole country is weary, don't you think? People need feeding up, after the years of tight rationing. I think the politicians will tread carefully over the next few months. And I think there will be a change of government when we get a general election.'

'What, chuck Winnie out after he's led us through the war?' Mayne mocked. 'Surely not?'

'He's a war leader. We need a peace leader now.'

'People at the unit seem to think the next war is looming already, but it'll be words and propaganda, they reckon, not bombs.'

'Yes. I heard what some of them were saying, but of course the senior officers didn't discuss any details with a lowly person like myself.'

Mayne laughed. 'There's nothing lowly about you, my friend.'

Victor insisted on buying the second round, then they settled down to discuss their plans.

Family first for Victor, who had a wife and child to go back to, though his wife had been ill for a long time. After a little well-earned R&R with his family, he'd come to Rivenshaw to help Mayne start the new business.

'I can't bring my family up north till we've found a decent house to live in, though,' Victor said. 'And help in the home. Susan's not strong. I don't think she ever will be.'

'I'm sorry.' Mayne knew there wouldn't be any more children for his friend beyond the one daughter; at least, not from this wife. Indeed, he wondered how long Victor's invalid wife would last. He'd met Susan a couple of times and she'd been like a wraith, pale and thin, with a lovely smile, but looking insubstantial.

When the two men parted, they were both smiling and relaxed. They didn't need to put their friendship into words. It had been forged in fire. Neither had wanted to go to war. Both had done their duty, and were now determined to make better lives for themselves.

That night, Mayne stayed at a good hotel and treated himself to a visit to the theatre, enjoying Ivor Novello's musical *Perchance to Dream*. He went back to the hotel with the song 'We'll Gather Lilacs in the Spring' running through his mind. Too late for lilacs this year, probably, and he had no one to gather them for. One day . . .

He was not the only person attending the performance on his own, was relieved not to bump into anyone he knew.

He'd always remember this time, a moment when he felt poised on the edge of the future, ready to take off and fly happily in a new direction, a direction he had chosen this time.

Next morning Mayne caught the early train to Manchester, from where he'd take a local train to Rivenshaw. All trains tended to be delayed and diverted, but to his surprise, his was only an hour late getting into Manchester.

He grew thoughtful as the shabby local train approached the small town nestled on the edge of the moors north of Manchester. He suspected that his family was in trouble financially, but his father had refused to discuss it with him.

Well, he wasn't going to sink his savings into Esherwood, let alone try to recreate old glories. An old manor house was a bottomless pit and death duties would hit the next generation just as hard as they'd hit his father. These days, families had to pay dearly to retain their privileged lifestyle in big country houses.

If Labour got elected next time, he suspected they'd find a way to take all such estates from the so-called upper classes.

The War Department hadn't handed Esherwood back to his family yet, or even said when they would do so, as far as he knew. He wished they would make up their minds. His whole future depended on getting that house back.

When you came down to it, he thought sadly, the crumbling old house was more reliable as a basis for the future he was planning than a crumbling old man to whom books and learning were more important than anything else, his family included.

Mayne had learned that you made things happen by hard work, careful planning and attention to detail. He was about to see if he could use his new skills to create a successful business.

He began to recognise landmarks and got his case and kitbag down from the rack.

The feeling he'd had last night after the show was still singing through him and he was looking forward to the future, eager to get started.

Helen didn't wake up until someone touched her good arm gently.

'What?' She jerked upright, staring at the man blankly till she remembered who he was and what they'd arranged. 'Oh, yes. It's you, Jan.'

'Are you all right, Helen?'

'I must have fallen asleep. I'm exhausted.' She looked beyond him, wondering where the neighbour was.

'Miss Peters has gone to have tea with a friend. She will come across later if you need her.' He gestured towards the kitchen table. 'Here is the food we bought. There are shortages, so there was not a lot of choice, but still, it is a start.'

She studied the loaf, a tiny piece of cheese, an egg, a small portion of butter and a reasonably sized bag of potatoes. It looked like they'd be eating a lot of potatoes.

'I didn't buy any tins because there are still tins here.' Jan pushed a lumpy parcel towards her. 'I got you a piece of hambone from the butcher. We can make soup with it and there is some meat and fat left on it.' He chuckled suddenly. 'Miss Peters told them you'd been injured serving your country and needed good food to build you up again. That was what got you the hambone. The other women in the shop were not pleased.'

'Good old Miss Peters. I was scared of her when I came here as a small child, but once I grew older, I began to appreciate how helpful she can be. You'll share the food, of course.'

He stared at the table. 'There is not enough for two, except of potatoes. Those I will eat.'

'If you're helping me, we'll share whatever there is, not just the potatoes.'

He opened his mouth to refuse, caught her eye and said only, 'I thank you.'

She saw him blinking his eyes as if her offer had brought him near to tears. He'd come home too, in a sense. At least, he'd come to make a home in England, if he was allowed. Though it must seem a foreign country to him still.

After a moment he recovered enough to give her a shy half-smile. 'Now I find some blankets to air for you, then I make account of my shopping. I have found a piece of paper and we will write it all down.'

'No need to do that. I didn't give you much money and I trust you.'

He drew himself up. 'There is a great need for me to keep accounts. I have to take your money now. I have only a few pennies of English money left. I apologise for taking yours. One day I shall repay you everything, every single halfpenny. That I swear on my grandfather's soul.'

'Oh. Well. All right. But you've already planted a garden

and there is food in it, so you're giving as well as taking. And you're going to help me in the house, and plant more food in the garden, I hope. So you will be earning your way, Jan.'

'I shall still keep the accounts,' he repeated stubbornly.

She stopped protesting. He had his pride, clearly. 'OK. We've food for the next day or two, then we'll go looking for more.' She glanced out of the kitchen window. Strange how that vegetable garden helped her feel she could trust Jan. As Miss Peters had said, villains didn't usually linger to make gardens.

Helen watched Jan leave the room, tall, too thin, gaunt even, but with eyes lit by intelligence. She listened to him run lightly up the stairs and watched him again as he came back with three blankets. She really liked his face. It was strong and yet gentle.

He held the blankets out to let her feel how damp they were. 'They don't smell very nice. We will hang them outside on a fine day. My mother liked to hang things outside in the sunshine.' He bit off more words, as if it'd hurt to remember his mother.

One day, Helen might tell him about her own mother, tell him how lucky he was to have good memories of his, even if his father had betrayed them.

Rain beat against the windowpanes as if to emphasise that it wouldn't be today that they hung anything out to air. Even as they both watched, the rain eased off, but the dark grey clouds were threatening more.

'Just a shower this time.' He went back to spreading the blankets round the kitchen. He hung the nicest one on the wooden ceiling airer, a contraption with wooden slats that hung from the ceiling in front of the fire and could be wound up and down.

Helen found herself admiring the neat way he did things,

never hurrying but always seeming efficient and in charge of a task, however small. His hands were long-fingered and elegant as he got out a teapot – clearly he knew this kitchen better than she did. He spooned a few tea leaves carefully into it, then poured in the boiling water.

While he waited for the tea to brew, he stoked up the fire then poured her a cup of tea. 'It is very weak. There is not much in the weekly ration. Miss Peters says to use the same tea leaves two or three times with a few fresh leaves added.' He grimaced.

'It'll still warm me. I'm very thirsty. Get a cup for yourself.'

'Thank you.' He did so, cradling the cup between his hands, sniffing the hot air rising from the straw-coloured liquid as if he relished even this weak brew.

'Don't you want a splash of milk in it?'

'No, thank you. I prefer my tea black. You call it black, don't you, even though it's barely brown?'

He took a sip, then another, before setting the cup down. 'Miss Peters got you a loaf. And I found some dried fruit in the pantry. It was in a tin box and must be quite old, but it wasn't mouldy, just dry and hard. I soaked it in water yesterday and then chopped it. We can use it like jam. It will be better than nothing. See, I will spread a little butter on the bread for you, then some fruit. You must eat something more.'

'Thank you. We call this a jam butty.'

'Butty? This is a new word for me.'

'Short for a slice of bread with butter thickly spread on it. I'm going to miss butter. We got more than our share at the farm, but the ration is very small elsewhere.' She looked at the dark smear with a few tiny lumps of fruit in it. She couldn't tell what sort of fruit it was, but was suddenly so ravenous she bit into the bread, relishing even that faint taste of sweetness.

As she swallowed her second mouthful she noticed he hadn't made a jam butty for himself. 'Don't you want something to eat?'

He hesitated, then nodded. 'Well, just one slice then. To keep my strength up.'

He ate very slowly and she guessed he was ravenous. He looked up and shrugged again. It was very attractive, that shrug and the wry expression that went with it.

She smiled. 'Have another slice. I will too. We'll see if we can make more of your sort-of-jam. At least bread isn't tightly rationed like butter and cheese.' She noticed that he only cut a thin slice for himself and a thicker one for her.

He was still studying their food supplies. 'For the evening meal, we will have sandwiches of lettuce leaves from the garden and maybe a radish or two. Not much is ripe yet, but soon other things will start to ripen. And I will plant other seeds. There are a few left.'

'Good idea. And tomorrow, we'll make some broth with the hambone. Maybe we can get some barley at the shop to put in it, or dried peas.'

He licked his lips involuntarily. 'There are some other jars in the pantry. We can find out what they have in them tomorrow.'

She leaned her head back. 'Yes, tomorrow.'

'And when you feel better, tomorrow or the day after, I will go to the police station and tell them about myself. Miss Peters made me promise to do this. She said she would come with me.'

'I'll go with you, too, and speak for you. If there are any problems, we'll do as she suggested and stretch it still further, say my aunt knew your grandfather before the war and you visited England with him.'

She smiled conspiratorially. 'I'll pretend to be much weaker than I am, say how badly I need your help.'

He looked at her speculatively. 'Sometimes it is necessary to lie but what if they find out?'

'How can they? You don't think they'll have enough time and people to investigate my childhood, do you? And my aunt is dead, so they can't question her. We'll just stretch the truth.'

'Thank you.'

After a few moments, he said, 'I wonder . . . There is a wheelchair in the shed. I could clean it and push you to the police station in it. Tell them you can't walk far.'

'Good idea. It's true, actually. I overdid it on the journey here and I'm not up to doing much for a while. If I don't have to *walk* into town, I can visit my lawyer as well as the police, and find out the details of what I've been left. I really am wretchedly weak still, Jan. We'll use that to help you.'

They both smiled at the same time.

'We are conspirators,' he said gravely. 'That is the right word, yes?'

'Yes.' She held out her hand. 'We should shake hands to seal our bargain. You'll work hard for your new country, I'm sure.'

They shook hands gravely, and again he didn't pull away immediately. Nor did she. He wasn't the only one who liked to touch a fellow human being now and then. His hands were beautiful, even with the calluses from all the manual work he must have done.

She looked down at her hands. Soft now, without the ingrained dirt, but with a few calluses still. They were beginning to look like a young woman's hands again. She was glad of that.

Then she got angry at herself for being vain. Except . . . she was a woman still, wasn't she? A young woman, who should be out in the world finding a mate.

She looked at Jan and an idea crept into her mind. No, she couldn't. Could she?

What was there about him that made her feel so safe and comfortable? She'd have to see if that lasted, if they continued to get on well.

The next afternoon, Helen got ready for a trip into town, then sat in the wheelchair. Jan had cleaned it and worked wonders with a little of the ham fat at getting the creaky old chair moving more easily.

Miss Peters was still keeping an eye on them and this morning she'd come across her garden to lean on the wall and watch Jan work on the wheelchair, asking why he was doing that. She'd laughed heartily when he told her.

As they left the front garden, their elderly neighbour came out of her gate, wearing an old-fashioned coat that almost reached the ground and a battered felt hat with two bedraggled feathers on it. 'I'll come with you to the police station, as I promised, and tell them I met Jan's father once.'

He scowled. 'Not my father. I do not speak of my father. I have disowned him. Anyway, my grandfather was the one who actually came here.'

She blinked in surprise at the vehemence in his tone. 'Your grandfather then. When did he come to England, Jan?'

'In 1935. He came on business. Before they stopped us travelling out of the country.'

'Ah!' she said softly. 'You're Jewish, aren't you?'

He froze and for a moment fear crept across his face.

They'd all read about Jewish people being killed by the Nazis and realised why he'd been concealing that, so Helen reached out to pat his arm. 'This is Britain, Jan. We don't kill people for being Jewish.'

'But there is some prejudice. I have met it already.'

'Only from idiots,' Miss Peters said in a bracing tone.

'Anyway, what you'd be facing as a Jew if you went back gives the authorities another reason for letting you stay here . . .'

'I thought . . . I should hide it,' he stammered. 'Even from you.'

'It doesn't make any difference to us,' Helen said.

Miss Peters nodded. 'No. Definitely not. Anyway, I shall tell the police for you. In fact, leave most of the talking to me and don't speak more than you have to. I know the sergeant in charge of the police station. He's a good man.' She smiled smugly as she added, 'And I have some influence with a few of the key people in this part of the world.'

Jan relaxed visibly. 'Thank you.'

It seemed, Helen thought, as though Jan had passed some sort of test with Miss Peters and she was going all out to help him. What a wonderful old lady she was!

And Helen was beginning to think Jan was pretty special, too. All those years on the road – it was nothing short of a miracle that he'd escaped.

And she had to respect his honesty and hard work. Now that he dared show himself, he'd got up early this morning and worked on the gate at the front of the house. It now hung properly on its hinges.

She'd watched him out of the front room window, admiring his utter concentration on the task at hand. But he was thin, far too thin. He needed feeding up.

7

Mayne strolled through the lengthening shadows of early evening, heading from the station to Upper Parklea and Parson's Mead. He thought he recognised one or two people in the town centre but didn't stop to find out if he was right. He didn't want to chat with anyone; he simply wanted to enjoy being back.

He stopped to stare at the Dower House, which looked even shabbier than it had last time he'd come here on leave. He paused to frown at the front gate, which was open and couldn't have been closed for a while, because grass was growing thickly round the bottom of it. Hadn't his father even noticed? Or his mother?

To the right of the Dower House, the double wrought-iron gates into its short carriage drive were closed and padlocked. The sight of that padlock reminded him of an argument he'd had with his father last year. Reginald had lent Mayne's car to an acquaintance just because he'd asked, and the fellow had not only scraped the paintwork but used up a whole tin of Mayne's precious petrol ration.

He wouldn't put it past his father to sell the car, since it wasn't something the old man valued. He seemed to think he owned everything in the house when, in fact, Mayne had bought that car.

He'd fixed padlocks on the gates and the garage door, and

had hidden the various keys in the attic, not even telling his mother where they were, because she didn't often stand up to his father. He'd left a set of keys with the lawyer 'in case', sealing them in an envelope. He'd given very clear instructions not to hand the package to his father unless Mayne was killed.

Without petrol, the car was useless, but Rivenshaw was a small town and he could walk to most places, so it wasn't urgent. The authorities would start letting civilians have petrol soon, he was sure, even if it was tightly rationed, so he could bring the car out again.

Mayne frowned. It had been a good while since the car engine had been run. He was skilled at woodwork, could lay bricks too, and thanks to his officer's training knew how to organise other people to do jobs, but he didn't understand car engines, he had to admit. OK. He'd find someone who did and get them to check the car and make it ready for use. He was definitely going to need a vehicle.

Perhaps he could wangle an extra petrol ration of some sort once he started his business. He'd either use the car for carrying stuff around or else sell it and buy a van or truck, which would suit his needs much better. He smiled grimly. How his mother would hate to see an Esher riding around in a truck! *Lowering standards*, she'd say. Well, she'd just have to lump it.

Come to think of it, there ought to be a bicycle somewhere too, one he'd used in his youth. If the tyres were still all right, he might get that out and blow them up. There had been a lot of riding on bicycles during the war.

He realised he had been standing for a while staring at the house. Taking a deep breath, he strode through the front gate and used the knocker vigorously before opening the front door and yelling, 'I'm back!'

There was a shriek from the kitchen and his mother came running down the hall to fling herself into his arms.

He gave her a quick cuddle then they both moved back. They weren't usually demonstrative.

She studied him. 'No uniform?'

'No. I'm a free man again. Though I'm wearing my own suit, not one of those dreadful demob suits, and you'll notice that I'm not carrying my things in a cardboard suitcase, either.'

'I still think you should have stayed in the Army. You looked so dashing in an officer's uniform and they pay officers well.'

'I told you: I'm not cut out for the military life and I feel like a change.' He was puzzled. It wasn't like her to worry about money.

'Well, too late to do anything about that now,' she said. 'Let's hope you'll take advice before rushing into anything. I wonder how quickly we can get our way of life back to normal.'

What would constitute normal now? Not the same as before the war, which was clearly what she expected. He changed the subject. 'Where's Father?'

'Where do you think? In his study.' She yelled up the stairs, 'Reginald, your only son has come home from the war. Are you not even going to greet him?'

'Just a minute.'

They waited, but there were no sounds to indicate Reginald moving about.

'He hasn't changed.' Mayne tried not to sound aggrieved.

'I doubt he ever will.'

'I don't know how you put up with it.'

'He's my husband. And at least he's not being unfaithful to me with other women, just books.'

Mayne didn't think his father loved any living person, not really.

'Your father found a new book about the Tudors in the WVS

shop and then some other documents when he went into Manchester, so I've hardly seen him for days. Never mind him. You and I will go and have a nice chat in the kitchen.'

As she put the kettle on, she frowned. 'You were demobbed quickly. The government tells us some men will have to wait for months or a year even.'

'It was easier for the Army to get rid of me than try to fit me back in the regiment temporarily, given that I'd been seconded to different work for over a year. I enjoyed it, too, much more fun than marching around firing guns. Luckily we'd just finished a project at the special unit and were cutting down on staff. I volunteered to get out.'

'So you'll be living at home again from now on.'

He'd not been looking forward to telling her this. 'Just for a few days, Mother. I'd like to find a place of my own.' He found her a bit hard to take for long periods, with her affectations and old-fashioned lady of the manor attitude to the world. 'I am thirty, after all, a bit old to be living with my parents. That is, if I can find somewhere to live.'

Her voice grew sharper. 'You're not married, Maynard, so it would look strange for you not to move in with us. What would people think?'

'Hang what people think. I need my privacy, Mother. It's been in short supply during the war years.'

'Privacy! I don't know what your generation is coming to with its strange ideas. Normal people live in families not on their own.'

'After years of living cheek by jowl with other fellows in the army, I want to be on my own. Can't you understand that?'

She shrugged and then looked thoughtful. 'You could move into the old housekeeper's quarters at the rear. It's like a small flat, quite separate, with its own entrance. But Mary and I can still cook for you and do your washing.'

'I can't chuck Mary out of her home.'

'She's not lived there for nearly a year. She comes in daily now and leaves at six. And only five days a week, too. She lives with her daughter and helps out with the grandchildren in the evenings and at weekends. She's even talking of retiring. It's very inconvenient.'

For whom? he wondered. Mary must be over seventy now. She was nearly a decade older than his mother.

As he still hesitated, his mother said more sharply, 'You won't find anywhere suitable to rent in Rivenshaw, Maynard. Women who've lived with their parents again during the war are desperate to find homes of their own now their husbands are coming back. Houses are snapped up before they're even advertised.' Her voice became coaxing. 'Come and look at the housekeeper's quarters, at least.'

'All right.' He followed her through the kitchen and into the two rooms to one side of the main house. He'd never done more than peep inside them before, because you didn't invade Mary's privacy.

'Look. That's the outer door.' His mother pointed across the largish room. 'And this is the bedroom.'

It was a small room but adequate, and already furnished. He walked over to a door on the right. 'There's even a small bathroom!'

'You'd better use ours. You'll never fit into that tiny bath!'

'You'd be surprised at what I've fitted into in my various postings!' He walked round the main room again, studying the details. There was a small alcove to one side, hidden behind a curtain. It had a double gas burner, a big stone sink and a couple of cupboards. 'Oh good! A kitchen. More than enough for my needs. I think this place will definitely do, Mother.'

He went back to study the door that led to the house. 'I'll put a lock on this tomorrow.'

She stared at him indignantly. 'Surely that isn't necessary?'

'Does Father still take things he needs without asking whether the owner needs them too?' His father had been like that all through Mayne's childhood and the boy had soon learned to hide his treasures away carefully.

She sighed. 'Yes. He's worse if anything.' She avoided her son's eyes as she added in a tight voice, 'He doesn't even try to manage the money these days. There are rather a lot of unpaid tradesmen's bills, I'm afraid.'

'Typical of him. I'm not paying the bills for him out of my money, but I will help you sort out the family finances – well, I will if he agrees to turn the business side of the estate over to me. I've discovered that I'm quite good with figures.' Mayne hadn't intended to broach the idea of taking over yet but he was pretty sure his mother would be on his side. 'Will you support me in that?'

'I'm no good with figures, so I can't do it. It's so embarrassing to owe money everywhere. We can't go on like this. Some shops are refusing to serve me now unless I pay cash and start paying off our bill.'

He was shocked. 'Are things really that bad?'

She nodded then changed the subject quickly. 'I'll just sort out something for tea. There's not much choice, I'm afraid.'

Mayne put his suitcase and kitbag into the bedroom and went out into the gardener's shed to look for a bolt. He wasn't wasting a minute in protecting his privacy.

He found plenty of tools and hundreds of smaller items like nails, screws and bolts rusting gently in the darkness of the shed. He wasn't surprised that no one had noticed these treasures, because they no longer had outdoor staff. The tools were piled in corners any old how, many of them hidden under sacks and debris of various sorts. They could be cleaned up again, though, the rust removed.

Mayne eyed them gloatingly. Tools like these were in short

supply for civilians, he knew, and there were waiting lists to buy new ones. These would come in extremely useful in his new business. He'd put a padlock on the door to this shed as well as the door to his new home.

He sorted out two bolts but couldn't find the right size of screw and his mother was growing impatient. He'd come back and have a proper look round in the morning. It was sad not to trust your own father, but there you were.

And he didn't want his mother just walking into the place where he was living because he didn't trust her, either. She'd seemed a bit vague the last few times he'd seen her, as old people sometimes did.

Footsteps sounded on the stairs and Reginald Esher wandered into the kitchen. 'Ah, there you are, Maynard. Glad to have you home, son.'

He sat down and allowed his wife to serve him a bigger portion than anyone else. That was going to stop, Mayne vowed. He put out his hand to block her spooning even more of the mashed potatoes on to his father's plate, then pushed it back in front of her.

'Share the food out equally, Mother. We're all hungry and need to eat, as I'm sure Father will agree.'

She glanced quickly at her husband but did as her son asked.

His father stared down at the contents of his plate as if he'd never seen it before. 'Is that all there is, Dorothy?'

'I'm afraid so, Reginald. Though there's plenty of bread. You and Maynard can fill up with that if you're still hungry.'

'I've heard that rations are going to be cut still further to feed people who are starving in Europe,' Mayne said. 'It'll take time to get our food imports from abroad increased.'

'Which reminds me, Maynard dear, you'll have to let me have your ration book.'

'We'll discuss that tomorrow, Mother.'

His father looked up. 'If your mother needs the ration book, you must hand it over immediately.'

'Maynard's going to live in the old housekeeper's rooms.'

'He can pay us rent, then. He must have saved some money during the war, being kept by the government like that. They treat officers well, even these days.'

And just like that, Mayne's good resolutions to approach his father tactfully went out of the window. 'I think I'd better find somewhere else to live, then. I don't see why I should pay rent in a house that'll be mine one day.'

Though he wondered if it really would come to him. He might be the only son, but if his mother was right and the finances were in such a bad way, the big house could well be repossessed by the bank before his father died.

Reginald looked down his nose at them both. 'I'm still master here, and don't you forget it.'

'A master who can't pay the bills, I gather,' Mayne threw at him.

His father scowled at his mother. 'What have you been telling him?'

'The truth. The butcher told me today in front of a shop full of people that he won't let us have anything else unless we pay cash, and he reminded me that we have outstanding bills. I felt so humiliated, I didn't know where to look. I had to leave the shop without buying anything.'

'What did you do with the housekeeping money? You've been extravagant with money, Dorothy.'

She looked at him in anger. 'No more extravagant than you, Reginald. And I didn't do anything with the money this month, because *you* never gave me any. You said you'd had some rather large book bills.'

He looked surprised, frowned and muttered to himself. 'Ah yes, the Tudor manuscripts. I had to have them. A man has to feed his brain as well as his stomach, even in wartime, and they were crucial to my research.'

His father hadn't changed a bit, Mayne decided. Still utterly selfish and focused only on his own needs. And his mother seemed less capable, somehow, as if her mind was on other things.

She burst into tears and threw her napkin at her husband. 'Then you feed your brain, Reginald, but don't expect me to feed your body. I can't buy food without money. I daren't go into any shop in town unless you give me something to pay them on account. I've even been thinking of selling my mother's bracelet, only you'd take the money away from me, I know you would. You kept all the money from that last painting we sold.'

Mayne sucked in his breath sharply. He knew how much she loved that bracelet. 'Surely there are other things you can sell?'

'Your father has already sold most of my jewellery.'

'You're exaggerating,' his father snapped. 'We only sold a few pieces. And you sold some others without asking me.'

'Well you didn't use the money to pay the outstanding bills as you'd promised! And you're not the only one who needs things sometimes.'

'Those damned shopkeepers can jolly well wait. They've done well out of the Esher family over the years.'

'There's nothing special about an Esher who doesn't pay his debts,' Mayne said.

'And you haven't paid Mary's wages for three weeks, either,' his mother went on, dabbing at her eyes. 'How dare you take advantage of her like that after all she's done for us over the years?'

'You should be paying her wages out of the housekeeping. Anyway, she knows we'll pay her eventually.'

'No, she doesn't. You've skipped paying her before, and

she persuaded me to forget it, but this time I won't put up with it. It's *stealing* her labour, that's what it is.'

She turned to her son. 'Maynard, if you can find somewhere else to live, you take it. After what your father has just accused me of, I shall leave him to his books and he can eat *them* when he's hungry. I shall only be taking care of myself from now on and I shall tell Mary not to come back to work here till she's been paid.'

There was dead silence as Reginald gaped at her.

'I mean it,' she said. 'I've had enough.'

'This is your fault,' he shouted at his son and shoved his chair back so hard it fell over. Ignoring it, he walked out, slamming the door behind him.

Dorothy looked at Mayne, then stared into space. After a few moments, she said, 'What am I going to do?'

'Don't do anything rash. I'll go and see our lawyer tomorrow. I know Mr Lloyd died last year so I suppose it'll be Mr Graveston I have to deal with.'

'What?'

He repeated it.

'No. He's retired because of poor health and left the town. There's a new man taken over now. He's called Gilliot. Well, I think he is. I keep forgetting. I don't like him. I do remember that.'

'I'll have to go and see him, whatever he's like, to find out the facts. But I won't give Father any of my own money, not one penny. I'm sorry if this hurts you too, Mother, but he'd not pay the bills with it. And if I gave you money, he'd take it off you, you know he would.'

She flushed and glanced upstairs as if to make sure her husband couldn't hear what she was saying. 'He's stolen money from my purse several times now. I have to keep it hidden.'

'That is unconscionable.'

'I'm sorry. This is a terrible homecoming for you. I hadn't meant to tell you yet.'

'*You* have nothing to be sorry about and the confrontation with Father was inevitable, given the circumstances. Have you heard from the War Office yet about when they'll give us back the big house?'

She looked at him in puzzlement. 'Your father said he'd written to tell you. They informed us last month that they were moving out, then left soon afterwards. The commandant came to see us, only your father refused to come out of his study to talk to him.'

'Typical!'

'The commandant spoke to me instead. He said the house was in a bad state and apologised for any damage. He said in wartime the greater cause has to come first, and they didn't have time to repair anything.'

'Damn. I was hoping the house wasn't in too bad condition, since neither you nor Father mentioned serious damage. I gather a War Damage Commission has been set up and will pay compensation, but that'll probably take time and I doubt they'll be generous. What's the old place like inside?'

'I haven't been there since the Army took over. It wasn't allowed.'

'But now that the Army has handed it back, surely one of you has gone up to have a look?'

'I couldn't bear to see it until it's been set to rights.'

Mayne wasn't surprised at that. She'd always tried to avoid unpleasant situations. He'd hoped the war would make her more practical. 'And Father? Has he been up to inspect the big house? He claims to love it, after all.'

'Not yet. He says he's at a crucial stage in his research. He did get permission to fetch some books last year and complained that the boxes had been put in the cellar and some books were mildewed, but he didn't seem to notice anything about the house.'

'No. He wouldn't!'

Mayne was glad the books had been put in the cellar. If they'd been lying around, they'd probably have been torn up and used to make paper darts. He'd heard of that happening when men got bored. And some places had been utterly ruined by the troops billeted there, which seemed incredible to him. Why had the officers in charge not stopped it? He would have done so if it had been his men.

Worry settled in his chest like a lead weight. Had he lost his new business before he even started it up? As long as the house was still structurally sound, surely the inside could be made habitable again. It was too dark to go and inspect it now. And he didn't suppose the electricity was still connected there.

He would get up at dawn tomorrow and check it out, then call on the new lawyer in the morning and contact the electricity people to switch on the power.

He finished his meal, but his mother left half hers. She scraped it into a dish and covered her husband's meal with a plate, putting them both on the cold stone shelf in the pantry, muttering, 'We mustn't waste anything.'

Then she left without a word.

She was in a strange mood tonight. Very strange.

When he retired for the night, Mayne didn't try to unpack his bags, just fished out his pyjamas and a change of clothes for the morning. He wasn't sure how long he'd be staying, whether this little flat really was private enough. He had to make time tomorrow to put those bolts on the connecting door.

He snuggled down in bed with a tired sigh, feeling his body relax bit by bit. No need to set an alarm clock at this time of year. After his years in the Army, he'd wake automatically at dawn.

They'd said on the radio that it would be a fine day in the north-west. It was nearly June now, a lovely time of year, and he was looking forward to seeing the grounds of Esherwood as well as the old house.

May had been memorable, in more ways than one. What would his first weeks of peacetime freedom in Rivenshaw bring? Who knew with his father? The old man might agree to hand over the estate to his son, but if so it'd better be done quickly. He often changed his mind on a whim.

The war might be over, in Europe anyway, but Mayne would have some personal battles to face on the home front. He was quite sure of that.

Helen sat in the wheelchair, feeling like a fool, but actually quite glad not to be walking into town and back on top of the calls she had to make there. She felt she'd well and truly drained her reserves of energy getting home to Rivenshaw, and was deeply thankful for Jan's help.

And for Miss Peters' help. She glanced sideways at the old lady, who was walking beside them, nodding to people now and then, looking ready to take on the world.

The police station was open but there was no one to be seen. From a room to one side came the tapping of a typewriter, from the office behind the counter the sound of a chair being pushed back.

'We're lucky. There's no queue at the moment,' said Miss Peters. 'Ah, Sergeant Deemer. How nice to see you again!'

A burly older man in police uniform came out of the back room. 'Miss Peters. How nice to see you, too.'

Was it her imagination or had he greeted Miss Peters with a touch of wariness? Helen wondered.

'I've brought my young friend and neighbour to register with you,' she said cheerfully.

He looked from Jan to Helen and then back to Jan again, eyes narrowed as if suspicious.

'Jan is a displaced person,' she said, 'and I gather he must register. Which he's very willing to do.'

'You're not registered anywhere else, sir?'

'No.'

'Where have you been till now?'

'Travelling, Sergeant, fleeing from the Nazis when and how I could.'

'Well, you seem to have succeeded.'

'He's come over from Ireland,' Miss Peters put in.

'How did he get into this country, then?' Deemer asked. 'And can't he speak for himself?'

'Of course he can, but I speak better English, so you'll be quicker dealing with me, since I know all the facts. But if you want to take all day about this, Sergeant, go ahead.' She waved one hand dismissively.

He let out a growl of annoyance. 'Very well, then. You tell me.'

'Jan didn't know England was another country from southern Ireland. He comes from Poland and didn't learn much about Great Britain at school.'

'The government is sending refugees back to Poland, so—'

She interrupted quickly. 'Not the Jewish ones.'

'Ah.'

'If he goes back, they'll put him in a work camp and probably work him to death. You've heard about those camps, I'm sure. That's why he ran away, to avoid them.'

'Then why did he come to Rivenshaw?'

'Because his family knew Miss Bretherton's family. Oh, I didn't introduce you, did I? Sorry. Sergeant Deemer, this is Helen Bretherton, just demobbed from the Land Army. She was injured in the course of duty and she hasn't recovered yet. She inherited Ethel Bretherton's house next to mine. I knew Helen as a child.'

His expression softened. 'Welcome back, miss.'

'Jan came to the Brethertons for help, but didn't know there was no one left, so I've been keeping an eye on him for a few days, just till dear Helen got here. He's been doing some gardening. Such a useful, hardworking young man.'

She patted the younger woman's shoulder. 'It's a good thing he is here, because Helen needs help and I'm not strong enough to look after her till she recovers. I have to manage without a maid these days, and I'm not as young as I was.'

He frowned, trying to think his way through this maze of information. 'So he's helping Miss Bretherton?'

'She's offered him a job doing the gardening and helping her to make the lower part of the house habitable.'

'Is that true, Miss Bretherton? You've offered him a job?'

'Oh, yes, Sergeant. I won't be able to manage without help for some time. This is quite a serious injury. A major muscle and some nerves were sliced open in an accident on the farm where I was working.' She gestured to her bandaged arm.

'Well, that might just be reason for allowing him to stay here. I'll have to consult the area inspector, though. This man can't settle here without permission.'

'Of course he can't,' Miss Peters said. 'That's why we came to see you today.'

'There is that in his favour. But still, you know what they're like at area headquarters. *I* can't make that decision, Miss Peters, no matter what you tell me.'

'I will be a good citizen,' Jan said suddenly. 'This is a free country. It has won the war against the Nazis. I will work hard to make a new life here.'

His accent sounded twice as thick as usual, Helen thought. Clever of him. She had trouble preventing herself from smiling.

'Who is your area inspector?' Miss Peters asked.

'Inspector Upham.'

'I thought he was dead.'

'Came out of retirement to do his bit.'

'I'll write to him. I'll bring you a letter this afternoon to send with the paperwork.'

He looked at her steadily. 'For some reason, you're on this chap's side, Miss Peters, and that speaks for him better than anything else, as far as I'm concerned. I've never known you help a wrong 'un.'

'Thank you, Sergeant. I appreciate that compliment. I do my best.'

'But I still can't speak for the inspector.' He reached under the desk and slapped two pieces of paper down. 'Here you are, young man. One week's emergency ration coupons, for the grocery and butcher's shops. You must report to me here next week at the same time.'

Jan nodded. 'Next week. I remember the way.' He took the papers that were pushed across to him. 'Thank you.'

'See you look after that young lady. *And* that you work hard,' Deemer called after them.

Jan turned. 'I will. Her family has been very good to my grandfather and me before the war.'

Outside Miss Peters looked at them smugly. 'That's an excellent start.'

Jan's heavy foreign accent had almost vanished. 'It's kind of you to write to the inspector.'

'I played with him when we were children. His mother and mine were friends.'

The Town Hall clock struck the hour.

'Oh, my goodness! Is that the time already? I'll leave you two to register Jan's ration books at the shops. Don't forget to see your lawyer, Helen. He needs to know you're back.'

And she strode off down the street without waiting for an answer.

'She is a very clever lady,' Jan said. 'As well as kind.'

'She doesn't like to be called kind, but she is, in her own way. I think I'd better stay in the wheelchair. Are you all right to push me?'

'Yes. I like to look after you. And I remember the way to the grocer's and butcher's from when I went there with Miss Peters. Only . . . I don't have any money to buy food.'

'I'll lend you the money.'

'I must take it now, but I will pay you back one day. Now we can share my food rations as well as yours.' He gave a satisfied nod that spoke more eloquently than words.

She settled back in the chair, feeling a sense of satisfaction at how the morning had started.

People like Miss Peters were what had made England refuse to give up in the war. The government could be so proud of them and what they'd put up with all these years.

At the lawyer's, Helen insisted on getting out of the wheelchair, which they left in the entrance hall. She went inside the lawyer's rooms and found a very old man sitting at a desk.

'Yes, miss?' He looked up but didn't stand.

'I'd like to see Mr Gilliot. I gather he's taken over the practice.'

'And you are?'

'Helen Bretherton.'

He relaxed his haughtiness slightly, but only very slightly. 'Ah, yes. I knew your great-aunt well. I'll find out if Mr Gilliot can see you now.'

He eased himself up out of his chair and walked stiffly through a doorway. He would be another of those who'd come out of retirement, she guessed, to fill jobs left vacant by those who'd gone to war.

He returned at the same snail's pace. 'Mr Gilliot will see you now, miss.'

'I'll wait for you here,' Jan said.

'Please take a seat, sir.' The old man led Helen into the inner sanctum. 'Miss Bretherton, sir.'

Henry Gilliot was a thin gentleman who looked to be in his forties. He had a scar on his cheek and held his right arm stiffly, so she guessed he'd served in the armed forces and been invalided out.

He came from behind the desk, left hand outstretched. 'I'm delighted to meet you, Miss Bretherton. You should have let me know you were coming and I'd have sent someone to meet you at the station.'

'I arrived late – you know how uncertain travel can be – and as I knew where there was a key, I let myself into the house.'

'Good heavens! Was it habitable?'

'Downstairs, yes.'

He was staring at the heavily bandaged arm. 'You've hurt yourself. How are you managing?'

'I've hired help, someone my neighbour knows. You've probably met Miss Peters.'

He relaxed visibly. 'Yes. A redoubtable old lady. She's been keeping an eye on the house. Is the woman she found going to stay on as your maid? If so, you'll want to arrange payment of her wages. We can do that for you.'

He was pleasant but somehow she didn't think he liked her having taken possession of the house without his say-so, and now was trying to take control of the situation. 'It's not a woman. It's a man to do the garden and the heavy lifting. He's a displaced person.'

Mr Gilliot didn't attempt to hide his disapproval. 'Are you sure that's wise?'

'Miss Peters thinks so. She met his family before the war.'

'Nonetheless—'

'I haven't come to discuss my home arrangements, which are, after all, my own business, Mr Gilliot. I gather I've been left some money as well as the house. I'm hoping it'll be enough to have the house repaired. The rain's getting in where the bomb knocked out part of one wall and window, so there's considerable damp upstairs.'

He took a file out of a drawer and opened it, pulling out a sheet of paper and handing it to her. 'This is a summary of what your aunt left you. I can arrange to have a copy made for you now that you're here.'

'I'll do my own copy and return this one to you.' She thought he was going to snatch back the piece of paper, so folded it and put it quickly in her handbag.

'Very well. But please take care of it. I'll accompany you to the bank, so that you can gain access to the accounts there.'

'That'll be very useful. I do have some money saved, but they didn't pay us Land Girls generously and I need some new civilian clothes, as well as money for repairs. Good thing I've got some clothing coupons saved.' She had been wearing her uniform on the farm. 'I can't imagine the government stopping the rationing for a while, can you?'

'I'm afraid not. My wife is very concerned about our own clothing situation.' He pulled out a large, old-fashioned pocket watch and flicked the cover open. 'If we go to the bank now, I've just got time to introduce you to the manager before my next client arrives.'

Outside, Jan stood up and she beckoned to him to join them. 'This is Jan Borkowski, who is helping me. Jan, this is my lawyer, Mr Gilliot.'

It was as if the air had suddenly turned icy. The lawyer stared as if in shock, then nodded his head slightly but made no attempt to shake hands or speak to Jan. 'Shall we go?'

They left the office and she decided to sit in the wheel-chair to emphasise that she needed Jan's help.

The lawyer stopped in surprise. 'I didn't realise you needed a wheelchair.'

'I'm not long out of hospital and tire easily. Jan has been wonderful about helping me get about. Luckily he's very strong.'

'Um. Yes. Good.'

But the lawyer still looked as if he was upset, and it was easy to see from the way he kept glancing sideways that it was to do with Jan.

Mr Gilliot introduced her to the bank manager, signed some papers handing over the accounts to her and left her to it without saying goodbye to her companion.

When they got home, she suggested a cup of tea, and as Jan handed it to her, she said, 'Sit down and have a cup yourself.'

She waited for him to take a couple of mouthfuls, then said, 'Now, tell me why Mr Gilliot was like that with you. It's obvious you know why.'

'Better not to talk about it. There is nothing we can do.'

'Better that I know, or how can I continue to help you?'

Jan grimaced. 'He has guessed from my appearance that I am Jewish. Hitler was not the only one to dislike the Jews. There are people in all countries who feel the same.'

'Oh. I didn't realise it was that bad here.' She didn't see that his religion was anyone else's concern. 'I don't think there's a synagogue in town, so I don't know how you're going to worship.'

He set his cup down again, stared at it then looked her in the face. 'I am Jewish by birth, Helen, but after the horrors

I've seen, I have no belief in religion. And if I have to declare myself, Miss Peters told me a while ago to put Church of England.'

'I thought we'd fought for freedom,' she said bitterly. 'I gave up three years of my life for that struggle against the Nazis. I apologise for Mr Gilliot's attitude. I shall be changing my lawyer.'

'There is never freedom for all. I don't think it is possible.'

'Nonetheless, I shall change lawyers. I didn't like that man's attitude to me, either.'

Jan smiled, such a lovely smile it transformed his face and she realised if he were well fed, he might be quite attractive.

'Thank you for your concern, Helen, but it is not worth bothering about it. There are people with prejudices everywhere, but there are also people like you and Miss Peters to make up for it.'

Without thinking, she reached out to take his hand. 'I'm glad I met you, Jan. I definitely couldn't manage without your help, so I thank you for staying with me. I overestimated how quickly I'd recover if I could only get away from hospital.'

'You will be fine, Helen. Already you have more colour in your cheeks than when you arrived. But deep wounds take a long time to heal properly so you must be careful with your arm. And it is I who must thank you. I have nowhere to go and you are letting me stay in your home.'

He added, 'Nowhere in the world,' in a low voice as if thinking aloud and her heart went out to him.

There was a tap on the back door and when Jan opened it, Miss Peters was standing there.

'How did it go, my dears?'

'All right till Mr Gilliot realised Jan was Jewish. I was embarrassed by his behaviour after that.'

'I'm not really surprised. You can't change the world and

its prejudices. You can find another lawyer once things settle down, and I may do so too. Gilliot talks to me as if I'm senile.'

She held out a paper bag. 'I was given some goose-berries, which are overripe and won't keep, so I brought you a few across. I don't have enough sugar to turn them into jam.'

'There is some sugar in the pantry. It's been stored there all through the war, I think, and has gone hard,' Jan said.

'Good. Then you can have a dessert tonight.' She frowned at Helen. 'And be sure to get an early night, my dear. You look tired out.'

'I can pick a few lettuce leaves for you, Miss Peters,' Jan said, then turned to Helen as if asking for permission to give them away. When she nodded, he said, 'If I pick the outer leaves, the lettuce lasts longer.'

'Good idea.'

Miss Peters waved one hand in farewell to Helen and followed him out.

Jan came back a few moments later. 'Why don't you go and lie down for an hour? I can dig over some more ground. Now that you're here, I shall plant other things to eat.'

Helen didn't intend to sleep, but she could feel herself getting drowsy as soon as she lay down on the big sofa in the front room. She didn't attempt to resist. It had been an eventful few days.

But she thought she could turn this house into a home again.

With Jan's help. He seemed a very decent sort. Nice-looking too.

She had almost forgotten that she was a young woman in need of a mate till she met him. Would he be interested in her? It might be worth finding out. She very much wanted to have children, would dare anything for that.

It surprised her how quickly she had started thinking about Jan in that way. The attraction hadn't been this immediate with Wilfred.

8

Mayne got up even before it was light and went into his mother's kitchen. There was so little food in the pantry, he didn't take any of it. He'd find somewhere to buy a late breakfast when he went into town, and get a loaf from the baker's.

Maybe the British Restaurant in Rivenshaw opened for lunch or, as the locals called the midday meal, dinner. If he remembered correctly, they ran the wartime meals service in the hall of the Methodist Chapel. You didn't need ration coupons to eat in a British Restaurant, just money and an ability to eat anything set before you, because they weren't famous for their wonderful food.

If he found somewhere to eat a cooked meal most days, it would save him a lot of time and trouble while he sorted out the business of the family estate one way or another.

He decided to fit the bolts later, so jammed a chair against the door from his flat into the rest of the house, balancing a teaspoon on it so that he'd know if someone tried to force their way in. He went outside, stretching and turning his face up to the bright morning sunlight. Just as he was about to cross the gardens to get to the big house, the kitchen door opened, so he stopped to say, 'Good morning, Mother.'

'Have you had anything to eat, Maynard?'

'No. I'll buy something in town later. You haven't enough food to spare.'

'Have a slice of bread, at least.'

He hesitated but he knew she'd take a huff if he didn't eat what she offered. Anyway, bread wasn't rationed. 'All right. I'll bring another loaf back with me.'

'And you'll have a cup of tea?'

'I haven't time, Mother. I need to find out what state the big house is in.'

'Why the hurry? Are you planning something?'

'Yes. I'll tell you about it later.'

She looked annoyed but didn't pursue the matter, just cut him a slice of bread. 'Sorry. Your father ate the last of the margarine.'

'Doesn't matter.' Mayne ate the dry bread to please her and drank a glass of water quickly.

He was glad to get out into the fresh air and smiled as he heard birdsong while he walked across the back of the house to the main drive. His smile faded as he saw the ugly concrete bollards on either side of it, with big rusty chains padlocked across to prevent entry. Why hadn't the occupiers thought to remove those, at least, before they left? He'd have to get someone to cut the padlocks.

If this had been a civilian establishment, the chains would have been taken for scrap long ago. He got out his notebook and jotted down a reminder to remove bollards and chains, and keep them. He could sell them for scrap if nothing else.

The gardens near the Dower House looked much the same as they always had, though they were rather overgrown.

When he rounded the curve in the drive, however, he stopped in shock at the devastation. Trees had been felled, bushes pulled out, for no reason that he could see, and flower beds flattened into hard, bare earth.

Closer to the house, at the far end of this desolation, stood a large Nissen hut with a ramshackle wooden shed beside it. He tried the doors of both the shed and the Nissen hut, but they were locked. He'd come back later with tools to break in. The War Office had handed the house and land back, so presumably everything belonged to the family now.

The other outside area left more or less intact was the kitchen garden and, from the sight of it, someone had kept it planted. However, someone had been raiding it recently, trampling on plants to get at the stuff that was edible now.

That was going to stop. If there were fruit and vegetables ripening, they would belong to the family.

He decided to go into the big house first, then look at the rear outhouses, so he unlocked the front door, stopping in shock at what he saw. 'Dear heaven! How could they let this happen?'

The place looked as if it had been sacked by the Mongol hordes. As well as piles of rubbish dotted about the floor, the seventeenth-century oak panelling in the entrance hall had initials carved on it, and words you didn't use in women's company. He walked round, feeling sick as he saw stray gouge marks and cracked panels everywhere. One neat circle of intact panelling was surrounded by a myriad of small holes. It took him a minute to realise that a dartboard must have been hung there.

A few panels had been hacked out completely. There was no sign of them. Why? What sort of men destroyed the house that had been lent to them to convalesce in?

It took only a minute to work that out: probably the sort of men who resented some people being privileged enough to own such a large dwelling. Or . . . he remembered things he'd seen himself during the war years . . . men bored and frustrated beyond bearing by having nothing to do and taking out their anger on anything handy.

He went quickly around the ground floor, noting cracked

windows, which looked as if something heavy had been thrown at them from inside. Doors had been pulled off their hinges, furniture damaged and left in careless heaps.

He also found stacks of metal army beds and flock mattresses, most in a decent condition. He made a mental note to retrieve anything that was reusable and hide it away – if he got his father to agree to his plans, that was.

The kitchens weren't quite as bad as the rest of the house, presumably because people still wanted to be fed properly. Or maybe the occupants had been moved out so suddenly, they hadn't had time to wreak havoc here in the final days.

There seemed to be a few supplies of dry goods left in the pantry. They would come in useful if he could prevent looters from getting in.

He switched on his torch and made his way down to the cellars, dreading what he'd find.

Most of the family's stores of everyday dishes, bowls and buckets had gone, but there were all sorts of wooden crates, stacked, or lying on their sides. Some were empty, some unopened. He'd deal with them another time, but even the wood of the empty crates would come in useful.

His objective now was a small storeroom, which wasn't visible unless you went into the far corner of the cellar and moved some broken furniture out of the way. He had personally moved various family treasures and smaller pieces of furniture into it before the house was handed over. He'd had just one day to do this and hadn't asked anyone to help so that it would remain a secret.

His father hadn't seen the need to hide anything, sure the government would respect his property, so Mayne had worked all night on his own. He couldn't now remember exactly what he'd hidden.

He wondered if his father remembered that this cache existed. If he asked, Mayne would tell him it had been looted.

He had the keys, so his father wouldn't be able to check the storeroom.

Much of the broken furniture hiding the entrance to it could be repaired, he decided as he lifted a few of the pieces aside. How people had changed about what they considered worth keeping and using, him included! *Make do and mend* was more than just a slogan these days: it was a way of life.

He took out the huge bunch of keys and tried to unlock the door to the storeroom. After finding the right key, he made several attempts, but it wouldn't turn. He decided he'd have to come back with oil and try again. He didn't want to break the door open, because it was useful to have a hiding place.

There was another hidden chamber in the attics. He must check that it hadn't been discovered, either.

He put back the broken furniture, rubbing out his footprints on the dusty floor with an old broom and studying the area. He hefted a couple of empty crates across as well, then nodded in satisfaction. No sign of the entrance to the inner cellar now.

He went to check the first floor. There were eight bedrooms in the main building, the five larger ones having dressing rooms attached, and – goodness! – two new bathrooms had been installed, as well as the old one being refurbished.

'Damnation!' The ceramic suite had been stolen from one of the new bathrooms, with the pipes left jutting up forlornly where the sink and bath had been taken away. Someone had sealed the pipes to stop them leaking. The theft made him angry, though. It had been a professional job. Such items were hard to get hold of. If they came back for the other bathroom suites, they'd find him waiting.

He walked along to the east wing, where there were three further bedrooms, without dressing rooms, together with what had once been the second bathroom, an old-fashioned room. He tried the taps and flushed the toilet. Everything still worked, though it needed a good clean.

At least the military occupiers had been generous with bathrooms, as you might expect in a convalescent home, which would save him some money. Or it would do if he got his father to hand over the house and managed to keep further looters out of it.

He told himself not to count his chickens till they hatched, but he and Victor had been planning this building project for several months. It mattered a lot to him, not only as a way of preserving the old house, but as a way of earning a living.

He decided to sleep here tonight. Yes, and bring his revolver with him in case he was attacked. He was determined to prevent the theft of anything else from his family home.

He'd need help, though. One person wasn't enough to keep watch on such a large house and several acres of grounds. Who could he find to do that? He wasn't even sure which chaps from the town had been demobbed. Maybe he should write and ask Victor to join him as quickly as possible, to help him guard and salvage things.

Up another floor and he was in the children's area, where he'd led a privileged and lonely life with his nanny till he was old enough to go to school. There were rooms enough for several children, but his mother had only had one child. He'd gone into the other bedrooms sometimes when he was younger and imagined having brothers and sisters, even giving these imaginary siblings names.

He'd been completely on his own up here as often as not, sometimes with a young maid to keep him company, increasingly left to amuse himself as he grew older. Which was why he knew all the house's hiding places.

During his childhood, his father had taken his mother off on research tours, which had been more like little holidays for the pair of them. Once or twice she'd suggested taking Mayne with them, but his father had refused point-blank. He wanted her to take notes for him, not look after a child.

She should have stood up for her son more, Mayne thought. But probably she hadn't cared enough. Even when she was at home, she'd only been an intermittent presence in his life. In her own way she was as selfish as his father. What she seemed to enjoy most was her social life.

The attics were the last place to visit. He'd always thought of them as his territory, and very few other people had bothered to visit them in the old days, except the maids who'd occupied two of the small bedrooms above the east wing when he was smaller. It wouldn't have occurred to his father or his mother to come up here at all. They considered it an area for servants and storage, not for 'the family'.

The row of small bedrooms had been unused for years, as the family grew short of money and stopped hiring live-in maids, instead paying charladies to come in by the day. Mary had kept her title of 'housekeeper' and until a year ago had lived in the downstairs rooms, which Mayne now occupied, plus there had been a daily housemaid and scrubbing woman to help her.

From the doorway of the vast storage area, all you could see was more broken furniture, boxes of who knew what, ancient travelling trunks, battered chests of drawers. Why had none of this rubbish ever been thrown away? He'd probably benefit from that now.

He'd spent many hours up here as a child, knew every inch of the place, and he was probably the only one now who knew about the secret room. He found a place to one side where old trunks had been used to sit on. A lot of cigarette butts were strewn about on the floor and beyond it were three slightly charred floorboards where someone must have set the place on fire – accidentally, he hoped. Thank goodness they'd bothered to put it out again!

He went into the secret room after manipulating the nearby shelf to open it, sighing with relief when he saw the paintings he'd hidden before he left for his Army training. These were the most valuable possessions of all, and if he sold them, he'd not use the money to buy dusty old books, you could be damned sure of that.

There were some leather drawstring bags of jewellery in a casket, too, but after glancing inside a couple to check that their contents hadn't been tampered with, he hid them again. These weren't his mother's but old pieces that had gone out of fashion. They'd been left to him by his godmother and his mother had turned up her nose at them, saying they weren't worth much and he should sell them to a jeweller to break up and reuse. He hadn't followed her advice. Another thing to keep quiet about.

He hadn't had time to fill up this secret chamber, and it was quite large, so there was still room if he wanted to put anything else in a safe place – maybe some of his tools and supplies when he started building.

If he started building.

Mayne went downstairs again with a lot to think about. When he looked at his wristwatch, he realised it was nearly ten o'clock, so hurried home to dress more smartly for his visit to the lawyer's.

His mother immediately rapped on the connecting door and when he opened it, offered to make him a cup of tea.

'There isn't time.'

'Just tell me quickly how the house is, then.'

'In a dreadful state. Rubbish everywhere, panelling destroyed, lots of damage. Oh, and they've built a Nissen hut next to the vegetable garden. Its door is locked so I can't get inside to see if there's anything useful. Where's Father?'

'In his study.'

'He'd stay in there even if this house caught fire.'

'He feels safe there. He's very upset about how the world is changing, you know.'

'Not too upset to eat half your food rations as well as his own. Did you cave in and make him any breakfast?'

'No. I meant what I said.'

'Good for you. Keep to your resolve, Mother. I'll cater for myself. Father has to learn what our Brave New World is like.' She obviously hadn't read the book, so he didn't explain that his allusion was not to Shakespeare's verse from *The Tempest* but to Aldous Huxley's intriguing views on what the world might become in the future, a place where people were controlled in every aspect of their lives.

Britain had come close to that during the war, with even the styles of clothes mandated to save fabric, not to mention how much food one person could buy at a restaurant.

'You shouldn't go to see the lawyer on an empty stomach, Mayne. You need to have your wits about you.'

'I'm fine, Mother. Is the British Restaurant still operating?'

'I suppose so. *I* have never gone to it.'

'I'll get something to eat there after I've seen this Mr Gilliot. Shall I bring you a loaf back?'

'Yes, we do need another loaf. Thank you.'

There was silence for a moment or two, then she said sadly, 'It's going to be difficult setting the house to rights, isn't it? Peace may be even harder than war for some people.'

He didn't pretend. 'Yes. It'll be very difficult for our family. And if you're in debt, even Father will have to face facts.'

'Perhaps we should sell the Dower House and use the money to repair the big house. I'm so looking forward to getting my old home back.'

He looked at her in surprise but didn't comment. There was no way things could be the same again. Even if they'd had the money, materials to make repairs with were scarce, and replacement furniture simply wouldn't be available.

One of the government's priorities was building houses to replace those lost in the war. There was a huge shortage of places to live after all the bombing losses. The authorities didn't care whether people like his parents were struggling to set stately homes to rights. He'd known that for a good while, but neither his father nor his mother seemed to understand the practicalities of the situation.

One step at a time. First he must find out exactly how things stood.

The new lawyer received Mayne with a flattering degree of attention. He cut short the fuss. 'I need to talk to you frankly about Esherwood and my family's financial situation, Mr Gilliot. Don't try to be tactful, just tell me the truth, if you please. I've learned to be businesslike in the Army, where I was managing major projects, so I'm not like my father.'

'Ah.'

Mayne waited.

'Things are bad. Your father owes a lot of money, more than he can ever pay back, and I fear the bank is likely to foreclose on Esherwood soon.'

'Does the estate still have any decent value? I've been up there. The interior of the house has been very badly treated, but I think it's still structurally sound. The grounds near the house look as if they're in a war zone. It's disgusting that the War Office allowed the place to be so badly damaged, but I hear it's happened all over the country.'

'Oh, dear. I haven't been up there myself, and I grew up in Manchester, so I've never actually seen the house. Your father refused point-blank to discuss selling Esherwood, though I went to the Dower House to see him, at the bank's request.'

'He'll discuss it now, I'll make sure of that. He and my

mother are still living in a dream of returning to pre-war ways, I'm afraid. Which is not going to happen, in my opinion.' Mayne stood up. 'I'll find out how much the land is worth before you come to see us, and—'

'If you would just sit down again for a moment, Mr Esher. I've already received an offer to purchase Esherwood.'

'Have you indeed?' He sat down.

'Not a very generous offer, I'm afraid. Only five thousand pounds.'

Mayne winced. 'That little?'

'Sadly, yes. The gentleman in question has made good money from the war and intends to knock down the old house and build himself a new one. He's a shrewd bargainer, but I'm sure we can get him to raise his offer a little.'

'Who is he?'

'I can't tell you that. I promised to keep his name secret.'

Mayne ran quickly through the prominent citizens in his mind and settled on the one who'd be most likely. 'I bet it's old Ray Woollard.'

Gilliot gaped at him. 'How did you—?' He broke off abruptly. 'I can neither confirm nor deny that.'

'You don't need to. Your reaction has already confirmed that I've guessed correctly. He's got to be one of the richest men in town now, anyway.'

'To be frank, I doubt your father will have much choice about selling. His debts are considerable, I believe, but he won't disclose the total.'

Mayne was annoyed but didn't comment. 'He probably doesn't know how much he owes. He's not very practical. I'll find out, though. In the meantime tell Woollard to get back to me when he has a serious offer to make.'

Mayne left the lawyer's rooms and walked slowly along the street, stopping at the baker's to buy a couple of loaves.

When a street seller accosted him with black market bits and pieces of food, he abandoned principles and bought a jar of jam, a couple of tins of peaches and one of corned beef, all at grossly inflated prices.

The seller put them in a sack for a small extra charge. The items were, from the labels, made in America, and had no doubt been bought or even begged for nothing from the American troops stationed in the country. A lot of that went on. Some of the Americans were very generous; others were out to make money.

He began walking back to the Dower House, taking a slightly roundabout route that would lead him along the even-numbered side of Parson's Mead.

He wasn't sure how he'd persuade his father to hand over the house to him and let him sort out the finances. But if he didn't find a way, they'd lose Esherwood and he'd lose a golden opportunity to set up in business.

He had to set aside his scruples and use every method he could to win Esherwood.

When he got home, his father was in the kitchen, yelling at his mother. He didn't go inside, but stood listening through the half-open door to his flat.

'I have to eat something,' his father said angrily. 'Get me whatever there is.'

'There isn't anything left and I can't buy food without money.'

'You always have stuff in the pantry: stores, little tins of this and that. I don't mind what I have for my luncheon.'

'You can't eat food we haven't got.'

Mayne watched his father open the pantry door, vanish inside and come out again almost immediately, looking surprised.

'Are you sure there's nothing elsewhere? In the cellar, perhaps?'

'There are a few potatoes left down there, half a loaf here, some flour too, I think, and today's milk. You can have dry bread or boiled potato for your lunch.'

'You know I don't like that British loaf. It's peasant bread, nasty brown stuff.'

'There isn't any much else being sold these days.'

Mayne judged it time to make his presence known. 'If Mother says there isn't food, then there isn't, Father.'

'Mind your own damned business. What do you know about it?'

'If you'll give me some money, Reginald, I'll buy something,' his mother said.

'I don't have any cash left, Dorothy. You'll have to lend us some, Maynard. I owe the bookshop and they won't send me a book I need unless I pay something off their bill.'

'I won't give you one penny to spend on books.' Mayne took a deep breath and tried to speak more calmly. 'Anyway, there's something far more important for us to discuss.'

'What do you mean?'

'I've just come back from speaking to our new family lawyer. Why didn't you tell me we were nearly bankrupt?'

His father stopped dead. 'Why did Gilliot say that? We're not bankrupt. We still have the house.'

'I went to look at it this morning. It's in a terrible state. The soldiers vandalised it, goodness knows why. They even destroyed the oak panelling in the hall.'

His father stared in shock, then asked in a shaky voice, 'They destroyed the seventeenth-century panelling?' He sat down suddenly on a chair. 'Are you sure?'

Mayne followed suit and gestured to his mother to join them. 'Yes. I went round the whole house this morning before I went to see the lawyer. Why didn't you tell me the Army had moved out?'

'I thought I had. I don't understand why the house has been damaged. When they requisitioned it, the man from the War Office said they'd look after it. He *promised*.'

'I don't think they knew when they requisitioned houses how all-out the effort for Britain to win the war needed to be. A lot of big houses have suffered badly, some far worse than us, I gather. A few have even burned down, thanks to careless smokers and the like.'

'Destroyed the panelling!' his father repeated.

Was the old man listening? Mayne wondered. 'Apparently there's someone who wants to buy the house and you're going to have no choice but to sell it. This person intends to knock Esherwood down and build a modern mansion in its place.'

His father's head came up and he asked sharply, 'Who is it?'

'Ray Woollard.'

'I'm not selling it, not to him, not to anyone.'

'You won't have a choice if you're declared bankrupt.'

'I'll write to the War Office and demand they pay us compensation to repair the damage.'

'The War Damage Commission will be paying some compensation to cover necessary repairs, I gather, but it'll be a while before that happens, so you won't get it in time. And I doubt it'll be generous. There are too many damaged houses to deal with.'

Mayne hadn't expected to feel sorry for his father, but now he did. But he felt angry too, because his father had made no effort to watch over his inheritance.

Reginald shook his head sadly, his eyes blank, like a blind man's. 'What do I know about business? I was waiting for you to come home. You have your annuity. I thought we could sell that and live off it for a while.'

'And after that money was used up? What did you think we'd do, then?'

Silence, then Reginald thumped the table and yelled, 'I don't know, damn you! I'm not a businessman, I'm a scholar.'

'Well, I need my money and it's not an annuity, so we couldn't use it in that way, even if I did want to sell, which I don't.'

'Not an annuity? What is it then?'

'It's various investments my godmother made over the years. She was a very astute woman financially. Many of her investments have even continued to make money or at least maintain their value during the war, though a couple of houses in London were destroyed early in the war in the Blitz. The land will still be worth something once things start to pick up and people begin rebuilding. But that won't happen for a while.'

His father's voice took on a pleading tone. 'You can sell the investments, surely.'

'I won't do that and there is nothing you can say or do that will change my mind. I shall need an income myself.'

'That's very selfish.'

'I'd call it practical. Let's get back to Esherwood. Gilliot told me how much Woollard had offered for it: a ridiculous amount. Will you give your inheritance away so that you can continue buying books, then hide in your study here while the family home is knocked down?'

'Of course not. The man's nothing but a jumped-up prof-iteer! His father was a gardener, and Woollard started life working in a foundry.'

'Then he's done very well for himself, hasn't he? I admire that. To get back to my main point: you'll have to sell to someone. And he's got a lot of money.'

All the fight suddenly went out of his father and he buried his face in his hands, shaking with emotion, so that Mayne's mother went to stand behind him, her hands on his shoulders.

'Do you have a better plan, Maynard?' she asked.

'Yes. I do. And luckily for the family, I also have a good head for business.'

'Does that mean you can borrow the money to pay off your father's debts?'

'No, not in the way you mean. I'll need every penny I can rustle up to start up my business. I have a couple of friends who are willing to go in with me. One's an architect. Together we could convert Esherwood into flats and sell them at a profit.'

His father brightened just a little.

'But we'll only do that if Father will sign the estate over to me permanently. My friends would find it too risky an investment otherwise.'

His father sat up straight, his voice shrill with anger. 'Turn Esherwood over to you? I won't do it.'

'Owners of stately homes do it all the time to avoid paying death duties. Turning it over to me will allow you and Mother to continue living here in the Dower House, and once the estate is mine, I shall be able to scrape together the money to pay your debts.'

'But we'd have no income.'

'I'd make you a small allowance. And Esherwood would be saved, even though it wouldn't be a private residence any longer. It's your only chance, Father.'

'Esherwood is a family home, not a damned business.'

His mother gestured towards the door and he realised she wanted him to leave them alone. As he moved, she left her husband to whisper, 'Go out and buy yourself lunch. Give me a few hours. I need to have a think about this. You've taken us both by surprise. Let me talk to your father and let this rest for a few days. We surely don't need to rush into anything.'

Mayne would rather have settled it today, but he nodded and left her to attempt the impossible: persuading his father to see sense. He'd be keeping watch at the big house, so wouldn't need to sit with his parents in the evenings. Given the long hours of daylight, he could do all sorts of jobs there. But most of all, he could prevent looting.

If anyone could persuade his father to hand over the house, she could.

But would she? She didn't love Esherwood as he did, never had.

She'd have told him if she disagreed with what he wanted to do, surely?

But as the days passed and she said nothing, not even giving him a hint of how things were going, he began to wonder. Was he working in vain on clearing up the rear of the big house ready to store his building supplies there?

Were his hopes going to be disappointed?

On May 23rd, Mayne and his parents forgot all about the discussion they'd planned about his project, because Churchill announced that the coalition government had been dissolved and a general election would be held on Thursday July 5th.

It was the main topic of conversation in the town.

Mayne's parents were quite sure that Churchill and the Conservatives would romp home. He wasn't so sure, however. Men in the forces weren't nearly as enthusiastic about Churchill's party. The ordinary soldier in particular considered the Conservatives responsible for the dark years of the 1930s, and Mayne had heard them talk bitterly about dole queues and unemployment.

He knew better than to say that to his parents, so pretended not to be interested in politics and got on with his work at the big house. When it rained, he worked indoors, clearing a path through the rubble in the hall.

One day he decided to tackle the Nissen hut, for a change,

and took some tools along to unscrew the lock and get the door open.

As the door creaked open, he gasped in surprise. The place was chock-full of stores. He couldn't even begin to assess what was there, but boxing in the entrance were piles of wooden planks, used, but in good condition, going right up to the ceiling. To the right were the backs of metal cupboards, continuing the barriers.

He decided to peep over the top and pulled down a few planks. Behind them were boxes and to one side some sheets of corrugated metal. It took him a minute or two to realise what they were: some of the interior fitments for building other Nissen huts. This must be a project that had been started, then abandoned before it was finished; and no one had bothered to clear it, so again, it was his.

He was thrilled. This would give him a good start with his building. Well, it would if his father handed over the estate to him.

He made sure his presence at the big house was known about in the town, and thought that would deter looters. But he only had a day's peace, then it started again and twice he had to chase away intruders.

This couldn't go on, Mayne decided. He couldn't keep watch at night and function during the day. It was time to have a showdown with his parents, get this matter decided and then hire men to keep a proper watch over the old house at night.

Surely even his impractical father would realise Mayne's plan was the best option for Esherwood?

9

On Friday the first of June, the foreman summoned Judith to his office and told her she would lose her job at the end of the following week. She looked at him in dismay. 'You can't mean it!'

'I'm sorry, Mrs Crossley, but I do. You've been a good worker and we'll give you an excellent reference, but the manager thinks it only right to give the jobs back to the men coming home from the wars.'

He added briskly, 'They're starting to demob people already. We've heard from two who'll be returning in the next week or two. We can't let them think we don't care about the sacrifices they've made.'

'What about me? Haven't I done my bit in the war?'

'Yes, of course you have. But you've got a husband and he'll be coming home soon, so you'll be all right.'

'I'm going to leave him, so I need those wages to live on.' Even then, she was paid less than a man doing the same work, so it'd be a struggle to survive.

He looked at her sympathetically. 'Has it come to that?'

'Yes. I only stayed in the same house because Doug was overseas. Surely you can find a job of some sort for me?' Her suggestions had saved money for the mill, but the foreman had never given her credit, pretending to the manager that they were his ideas.

'I can't change what the boss tells me to do. And there won't be as much work here anyway, now that we won't be manufacturing uniforms and assembling kits. It'll take a while to get back to full peacetime production. Come back then and I'll see what I can do.'

She gave up trying. The only thing left would be to throw herself on her father's mercy. She'd go and see him at the weekend. And if he said no, she didn't know what she would do. She realised the foreman was still speaking.

'We'll give you a good reference. You'll find something else.'

She forced herself to say thank you for that.

Two other women were sacked as well as Judith. But they got on OK with their husbands, and were looking forward to having a normal family life again.

That evening she walked slowly home from the mill, worrying. She'd have one more week's wages to come and that'd be it.

When she got home, she hid most of this week's money. She'd taken to doing that straight away every week, just in case. She knew the kids wouldn't steal it, they were good kids, but Doug might come home any day and he'd take her money without hesitation.

She'd not forgotten how he'd eaten the entire family's meat ration that last time he was here; strange how some things upset you more than others. Well, he wasn't going to treat his friends to drinks while his kids went hungry, not any more.

On the Saturday afternoon Judith was in her bedroom, getting ready to visit her father, when Kitty came running into the house, screaming, 'Dad's come home. I saw him in the next street and ran to warn you.'

'I'm up here.' For a moment Judith froze, then she took

her purse and emptied nearly all the coins into a handkerchief. When Kitty came into the bedroom, she held it out. 'Here's my money. Put that in your knickers and don't tell anyone you've got it.'

Kitty did as she was told, glancing out of the window towards the street. 'He's not in sight yet. What are you going to tell him? About leaving, I mean.'

'The truth. I can't pretend. I won't live with him again. Once I've told him, I'm going round to beg my father to take us in.'

'Dad will thump you.'

'Which will prove to my father that I need his help.' She said this as bravely as she could, trying to brace herself for being bashed, but her stomach was already churning at the prospect. Doug knew how to hurt you without it showing, and only hit out where it showed if you made him angry.

She went downstairs to wait in the kitchen. 'Go round to your grandad's, love. Take Gillian with you.'

'He'll see us going.'

'You can slip out the back way and go down the alley. Wait at the end of the street till he's come into the house then run away as fast as you can.'

'I don't want to leave you.'

'Better for me if you're not around, then he can't threaten you to force me to do something.' Judith made a shooing gesture with her hands. 'Go on! He'll be here in a minute. If you see Ben, tell him what's happened and tell him to stay away, too.'

She wasn't feeling as brave as she'd pretended. In fact, she was scared stiff. She sat down behind the table and waited, her heart beating faster, her nerves on edge.

Five long minutes later the front door banged open and an angry voice yelled, 'Where are you?'

As if he didn't know. 'I'm here.' She didn't get up. She

waited, clasping her hands together to stop them shaking so obviously.

Doug stood in the kitchen doorway, dressed in an ill-fitting demob suit and cheap shiny shoes. He slung a cardboard suitcase to one side and stared at her.

How had he got out of the Army without her finding out he was coming? Then she saw that one hand was bandaged.

'Get me a cup of tea.'

She hesitated, but she'd have got one for a neighbour, so she wouldn't start by antagonising him over something so unimportant.

As she passed him, he put his good hand up her skirt and she pulled away. When he stood up, smiling *in that way*, she grabbed the frying pan. 'Don't touch me.'

'You're my wife. I'm allowed to touch you any time I want, and I want it now.'

She used the trick Irene had told her about, the one her friend said terrified men. 'I'll fight you all the way. I know I can't win, but neither can you, because as soon as you're asleep, I'll take my sharpest knife and cut off your manhood.'

He gaped at her in amazement.

'I mean it. If you force yourself on me, you'll never sleep soundly again Doug Crossley, for wondering when I'm going to take my knife to it. It's very soft. A knife will slice through it easily.'

She saw him put his hand over his private parts in an instinctive gesture.

'You'd never dare.'

'I would. You've been unfaithful to me and, for all I know, you're diseased. I don't want you coming near me again in that way. It'd make me vomit if you touched me.'

'You rotten bitch! Dewhurst said you'd been having it off with someone else. Who is he?'

'Dewhurst is wrong. *I* haven't been unfaithful. I wouldn't.

No man's touched me since you forced me last time and if I have my way, no man will ever touch me again.'

He sat down suddenly and she saw that he was pale, so guessed he mustn't be well. Perhaps he was still weak from the injury. Good. If they were lucky, he wouldn't have the strength to knock them around yet.

But he got up just as suddenly and without warning gave her a backhander that sent her flying across the room to lie sprawling in one corner.

'Dad, don't!'

Ben was standing in the doorway.

'Go away!' she told him urgently as she scrambled to her feet. 'Leave me to sort this out, son.'

'How can you sort it out? He just hit you. He's bigger than you. He'll do it again.' Ben picked up a chair, using it as a barrier. 'Is it true what she said, Dad? Have you had other women?'

'How the hell did you find out, you bitch?' Doug muttered, looking uneasily at his son who was holding the chair like a weapon.

She glared at him. 'You let it slip last time you were home, when you were drunk. That's when I decided to leave you. Only you were posted abroad, so we didn't move out. It'd be fairest if *you* got out of here, for your children's sake. There are four of us, only one of you.'

That nasty smile returned. 'I'm not going anywhere and it's my name on the rent book.'

'Then we'll leave.'

'Oh no, you won't. I'm still stronger than you. You'll do as I tell you or get what you deserve.'

'You're not stronger than us both together,' Ben shouted.

The back door opened and Kitty came in. 'I'll fight you as well, Dad. That's three to one.' She went to stand beside her mother.

'We won't let you hurt Mum any more,' Ben said. 'She's done nothing wrong.'

'What do you know about it? You're a child still. Wait till you're a man and then see how you control your woman. This is the only way they understand.' He made a sudden lunge towards his son, but Ben jabbed the chair at him and held it between them.

With a confident laugh, Doug grabbed it with his unbandaged hand and tried to pull it away from him, but Ben held on, backing round the table towards his mother. In the end, his father's strength won and he pulled the chair away, tossed it aside and raised his fist to thump his son.

Judith wasn't going to let him hurt Ben. She picked up the nearest heavy object, a frying pan, and swung it at Doug. It took him by surprise and knocked him off balance.

As he fell, he banged his head on the corner of the table and when he hit the floor, he didn't move.

For a few seconds she stood motionless, terrified she'd killed him, half-wishing she had. Then she saw his chest rise and fall. Relief flooded through her. 'Quick, Ben, get me the washing line. I'm going to tie him up while we pack our things and get out. He'll never let us go otherwise.'

'Good idea, Mum.'

She picked up her sharpest knife to cut the washing line and her son, her wonderful brave son, took it and ran to do her bidding.

As she was tying Doug's hands behind his back, Ben took the rope out of her hands. 'Not like that, Mum. They showed us how to tie knots when I joined the Boy Scouts at school.' He made a tighter, better job of his father's hands, cutting off that part of the clothes line. 'Shall I tie his feet together as well?'

She stared down at Doug, imagining him coming after them. 'Yes. And we'll fasten the end of the rope to something or he'll get away. How about the table leg?'

'No, not the leg, he could knock the table over and get the rope away from it. Tie him to the crosspiece under the table.'

'Good idea, love.' The kitchen table was a heavy old-fashioned one she'd picked up second-hand. She and the children had had the devil of a job getting it back home, moving it a few yards at a time along the streets till some men passing by had come to their aid.

Satisfied Doug couldn't harm them or stop them leaving, she turned her back on her husband. 'Right now, children, go and put your clothes into pillow cases, *all* the clothes you can fit in.'

They were still gaping at her. 'Go on!' she yelled. 'He's coming to already. We have to hurry. Just a minute, Kitty. Where did you leave Gillian?'

'I told her to go round to Grandad's. But I wanted to be with you.'

'That's all right then. You pack her things, then you two can keep watch over your father while I pack mine.' She'd take her money out of its hiding place while she was at it. Even the children didn't know where that was.

They pounded upstairs, their feet echoing on the bare boards up there even more than usual. As Judith waited, she went round the kitchen, picking up one or two items to take with her, like her favourite knife and three sets of cutlery. Heaven knew how she'd be able to buy more things for them without a job.

She stopped to look down at her husband, worried that he hadn't regained full consciousness. She'd really be in trouble now. He'd never forgive her for this.

Well, no going back. She didn't know where she and her children would be sleeping tonight, but she wouldn't willingly live in a house with Doug – never, ever again.

In one way, it was a relief to have the waiting for his return over.

Now the hardest part of her struggle for the children's future would begin.

After what seemed ages, Doug opened his eyes and she watched him warily. It was a minute or two before he was able to focus properly, then he saw her sitting on a chair nearby with a knife in her hand. He tried to get up and attack her, and it took him a minute to realise what was stopping him, that he was bound hand and foot.

'What have you done, you bitch?' He strained to break his bonds, but couldn't budge Ben's knots. Then he banged his head on the table leg as he tried to move away from it, yelping in pain.

'What I've done is defended myself and my children against you, you big bully.'

'Get these damned ropes off me. You can't keep me here like this.'

'I can keep you here till we're ready to leave.'

'You'll regret it. I'll soon find you and come after you.'

'And we'll fight back again,' she said as steadily as she could manage. She felt literally sick at the sight of the hatred on his face.

'You've turned my children against me.'

She indicated her black eye and swollen cheek. 'No, you've turned them against yourself, beating me as soon as you got back. You haven't changed a bit. I'm not stupid enough to live with someone who keeps hurting me.'

'A man has a right to chastise his wife *and* children.'

'Other men don't beat weaker people for nothing, like you do.' She looked at the area between his legs. 'I meant what I said, Doug. If you touch me again, *or* the children, you'd better watch out for your manhood.'

'You wouldn't dare. They'd lock you away in prison if you did that.'

'Oh, wouldn't I? Try me. A desperate woman will dare anything. It'd be worth going to prison to save other women from your attentions. Just think, you'd never be able to have a woman again.'

He lay there, staring at her as if he'd never seen her before. 'You've run mad.'

'You're the one who changed after I had Gillian. You're the one who's run mad.'

There were steps on the stairs and Ben came in carrying a big bundle. 'Did you want me to bring the sheets and blankets as well, Mum?'

'Yes. I should have said. I wasn't thinking straight. Then come down and keep an eye on your father while I pack my things.' She banged the frying pan down on the end of the table. 'Hit him with this if you think he's likely to escape.'

Ben nodded and ran off, clattering down again a couple of minutes later with a roll of bedding tied together by his school scarf.

'Call me if you need help.' She ran up the stairs. 'How are you going, Kitty?'

'Nearly finished.' She came closer to whisper, 'Do you want the money back?'

'Keep it hidden for now.' She shut her bedroom door and got her savings out of their hiding place, putting the small roll of notes inside her brassiere, for lack of anywhere safer, and the coins into her purse.

'Son, you need to untie me before she gets back,' Doug said in a low voice.

'Why? So you can thump Mum, bash me and smack Gillian?'

'Because we're men, you an' me, that's why. And us men have to stick together to keep women in order.'

'You can keep people in order without thumping them.

It's bad enough when you hit me, but to hit a little girl like Gillian, that's cowardly, that is, and it sickens me.'

'Well, I'll promise not to hit *you* again if you untie me.'

'You never keep your promises. We've all seen you break them time and time again. Yes, and you eat other people's share of the food, too. I haven't forgotten how hungry we used to get when you lived at home. Mum's right to leave you and if anyone tries to force me to come back to you, I'll run away on my own. I'll go right across the sea to Australia to get away from you, if I have to. I hate you and I wish you weren't my father.'

Kitty entered the room and came across to stand at the end of the table with her brother. She looked at her father only once, as if to make sure he was still tied up securely. 'I've been listening to what you said, Ben, and I agree. He's just as horrible as he always was. I hate him too.'

'It's that bloody school,' Doug yelled, struggling in vain to get free. 'Your mother should never have sent you to it. It's spoiled you for being a wife, that place has, Kitty. You don't even talk properly now, you talk daft, trying to be posh, only people like us can't be posh. Folk will scorn you for trying. You'll see.'

Kitty glared at him. 'It's a wonderful school. And it's *you* who's spoiled things. I've seen how you treat Mum. I'm never going to get married. I'm going to be a teacher when I grow up and live on my own with a little dog.'

Ben put his arm round his sister, who clung to him tightly for a moment. He continued to gaze steadily at his father. 'I go to the grammar school as well, now.'

'What? How did you get in? How can *she* afford the fees? Why did no one tell me?'

'How could we? You never wrote to say where you were, never once asked how we were, so Mum couldn't have written to you, even if she'd wanted to. I was awarded one of the new council scholarships, that's how I got in. It pays my fees. Only three of them are given out each year to lads from poor families who've done well.'

Ben was very proud of that scholarship. He knew he wasn't as quick to learn as his older sister, but he had worked harder than Kitty had ever needed to, and it had given him great satisfaction to gain it.

His father tried again. 'You're betraying the Crossleys, Ben, betraying your father and grandfather. People will laugh at you for trying to be what you're not.'

'No, they won't. The teachers and other kids are nice to me. You're the one betraying your family. You should be proud of us kids, and not try to stop us improving ourselves.'

'I see how it is; *she* has turned you all against me. So I'll tell you what I told your mother: I'll make you sorry for this. I'll bring you lot to heel if it's the last thing I ever do.'

Ben bent down and shouted right in his father's face. 'You'll have to catch us first and don't forget I'm growing bigger all the time, because Mum sees we get enough to eat. I'll soon be bigger than you. And I'll be a lot stronger too, because I won't booze like you do. You'll go to fat now you're out of the army. I heard some men talking about how that happened after the First World War. I'll laugh when I see you staggering down the street, drunk and fat and stupid. They laugh at you now when you get drunk. I've heard them many a time.'

He turned as he heard his mother coming down the stairs.

She smiled across at the children, feeling the swollen skin on her face pulling as she did. She had a black eye already and Doug hadn't been home an hour. Oh, the shame of it! 'Are you ready, children?'

'Yes, Mum.'

'Come on, then. No, just a minute.' She picked up the frying pan and hung it neatly in place over the cooker, glanced quickly across at the outer kitchen door and saw that it was closed. 'Don't want to leave things untidy, do we?'

'Oy! You're not leaving me tied up,' Doug yelled.

'If we untie you, you'll stop us going. I'll send someone tonight to tell your friends at the pub where you are.'

Doug swore long and fluently as they left the kitchen. 'Come back, you cheating bitch! Come back. Help! Someone help me! She's trying to kill me.'

Judith shut the front door firmly and locked it, then tossed the key down the nearest drain, before leading her two oldest children off down the street. She was never coming back here if she could help it.

All of them were struggling with their heavy loads, unable to walk as fast as she'd have liked. She kept looking round, worrying that Doug would get himself free and break down the front door.

'We'll go along by the park,' she said. 'That way fewer people will see us. It's just as quick to get to Dad's that way. I hope Gillian is still waiting for us there.'

It worried her not to have her youngest where she could keep an eye on her. The whole situation worried her, but she had no choice. She and her son would have been beaten senseless if she hadn't got to Doug first.

Mayne went out to get away from his parents. He was still hoping his mother could persuade the old man to see sense, but the waiting was getting on his nerves.

He heard something that sounded like a cat mewing and looked round. A girl was sitting on a bench near the top of Parson's Mead, crying bitterly. He hesitated, but he couldn't walk past her, she sounded to be in such distress.

She was crying so hard, she didn't see him coming. 'What's wrong?' he asked.

She jumped in shock and flinched back, terror on her face.

He took a quick step backwards. 'I'm not going to hurt you, love.'

But that made her sob even more.

'If you tell me what's wrong, maybe I can help.'

She hiccupped to a halt, staring at him as if uncertain whether to trust him or not.

'Go on. Give me a chance. Tell me what the matter is.'

'It's Dad. He's come back from the war and he's going to hit Mum, then he's going to hit all of us. She sent me to my Grandad's to hide but he's been taken to hospital and there's a lady living at the house with him and she won't let me go inside. I daren't go home, though. What if Dad catches me?'

He remembered earlier in the war a woman sitting on this bench, a woman who'd had her face bashed. He'd managed to help her. Surely he could do something for this child. 'What's your name?'

'Gillian.'

'And your surname?'

She looked round as if scared to say it aloud, before whispering, 'Crossley.'

Good heavens! It was the same family. 'Are you Kitty's sister?'

She relaxed a little. 'Yes. Do you know our Kitty?'

'No, but I met your mother a few years ago and got my father to help your sister go to the grammar school.'

'You must be old Mr Esher's son come back from the war. Mum told us about you. But you can't help her today. He's stronger than anyone, Dad is, and he's her husband. He says husbands are allowed to hit their wives. But even if they are, it's still not *fair*. She hasn't done anything wrong. She's the best mother in the whole world, our mum is.'

'Well I don't agree that husbands should hit wives. Let's see if I can think of something to stop him.'

He'd remembered Judith Crossley on and off over the years, even after only one meeting. She had such a vivid face, filled with intelligence, even if she hadn't had a formal education as her daughter would have had by now. It had been such a good memory, knowing he'd been able to help a clever girl and her mother, knowing he'd done something other than killing in a crazy, war-torn world.

He held out his handkerchief, smiling as he remembered doing the same thing for her mother.

The girl mopped her eyes and stood up, offering it back to him. 'Thank you.'

'It's a bit soggy. You'd better keep it. Come on. We'll go round to your house, but you can wait for me at the end of the street if you're afraid.'

'You won't let him hit me?'

'No, definitely not.'

She studied him. 'You're nearly as tall as he is, but you're not as fat. Are you strong?'

'Quite strong. But I don't like to hit people. I'd rather talk to them, persuade them to behave properly.'

'No one can persuade Dad about anything. He just shouts you down.'

'I don't think he'll thump me.' Mayne led the way down the slope, but just as they got to the footpath, a sad procession came into view. A woman and two youngsters, carrying huge, lumpy bundles and moving slowly.

The poor woman looked worn out and had a big black eye where her husband had hit her.

History repeating itself, he thought. Perhaps he was fated to help Judith Crossley at regular intervals in his life.

10

As the front door banged shut, Doug continued yelling for help at the top of his voice. At the same time, he rolled his upper body to and fro. 'Ah.' The heavy table had moved a bit.

The bitch had tied the rope too tightly for him to get his feet free of the table, but it wasn't far to the back door. Inch by sodding inch he dragged himself and the table across the kitchen floor, yelping when he hit his hand where two of his fingers had once been. When he got to the back door, he lay panting for a moment or two as he stared up at the door handle.

Then he saw something and said 'Ah!' again. It was his lucky day. The door latch hadn't slid into its slot but was balanced on the edge. If he could just jerk the door, it might jump away from the slot. It was worth a try, anyway.

With difficulty he managed to ease his body slowly up the wall into a sitting position, taking care not to touch the door. Gathering his strength he thumped his torso sideways against the door, cursing as he banged his head.

For a moment all hung in the balance, then the latch fell down outside the slot, freeing the door. With a laugh of triumph, he edged the back door open and began yelling for help at the top of his voice, stopping and starting till he heard footsteps running towards the house along the back alley.

'It's coming from here,' a woman called.

Doug raised his voice again. 'Help me! Help!'

'The back gate's bolted,' the woman said.

Oh, hell, it was that bitch next door. She'd never been a friend of his.

'I'll climb over and unlock it,' a man's voice said.

The voice sounded familiar but Doug couldn't place it.

There was the thud of feet landing on the flagstones of the back yard and someone came to the back door, peering inside and jerking back as he saw Doug half-lying below him.

'Damned well untie me!' yelled Doug, unable to move further away from the door.

The man squeezed through the half-open door and round him. 'What the hell's happened to you, Crossley?'

'That sow I'm married to knocked me out with the frying pan. It's over there on the floor.' He jerked his head to indicate the other side of the table. 'There'll be blood on it.'

The woman came inside to join them. She looked round the floor, then saw the pan hanging on the wall. 'That pan is where it belongs and it's perfectly clean. Are you sure she hit you with it?'

'Of course I'm sure, you stupid twit.'

'Well! I see your manners haven't improved, Mr Crossley. Not even a thank you for rescuing you. *I'm* not untying you. In fact, I'm not staying here a minute longer.' She marched out of the back door.

The man hesitated. 'I suppose I'd better untie you.'

'Never mind untying me, cut the damned rope.'

'Where's your sharp knife?'

'In the top drawer.'

He went over to look. 'It isn't there. The drawer's nearly empty.'

'She's took my cutlery, then. There must be something else. Scissors.'

'No scissors.' He grinned, seeming to be enjoying the situation.

That annoyed the hell out of Doug, but he didn't dare offend his only remaining rescuer, a man he knew by sight but didn't go drinking with. What the hell was he called? Doug couldn't remember.

In the end the man had to use an old blunt table knife and pull the ropes even tighter to get it under the rope and saw it to and fro. This made Doug yell, especially when it was his bad hand that was being twisted about.

'What happened to your hand?' his rescuer asked.

'Lost two fingers in an accident with a gun.'

'Bad luck. Just as the war ended, too.'

'Just *after* the war ended. Some damn fool was playing around with his gun to celebrate an' shot me. If they hadn't of took me away to hospital, I'd have chopped his fingers off. See how he liked it.'

He moved towards the front door. 'Um . . . thanks. I'll buy you a pint one night. I'd better get after her.'

'You should just let her go.'

That was enough of being polite. 'Mind your own damned business.' Doug walked stiffly to the front door, still having trouble moving his arms and legs properly. He tried to open the door, but it was locked. And the key wasn't in it.

He thumped his shoulder against the door, but bounced off and remembered that it opened inwards. He could do nothing to budge it.

Cursing he went back into the kitchen and left the house by the alley. There was no sign of the man, but two neighbours were standing talking in the alley. They stopped when they saw him coming.

'She's locked the front door and taken the key, damn her!' he yelled as they stared at him.

'I don't blame her,' Mrs Needham said tartly.

He stopped and swung round. 'You mind your tongue, missus.'

She folded her arms and stared at him defiantly. 'Who do you think you are, talking to me like that? This is England. We just fought for our freedom, us on the home front as well as you lot in the forces. And now we've won our freedom, I'll say what I like to anybody, even the king.'

She took a deep breath and continued to shout at him. '*And*, Doug Crossley, if you so much as lay one finger on me, my sons will come and punch a bit of sense into you. I have three grown sons left still, if you've ever noticed anything beyond your beer. Good lads, they are, and won't let anyone hurt their mother.'

He gaped at her and walked on. What was the world coming to when women talked to men like that? What the hell had happened to England while he was away?

Whatever it was, he wasn't going to change the way *he* behaved. He'd risked his life for his country, he had, and lost two fingers. He deserved some respect.

No need to tell them he'd mostly been stuck in the desert, driving officers around sometimes, bored to tears.

He reckoned he'd earned the right to live his life as he always had, and let anyone try to tell him different.

Judith stared at the man standing next to Gillian. It took her a minute or two to realise who it was, because he'd changed, had a frosting of grey in the hair at his temples now, and an air of quiet authority about him that she couldn't remember from their other encounter.

'It's Mrs Crossley, isn't it? I'm Mayne Esher.'

'Yes. I recognised you from last time.'

As their eyes met in acknowledgement of that moment, he held out his hand and shook hers.

Then Judith noticed how red her daughter's eyes were.

She dropped her bundles and pulled Gillian close. 'What's happened, love? You were supposed to wait for us at your grandad's.'

'A lady came to the door of his house. She said she was a friend of his and she's staying with him. Oh, Mum, they've taken Grandad to hospital.'

'Hospital? What's wrong with him?'

'*She* said it was appendicitis and it happened in the middle of the night. She went to hospital with him and she's just come back.'

'What did she look like?'

Gillian wrinkled her nose in disapproval. 'She had red hair, only it wasn't really red and you could see the grey roots, so it looked silly.'

Mrs Walmsley, Judith thought. That woman has been trying to get her hooks into Dad for a while now. He couldn't be so stupid as to marry her . . . could he? 'Go on, love.'

'She wouldn't let me into the house, said she lived there now and was going to have a sleep now. She wouldn't *listen* to me. She said to tell you not to come round to the house and not to visit Grandad at the hospital until tomorrow. They're operating on him this afternoon and he'll be too woozy for visitors after that.'

'But he's going to be all right?'

'She said they got him there in time.'

Judith hadn't realised the woman had moved in with her dad, because they were in another part of the town. There wouldn't be room for him to take in her and her children now. No wonder he'd not wanted her to leave Doug.

She put one hand over her eyes, trying to hide how close to tears she was at this disappointment. She had to work out where else to go.

'What am I going to do?'

She didn't realise she'd spoken out loud until Mr Esher

said quietly, 'Why don't you sit down on that bench and tell me about it? Clearly you're in trouble. I was just telling your daughter I'd like to help, if I can.'

She looked at him bleakly. 'Kind of you, but unless you can find us somewhere to live that has furniture and won't charge us rent, there's nothing you can do. They're sacking us women from the mill now the men are back, so I've lost my wages. But my husband just came back from the Middle East, so I had to leave or he'd have killed me.'

For a moment her hand fluttered up to the painful swelling on her face, then she sighed and went on, 'I thought my dad could put us up till I'd worked something out. Only he's got his lady friend staying with him and we've no other relatives in Rivenshaw.'

He didn't think he'd ever seen a woman look so weary and downtrodden, and the bruise was even worse than the one she'd had last time. Did the husband do nothing but punch her? Mayne's heart went out to her. He shouldn't stay, there was nothing he could do to help with this sort of problem and he had to find someone to keep watch with him at Esherwood or the thieves would take more of his precious goods.

Then an idea suddenly hit him and he studied the sorry little group. 'Actually, I think I can help you with accommodation, if you'll help me in return. It's rather a rough place, but it's weatherproof.'

She looked at him doubtfully. 'Tell me about it.'

'Let's get you off the streets first. You won't want to sit here with every passer-by staring at you. Let me help you with your baggage.'

But she put out one hand to stop him and said in a firm voice, 'I'm not going anywhere till you tell me where and what exactly I have to do to put a roof over our heads.'

The lad went to stand beside his mother protectively, and the older girl put an arm round her little sister.

Quickly, Mayne explained his problem. 'I don't know how long I'll be able to give you somewhere to stay, but at least for a night or two.'

'I can help you keep watch,' Ben offered eagerly.

'Won't you have to ask your father first, Mr Esher?' she asked.

'I'll go and tell him after I've got you out of sight, but I don't think he'll complain if I tell him Kitty needs help. I sometimes think education and books are the only things he cares about. Now, we don't want your husband catching up with you, so let's be off.'

They picked up their bundles and set off along Park Gardens, heading up the last of the slope towards the big house.

They'd only gone about fifty yards when a voice behind them yelled, 'Hoy!'

Judith stopped dead and turned round, her heart sinking. Doug was striding towards them, a triumphant look on his face. And he wasn't alone. One of his drinking pals was with him.

Well, he'd have to kill her to make her go back.

And he probably would.

Helen was sitting on the wooden bench in the back garden watching Jan dig and weed, so that he could plant more seeds, when she heard someone yelling and cursing in the street. 'What on earth's going on?'

She hurried to the front of the house to look, afraid it'd be someone with prejudices against displaced persons. She heard Jan following her.

But it was nothing to do with them. A fleshy lout with his hand covered by a dirty bandage was yelling at a woman and some children. A shorter man next to him was grinning as if it was all very amusing, but the two girls looked terrified. Helen hated to see that look on children's faces.

Maynard Esher was standing beside the woman, trying to get a word in edgeways. Helen quickly explained to Jan who he was, then turned back anxiously to see if sense would prevail. You didn't usually see such rough types or hear such language in this part of town.

'Get away from her, you!' the horrible man yelled. 'I don't care if you are her fancy man; she's *my* wife and she's coming home where she belongs, yes, an' bringing my children with her.' He raised his fist again.

The smaller girl was sobbing. 'Mum, don't let him hit me.'

Mr Esher was outnumbered, but wasn't giving ground. 'Your wife's left you, Crossley, for obvious reasons.' He pointed to her face. 'How long had you been home before you hit her? Ten minutes? Fifteen?'

The man behind Crossley joined in. 'If you grab hold of her, Doug lad, I'll take on Esher. I'd be glad to have a punch at that damned family.'

'Shall I help your friend Mr Esher?' Jan asked suddenly. 'I have seen men like these when I was travelling, men who take pleasure to hurt people.'

'Would you mind helping him? You might get hurt yourself.'

'I am a good fighter. I don't like to see children beaten for nothing. If there is trouble, try to get them and their mother into the garden and close the gate.'

'We can run into the house if that brute looks like winning.'

Jan smiled, not a nice smile. 'Oh, I don't think he'll win.' He moved forward, calling out, 'Mr Esher, may I be of assistance to you?'

Mayne was surprised by this offer from a complete stranger, but wasn't going to turn it down. 'I'd be most grateful. I can't shake hands at the moment, but I'd be glad to know your name.'

'Jan Borkowski. I'm working for Miss Bretherton.'

Doug had stopped yelling to listen to this and now erupted into speech again. 'You can bloody well stay out of this, you foreign git. She's my wife and these are my children, so it's none of your business. She's coming home where she belongs.'

'So that you can beat her again?' Mayne's quiet tone was in great contrast to Doug's yelling.

'She's my *wife*. A husband is allowed to beat his wife – as long as he doesn't kill her.' His smile at Judith was an open threat. 'It's nothing to do with you. She should do as she's told for once.'

'I'll never again do as you tell me, Doug Crossley,' Judith shouted. 'And I won't come back, whatever you do to me.'

'We'll see about that. When I fetch the police, they'll take the children off you because you don't have nowhere to live, and then I'll be the one to look after them and make them toe the line. You'll come back then to try to mollycoddle them, I know you.' He suddenly lunged for Judith, yelling, 'Get him, Bert!' to his friend.

But she twisted out of his way and somehow Jan managed to trip up the other man before he got near Esher.

'Come with me, children,' Helen called.

'I'm not leaving, Mum,' Ben said. 'Stop it, Dad. Let us go. We all hate you.'

The veins bulged on Doug's forehead and he put all his strength into a blow that sent his son spinning backwards into a nearby tree trunk.

There was the dull sound of a body hitting wood and Ben dropped to the ground to lie still.

With an anguished cry, Judith ran to kneel by him.

'Don't move him!' Mayne said urgently. 'You can do more harm than good if he's broken something.'

Miss Peters had come out of her house to watch the incident and now left her garden to join the group. She was five feet high and not showing a sign of fear as she approached

Crossley. 'You've killed your son now. How does that feel, you damned coward?'

Doug backed away. 'I haven't killed him. Any road, you all heard him cheek me. I just gave him a tap, to show him who's in charge.'

By now a few other people had gathered round them.

'That was more than a tap,' a man called out.

'Shame on you!' a woman shouted, but took a quick step backwards as Doug's friend moved towards her.

'Someone fetch the nearest doctor!' Mayne ordered, kneeling next to Judith.

'He won't come unless you pay him,' a woman said.

'I'll pay.'

As a lad jumped on his bicycle and pedalled away furiously down the street, more people gathered, asking what had happened, staring at Doug.

He began backing away, but Mayne grabbed hold of his sleeve. 'Oh, no, you don't. We're having the police to you, and if you've killed that lad, you'll be facing a charge of murder.'

Bert suddenly started running and they didn't pursue him.

Ben whimpered just then and Doug jerked his sleeve out of Mayne's hand. But he was ringed by the bystanders so couldn't move. 'Well, I've not killed him, nothing like. He was only pretending to be knocked out.'

'He's not really conscious, just in pain,' Judith said. 'Oh, you brute, to hit a child so hard.'

It was ten minutes before an ambulance came, and for all that time, Mayne and Jan, with the help of the bystanders, made sure Doug couldn't get away. Judith went off to hospital in the ambulance with her son, while Helen took the two girls into her house.

At last a solitary policeman walked along the street. 'I hear there's been trouble here and— Oh, Mr Esher, it's you.' His tone at once became more respectful.

Doug feinted and tried to get away, but when Jan grabbed him, he glared at them all impartially.

'What's the problem, sir? The lad who came to the police station didn't seem sure, but said a gentleman had sent him and a boy was dead.'

Doug said loudly, 'This so-called gentleman is stopping me taking my wife home. He's her fancy man.'

'Don't be ridiculous!' Mayne snapped. 'As well say this policeman is her fancy man as me. I've only just come back to Rivenshaw.'

The policeman in question looked uneasily from one to the other. 'Now please, one at a time. Mr Esher, what happened?'

Mayne explained.

The policeman seemed uncertain what to do. 'She *is* his wife, though, sir.'

'She's left him. Is this a free country or not?'

'Well, we don't usually interfere between married couples. I mean, that's private, that is.'

'Even if a man nearly kills his son by his brutality and threatens to do the same to his wife? The boy's unconscious and has been taken to hospital, so his mother's gone with him.'

'Ah. Well, we can go and interview her there. I daresay she'll want to return home by now, if she has nowhere else to go, and I'm sure her husband will forgive her.'

'Forgive her? Have you been listening to what Mr Esher said?' demanded Miss Peters, who'd been standing nearby. 'The husband thumped her and nearly killed his son. I saw it myself. I'm coming with you to the police station. I think you're going to need a woman to help you deal fairly with Mrs Crossley, Constable.'

He looked uneasy. 'I don't think we need to trouble you, Miss Peters.'

'It's no trouble.'

The constable's expression said he didn't want her company, but he seemed afraid of her.

'You stay out of this, missus,' Doug told her. 'It's none of your damned business.'

'Mind your manners, fellow,' she snapped, nose in the air. 'I've seen your sort before. Cowards who hit people smaller than themselves.'

He took a step forward. 'Now, look here, Lady Muck, I—'

The constable grabbed his arm. 'Keep calm, sir, and mind your manners. We won't settle anything by quarrelling. We'll . . . um, take up your kind offer, Miss Peters, and see what the sergeant says. Did you say there were some other children? Where are they?'

'The two girls are with my neighbour, Miss Bretherton. She says they can stay with her and Mr Borkowski while we sort things out.'

'But he's a foreigner.'

Miss Peters set her hands on her hips. 'So were many of our allies in the recent conflict, don't forget. The question is, which sort of foreigner, friend or foe? This one is a friend.'

The constable threw Jan a sour look and turned to the group. 'Come along, then, Mr Esher. And you too, Crossley.'

'You know his name already?' Miss Peters asked.

'He was in one or two fights before the war. We've had to take him in.'

'That doesn't surprise me.' She stared up at Doug thoughtfully, not seeming in the least afraid of him.

It was he who looked away first and took a step backwards.

12

The walk to the police station took a few minutes and on the way people turned to stare at them, no doubt because of the tall policeman leading the group, the surly man following him, and Miss Peters next, her arm linked in Jan's.

Mayne brought up the rear, fretting at how quickly the afternoon was passing. He needed to find someone to stand guard with him on the big house. He wasn't even sure now that Judith Crossley and her family would be able to join him there. The policeman seemed reluctant to intervene and inclined to take the husband's side.

He shouldn't have interfered.

Then he remembered her battered face and knew he couldn't have let her get hurt again. He'd only met her twice and each time she'd borne the marks of her husband's heavy hand. Some things were just . . . wrong.

He glanced at Miss Peters, admiring her courage. The feisty old lady had given him the occasional sweet when he was a lad, had been a friend of his grandmother, was a well-known figure in the town.

When they got to the police station, the constable handed them over to his sergeant with a few brief words of explanation. As he moved to one side, he sighed in relief.

Miss Peters moved forward, smiling at Sergeant Deemer. 'In other words, this is a case of wife-bashing.'

'She *is* his wife,' the constable said, as if that excused it.

Doug smirked, expecting another official to be on his side, but the sergeant scowled at him. 'Oh, yes? Do we have proof that he attacked Mrs Crossley?'

'I saw the attack myself,' Miss Peters said.

'Where is the lady now?'

'At the hospital with her son. The boy was attacked by his father when he tried to protect his mother, and it was such a vicious blow, he was knocked unconscious.'

'He was hit so hard, I felt it best to send for the ambulance,' Mayne put in. 'He'll be in hospital now.'

Doug stepped forward, trying to elbow the old lady out of the way, but falling back in sheer surprise when she hit him on the side of the head with her heavy leather handbag. 'There was no *need* for him to go to the hospital, officer. Our Ben was recovering.'

Sergeant Deemer was famous for 'the look' and he fastened it on Doug now. 'Kindly keep quiet when I'm questioning other people and do not jostle them. Your turn will come.'

'But—'

'If you can't keep quiet, I'll have to lock you in a cell.'

Doug muttered in resentment, but closed his mouth.

Miss Peters finished her summary of what had happened while the sergeant listened attentively. Jan had moved to one side, but was also listening carefully to what was being said.

'Hmm.' The sergeant stared up at the ceiling, gathering his thoughts. 'I shall have to see the lady herself to confirm this, and to ask whether she wishes to charge her husband with assault. At the hospital, is she, Miss Peters?'

'Well, she was taken away in the ambulance, so she should be there by now.'

'The hospital's just across the road. Constable Farrow, go there and ask how badly the boy is injured. If his mother can leave him for a few minutes, I'd like to ask her a few questions. In the meantime I'll speak to these two gentlemen.'

Miss Peters put an arm out to stop the constable. 'I'd better go with him, Sergeant. We don't want to frighten her.'

'Thank you, Miss Peters. The poor woman will no doubt appreciate the support of a lady like yourself.'

'Give me your arm, Constable. I'm not as young as I was.'

Flushing in embarrassment he did that.

When they'd gone the sergeant asked, 'Would you mind answering a few questions now, Mr Esher?'

'I'm happy to.'

'But he isn't—'

'Crossley, do you not understand plain English? Keep quiet till you get your turn to speak.'

Doug caught Jan staring at him and glared at him. Damned foreigners. They should all be sent back to where they came from now the war was over.

His reputation with the lads at the pub was going to suffer if he let Judith get away with this. He'd better make sure that people knew he'd won once he'd dragged her home and punished her.

He'd had other women who were much more fun in bed than Judith, but she was a good housewife, and he needed her to do the cooking and washing, as well as looking after his kids till they were old enough to go out to work. No one could stretch a penny like she could.

Judith came out of the cubicle where her son was being examined, head held high. The bruise and swelling stood out lividly against her pale complexion.

'He must have hit her harder than I realised,' the constable muttered. 'That's more than a slap.'

'And would a slap be all right?' Miss Peters asked.

'It happens all the time.'

'Well, as you said, this is a great deal more than a slap.' Warming up to one of her pet obsessions, Miss Peters continued in a loud voice, 'The way some men beat their wives is disgusting! We won the war against Hitler, but we still have a war to wage against brutality at home.'

A nearby nurse and cleaner stopped their conversation to nod approval.

As Farrow looked uncomfortable and uncertain what to do, Miss Peters moved forward without him. 'Sergeant Deemer sent me to find you, Mrs Crossley. But first, how is your son?'

'Badly concussed. They want to keep him in for the night.' Judith stopped to gulp back tears. 'They may have to operate on his skull to relieve the pressure on his brain.'

'Oh, my dear, I'm so sorry!'

A sister came out of the cubicle, her starched headdress bobbing about as if she had wings on her head instead of hair. 'Are you still here, Mrs Crossley? Please leave your son to us now and take a rest for your own sake. We'll let you see him again this evening, after Doctor has examined him.'

Miss Peters walked across to the sister, hand outstretched. 'Mary Johnson. That's a fine uniform you're wearing. I always knew you'd make a good nurse.'

The sister relaxed as they shook hands. 'Nice to see you, Miss Peters, and looking so well, too.'

'I don't have time to be ill. There's always someone who needs help.'

'You do a lot of good. I've never forgotten how you helped my mother.'

A faint red stained the old lady's cheeks. 'Oh, pish! It was nothing. Now, would it be all right for me to take Mrs Crossley across to the police station to tell Sergeant Deemer what happened?'

'Good idea. And make sure that husband of hers is brought

to account. I'm tired of patching up battered wives.' She glared across the room at the constable. 'The police should be doing a lot more to help these poor women.'

Farrow shuffled his feet in acute embarrassment as other women nearby muttered, 'Hear, hear'.

Miss Peters put an arm round Judith. 'Come and tell the police your side of the story, my dear.'

'Is my husband there?

'Yes, but he won't dare touch you again. He'll have me to answer to if he tries.'

Judith looked down at the tiny old woman in awe. Miss Peters' eyes were sparkling with defiance. *She* wouldn't have put up with a husband beating her for even a minute.

At the police station, Judith stopped in the doorway, looking nervously across at Doug. She'd not really studied him when he burst into their house, but now she could see clearly that his years of boozing were showing on his face and body. She'd heard men in the forces could get beer when no one else could.

When he saw her, he straightened up. 'My wife fell over,' he said loudly. 'That's how she hurt herself. Clumsy, she is. Tell them, Judith.'

'I did not fall over! You hit me when I told you I was leaving you. And this,' she pointed to her face, 'is the reason I'm leaving. It's not the first time you've hit me. You hit the children, too.'

'I daresay he's sorry. He didn't mean to hurt you,' the police constable said soothingly.

Doug smirked at them and said in a falsely sweet tone, 'Oh, yes, Constable, I'm very sorry. I didn't mean to hurt her.'

The sergeant cleared his throat to get everyone's attention and glared at his subordinate. 'Leave the questioning to me, Farrow, and don't put words into the witness's mouth. The law does not approve of you attacking someone, Mr Crossley, whether you're married to her or not. And *you* would do well to remember that if you want to gain promotions, Farrow. King George is on the throne now, not Queen Victoria.'

Miss Peters intervened, tugging Judith gently forward towards the sergeant. 'Do you have somewhere to stay, my dear?'

Judith sighed. 'I was going to stay with my father but he's in hospital too, having his appendix out. They won't let me see him till tomorrow.'

'I know somewhere she and her children can stay,' Mayne said.

'There! Didn't I tell you? He's her fancy man,' Doug yelled.

The constable hastily moved between him and Mr Esher.

'I am not, and I never have been, anyone's fancy man, and certainly not your wife's,' Mayne said scornfully. 'I was talking about a job with attached accommodation for Mrs Crossley and her family.'

'Where would *she* find a job like that?'

'That is none of your business now, Crossley. She's left you.'

'I'll find her, wherever she goes.'

'It's no secret. She'll be working for my family. And I'll take this opportunity to warn you not to set one foot on our land or you'll be charged with trespassing.'

He turned to Sergeant Deemer. 'After I've shown Mrs Crossley the accommodation and explained about the job, she will no doubt wish to return to the hospital to sit with her son. I'll make sure she gets there safely. Are you going to charge Crossley with assault now, Sergeant?'

Deeming sighed. 'Not this time. I'm under orders from above to give offenders like him a final chance, with a strict warning not to do it again. However, if it happens again, I shall be able to charge him. You hear that, Crossley. You're to stay away from your wife or you'll find the law keeps you away.'

'Yes, Sergeant. Of course, Sergeant.' Doug's expression left no one in any doubt that he'd disobey that warning. 'Am I free to go now?'

'Yes.'

Doug gave Judith a look that said this wasn't finished and strode out.

'He won't obey you,' she said. 'He'll come after me.'

The sergeant spread his hands to indicate his helplessness. 'I'm sorry. Unfortunately I have to obey orders.'

'Well, you won't be on your own from now on, Mrs Crossley,' Mayne told her. 'I'll take you to Esherwood, shall I, and show you the accommodation?'

'And you can escort me home at the same time,' Miss Peters said. 'It's on the way.'

12

Outside, Mayne asked, 'Are you all right for a ten-minute walk, Mrs Crossley?'

'Yes, of course. But could you please call me Judith? I hate using his name. It doesn't feel like mine any more. I think I'll go back to using my maiden name, which is Maskell.'

'Good idea. We'll pick your daughters up from Miss Bretherton's on the way to Esherwood and show them their new home.' He saw a worried look on her face. 'I'm sure Ben will be able to join you in a day or two. It's a very good hospital and they didn't have their 'he might die' expression on their faces. I've seen that so many times during the war that I'd recognise it at once.'

'That's comforting to know. Thank you.'

He wanted to comfort her, it surprised him how much.

They found Gillian perched on a wooden bench at the rear of Helen's house, chattering away to Jan, who was gardening and smiling across at the lively child. She waved to her mother and continued chatting.

In the kitchen, their bundles were piled in one corner, which was a relief. Kitty was helping Helen make sandwiches and she too was talking happily. As soon as they were away from their old home and father, they were lively, normal girls.

Judith was determined to keep them away from him from

now on, somehow. 'We're going to see our new home, girls. Come along.'

Kitty hesitated, looking down at the food.

Helen guessed what the matter was. 'Take a sandwich to keep you going, then you can come back and have something else to eat afterwards.'

'Thank you. Mum, you can have half mine. You've not eaten much today.'

'Take one each,' Helen said. 'Mr Esher?'

Mayne declined the offer, knowing how short of food people were, but the girls and their mother accepted one sandwich each, eating them in small bites as they walked along Park Gardens, making them last, he guessed.

He didn't explain what he was planning to do with Esherwood. He wanted to surprise Judith and gauge her reaction to the old house and its possibilities.

When they came to the Dower House, he led the way past it to the drive, where they had to edge round the barrier.

In front of the big house, he stopped. 'I thought you could live here.'

'*Here?* Is the house still all right?'

'It's not been destroyed, but it's been badly damaged inside.'

'How sad for your family to see this happening and be able to do nothing. They must be pleased to think of moving back in. It's a pretty house, isn't it? I've never been past the entrance gate before.'

'It used to be pretty. I don't think Father has missed the house as much as Mother has, because they allowed him to take his books with him and that's what he cares about most. He might be a good scholar, but he's absolutely impractical about the rest of life.'

'I'll always be grateful to him for his help in getting permission for Kitty to attend grammar school.'

'That's his second love – education. Anyway, I'm not sure

he and Mother will ever move back here because it'd cost too much to run the place. Most of the rooms inside the big house are still habitable, though, or will be with some cleaning and repairs, so you could stay here temporarily.'

'You said we could repay you in return for staying here, but you still haven't said exactly how. I don't have any prospect of getting another job, especially now I've left Doug.'

'I need to have people living here to stop looters. You can keep your eyes and ears open and call for help if needed. I'm hoping that your living here will scare them off looting the inside of the house. Some things have already been stolen, I'm afraid.'

They followed him through the front door and Judith stopped dead at the sight of the mess and damage. 'Oh, my goodness! Did the looters do this?'

'No. The British troops who were convalescing here.'

'Our own people? Oh, that's shameful.'

The two sisters were standing close to each other. He heard Gillian whisper, 'Esherwood's so big.'

The older girl replied, 'It's nearly as big as our school. It must have been lovely before.'

Hearing her words made Mayne feel sad, but he didn't allow himself to dwell on that. 'Come and see which bedrooms you might be able to use. You'll have to clear them out first, I'm afraid, which is another thing that will help me. It's your choice which ones you use. Makes no difference to me.'

Judith was thoughtful as he finished a quick tour of the first floor. 'Will we be the only people in the house at night?'

'No. I'll be here too, downstairs, complete with revolver. I'm having to keep watch at night because of looters. I'll have to see if I can find a couple of men to hire as night-watchmen. My friend Victor will be joining me here soon as well – at least, he will if my father cooperates. You'll be able to stay here for a few days longer, I hope.'

Gillian edged forward. 'Mr Esher, I couldn't help overhearing, and if you're looking for someone to help you keep guard, Al Needham, our neighbour's son, came home from the Army two weeks ago and he hasn't got a job any more. I heard him telling his mother his old workshop had closed down. He sounded really angry.'

'Where does he live?' Mayne jotted down the address, then turned to Judith. 'I have to go and see him because I need some watchmen straight away. Can I leave you three ladies to sort out your rooms, do you think?'

'I've already decided that the bedroom at the corner of the first floor will suit me and the girls, and Ben can sleep in the little room off it. That way, we won't take up too much space.'

'Space is one thing we're not short of. Take the next bedroom for yourself as well.'

'Maybe I will if we find we're able to stay longer.' She flushed as she added, 'It'll look better if I'm sleeping with the girls.'

'Ah. Yes, right.' He should have thought of that. He glanced at his watch. 'Look, there are iron bed frames scattered all over the place. And bedding. They left an incredible amount of stuff behind. Just help yourselves. I don't think Doug will follow you into the house, now I've warned him off, though he's bound to find out where you are and try to catch you when you go out.'

The Town Hall clock struck the hour just then.

'We'll give ourselves half an hour to make a start,' Judith decided. 'Then we'll go back to the hospital and see how Ben and my father are getting on.'

Mayne stopped. 'I need to stay with you, then. Unfortunately, you can't walk the streets in safety at the moment.'

'You'll have time to see our neighbour if you hurry. I won't leave till you get back. I'm sorry to take so much of your time, but I must admit I'm afraid of meeting Doug until he's calmed down.'

'I just thought of someone else, Mr Esher,' Kitty said. 'Jan might help you keep watch at night, as well. He's the man who helped you when Dad was threatening Mum. He's helping Miss Bretherton in the daytime, but she can't afford to pay him, only give him shelter and food, so if he could work for you as well, and earn some money, that'd help him a lot.'

'You two girls are being very helpful. I'll pop in to see Jan on the way back.'

When Mr Esher had left, Judith said briskly, 'Come on, girls. Let's get started. Where were those bed frames?'

'I remember.' Gillian led the way, clattering down the curving staircase, which must once have had a carpet on it, judging by the screw holes, but which was now bare wood, badly scraped and battered by hobnail army boots. The bigger rooms on the ground floor seemed to have been used as dormitories and had a dozen iron bed frames in each. Some more frames were piled higgledy-piggledy in a corner of one room, and one was standing in solitary splendour, made up with sheets and blankets, corners mitred as if ready for an inspection by Matron.

'They haven't even emptied the chamber pots,' Gillian said in a horrified whisper.

'We'll clear all that out tomorrow,' Judith said.

'Can't we just throw the chamber pots away?'

'No, we can't. England is short of everything and that includes each and every pot. Waste not, want not. Today the main thing we need to do is sort out bedrooms for ourselves and make up some beds.'

'I'm going to pretend I'm a duchess living in a palace,' Gillian said, twirling round.

'Pick up the other end of that mattress, Duchess, or you'll have nothing to sleep on.'

Judith watched her daughters carry the mattress upstairs, and managed to take one on her own.

At least they had somewhere to sleep tonight.

Helen called Jan in from the garden, where he had been standing for a few moments, hands resting on the spade, staring blindly into space. 'Come and have something to eat. We can finish off that soup.'

He smiled at her as they sat down together. She didn't feel the need to speak, and he was still thoughtful. She suspected each of them was glad not to be living alone. She'd thought she wanted to get away from people, but now she realised it was the farm she'd been glad to leave, not her friends in the Land Army.

'I'll clear up,' Jan said when they'd finished. 'You must not get that bandage wet.'

'OK.' She watched him lazily. His movements were always neat and efficient, and he was gradually losing that bleached, starved look.

'I was glad you helped Mr Esher, Jan. It was kind of you to risk being injured.'

He stopped, cup in hand, his expression serious. 'Those two men were in more danger of being hurt than I was. I have had to learn to defend myself.'

'Yes, I suppose you have.' As he dried and put away the final plate, she asked, 'Where are you going to sleep? You can't stay on the kitchen floor. How about the dining room? It isn't being used. You could make up a bed for yourself in there. In fact, take it for your own room, where you can keep your possessions. We'll live in the kitchen during the daytime.'

'I don't own many things. Two changes of clothing is all. I must wash my clothes every couple of days to stay clean.'

'I wonder how we can find more clothes for you. There

must be a clothing exchange in Rivenshaw. That's where people in need usually find clothing. They've set them up everywhere else I've been. Or, wait a minute – have you checked all the bedrooms and attics for trunks of old clothes?'

He drew himself up proudly. 'No. I do not steal.' Then a faint, rueful smile crept across his face. 'At least, I do not steal from my allies.'

'Friends,' she corrected quietly. 'I would hope you and I can become good friends.'

'I too would hope for this.'

There was warmth in his gaze . . . wasn't there? Not just any sort of warmth, but the way a man looks at a woman he finds attractive. Well, she hoped she was reading him correctly. She liked him too, not only as a man, but she admired the way he'd survived against the odds.

She changed the subject. It was too soon to confront his feelings, or her own. 'Let's go and look round upstairs, Jan. I'm dying to see it, even if it is damp.'

'Will you not be better resting?'

'Jan, I'm fed up of resting. I'm used to keeping busy. Besides, I'm feeling better every day, as long as I don't overdo it.'

Upstairs, she found four bedrooms crammed with old-fashioned furniture. The two rooms on the left-hand side, nearest to the bomb blast, were very damp and badly affected by the weather, the other two weren't nearly as bad.

In all the bedrooms there were drawers stuffed full of old clothes. Had her great-aunt never thrown anything away? Sadly, some of the clothing was rotted by damp and mildew, but in other rooms things were merely damp and musty-smelling. They could be washed and aired.

Helen held up a pair of men's drawers, smiling. 'I remember the farmer's wife correcting me about her husband's under-wear. These are called drawers because they reach only to the knee, which is what her husband still wore, and they are called pants if they reach to the ankle, which is what my grandfather wore. I think these must have belonged to my great-aunt's brother. I could shorten them for you quite easily.'

'You are not embarrassed to deal with these?'

'Heavens, no. I've been working on a farm, remember, living with a group of people. You soon stop being embarrassed by bodies of any sort, or the normal activities of daily life. I'm quite good at sewing, actually. Most women have had to be, with clothes rationed so tightly during the war.'

He nodded. '*Make do and mend.* I have heard it said everywhere.'

'I'm sick of the phrase. I think I'll see if there are any women's clothes here that I can alter or remake for myself. Now I'm not wearing uniform, I'm quite short of clothes, too. I'm glad we came upstairs. Sewing will give me something useful to do with my time till I recover properly.'

'But your arm!'

'Will be all right, since it's my left arm. Anyway, I'll be mostly using my hands and fingers, not the bigger arm muscles. I'll be careful, I promise you. The wound is getting better every day. Can you carry that pile of clothes downstairs for me?'

She was about to lead the way down from the attics, but he moved in front to stop her. 'First I'll make sure *you* get down safely, Helen. These stairs are very steep.'

They were standing so close together on the small landing that she felt her breath catch in her throat. She had a sudden urge to reach out and touch his face, the skin sallow, the cheeks hollow from months of not eating properly, but still a nice face.

His eyes were devouring her and she was suddenly certain that he was attracted to her. It sprang up almost of its own accord, attraction between men and women did. You couldn't mistake it when it was this obvious.

He wouldn't say or do anything about it, she guessed, so it was up to her. She touched his cheek with her fingertips. 'I want to get to know you better, Jan.'

He didn't pretend. 'You should find a more suitable man to know. I haven't even got permission to stay in England.'

'I find you very suitable, and I'll make sure you do get permission.'

He took her hand and turned his head slightly to kiss her palm, sending shivers down her spine.

'We must not rush into anything, Helen. I will not take advantage of your kindness.'

In for a penny, in for a pound, she thought. 'Oh, what a pity! I was hoping you'd kiss me.'

He flushed slightly. 'I want to, but I am not an expert at kissing. I have been fleeing for years. I have not known any women in that way.'

'None at all?'

'No. I did not dare, for their sake.'

'Then let me show you how to kiss.' She put her arms round his neck, pulled him closer and stood on tiptoe to kiss him gently on the lips. Then she deepened the kiss, because it felt so good.

When she moved away, he looked stunned. 'You are sure about this getting to know one another, Helen?'

'Yes, of course, or I'd not have kissed you.'

'Then let us do it again, because I very much enjoyed the kissing.'

To her disappointment, the second kiss was interrupted by the door knocker sounding downstairs.

'Damn!' she muttered. 'Can you run down and answer it?'

She smoothed her hair and followed him more slowly,

feeling warm inside, smiling at her own forward behaviour, intending to behave like that again.

Mayne knocked on the door of the house next to Judith's old home, keeping his eyes open for Crossley, though he guessed the fellow would be in the pub now. He explained his purpose and the young man who'd answered the door brightened up at once.

'A temporary job? I certainly am interested. I'm Al, by the way.'

An older woman came out to join them. 'His name's Alan!'

'Ma, no one calls me Alan these days.'

'I do, because that's what you were christened. I didn't call you after one of those American film stars. Didn't *Alan* even invite you inside, Mr Esher?'

'I don't have time, I'm afraid, Mrs Needham.'

'Ma, he's offered me a job.'

She brightened up at once.

'I can't pay much at first, but it may have prospects if things turn out as I hope. I need nightwatchmen. If you can start tonight, Al— Oh, good! Bring anything you might need during the night and meet me near the kitchen door at Esherwood as soon as you can. I have to call somewhere else on the way back.'

His next stop was at Helen Bretherton's house. There he offered Jan similar work as a nightwatchman.

Jan looked at Helen questioningly. 'I could do that and still work for you. I don't need a lot of sleep. Will you be all right here on your own at night?'

'Yes, of course I will. There are good locks on all the doors, and they're old-fashioned doors, really solid. Besides, Rivenshaw is a peaceful little town.'

'Not so peaceful that I haven't had looting at Esherwood,' Mayne said.

'You will have no looting while I am there,' Jan promised.

'Meet me at the back door of the big house when you've had time to get ready. I need you to get there while it's still daylight, so that I can show you round the grounds.'

'I will not be long.'

'No need to rush. I have to escort Mrs Crossley – I mean Maskell – to the hospital to see her son.'

He'd found two men to help him and that should be enough, Mayne thought triumphantly as he took a short cut back across Parson's Mead, skirting the rows of vegetables and fruit and waving to an old man who was working on his plot.

They weren't digging for victory now, but digging for survival, because the shortages would continue for a good while and they'd still need to produce as much food as possible. He'd have to check that vegetable garden at Esherwood more thoroughly.

He found himself smiling as he strode back. If his father gave him the chance he wanted, he'd be a very happy man. Rebuilding homes for people was a very worthwhile way to earn a living and that mattered to him.

Mayne found Judith and her daughters ready to go to the hospital to see Ben, so he walked there with them and agreed to pick them up in a couple of hours. They would wait for him in the reception area.

She didn't argue with the need for an escort.

He hurried back and found Al and Jan waiting for him, so showed them round the grounds near the house and suggested one of them watch the front and one the back.

'I'm sorry to leave you but I have a most important meeting. Perhaps you can continue to explore?'

'I will learn my way quickly,' Jan promised.

'I trespassed a few times as a lad,' Al said with a grin. 'I know the main layout here quite well.'

'Good. I'll leave you to it.'

Now came the most crucial task facing him, Mayne thought. He had to talk to his father again, try to make him see that the family had no choice: they could either let Esherwood be taken away from them and sold for whatever was offered, or the old man could hand it over to his son, who would invest his money in converting it into flats.

Mayne prayed that his mother had managed to talk some sense into his father. She hadn't said anything, though. He was aching to start putting into operation all the dreams and plans that had cheered him up during that final gruelling year in the Army.

He stopped on the way to buy some more food to add to what he'd already purchased, hoping that would help soften up his father. As he entered the house through the kitchen, he found a touching scene, with his mother and father sitting in front of the fire together making toast. It was so unusual lately for them to be together like this that he hated to interrupt them. They didn't even notice him till he spoke.

'I've bought a few more things to eat. Black market again, unfortunately – there seem to be people selling oddments of food all over the place. As there was so little to eat here, I thought anything I could get hold of would come in useful.'

His father shrugged. 'One has to survive.' He went across to the table where he had already mashed up some tinned peaches from Mayne's previous purchases. He spread them thinly across a piece of toast, like jam. When he held the result out to Mayne, it felt like a step towards reconciliation.

'Thanks.' He took a bite and sat down, watching his mother examine the small jar of potted meat and the tin of sardines he'd brought this time, as well as the bread, pearl barley and Oxo cubes. 'It's been hard, hasn't it, making the food stretch?'

'Very hard. Mary used to do it better than me. I planted some vegetables this year, only I don't know much about that sort of thing and they aren't flourishing as they did when Jack Bright did the gardens. It's all he can do now to manage his son's allotment, his rheumatism is so bad.'

'Miss Bretherton is employing a displaced person as a gardener and I'm employing him as a nightwatchman. He seems to know his stuff. He won't have time to do your gardening, but perhaps he'd give us some advice.'

'It seems strange to have a new Miss Bretherton. Is this one a spinster lady, too?'

'She's too young to call her a spinster. Her name's Helen and she's been in the Land Army but got quite badly injured.'

'I suppose I'd better call on her. If she's our sort of person. Perhaps she isn't. Couldn't she have done something more ladylike than work in the Land Army?'

'I don't think her house is in a suitable state for her to welcome callers. It got a sideswipe from a bomb and the upstairs isn't habitable. She's letting Jan, the displaced person, stay there till he gets a permit to live in England. She can't do much physically and he's very handy. He's going to make the upstairs waterproof again if he can get hold of the materials. You have to go on a waiting list to get window glass, though.'

He was talking too much, but it helped fill the disapproving silence that had greeted his talk of Jan.

'Why are all these foreigners still here in England?' his father asked, sounding grumpy.

'This one can't go back to Poland because he's Jewish.'

He waited for some disparaging remark about Jews but, for once, his father surprised him.

'Ah, Jewish, eh? Very fine minds, some of those Jews had. What Hitler did to them was appalling, barbaric. We shall never know how much useful knowledge and future discoveries have been lost to humanity because of that vile monster.'

'And yet our lawyer apparently hates Jews.'

'Does he?' Reginald shrugged. 'That won't make him a worse lawyer for what we need, will it?'

'I will find it distasteful to deal with him. After all, his attitude is one of the things I've been fighting against.'

'Oh, just ignore it. People have been anti-Semitic throughout history. I have a book you could read if you're interested in the subject.'

Mayne couldn't ignore the lawyer's attitude, though. He didn't want to deal with the man because he'd seen too many photos of the horrors caused by extreme prejudice in the war during the past year. But now wasn't the time to argue about it.

'One day, when I have more time, I'd like to read that book,' he said tactfully. 'But not now. I'm hoping to be working very hard setting up my business. There is no life of privilege for my generation, just increased taxes on wealth and new paths to be found in life.'

His father looked down at the piece of toast his wife had just put on his plate, fiddling with it. 'Dorothy tells me I'm out of touch.'

'I'm afraid Mother's right.'

'She says I should sell to Woollard and take that burden off your shoulders.'

Mayne saw her nodding vigorously and was shocked to think how he'd mistaken what she was intending to do. 'Mother, no! *I* want Esherwood.'

She threw words at him like daggers, more angry and determined than he'd ever seen her before. 'And if you get it, you'll half kill yourself repairing everything, trying to make it what it used to be, and then after your father dies, the death duties will take it all away from you. If these Labour people win the coming election, they'll make sure you don't keep Esherwood. I won't let you waste your life, Mayne. I want better than that for my only son.'

He took a deep breath. 'I think you'll change your mind when I explain. I don't want to repair Esherwood to live in myself, let alone try to restore it to its former glory. I want to convert it into flats and sell them to people. I've done the calculations. You're right that we can't afford to keep it, but I do think we can make good money from it. I've learned a lot about organising big jobs in the Army, and I have partners who understand the building industry.'

His father looked at him with more respect. 'That might work, Dorothy. I couldn't do it. Never have been a practical sort of fellow. But Maynard might manage it.'

'Well, I still don't agree. I think that horrible house is jinxed and I've never liked it, never. It's not your decision, Maynard. It's your father's. You don't own the house yet.'

He was shocked by the virulence in her tone. 'But our family has to do something to save it.'

'No we don't. We can sell it. I've asked Mr Woollard to call and discuss a price. We should hear what he has to offer and if it's not enough, find someone else who will pay more.'

'Mother, no!'

'Yes, Maynard. I've watched your father sink under the burden of that house and I'm not having my only son go down the same path.'

'But I've been making plans about the house for over a year. I really want to do this.'

'Then you'll have to unmake your plans and find something else to do. Someone has to save the men of this family from that burden, and I'm going to do it.'

His father shook his head and spread his hands as if helpless to change her views.

Mayne stared at his mother in disbelief. He'd thought she was on his side. 'When is Woollard coming?'

'I've asked him to call tomorrow morning,' she said.

'I hope you'll let me be present. After all, it is my inheritance you want to give away.'

'I'm not giving it away. I want your father to *sell* it, then we can live comfortably in our old age. You won't change my mind. And your father's promised to heed me.'

'I've promised to think about it seriously,' Reginald said. 'I haven't promised to sell at any cost. We don't know what Ray Woollard is offering yet. He hasn't made all that money by paying generous prices for things. I think it's a good idea for you to meet him with us, Maynard. He's a dashed tricky fellow. We shall all have to keep our eyes on him. If we sell to him, we must make him increase his offer.'

'Thank you. I would like to be there.'

'It's our opinion that counts, remember, Reginald. *You* are the owner, not Maynard.'

'We'll see.'

'No. We won't. If you don't sell it, I'm leaving you. I've been a prisoner here ever since we married. I've more than earned my freedom.'

She glared at them both, then burst into tears and ran upstairs to her bedroom.

His father followed her.

Mayne was left feeling betrayed by both parents. One had let the family fortunes slip away without making an effort to do anything practical about the business side of the estate; the other had been planning to take the family home away from him.

In fact, he had to wonder what they'd done with the money. There was so little to show for the spending of it.

He waited, but his father didn't come down again, so he walked slowly back to the big house.

What would he do with his life if he didn't get Esherwood?

13

On Monday, Constable Farrow yelled suddenly from the front door of the police station, 'The AC is here!'

Deemer groaned. 'Oh, hell! Go and tidy up the back room and cells quickly. I'll try to slow him down a bit.'

Inspector Upham, the area commander, turned up unexpectedly at the police station every now and then, to check out every pernickety damned detail, something Sergeant Gilbert Deemer greatly resented. Had the man nothing better to do than count pencils and check for waste of government resources?

For once, the inspector wanted to talk first, though that didn't stop him studying the front area as he strode through it to the tiny sergeant's office, where he took possession of Deemer's chair without even asking permission.

'Sit down, man. Tell me about that displaced person who's living in Upper Parklea. Him turning up like that is a bit suspicious, don't you think? I've had a letter worrying about him from that new lawyer chappie, who is not happy about the DP's unexplained arrival in town.'

Deemer blinked and held back a protest. He knew why the letter had been sent. Oh, yes. He'd already seen how Mr Damned Gilliot resented Jews. It was as if he blamed them for the war that had cost him his health.

Gilbert Deemer saw a lot more than people realised. He

might not have a fancy university education, but he prided himself on his astuteness and understanding of mankind. Well, he'd seen enough of it, hadn't he? From all levels of the social scale.

The sort of attitude Gilliot displayed towards Jews was like blaming a rabbit for getting itself shot, if you asked him, or asked any sensible person. Deemer had seen the horrible photos from the concentration camps in recent newspapers. They'd turned his stomach, they had, and made him even prouder that his country had stood up to Hitler and the Nazis.

'What exactly is Mr Gilliot worried about?' He managed to keep his voice quiet.

'Apart from why the fellow came here? Wasting British resources on a foreigner who can perfectly well go back to his own country.'

'I checked Mr Borkowski carefully myself and I think he's more than earning his way.'

Upham stared at him. 'Oh? Gilliot suggested that you hadn't bothered to do that at all.'

'Well, sir, Mr Gilliot had only to ask me, which he didn't, and he'd not have needed to bother you. And actually, Mr Borkowski's services are greatly needed by Miss Bretherton, who was injured serving her country in the Land Army and has been demobbed early because of it. It'll be a few weeks before she can use her arm, which may have permanent damage.'

'She can find someone else to help her, surely? A woman would surely be more sensible?'

'No, sir. Her home here was struck by the side blast from a bomb that hit the next house, so it needs a lot of work if it's to be habitable upstairs. The DP is very good with his hands. He's started on the garden already and will be doing the repairs on the windows when he finds the materials to work with. With that injury, she's going to need help lifting and carrying things for a good while, and Mr Borkowski has to push her into town in a wheelchair till she's stronger.'

'Gilliot never mentioned any of that.'

Their eyes met and Deemer allowed himself a quick grimace. 'No, sir. He didn't ask *her* why she needed help, either. He's the sort of gentleman who is more used to telling people what to do than listening to what they *are* doing. Though why he thinks he can order *you* around, I don't understand.'

Upham's expression said that he perfectly well understood what his sergeant was hinting at. 'Nonetheless, the government wants as many foreigners as possible sent back to their own countries.'

'Even if they're likely to be killed there?'

Another thoughtful glance. 'Is that so? You don't happen to know why this Borkowski fellow came here to Rivenshaw, do you? You'd think he'd look for work in a city.'

'His family knew old Miss Bretherton. He came here with his grandfather to visit her a few years before the war when he was a lad, and I'm not sure but I think he and the new Miss Bretherton corresponded for a while after that. It's natural that Mr Borkowski would want to settle somewhere he had acquaintances. It's very hard going to live in a new country, I should think. I'd have done the same as him, gone to where I knew people.'

'Hmm.'

'And what's more, Miss Peters has vouched for him. She remembers meeting his family when they visited.'

'Ah. The lady is a good friend of my mother's. She wouldn't lie about that sort of thing.'

Oh, wouldn't she? Deemer thought. 'The old lady takes a great interest in town affairs. I . . . um, pay attention when she gets fired up about something because she's usually right.

She's helping another young woman at the moment who's been badly beaten by her husband. I've been instructed not to charge such men with assault, but warn them to change their ways, only this one will never change. He's a vicious fellow.'

'You sound as if you don't approve of that directive, Sergeant.'

'I don't approve of it being applied to everyone. This fellow is known for his violence to his wife. He came back from the Middle East and thumped the poor woman within an hour of getting home.'

The inspector gave him a rueful look. 'He does sound like a bad egg, but our hands are tied by area policy on domestic cases, I'm afraid.'

Gilbert breathed deeply. 'Crossley laughed at me when I gave him the required warning. He said he'd not do it again in a way that made it plain he didn't mean what he said.' The words burst out more forcefully than he wanted. '*He was laughing openly at an officer of the law, sir.*'

'Galling, I know, but I'm afraid I don't have the power to change that directive. Now, let's get back to this DP. Miss Peters has always shown herself to be an extremely shrewd judge of character. England could do with more like her. What's the chappie's English like? Is he the sort to settle in well?'

'Mr Borkowski speaks excellent English, though with a slight accent, so you can tell he's foreign. When I first met him, he'd come here voluntarily to register.'

'Voluntarily?'

'Hmm. I doubt this young fellow could have fooled Miss Peters.'

'No, sir. I doubt anyone could.'

'And you're a pretty shrewd judge of character too.'

'Yes, sir. I hope so, sir.'

'How about we allow this DP sixty days' grace and review the situation then.' He leaned back in his chair and rubbed his forehead. 'Got the devil of a headache today. Must be coming down with influenza or something. This isn't a formal inspection. I'm on my way to a meeting, but I was passing through and thought I'd call in. Costs us less in petrol if I kill two birds with one stone.'

'Always glad to see you, sir.' Deemer stood up and opened the door. 'And after the sixty days?'

'If this DP has settled down well, I'll recommend him for a permanent stay. You sound to be handling it well but keep careful notes on everything you do about him. You know what lawyers can be like when they want to get their own way about something.'

'Yes, sir. I'll definitely do that, sir.'

Gilbert let out a groan of relief when the inspector left.

Constable Farrow came sheepishly out of hiding in the back and went out on his rounds.

This wasn't the first time Mr Bloody Gilliot had interfered in police matters, Deemer thought. The man might be a lawyer, a respected profession usually, but Deemer hadn't taken to him at all. He much regretted the demise of old Mr Lloyd. Now there was a real gentleman.

He hadn't expected people to kowtow to him.

He hadn't shown prejudice against Jews, a feeling more suited to Nazis than honest Englishmen.

With a loud and scornful sniff, Deemer got on with his work.

When Judith went back to the hospital with her daughters, the sister in charge of that ward told her Ben was awake, but she must wait to see him till the doctor had finished his evening rounds.

At the sister's prompting, the doctor stopped to speak to

her. 'Good news so far about your son, Mrs Crossley. The swelling is going down and Ben is complaining he's hungry.'

She felt her whole body sag in relief. 'He's always hungry, that one. He's grown so quickly this past year.'

'If he's still stable in the morning, you can take him home, as long as you promise to keep him quiet.' He frowned at her bruised face and put one finger under her chin to hold it up to the light. 'I see you were attacked as well. You should report your husband to the police.'

'I did. They apparently have orders from above not to prosecute husbands like mine, just to warn them.'

He scowled. 'Have they, indeed? I shall complain to the area commander about that. Will your son be safe if we release him?'

'I've moved out of our old home, so Ben should be all right unless my husband breaks into our new home.' She didn't go into any details.

'I wish you well in your new life.' He turned to the nurse. 'Sister, I think we can make an exception to the two-visitor rule to let these girls stay with their mother, given the circumstances, don't you?'

'Yes, Doctor.'

'Go and see your son now, Mrs Crossley.'

'I'm going by my maiden name now: Maskell.' She put one arm round each of her daughters and walked into the ward.

Ben's face lit up when he saw them. There were ten beds on either side of the long room and his was in the middle.

'Can I go home now, Mum?'

'In the morning, if you have a good night.'

His face fell again.

'We're living at Esherwood now,' Gillian burst out. 'It's a huge house, but it's very dirty and the soldiers who stayed there have damaged it, but I don't care. I like it. *And* we have an indoor bathroom with a lavatory. It'll be lovely not having to go outside in the dark. What's more, if there's enough hot water, Mum says we can have a bath tonight. I've never had a bath in a proper bathroom before, only in our old tin one in front of the fire.'

When the bell rang for the end of visiting hour, Judith left the ward, stopping at the sister's desk to ask her to keep Ben safe from the father who had injured him. 'What time shall I pick my son up tomorrow?'

'Leave it till eleven o'clock, after Doctor's round.'

'All right. Thank you, Sister.' She took her daughters down to the reception area to wait for Mayne. It might be cowardly, but she didn't want to go home on her own, was afraid of Doug coming after them.

It was half an hour before Mayne came rushing into the hospital, apologising for being late.

'It doesn't matter. You're here now, so we'll feel safe going home.'

'Have you had anything to eat, Mrs Cr— er, Maskell?'

She could feel her cheeks growing warm with embarrassment. 'Why don't you call me Judith, to make things easier? And no, I haven't eaten. We couldn't get to the shops, so the girls and I have resigned ourselves to going to bed hungry. It doesn't matter, really it doesn't. The main thing is we're safe and Ben is on the mend. We'll go to the baker's first thing tomorrow morning.'

'Aha!' He waved a sacking shopping bag at her. 'I bought you a loaf and one or two bits and pieces, and my mother has invited you to have a meal with us tonight.'

'I can't impose on your family like that!' she protested. 'It's late and, anyway, what will they think of me?' She gestured to her face.

'I've told them why I've given you shelter. My mother was very sympathetic. She's been having a hard time managing, so I bought some eggs. Six will mean one each.'

'You must have spent a fortune to get six. But we shouldn't have an egg each. That'd be wasteful. We could make an omelette tonight, or pancakes and then your mother can use the other eggs in cakes. It'll make them last longer.'

'Very practical. Our normal cook isn't well, so my mother might appreciate some help with the cooking. I doubt she's very good at omelettes or baking cakes, and her cook/house-keeper has illness in her family and can't come in for another day or two.'

'I know how to make an omelette, though I haven't had the eggs to do one for a while.' Judith licked her lips invol-untarily.

'We'll have to change over your ration books tomorrow, and keep Doug's separate.'

Her face fell. 'Oh, no! I haven't told the shopkeepers. What if he goes and spends all my coupons? He's eaten all our food several times when he's been hungry.'

'We'll knock up the grocer and butcher on the way home, if necessary, though if we hurry, the shops may still be open.' He'd do almost anything to take that anxious, harried look off her face.

The shopkeepers were just putting their few display goods away, so Judith explained quickly and they promised to keep her and the children's ration books separate from Mr Crossley's from now on.

'You won't believe him if he tells you something different?' she said.

'No, Mrs Crossley. I remember him from before the war,' one of them told her. 'After he married you, he settled down for a bit. But a leopard doesn't change its spots and I saw him gradually go back to his old ways.'

Judith smiled as she came out of the shop and saw Gillian in animated conversation with Mayne. That child should be an actress, because she could bring a story to life. But acting was a chancy life and Judith hoped Gillian would one day find a nice man to marry who would love her and support her in reasonable comfort – but an educated man, not a rough fellow. She didn't want either of her daughters to have the hard life she'd had.

The Eshers were horrified by Judith's bruised face. When Mr Esher realised who Kitty was, he was delighted to meet his protégée and asked how she was getting on at the grammar school.

Mayne's mother was a bit stiff with her son at first, after their recent disagreement, but with guests to tea, she kept it to herself.

Judith wound up taking charge of the kitchen, and his mother let her, as if Judith was a servant.

While Judith was preparing the meal, Mayne nipped up to the big house to check on his two nightwatchmen but was back in time for what Mrs Esher called dinner, but Judith called late tea.

They ate what seemed to the three visitors a splendid meal, then Mayne explained that Judith and her daughters hadn't even sorted out bedrooms to sleep in yet and must do that before daylight faded completely, since there wasn't yet any electricity at the big house.

He left his mother to wash up, though she didn't look happy about that. To his surprise, his father picked up the tea towel to dry the dishes.

Mayne's mother rolled her eyes and muttered, 'Wonders will never cease.'

Reginald looked across at his son and winked.

They walked up to the big house, listening to the sleepy twitters of birds. Shadows were lengthening as the sun dipped towards the horizon.

Gillian expressed everyone's feelings. 'It's so beautiful here. I wish I could stay for ever.'

Al was patrolling the front of the house, armed with a stout stick. He smiled and nodded as they passed.

Inside, it was much darker and the girls fell quiet as their footsteps echoed eerily on the battered tiles of the high-ceilinged entrance hall. Since Judith had only a battered old torch, Mayne took them through to the kitchen, where he'd seen oil lamps. He filled and lit three from supplies of oil that the Army must have left, then carried two of them upstairs. He set one on the landing turned down low in case they had to go to the bathroom in the night.

As he carried the other into the bedroom, he was surprised at how much Judith and her daughters had accomplished in the short time they'd had that afternoon. 'You must have worked hard.'

'We had something worth working for.' She surveyed the large room the three of them would be sharing, with its three iron Army bedsteads. 'I can't thank you enough.'

'You'll probably hear Jan and Al patrolling outside. I'll be sleeping downstairs, keeping an eye on the inside of the house. Though I don't think Jan will be easily bypassed.'

'He's had a hard life, hasn't he?' Gillian said. 'He told me he's been moving round Europe since he was sixteen. Just imagine that.'

'That means he was only a year older than me when he started,' Kitty said. 'He must be very brave and resourceful.'

'Which is why I'm happy to give him a job,' Mayne said.

Judith followed Mayne as he went to find windows from which he could keep an eye on the outside. 'We'll make a start on clearing up the other rooms tomorrow evening,'

'No need to run yourself ragged. Wait till your job ends.'

'I like to pay my way.'

'How will you get to work tomorrow?'

She shrugged. 'I'm hoping I'll be all right during the busy times of day. Even Doug wouldn't attack me on a busy street.'

'I think it'd be better if I escort you from the house to the town centre at least.'

'I don't want to be any trouble. But I can't stay away from work because it's my last week there and I'll need the money.' She hesitated. 'I do have some savings, but I need somewhere to hide them. Is there anywhere in the house that you know of?'

He stood for a moment, then smiled. 'Lots of places, but my childhood hidey-hole might be best. Come up to the nursery floor and I'll show you.'

She looked round. 'This area doesn't seem to be as badly damaged as the rest of the house.'

'The second floor was probably used for bedrooms for the medical staff,' Mayne said. He showed her the secret panel and she put most of her money into the space behind it. 'I'm honoured that you're trusting me with your savings.'

'I trust you absolutely.'

'That's a lovely compliment.'

'You've been a good friend to us, Mr Esher.'

'If I'm calling you Judith, you must call me Mayne.'

'Are you sure? All right.' She yawned suddenly. 'My daughters and I had better get to bed now. We've had a long and tiring day.'

He said goodnight then walked back to the Dower House because he'd forgotten to bring some supplies for the night ahead. He would set an alarm clock and check the inside of the house every couple of hours. Fortunately, he had learned to snatch sleep on and off during his years in the Army. He'd make tea for his watchers, and maybe give them a slice of bread. He had nothing to put on it, but knew Jan wouldn't worry about that. The poor fellow looked permanently hungry, as if he hadn't eaten properly for years. Which he probably hadn't.

His mother seemed in a better mood when he popped in to say goodnight.

'Miss Maskell's had a hard life, hasn't she?'

'Very. But she's a good mother.'

'I can see that. But make sure you don't do anything to give people ideas about you and her.'

He was surprised by her saying that. 'Of course not. I need people living at the big house to keep intruders out.'

As he walked back up the drive, he admitted to himself that if Judith hadn't been married, things might have been different. He really admired her and found her attractive, with those lovely green eyes sparkling with intelligence. How a man like Crossley could father such clever children, though, was more than Mayne could understand.

His thoughts turned to his future. It was going to take years to get Britain back to peacetime arrangements and freedom, and he couldn't see how the government would be able to end rationing for a good long while. You couldn't conjure food up out of nowhere, and even if you shipped it in from abroad now that there was no worry about the ships being torpedoed, the people there still had to grow the extra crops.

He very much wanted to play his part in the rebuilding of the country and his old home.

14

Judith woke with a start, unable for a moment to work out where she was. Then she realised she was at Esherwood. It wasn't quite dawn yet, but she could make out the mounds in the other two beds, where her daughters were still sleeping soundly. And there was a faint light under the door from the oil lamp on the landing.

She hoped Ben was sleeping peacefully too in the hospital. And her father.

She was looking forward to fetching her son and— Oh no! She'd have to get more time off work to bring him home. She'd lose more of her precious last week's money.

Deciding she'd plan her day better with a cup of tea inside her, she belted her raincoat on over her nightdress and went down to the kitchen.

Mayne was sitting there, cradling a tin mug in his hands.

'Oh!' She could feel herself blushing. What must she look like? But she didn't own a dressing gown because Doug had cut up her old one in a fit of rage and she'd never bothered to replace it.

Mayne didn't seem to notice her appearance. He looked as if he'd been thinking hard as he gestured to a battered enamel teapot. 'There's tea just brewed.'

'Wonderful. Did you have a quiet night?'

'Jan thinks he disturbed two people but they ran off when

he shone a torch in that direction. Al didn't hear anything untoward.'

'Then people are still trying to loot Esherwood.'

'Yes. But I'll have help stopping that from now on, at least.'

He fell silent, giving such a heavy sigh she had to ask, 'Something's still wrong, isn't it?'

'Yes. My mother is insisting my father sells this place to Woollard. She and I had a big row about it yesterday, because instead of saying what she thought a while ago, when I asked her help, she kept quiet. She used the time to try to persuade Father to sell the place and move to somewhere like St Anne's or Scarborough.'

'Why on earth would she want to do that?'

'She says the house has been a burden on the family, spoiling the lives of generations of Eshers and now that it's so run down, we should be done with it. She says it's blighted her life and she deserves some pleasure from her final years. She's quite adamant about it.'

'Oh, dear.'

'Never mind that. What time do you need to pick up your son?'

'The hospital said eleven o'clock, but it also depends on what time they'll let me take an hour off work.'

He looked at her shrewdly. 'And that means you'll lose money.'

'I'm afraid so.'

'I'd offer to help but I have to be at the meeting with Woollard and I don't know how long it'll last.'

'I'm torn both ways. I do want to see Ben and speak to the doctor, but I need the money desperately.'

'Can I ask how much you're paid?'

When she told him, he looked at her in shock. 'Goodness, that little?'

She shrugged. 'Women's wages are always lower than men's.'

'I don't mind keeping an eye on Ben for you after we've finished with Woollard, if that'll help. I'll be pottering around here anyway, in case I get my father on my side.'

'Would you really keep an eye on Ben? That'd be a big help. If he's all right, I'll bring him home and go straight back to work. At thirteen, he considers himself grown up anyway.'

There was a knock on the half-open door and Mayne made a beckoning gesture to the two men standing there. 'Come in and have a cup of tea before you go home.'

'I'd rather get straight back if you don't mind,' Jan said. 'I don't want Helen overdoing things.'

'I don't mind at all. Al? Do you want a cup of tea?'

'If you've got one to spare.'

When he heard about Judith's dilemma, Al said, 'I can pick up your son for you, Mrs Crossley. I've nothing else to do.'

She hesitated. 'Well. If he's all right, that would be a big help, but if the nurse needs to see me to give special instructions, you must come and fetch me from work. Ben is far more important to me than the money.'

'Can do.'

She'd noticed before that he was fond of Americanisms, well, that's what she thought such phrases were. She didn't have the money to go to the cinema very often, but other women at work had told her about various films and shared the new phrases they picked up there. 'I'm very grateful, Al.'

'If I grab a couple of hours' sleep, I can get to the hospital by eleven o'clock, Mrs C— no it's Mrs M now, isn't it? Don't blame you.'

'Yes. And eleven would be perfect. Would you mind asking about my father while you're there?'

'No prob.'

When Al had gone, she wiped her eyes and saw Mayne looking at her sympathetically. 'You're all being so kind to me. I hadn't expected anyone to help.'

'Judith, I—'

Footsteps on the back stairs announced the arrival of the girls, hungry and thirsty, filling the air with their chatter.

But Judith couldn't help wondering what Mayne had been going to say to her.

Later, the two of them walked to the mill together, but didn't talk. She liked the way he didn't fill every second with chat. Sometimes silence was a blessing. She was feeling guilty because she should be the one to pick her son up. But she had little choice about that. Necessity is a harsh master.

And of course, she continued to worry what Doug might do to them next. She couldn't impose on Mayne to escort her everywhere.

How was she to protect herself and the children in the coming years? Doug wouldn't give up easily. He'd consider it a point of honour to get back at her.

At ten o'clock, Mayne was waiting with his parents in the front room of the Dower House for Ray Woollard to arrive. The luxury car didn't draw up outside until a full five minutes past the hour, however.

'Bad manners, that,' his father muttered. 'With a car and chauffeur, and him living only a few streets away, there's no excuse for being late.'

'Reginald!' his mother said in a warning tone of voice.

'You can't deny the truth, Dorothy. Fellow's a boor and a bully.'

Mayne went to answer the door.

When he opened it, Woollard held out his hand, so he

couldn't refuse to shake it. As he'd never liked the man, he let go as quickly as he could. 'Do come in.'

Woollard turned to shout to his chauffeur, 'Half an hour.'

More deliberate rudeness. Mayne watched Woollard saunter into the house and stand staring round the hall with the air of a man costing every article in it.

'I'd like to look round this place before we finalise the sale,' the visitor said in a particularly loud voice. 'I haven't been inside it before.'

'There's no need for that. The Dower House is my parents' home and it isn't for sale.'

Woollard let out an amused snort. 'Let's stop pretending. They need to sell the big house, and sell it quickly, so they'll agree to whatever I ask for. *If* I want the Dower House as well. I'm not sure yet. I'll remind you that I'm a busy man, so I don't take kindly to people messing about.'

Mayne didn't allow himself to respond to that provocative statement. He showed the visitor into the sitting room.

His father was wearing his snootiest expression, and Mayne guessed his parents must have overheard what Woollard had just said. Well, you could hardly avoid hearing it. The fellow must be going deaf to speak so loudly.

His father didn't offer to shake hands, merely gestured to a chair. 'Please sit down, Mr Woollard.'

Instead the visitor went to stand by the window, muttering. 'Right next to the street. Knocks the value down being so close to people passing by.'

He swung round and took the nearest chair. 'Right, then. Let's get down to brass tacks. I'll pay you £5,000 for your property, the big house *and* this one, and all the grounds. I shall want you out of here within a month of us signing the contract.'

Dorothy gaped in shock for a few seconds at this low price, then looked at her husband, as if expecting him to respond. When he simply folded his arms and stared at her, raising one eyebrow, she turned to Mayne, who also remained silent.

Taking a deep breath, she said in a nervous, fluttering voice, 'That isn't nearly enough, Mr Woollard.'

Silence, then, '£6,000 then.'

Reginald surprised everyone by saying, 'If you can't be serious about the sale, I'll ask my son to show you out, Woollard. I've taken advice about the price and been told £12,000 would be a reasonable figure. And the Dower House is not included in that.'

Woollard scowled at him. 'The big house might be worth a bit more than I offered – though not nearly £12,000 – if it was in decent condition. But I hear it isn't.'

'As you are going to knock it down anyway, the condition is irrelevant, but my son tells me the structure is still sound, even though the interior has been damaged somewhat. And there are several acres of land with it.'

'The grounds have been damaged too. There's a ruddy great Nissen hut near the house, and the stables are in a bad way, been used for target practice, I hear.'

'The damage, I will remind you, is because we ceded the use of that house to our country in a time of war. I hope you don't intend to take advantage of our patriotism. That wouldn't look well at all if people heard about it.'

Mayne stood up. 'Perhaps you need to go home and think about it more seriously, Mr Woollard?'

'£8,000, and that includes the Dower House.'

'Maynard, please show our guest out.'

Their guest didn't budge. '£9,000 then.'

'£10,000 and we'll consider it.'

'*Consider it?*' Woollard roared. 'You should snap my hand off. No, nine's my final offer.'

Mayne was glad to see that his father had at least had the

wit to hold out for a higher price, but this latest offer made selling Esherwood a more attractive proposition, so he was starting to feel even more anxious.

It was his father who broke the impasse by standing up. 'We'll let you know our decision in a day or two, Mr Woollard.'

'Nay, I want a decision here and now. I'm a busy man. I can't be toing and froing while you dither about. I've got other irons in the fire. *You* need to sell, I want to buy, so let's get on with it.'

'In that case, our decision must be no,' Reginald said firmly. 'I cannot sell my son's birthright without serious consideration of the step.'

Dorothy made a faint sound of protest and Woollard swung his head round to stare at her, eyes narrowed. 'The lady seems more willing to sell than you, Esher. Perhaps she's of a more practical turn of mind. Dammit, man, even if you set the house in order, you couldn't afford to run it!'

'Nonetheless, I will not rush into things.'

'Oh, all right, I'll give you a day or two to consider the matter. For Mrs Esher's sake.' He inclined his head towards his hostess, then moved towards the door.

Mayne overtook him and led the way out, resisting the urge to slam the front door behind their unpleasant visitor.

For a moment he leaned his back against the closed door, seeing things in the hall that seemed to have been invisible to Woollard: the delicately turned banisters, the elegant tiled floor, the plasterwork on the ceiling so beautifully done, with its wreaths and flowers, a copy of earlier Adam plasterwork. It was a work of art in itself, that ceiling.

Shaking his head sadly, he went back into the living room.

'I need to speak to Maynard alone,' his father said. 'Can you please give us a few moments, Dorothy?'

She folded her arms. 'No, I can't. I'm not having any secrets between the three of us from now on, and I still insist on you selling the house, Reginald. If you didn't intend to do that, why did you bargain so firmly with Mr Woollard?'

'To see how high he'd go. To see if I could manage to do the bargaining. I've never tried it before but I'd read how to do it in a book and I followed their suggestions. It worked too. You know, if Woollard is willing to pay £9,000, I should think the house is worth a good deal more.'

'But Mayne went to inspect it and he said it was in a disgraceful state,' Dorothy protested.

'The building itself is basically sound, Mother, except for the far end wall and some of the outhouses. It's the inside, the decoration if you like, that has been badly treated.'

'In other words, it's not fit to be lived in.'

'Not as it stands.' Not for people like her, anyway, though Gillian and Kitty seemed to think their accommodation and use of bathroom luxurious.

Reginald began pacing up and down. 'I can't think what I will do with all my books if we sell the house to that man. There's barely room for the main ones I need at the Dower House, and if we had to move to a smaller house than this, there would be no room at all.'

'You could store some of the ones left in the big house in the attic here. It's not damp,' Mayne suggested.

'Isn't it? I must go up and check.'

'Well, you can make a bonfire of those books, for all I care,' Dorothy snapped. 'You think more of them than you do of me, and you always have done.'

Reginald's mouth fell open in shock. 'No, I don't. My dear, how can you possibly think that? I've loved you since the first time we danced together.'

'Well, prove it. If you really love me, you'll sell the house and all that goes with it.' She paused, then said loudly and slowly, 'If you don't sell it, I'm leaving you.'

Mayne watched his father sink down in an armchair, as if defeated.

His mother's threat seemed like the final nail in the coffin of his own plans for the big house. He'd never seen her so determined about anything. Had her dislike of Esherwood been festering ever since she went to live in the big house after his grandparents died? Why had she not said something before?

Perhaps she had. His father was good at playing the absent-minded professor, not hearing things he didn't want to deal with, and always had been.

Mayne seemed to be the only one to love the old house. He'd played in the cellars and attics as a child, helped Cook make pastry and little cakes, slid down the banisters when no one was looking. He had so many wonderful memories of the place.

It was bad enough that he'd have to turn it into flats and sell them off to strangers, unbearable to think of it being knocked down by a philistine like Woollard. What would he do with his life if he didn't get the house? Go into building on a much smaller scale, he supposed, but then he'd not be building the sorts of dwellings he could care about.

He had to find some way to persuade his parents not to sell. But what?

Jan went straight home when he left Esherwood. He stopped in the street for a moment to stare at Helen's house before going inside. How quickly he'd come to consider it his home, too! Even before she arrived, it had felt welcoming.

He must guard against that. It wasn't his home, could never be permanent, was just a temporary refuge, as so many places had been before. The house belonged to Helen, not him. He hadn't even got permission to stay in England, so might have to flee again.

Only . . . they'd kissed, he and Helen. And it'd been wonderful, the warmth, the closeness, the softness of her body against his. He'd thought about that several times during the night, remembering, longing to do it again.

Would she have changed her mind about him? He couldn't imagine changing his mind about her. Perhaps he could court her. If fate allowed him the privilege he was daring to dream about, he would work his fingers to the bone for the rest of his life to prove himself worthy of her.

He went round to the back of the house and, early as it was, she was up, sitting in the kitchen at the table. She looked well rested and her face had more colour today. If it weren't for that heavy bandage on her arm, you'd take her for a woman in excellent health.

Of course, she hadn't had the same food restrictions as most people in Britain, from the sounds of it. Well, you wouldn't on a farm, would you? He too had eaten better whenever he worked on farms.

Helen glanced up as he came in, giving him a glowing smile. 'How did it go?'

'It went well. I disturbed some looters, so I earned my money.'

'Good. Are you hungry? I was just thinking about breakfast. I know it's early, but I'm used to eating around this time and then starting work straight away. You'll need to sleep before you start work, of course.'

'I can manage.'

Her voice grew gentler. 'You don't need to manage without sleep, Jan. I'm not a slave driver.'

'Well, I will take a little sleep, then, just to refresh myself, and I'll have something to eat, as well.' He had earned that, as well. It was important to him to earn his way in the world.

She insisted he share everything they had equally. Her

company made their simple meal a feast for a king. Afterwards, he washed the dishes while she tidied the kitchen.

As they were finishing, she caught him yawning. 'Go on! Off to bed with you. I'm going to do some sewing.'

He didn't know whether he was pushing his luck, but he couldn't resist leaning across to kiss her cheek. Only somehow his mouth found her lips and by the time the kiss ended, she was standing in his arms, smiling at him.

'I'm glad you did that, Jan. I needed reassuring that you still wanted to.'

'Of course I want to. Every time I see you, I want to kiss you.' When she continued to smile, he took it as permission and did it again.

She pulled away after a while and patted his cheek. 'I like kissing you. We'll do it often, I hope. Now, away you go to bed.'

He heard her call 'Sweet dreams' as he went along to the dining room. Sweet indeed: a home of his own and a lovely woman sharing it with him, to hold and kiss.

He woke just after noon, as he'd planned. Five hours' sound, uninterrupted sleep was plenty.

When he went into the kitchen, he found a neat bundle on the table.

She came out of the pantry and gestured to it. 'I shortened some of the old-fashioned drawers from the attic and there are two short-sleeved vests there as well that just needed a little mending. But you'll have to wash them before you wear them, because they smell musty. I daren't put this arm in water yet.'

He beamed at her. It had been so long since he'd had any new clothes, and these were hardly worn at all. 'Thank you so much. I shall wash them straight away. There is a wringer so they'll dry quickly in the sun.'

'You're not doing anything till you've kissed me, which is

a much nicer way to say thank you.' She blushed slightly, but her eyes met his, so he obliged.

Afterwards, she said, 'Now we have to eat something. You can put a pan of water on to boil for the washing while we're eating. We really need to get a gas hot-water geyser fitted in the kitchen. There is gas supplied to the house already. The trouble will be finding a geyser for sale. There are not only queues at the food shops, but long waits to obtain anything in England. Over a year's wait to buy a car, I heard.'

She turned away, then swung round to add, 'Oh, and I'm afraid you'll have to be very careful indeed with the soap. The ration is tiny. If we can buy your soap ration next time we go to the shops, that'll help. There are so many things here that need washing.'

During the afternoon, Jan finished digging out a new vegetable patch and began planting his remaining seeds in it. Miss Peters popped across from her garden to see what he was doing, as she often did, and noticed how few seeds he had, how carefully he was planting each one.

'I'll ask a friend for a few more seeds. She has an allotment and always has some to spare.'

'That would be wonderful. Anything would be welcome.' He indicated the spring onions in the first vegetable patch. 'Would you like one? And a couple more lettuce leaves?'

'Yes, please. I do miss onions. They've been so scarce since the war began, I don't know why.'

He watched her smile as he passed over his small offering. He could understand how the years of tight food rationing had made people appreciate anything extra. He felt the same about a lot of things that were still available in England, very appreciative even of something as simple as bread.

As evening approached, he put away the garden tools and looked at the newly extended vegetable patch with satisfaction. Twigs marked the ends of each row. The earth looked smooth, dark and fertile. It was so satisfying to make things grow. His grandfather had taught him about gardening when he was quite a small boy.

'Penny for them.'

He swung round, frowning in puzzlement. 'Penny for what, Helen?'

'It's what we say when someone is lost in thought. A penny for your thoughts.'

'Oh, I see. You can have mine for free. I was just enjoying the sight of the vegetable beds. And I gave Miss Peters another onion and a couple more lettuce leaves. Is that all right? I didn't think you'd mind.'

'Of course not. She's welcome to share all we have. She helps everyone else, so it's good to help her in return. Anyway, she's a bit old for heavy gardening.'

'It will soon be time for me to go and keep watch at Esherwood, so I must get something to eat now.'

When he was ready to leave, she said, 'Be careful tonight.'

'I always am. I have had to learn to be careful at all times.'

'Yes. I do understand that, but I still like to say it.'

He liked her to say it, too. It showed someone cared about him.

As he walked across Parson's Mead to the big house, he smiled. He had accomplished a great deal today, small fixing jobs here and there in the house, as well as the gardening. Oh, and the washing. His new underclothes had spent the afternoon hanging outside in the sunshine and were now airing gently near the fire.

He'd washed some of his other clothes too, ashamed of how ragged they were. But he wouldn't pretend with Helen, not about anything. And at least his clothes were clean now. There had been times when even staying clean had been an impossible luxury for him.

The sun was setting in a blaze of crimson and gold. It felt as if it had shone all day – in the sky and in his heart.

Al turned up at the hospital at five minutes before eleven, the appointed time for release of patients. He greeted the nurse on the reception desk, who was a distant cousin of his mother's, and explained why he was there.

'Ben's father just went up to get him, Al. Didn't anyone tell you?'

'It was the father who thumped him and put him in hospital. The mother has left her husband and the son is only to be released to *her* care.'

'Why did no one tell me that? I'd have refused to let that man in. Still, he hasn't come down yet, so you're in time to stop him taking that poor boy away.'

There was some shouting from upstairs and Al started up them, yelling over his shoulder, 'Send a porter to the police station for help. I bet that's Crossley. He can be violent and he won't back off easily.'

He didn't need to ask the way at the top of the stairs, just followed the noise into the ward on the right.

A sister was standing protectively in front of a bed in the middle of a long row, while a burly man ranted and raved at her, threatening her with one fist.

Ben, looking pale and still not back to normal, was sitting pressed against the bedhead, clutching the iron bars tightly. The other patients were staring in shock, and those from the two nearby beds had moved to sit further away.

'He's *my* son and he's coming home with me!' Crossley yelled. 'Ben, pick up your things. And you get out of my way, woman, or I'll move you aside.'

'I'm not coming home with you, Dad. You'll have to drag me every step of the way. And I'll run away again as soon as your back is turned.' The lad gestured to his own head.

'You'll probably kill me next time, instead of just knocking me out.'

'That was an accident.'

Ben's voice was bitter. 'You have a lot of accidents like that, don't you?'

The sister spoke crisply, using a tone of icy command that would have worked with most people. 'Go home, Mr Crossley. We can't release the boy into your care.'

A man in a white coat who looked like a doctor pushed past Al and joined the nurse. 'What on earth is all this shouting about?'

When she explained, the doctor turned to Doug. 'You should be ashamed of yourself, Mr Crossley, and I certainly won't authorise a man who injured his son to take him away, so you're wasting your time.'

'Oh, am I?' Doug shoved the doctor out of the way so hard he fell on the floor. The doctor was a small man and, as he struggled to his feet, could only bleat at his much bigger attacker to stop this at once.

Doug faced the sister again. 'Are you going to get out of my way or do I have to make you?'

Afraid Doug would hit her next, Al took advantage of the other man's attention being on the nurse to creep along the side of the ward, step by slow, silent step, not drawing attention to himself.

When he got near enough, he flung himself across the central space, taking Doug by surprise and yanking him backwards by the collar of his jacket. 'The doctor told you to stop this!'

Doug tried to wriggle out of Al's grasp, but the younger man twisted his arm behind his back before he realised what was happening.

Al managed this more easily than he'd expected. Doug must be out of condition and not nearly as tough as he looked, especially when faced by someone his own size. Too much drinking, probably. He had that puffy look to him. And he was favouring the bandaged hand now.

'Let go of me, damn you!'

'Not till you stop this.'

In the struggle, they crashed into a screen, sending it flying.

Al clung on to the arm, slowing Doug down. 'You heard— the doctor. You can't— take— Ben.'

'He's my son. I bloody well can.'

More footsteps sounded and someone else ran along the ward. Even Doug stopped struggling violently when he saw who it was.

Sergeant Deemer strode up to the two men. 'What's going on here?'

The doctor stepped forward, dusting down his white coat. 'This fellow just knocked me to the floor and would have done the same to the sister if this young man hadn't stopped him. I want the fellow charged with assault. I don't know what the world's coming to when people think they can walk into hospitals and attack members of staff.'

Al saw Sergeant Deemer's eyes gleam with relish as they settled on Doug. 'Are there any witnesses to this assault?'

There was an immediate chorus of patients offering to bear witness.

'Thank you. I'll send someone to take names and statements later, gentlemen.'

The sergeant drew himself up to his full height. 'Douglas Crossley, I shall have to ask you to come to the police station and answer a few questions regarding this incident. If this man releases you, will you come quietly?'

Doug breathed deeply, then nodded.

When Al let go of him, however, he immediately tried to break through the group, lashing out with fists and feet. The sergeant ducked a blow to the face and piled into the fray. With his help, Al managed to trip Crossley up and sit on the struggling man.

'You'll also be charged with resisting arrest and assaulting a police officer,' Deemer said in tones of deep satisfaction.

The man on the floor glared at him, unable to get up because he was locked in a wrestling hold.

'You're in serious trouble now, Crossley. Don't make it worse.'

But Doug wasn't giving in, so the sergeant produced some handcuffs. He needed both Al and the doctor's help to fit them on the still struggling man. When this was done, he turned to Al. 'I wonder if you'd kindly help me to escort Crossley across the road to the police station, sir, then we can take your name and address at the same time?'

Al looked across at Ben. 'I shan't be long, lad, then I'll come back and walk home with you. Your mother didn't want to take time off work, but she sends her love.'

Ben, who was still huddled against the bedhead, let out a shuddering sigh of relief that showed he wasn't as tough as he tried to make out, and said gruffly, 'I'll be waiting, Mr Needham. Thanks for your help.'

'We'll keep an eye on the lad till then,' the sister said.

'I think his mother would want me to express her thanks to you for keeping that brute away from her son till help could arrive.'

She inclined her head graciously. 'We pride ourselves at this hospital on taking the best care we can of our patients.'

'I can see you do. You were very brave.'

Al winked at Ben and turned to help Sergeant Deemer take Crossley away. The fight seemed to have gone out of their prisoner now.

Behind him, Al heard Ben's muttered, 'I hate him!' and his heart went out to the lad. What a way to feel about a parent! Al's own mother nearly drove him mad with her fussing sometimes, but he knew it was done out of love, and he loved her dearly in return.

As Mayne left the Dower House after Woollard's departure, he saw Ben and Al walking slowly along the street towards him, so stopped to wait for them. 'Feeling better now, lad?'

'Yes, sir.' But the boy's voice sounded despondent and he was rather pale.

Mayne looked quickly at Al, who shook his head as if to tell him not to ask. 'I'm just going back to the big house. Shall I show you round it, Ben? I promised your mother I'd keep an eye on you till she gets back from work, and I'd certainly welcome some company. Al, you must need some sleep.'

'Well, I wouldn't mind another hour or two,' the younger man admitted. 'See you tonight, Ben. Mayne, could I have a quick word, please?'

Taking his employer aside, he explained in a low voice what had happened at the hospital, then left.

Ben was standing near the barrier to the drive, shoulders slumped.

'Let's go and have a cup of tea and a piece of toast. Your mother left some food out for you this morning.'

'I'm not really hungry, thank you, Mr Esher.'

'Well, we'll look round the house first and I'll show you your bedroom but, after that, I'm going to insist on you eating something.'

By the time he'd been shown round the ground floor, however, Ben admitted he was tired and agreed meekly when Mayne said it wasn't worth looking round upstairs yet.

He seemed glad to sit quietly in the kitchen with a book. He drank his tea and ate a piece of toast, when Mayne set them in front of him and insisted, but didn't ask for another.

Like his mother, he was sporting an impressive bruise on his face. But he was also, from what Al had said, bruised inside because of the way his father had treated him.

Al said Crossley hadn't even looked at his son as he argued with the nursing sister. It was as if the boy was just a possession, a bargaining counter.

Later that afternoon, as Mayne was investigating the main rooms one by one, he heard footsteps and Ben came to join him in the old library.

It was a shambles, its empty bookshelves overturned and lying on the floor. Many of the shelves on the few bookcases still upright were badly marked by something, probably mugs of hot tea. A few books had been left standing neatly on the upper shelves. Most of the remaining books were piled in the inner corners. It all seemed to have been done without rhyme or reason.

Fortunately, his father had removed his most cherished reference books, either to store or take to the Dower House.

'Want me to find you something else to read, lad?'

'Yes please, Mr Esher. I wish I wasn't feeling so weak. I should be helping Mum more. She never gets a chance to rest.'

'Life can be busy at times. It was like that for me during the whole of my final year in the Army. I've never worked as hard in all my life, but it was a very important project, so we all did the best we could.'

There was the sound of the front door opening and Mayne jumped to his feet, striding across the room to look down the hall and check who it was.

He was surprised. 'Dad! What are you doing here?'

'I've come to find out what the place is like,' Reginald said. 'Woollard wants to knock it down. You want to change it. I'd rather keep it the same, if that's possible.'

He turned round on the spot, studying the spacious entrance hall and stairs, looking shocked rigid. 'This is dreadful! Utterly appalling. How could the officers have allowed their men to wreck the place? I came here one dark winter's evening last time so I didn't see how bad it was.'

'I'd better warn you that it gets a lot worse in parts.'

'Show me.'

Mayne turned round. 'Ben, would you come with us, please? I don't want to leave you on your own down here till we're sure your father won't be released.'

The lad shrugged and trailed along behind them.

After a few exclamations at the beginning of their tour, Reginald fell silent, his expression becoming grimmer with each room they visited.

'Do you want to see the nursery floor and the attics, Dad?' Mayne asked gently, some time later.

'Are they worth the effort?'

'Well, it's more of the same, though these hooligans don't seem to have destroyed quite as much up there.'

'I don't think I'll bother.' He turned to Ben. 'What do you think, young fellow? Is it worth saving this old house?'

Ben looked surprised at being asked his opinion, but Mayne gave him a little nod, to encourage him to speak.

'I think your son has the right idea, Mr Esher,' the lad said thoughtfully. 'I've read in the papers that rich people can't find enough servants, and you'd need a lot of servants to keep a huge house like this clean, which would be expensive. And it'd need a lot of coal to heat even one of these big rooms, wouldn't it? Coal's still rationed. You wouldn't be able to get enough.'

Reginald nodded. 'Even in the old days, we could never get the place properly warm in winter.'

'It'd be freezing, I should think,' Ben said. 'So really, Mr Esher, your son has the right idea for these modern times.

And that Mr Woollard is a horrible man, you know. You don't want to sell your house to him. Who knows what he'd use it for?'

Reginald exchanged surprised glances with his son. 'Why do you say that?'

'He used to pay people for things they'd stolen. That's how he got rich at first. He didn't pay them much, either.'

'How on earth does a lad your age know that?'

'I overheard my dad talking to one of his friends, who used to sell things he'd stolen to Mr Woollard. He was complaining how little he got paid for them and Dad said,' the boy's voice faltered, 'he wished someone would give him the chance to nick a few things from rich sods. He'd welcome some easy money.'

Both men were silent. Ben was staring down at his feet now.

It was Reginald who patted his shoulder. 'Thank you for telling me that. I think you're a very shrewd young fellow and what you said has been a help to my thinking.'

He turned to his son. 'How much can you afford to pay me for the house, Maynard? Can you match Woollard's offer?'

'No, nothing like. I hadn't expected to have to pay you anything. I thought you might consider passing the house on to me early and living in the Dower House. I'd make you an annual allowance, of course.'

'Your mother's got her heart set on us enjoying life a bit more, and for that we'd need some money. I wonder how much would satisfy her? *I* don't want to travel, but she does, so I suppose I'll have to humour her. I don't want her to leave me. Hmm. I don't expect you to pay as much as the place is worth, but surely you can spare something.'

'I don't have much money to spare and I won't have for years. Even if I did, would Mother agree to passing the house to me? She sounded adamant. I hadn't realised how strongly she felt about it.'

'I hadn't either. However, the law gives me the final say, since I'm the owner, and if I decide to pass the house to you, she'll have no choice. Only to be fair, she's scrimped and saved for years without complaining, so I do think she deserves some rather more comfortable years now the war's over.'

'Dad, I'll already be risking everything on the conversion. The house is in much worse condition than I'd expected.'

'Is the project really risky? Surely people will be queuing up to buy the flats?'

'I believe my idea for converting the house into flats could be a success, and if it were done properly, a very big success. The trouble is, the post-war building rules and regulations are bound to hamper me and suck away my profits. And of course, there will be problems as to whether we can get hold of the materials we need.'

'Yes. I see.'

'Everything is going to be in short supply for years yet. We drained the country's resources to fight the war. That's what makes Esherwood such a good prospect. The main structure is all right. There are a lot of outhouses we can pull down and use their bricks and roof timbers, not to mention all sorts of smaller resources we can tap into from inside the house itself.'

His father nodded thoughtfully. 'You do sound to have thought it all out.'

Mayne kept quiet with some difficulty, feeling this was a crucial moment.

It was a while before his father spoke. 'Look, if I agree to hand it over, I'll make one other stipulation, besides some annual payment. I don't want you to build mean little flats for working people. They should be decent flats for people of the middling sort.'

'That's actually what I was intending.' He didn't say that his father wanted this from sheer snobbery, while *he* wanted it because he'd make more money that way.

'Another thing: you talk about working with friends. Does that mean you'll be starting up a company?'

'Yes, of course.'

'But you'll still hold the majority share in it, won't you? We might as well sell the house outright as not have an Esher in control.'

'I'll definitely keep control. It was my idea in the first place, and I'm providing most of the land and building for our investment. Besides, I love this house. If I had any other choice, I'd live here and restore it.'

After a pause, Mayne added, 'I don't think you love the house, not really.'

His father stiffened. 'I respect my heritage.'

'I know you do. But that's not quite the same thing. Anyway, I believe I can turn it into a very special sort of place for people to live in. I was hoping to provide a flat for myself, too. Would you want one or would you rather stay where you are?'

'Heavens, I'd far rather stay in the Dower House than live in a block of flats, cheek by jowl with anyone who has the money to buy. I'm settled there now, and have the main books I need for my research. They wouldn't fit into a flat.'

'And Mother?'

Reginald waved one hand dismissively. 'She'll continue to live with me, of course. She and I will get over this little hiccup, I'm sure.'

Mayne wished his father showed more concern for his wife's needs. 'How about I modernise the Dower House a bit while we're at it? That might make her feel better. The kitchen is very old-fashioned and inefficient, and so is the bathroom. I'll have to do it gradually, as materials come to hand.'

'I suppose that would appeal to a woman.' Reginald looked

at him with a wry smile. 'It *is* my decision, you know, what to do with the house. *I* inherited it from my family. Dorothy didn't bring very much to the marriage financially, but she was pretty and . . . I wanted very much to marry her.' He sounded surprised at his own statement.

Mayne didn't comment. Whatever the rights and wrongs, he could see storms ahead between his parents.

'Another important thing about your plan,' his father went on, 'is that if I deed the house and land to you now, you'll not have to pay death duties to the government when I die. At least, I hope you won't. But if the Labour party wins the coming election, they'll be even more eager to wipe out people like us and who knows what drastic measures they'll take to do that?'

'We'll only escape paying death duties if you survive for a certain number of years after handing the house over, Father. I believe it's seven years.'

'Oh, I'm in pretty good health. Never ill, except for the odd cold. I'll try my hardest to live for seven more years. Seventeen would be preferable. I'm getting to the end of this book now, but I have a second one in mind.'

He stopped and held out his hand. 'So that's agreed. I'll hand over the house to you.'

The two men shook on the bargain, while Ben watched solemnly from a nearby chair.

Mayne was pleasantly surprised by his father's firmness about this decision. He'd feel more secure, though, when the handover was complete. His mother didn't give in easily when she wanted something.

After everything was signed, sealed and delivered, he'd do whatever it took to get his new business started, even if it alienated his mother. They were not the most affectionate family, never had been, but surely she'd not break the family up?

If he ever married, he would hope to enjoy a happy family

life, with a woman who'd love him and their children. He'd not send them away to face the rigours of boarding school at a tender age, or shut them up in another part of the house during the school holidays.

15

Judith was all set to hurry home after work when she saw Mayne waiting outside the mill, looking rather serious. He raised one hand to beckon and she ran across to him, her heart thumping in her chest. 'Is something wrong? Ben's not worse?'

'No, no. He's fine. I've left him at Esherwood with the girls, and Al is keeping watch on them. This is about your husband. I thought I'd better warn you.'

Her whole body sagged. 'What's Doug done now?'

'He's under arrest and has been detained at the police station.'

'*What?*'

Mayne explained, then added, 'Al went there before he brought Ben to Esherwood to make a statement. Sergeant Deemer is going to keep your husband locked up till he's brought before the magistrate, because he reckons Crossley will be a danger to you and the children – and to anyone else who gets in his way, like the doctor.'

'Doug's locked up? Oh, thank goodness!'

'Unfortunately, Deemer isn't sure how the new magistrate will handle this case. This one is, in the good sergeant's opinion, rather soft with offenders generally, and is so strongly against divorce, or even married couples separating, that he tries to make decisions that will keep them together, regardless of whether he's being fair, or whether the woman will be safe.'

'Oh, dear. I *can't* go back to Doug. Or let him get hold of the children.'

She realised the last of the people from work had left and looked up at the big mill clock. 'I'd better get going. I'm dying to see Ben, but I have to buy some food on the way home, which will mean queuing. If Doug is locked up, I'll be all right, so I won't need to trouble you for an escort. I'm sorry to have taken up so much of your time and thank you for coming to warn me. I appreciate that.'

'It's been my pleasure. I enjoy your company.'

She looked at him, startled by this.

His smile was sad. 'It's not a good time to tell you that, is it? You're still married and I have a new business to set up.'

She didn't know what to say. She liked Mayne too, but hadn't dared think of him as more than a kind friend. Well, how could she, in her situation? Best to change the subject. 'How did your meeting go? Are your parents still intending to sell Esherwood?'

'Let's get in line. On the way home, I'll tell you about my family problems.'

But when they joined the end of the queue, the other women waved Judith to the front.

'Sorry about your son, love,' one called to her.

'You'll need to get home to the lad,' another added. 'We don't mind you going to the front of the queue.'

There was a chorus of agreement from the other women but they looked curiously at Mayne.

He decided on frankness, knowing how closely most people from Lower Parklea stuck together in times of trouble. 'I'm on escort duty today, ladies. A few of us men have set up a roster so that Mrs Crossley won't get attacked by her husband on the way home.'

There were nods of understanding, but a few still looked at him suspiciously and whispered to one another.

The shopkeeper nodded to Judith but gave Mayne a dirty look, so he pulled a five-pound note out of his wallet and handed it over. 'This is to start paying off my family's account with you. I hadn't realised things had got into such a tangle. I'm sorting it all out bit by bit, and will pay you the rest in due course, I give you my word.'

The note vanished quickly and the shopkeeper gave him a friendlier nod. 'Someone needs to sort the accounts out, that's for sure. I'm not the only one in this town who's owed money. Now, Mrs Crossley, I've kept your ration books safe, as you asked, even though your husband tried to tell me you'd sent him to collect them.'

Judith could feel her cheeks growing warm with embarrassment. 'Thank you.'

'What was it you wanted today, dear . . .? I could let you have a tin of tomato soup. Just received a delivery today.'

The other customers looked at him eagerly when they heard that. How hard it had been for women, Mayne thought, trying to feed their families on such restricted rations. He hoped rumours that the government would have to reduce rations of some foodstuffs yet again to help feed the hungry people in Europe were not correct. But then, he wouldn't think much of a government that didn't try to help people who were literally starving to death.

As the two of them walked back, he told Judith what had happened with his parents, then they fell silent, each with a lot to think about.

At Esherwood, they found Kitty and Gillian sitting chatting to their brother in the kitchen.

Judith dumped the shopping bag on the table and gave Ben a big hug, which for once he didn't try to wriggle out of. In fact he clung to her for a moment or two.

'You all right, love?' she asked as she pulled back.

'I've got a bit of a headache, and I feel tired,' he admitted.

'Well, you're supposed to take it easy for a few days. You'd better not go to school till next week.'

Kitty looked at her brother and sister, then asked, 'What about Dad?'

'He's locked away at the police station for the moment,' Mayne said.

The children's sighs of relief were all too audible in the big, echoing kitchen.

He turned to their mother. 'Will you be all right now? Jan and Al will be patrolling the grounds all night and word seems to have got out about them, so I'm going to sleep in my own bed at the Dower House tonight.'

'We'll be fine,' Judith said firmly.

He didn't want to leave them. But he knew he didn't dare continue spending the nights here, for the sake of her reputation.

He was going to try to persuade his friends and potential partners to come to Rivenshaw sooner than planned. After all, his father had now promised to hand over the house. Surely he'd keep that promise?

Mayne went back to the Dower House to scrawl a quick letter to Victor, outlining the situation and asking him to come to Rivenshaw as soon as possible. He also mentioned that they might need to find some extra money to placate his mother.

He looked at his watch and reckoned he had just enough time to catch the last post, so hurried through the streets to the Post Office, relieved to make it in time.

As he walked away from the postbox, he nearly bumped into a young woman who'd deliberately stepped in front of him. She stopped him moving on by putting her hand on his arm.

'Mayne, darling, are you really home for good?'

He stepped back, dismayed to see her. 'Caroline! I thought you and your husband were living in Scotland.'

'We were, but poor Stephen died of a heart attack a month before the war ended. He was only forty-eight, too. It was such a shock. So I came back to Rivenshaw to work out what to do with myself. I'm staying at my brother's. Accommodation is such a problem these days.'

Which meant, he supposed, that she hadn't got as much out of the marriage as she'd expected. Once again he tried to step back; once again she stopped him, holding tightly to his arm. He couldn't bring himself to shake her off, because he could see one or two people staring at him. Well, folk knew he and Caroline had once been engaged.

Her voice was even huskier than it used to be. 'Mayne . . . I'm sorry for dumping you like that. I was dazzled by Stephen and terrified of the war.'

'Well, you got away from the bombs and found yourself a rich husband into the bargain when you married McNulty, so you should be a happy woman now.'

Although Mayne knew the time perfectly well, he looked at his watch so that he had an excuse for shaking her hand off that arm. 'It was nice to see you again, but I have to get on now. I've a lot to do.' He took a quick step backwards as he spoke to prevent her grabbing him again.

'Surely you can spare me half an hour, Mayne dear? Can't we go and have a drink at the Crown, like we did in the old days? I'd love to hear what you've been doing. I've often wondered.'

So he spelled out exactly how he felt. 'I don't think we have much to say to one another now, Caroline, given the circumstances in which we parted.'

'I just explained that. Oh, Mayne, I didn't think you were the sort to hold grudges.'

'I'm not holding a grudge. Whatever we once were to each other is over and done with. Completely finished. I wish you well, but I have nothing more to say to you.'

She pouted and looked up at him through her eyelashes. He'd once thought that childish gesture attractive. Now, it made her seem like a spoiled schoolgirl. He'd grown up quickly during the war, as you do when you face death day after terrifying day: death of the men under your command and the likelihood of your own death too.

How could she not have changed during a war?

He suddenly thought of Judith, comparing her to Caroline. How badly life had treated Judith yet she still got on with caring for her children, working hard, never complaining.

He knew which woman he preferred.

'Tell your mother I'll drop in to see her soon,' Caroline called after him.

He spun round to tell her not to, but she'd already moved away. And though he called after her, she pretended not to hear what he'd said.

He didn't want to spend time with her ever again. He knew his mother had thought Caroline would make a highly suitable wife for him, and had been sorry when their engagement was broken. She'd even told him it was his own fault and he should have paid more attention to his fiancée. As if his war work were a secondary consideration. As if it'd have made a difference anyway, once Caroline got a much richer man in her sights.

Why the hell had she come back to Rivenshaw? She'd told him she never wanted to see such a dreary old town again.

It had to be for financial reasons. Money had always been her *raison d'être*. Hadn't dearest Stephen been as rich as she'd thought? Or hadn't he left her as much money as she'd expected? Well, the man already had three grown-up children by his first wife, one of them the heir, and a man usually left most of his money and possessions to his heir.

Mayne sighed. He was quite sure Caroline would cause trouble for him.

Damnation! He didn't need another problem dumping on his plate.

Caroline walked away, annoyed by Mayne's attitude. Still, she'd always been able to bring him round and she would do it again.

She wasn't stupid enough to call openly on Dorothy Esher, but continued to wander round the town centre, meeting one or two old acquaintances and displaying great delight at catching up with them.

They were not, she could tell, equally delighted to see her. Maybe she'd been a bit too abrupt with them when leaving Rivenshaw. She'd been so sure she'd never return.

On her return, her brother's wife greeted her coldly, so Caroline set out to win Joanna over. 'I can't thank you enough for putting me up till I can see my way clear.'

'It can only be for another week or so, I'm afraid. I have enough difficulty keeping staff without loading more work on them. And you haven't given me your ration book yet.'

'I forgot to bring it.'

'Then you'll have to eat out at the British Restaurant every day, because we don't have anything to spare from our rations, apart from bread and potatoes.'

Caroline looked at her in shock.

'The war might be over, but the food shortages aren't. Surely you've noticed that? And while we're discussing arrangements, you'll need to deal with your own bedroom. You must dust and tidy it every day, and empty the dirty water from your morning's ablutions; the chamber pot, too, if you've used it. That room is in chaos already and you've only been here two days.'

'Did you go into my room?' Caroline asked, outraged.

'Of course I did. This is my house, after all, and I remember you of old. You don't seem to have changed much, but we've had to. This is a different world, with fewer servants and less money. Your brother might not have been fit to fight, but he's worked hard all through the war, serving his country in other ways, and keeping fire watch at night. He's tired now and needs a good rest.'

'So do I. I'll remind you that I lost my husband recently.'

'If what I hear from one of my Scottish friends is correct, you lost him well before that. You were very stupid to be so rude to his children.'

Caroline swallowed hard. Who had told Joanna that she and Stephen hadn't been getting on, that he'd died in the middle of a quarrel with her? Not knowing what to do to mend the situation, she said coldly, 'I'd be obliged if you'd respect my privacy while I'm here.'

'Well, you'll have to stay unobliged, then, because I shall be checking your room daily. What's more, anything you leave lying around on the floor will be put straight into the clothes exchange. We've still got a need for that till clothing comes off the ration.'

'You wouldn't dare!'

'Oh, but I would. I've learned not to waste things during the war, and also not to take servants for granted. I intend to keep mine and I won't do that by expecting them to clear up your messes.'

Caroline breathed deeply but didn't dare say what she thought.

'I gather you spent the last three years of the war at your husband's country estate,' Joanna went on. 'Weren't you doing *any* war work? He was, I know. And why aren't you still living there? Surely the family didn't throw you out after his death?'

Caroline decided to burst into tears, an art she'd perfected, but Joanna merely folded her arms and waited for her to stop crying. Her sister-in-law had grown very hard since her eldest son was killed. It had been a great tragedy for them to lose Billy, of course it was, but it shouldn't have made Joanna neglect what family she did have left.

Over dinner that night, her brother Michael chatted mainly to his wife. When the meal ended they looked at one another and gave slight nods.

'We'll take coffee in the sitting room,' Joanna said. 'I have the tray ready. It's Peg's night off.'

'You and I will clear the table while we're waiting for the kettle to boil, Caroline,' Michael said at once. 'Come along. Collect the plates together. No, not like that. Scrape the leftover food on to the top one. Then the food goes into the pig bin near the garden gate.'

'You don't expect *me* to touch that smelly thing!'

'You helped eat the meal; you must help clear up. Which means doing whatever is needed.'

Fuming, she carried things out to the kitchen, looked at him pleadingly. When he simply pointed to the door, she went out to scrape the leftovers into the disgusting pig bin for the farmer to collect. She had to wash her hands as well as she could without soap and then they even expected her to dry the dishes.

Once that was done, she followed them into the sitting room, because she didn't know what else to do.

'Righty-ho,' Michael said, 'we are going to have a frank talk. Why did you need to come to us so urgently, Caroline? Surely Stephen left you somewhere to live?'

'And don't start crying,' Joanna said sharply. 'We both know how easily you can produce tears.'

'All he left me was a nasty little cottage in the village, and a miserable income.'

'How much do you consider miserable?'

She scowled at him. 'That's my business.'

'Not if you want to stay with us, it isn't.'

'Five hundred pounds a year.'

'Good heavens, woman! That's a comfortable income by any standards.'

'Not by mine. By the time I've paid rent on a house and hired a maid—'

Joanna looked puzzled. 'But you just said you'd been left a house.'

'In a small village in Scotland miles from anywhere. I don't want to live there now the war's over. I'd go mad. I intend to rent a house in a more civilised area.'

'Well, you can sell your cottage and buy a house somewhere else. No need to pay rent.'

'I can't sell it. The cottage goes back to the estate after I die, or after I remarry.'

'They must have realised what you're like with money.'

Caroline opened her mouth to protest, saw her brother's eye on her and sagged down in her chair. Why was everyone being so unkind to her?

He leaned back, studying her. 'You haven't changed a bit. You're still a spoiled brat. And just to get things straight, you're not staying with us permanently. We'll put you up for a week, maybe two if you muck in and help. That'll give you time to sort out what you want to do and move on.'

She didn't dare shout at him, didn't dare confess she had debts, couldn't manage to pay them off and live on the miserable amount of money Stephen had left her.

She had to find another husband quickly. It was the only way out of this terrible nightmare that had started even before Stephen died.

Mayne Esher was still unmarried and had come back to Rivenshaw. Surely he'd be able to keep her in reasonable style? He wasn't nearly as rich as Stephen had been but he was still the heir to Esherwood, a house she'd always liked. She'd find a way to coax him into wanting her again. She knew a lot more about what men liked now.

But she wouldn't say a word about her plans to her brother. Michael hadn't even mentioned Mayne, though the two of them had been friends once.

The first thing she would do was work out a way of bumping into Mrs Esher in town. The old witch was very sharp-tongued but had always been on her side where Mayne was concerned.

16

The following morning, Mayne got up early, determined to make a start on sorting out the rubbish in the various rooms in the big house now that he'd inspected the larger rooms and cleared some places outside to dump things from them.

Apart from the filth and debris, which needed to be cleared away, there might also be things he could sell, like the iron bedsteads. And of course, every item that could be reused in the building alterations would be.

He couldn't avoid seeing his mother because it would be rude not to go in and say good morning to her.

She was waiting for him in the kitchen, her expression furious. 'What did you say to your father? How did you persuade him to hand Esherwood over to you?'

'Father didn't need any persuading. It *is* our family home, after all, and I'm the only son, so why should it go to a stranger? What's more, if I do this right, I'll still be able to live there. That matters very much to me. I love the old place.'

'Well, I don't. I meant what I said. I won't stay here if you take over the big house. I won't watch another Esher give his life to that crumbling heap of stones. We'd have had a far better life if your father had gone on to study at university and then got a job there, as he could have done. He had offers of places to study. But no, he had to stay here to look after Esherwood and do his own research. Well, *I* don't have to stay now the war's over, so if he stays on, I shall go to live with my cousin Gloria.'

'Surely you won't really leave Father?' Mayne was shocked, had thought she was making empty threats before.

'*Leave* him? Ha! How much do you think I see of him? He's immersed in his rubbishy research day after day, and he's grown worse lately. He doesn't even remember to come down for his meals much of the time.'

'He is rather well known as an expert on Tudor Lancashire. He's had a couple of academic papers published, in spite of his lack of formal qualifications, and he must be close to finishing his book.'

'Who cares about that? Even if his stupid book is published, it isn't going to make us any money, is it? I doubt it will be published, either, because he's just a dabbler.'

'From what I've heard, he's far more than that. He has a good reputation.'

She made a scornful sound and waved her hand dismissively. 'Now the war's over, I want to enjoy life while I can. At my age, there aren't many years left, Mayne. My younger brother didn't even make it through the war.'

Her voice broke on the last sentence, which had echoed with anguish. He could understand that. He too regretted his uncle's death. 'I've told Dad I'll try to make him an allowance, so you will be able to do more things, even travel a bit. It won't be lack of money that stops you, but post-war rules and regulations.'

'If you give him money, he'll only spend it on more books and manuscripts.'

Sadly, she was right. 'What if I gave half directly to you?'

She sniffed scornfully. 'Would it be enough to buy a decent house in a place where I could have a good social life? No,

I thought not. I can't remember the last time I went into Manchester to the theatre, let alone to a dinner party where the conversation was lively and interesting. No, I'm going to go and live with my cousin Gloria in Newcastle. She's part of the county set and has a wonderful social life. I visited her last year and enjoyed myself immensely, in spite of the war.'

'Does she know?'

'She said I could live with her if anything happened to Reginald. And I could visit any time. She gets lonely as well.'

'Mum, if you leave Father, what will people think? The county set might not want to associate with you.'

'The war has changed such snobbish views. I don't think I'll be ostracised these days for spending most of my time away from a man who can't see beyond his books, not if I come back here every now and then. It's not as if I'm leaving him for another chap.'

She glared at her son. 'And when I'm gone, see how *you* like being responsible for your father. Mary's retired and even if she hadn't, she wouldn't work for him without me here to keep him in order.'

He was horrified at the viciousness of her tone. 'Don't do this, Mother.'

'It's you who's doing it. You and your father are planning to ruin my life. I put up with things during the war, but I won't put up with it any longer.' With a handkerchief pressed to her mouth, she ran out of the kitchen and up the stairs.

Mayne heard her bedroom door slam, which muffled but didn't conceal the sad sound of her sobbing. He was sorry for her, but he wasn't going to let her give the big house away, and if that made him a heartless son, so be it. She hadn't stinted on spending what money the family did have before the war. It wasn't just his father who'd been extravagant.

He got some breakfast, missing the food in the officers' mess. He hadn't had any bacon for ages. Toast again today, and his share of a few raspberries and strawberries Jan had found in the garden of the big house, half-hidden by weeds. It showed the man's honesty that he'd handed them over instead of eating them himself. In fact, Jan might make a very good full-time employee once they started work on Esherwood.

Mayne turned as the door opened behind him.

'I heard what your mother said,' his father whispered.

'She's more upset than I'd expected.'

'She's run down, tired of making do, needs some good food to build her up. We all do.'

Mayne could see that in the people he passed on the street. He'd heard them chatting about shortages, about what they longed to eat again. The civilians had had a hard time during the war. They'd certainly done their bit.

Rivenshaw had been spared the worst of the bombing. He'd seen the bomb crofts, as they called them, in Manchester. Whole rows of them sometimes, ruins of houses or craters where buildings had once stood. If you looked closely, you could see fragments of people's lives, wallpaper, a painting on the wall, ragged remains of curtains.

It would take a long time to clear up the bomb crofts and build more houses. He very much wanted to be part of that.

'What are you going to do about Mother?'

Reginald shrugged. 'Wait. See if you can find some money and try to persuade Dorothy not to leave me. In the meantime I'll get on with the book. She's wrong about it, you know.'

'Oh?'

'It will be published. I have a publisher waiting for it. He thinks it'll find a market.' He looked at Mayne, imperfectly hiding his pride. 'I know you all think I'm batty about my research, but I not only know the facts, I can write about them in a way people relate to.'

His father's eyes were glowing with enthusiasm as he spoke about his book. Mayne hadn't seen him look like this in a long time.

'The publisher wants to bring out two books, a learned tome and a shorter, popular history of Tudor Lancashire. He thinks the latter will sell well in schools.'

'Does Mother know?'

Reginald shook his head. 'I was going to surprise her when it was a fait accompli. I only got the letter from the publisher a few days ago. It's not certain, mind. There's still an *if*. He's only seen the academic version and the first three chapters of the easier book. But he liked them both. So if the rest is as good, he'll publish them at the same time. Well, he will as soon as supplies of paper improve. They've been very limited by that during the war and haven't been able to publish nearly as many books as they wanted to.'

'Will he be paying you an advance for it?'

'A small one, maybe two hundred pounds.'

'Well, congratulations.' It didn't seem much payment for all those years of hard work, but his father's happy expression showed it meant a lot to him to have the books published.

Reginald looked round the kitchen. 'What about breakfast?'

'I can't hang around to wait on you. I'll put out your share and you can get it ready yourself. There is one rule: you mustn't take any more than what I put out. We have to share what there is carefully.'

'I'm not very good at dealing with food.'

'Then you'll have to learn. You can't sit in your ivory tower all the time, you know, Father, even if you are a good writer. You can always go to the British Restaurant for lunch. You and Mother could make an outing of it.'

'All right.' Reginald sighed and came across to the table. 'What must I have?'

There was no sign of his mother, so Mayne gave him the food and a smear of butter – he even put the butter on the side of the plate. He wasn't going to eat breakfast with them from now on, didn't want to start his days by arbitrating their disagreements.

'That's not enough even to cover one slice, let alone two,' his father protested.

'That's all we get. It's rationed.'

Silence, then, 'Your mother must have been sharing hers with me, mustn't she?'

'I wouldn't be surprised.'

His father spoke in a low voice. 'I'll think of a way to change her mind. I do love Dorothy, you know. I've never looked at another woman.'

No, but he'd looked at an awful lot of books, Mayne thought, only he didn't say that. You couldn't sort out your parents' relationship for them.

When Judith arrived at the mill on the Wednesday morning, the foreman beckoned to her. 'Mr Walker says there's no more work for you this week. You're to go to the office and get your pay, then leave the premises. Sorry, love. You know how it is with returned soldiers, only this time it's returned air force.'

'But you said I could work out the week!' She felt like bursting into tears. She'd have even less money than she'd expected. She was already having nightmares about managing, about using up her savings.

When the manager's secretary passed her a small envelope containing her wages and asked her to sign for them, she took out the money and counted it first.

'It's a day's pay short.'

'There were fines.'

'I've done nothing to be fined for. And if I don't get my money, I'll complain to the police about theft.' She was quite sure they wouldn't do anything but it was worth a try.

A door opened behind her and the manager came in. 'Causing trouble, Mrs Crossley?'

'No, Mr Walker. I just want the money I'm owed.'

'It's there.'

'No, it isn't, so I'm going to the police station.' She had a sudden thought. She knew Walker had made good money during the war and was trying to get in with better-class people. '*And* I'll tell Mr Esher you've diddled me. Me and my children are living at the big house. I see him every day.'

All hung in the balance for a moment, then Walker held out his hand for her wages packet, pretended to scan the figures on the tiny slip of paper. 'Someone's made a mistake. She is owed another day's pay. See to it, Miss Perting.'

His expression as he looked back at Judith said he was angry. It was suspected that he took the so-called fines money for himself. She had been going to ask for the reference the foreman had spoken of, but knew the manager would not supply a good one now. Pity. She wasn't sure how long the job with Mayne would last . . . or the accommodation.

She had only been hired at the mill because of the war, so had no training in anything else. She wondered sometimes how Walker would get on with the men who'd been away fighting. She'd noticed how the war had changed some men, given them an edge. They wouldn't put up with the sort of treatment their fathers had endured. Look at Al Needham. He was polite but not servile.

She walked slowly back to the big house, feeling weary of struggling. She'd make herself a pot of tea, just a weak one, give herself a quiet hour, then plan how to find work, even if it was only going out as a charlady. There was always a need for those, surely?

She stopped for a moment to wipe away a tear.

No matter what she did, however hard she tried, things seemed to go from bad to worse.

Mayne was standing outside looking up at the damaged end wall of the big house. He saw Judith coming along the drive before she noticed him and watched her for a moment. She looked utterly miserable, poor thing. What had brought her home at this time of day?

Then she stopped to wipe away a tear and he couldn't keep away. She wasn't the sort to cry over nothing. He hurried across to join her. 'What's wrong?'

'I lost my job today, instead of Friday. Mr Walker wouldn't even let me end with a full week's work, though he knew how much I needed the money. What am I going to do now? How will I find the rent for a home? How will I feed the children?'

A sob escaped her control and Mayne couldn't bear it. He put his arms round her and held her close for a moment. 'We'll think of something.'

Her voice was muffled. 'There aren't a lot of jobs going in Rivenshaw for women. I've been asking round.'

'Come and have a cup of tea.'

She let him keep one arm round her shoulders as they walked into the big, echoing house, but she was moving like an old and weary woman today.

She'd had too much to bear, he thought, with no one to help her through the bad times.

In the kitchen she pulled away from him and turned towards the gas cooker.

'You sit down,' he said gently. 'I know how to put a kettle on.'

When he'd made the tea, he sat opposite her, deliberately.

He shouldn't have cuddled her outside. What if someone had seen them? The last thing she needed was to have her reputation blackened.

'Have you any idea at all about what you're going to do, Judith?'

'Looking for work as a cleaner seems the only thing, doing jobs here and there, as needed. It'll be difficult to manage. I hope you'll let me stay here for a while. I won't be able to pay you much rent, but I'll try to help with the cleaning of the house in the evenings instead and—'

He let out an exclamation as an idea struck him.

She stopped speaking and looked at him inquiringly.

'I believe I know of a job for you.'

'You do? Does your mother need help in the house?'

'No, I do.'

'I don't understand. What exactly do you mean?'

He gestured widely. 'Well, we've pretended to people that you're going to work for me, to explain why you're here. Why don't I actually hire you? This house needs clearing out and cleaning from cellar to attics; all the cupboards need going through too.'

She stared at him, mouth open in surprise.

'If you don't mind dirty cleaning jobs, why not take mine? I'd pay more than Walker did. I think it shameful how little he gave you. In other words, you'll be earning something closer to a man's wage. After all, you have three children dependent on you.'

He watched her expressive face. Doubt chased across it, then hope, then something more like fear.

She looked him in the eyes. 'I have to ask this, have to be sure, even if I lose the chance of this job because of it. If you're wanting to install me as your mistress—'

He cut her off, '*No!* I'd *never* ask you to do that. I'm offering you a real job as my . . . my assistant, we'll call it.

I can't say exactly what you'd have to do. Anything and everything that's needed.'

She buried her face in her hands and began to weep again, shoulders shaking with the violence of the emotion.

He half stood up. 'Judith, what did I say to upset you?'

She gulped to a halt and looked up, her smile glorious even though her eyelashes were still wet with tears. 'Sorry. I don't usually weep for joy. I can't tell you how relieved I am. Mayne – are you sure you still want me to call you by your first name? – I'd love the job and I promise I'll work really hard to give satisfaction.'

He made himself sit down again. He wanted to rush round the table, sweep her into his arms and dance her round the kitchen. Mustn't do that. He wanted . . . a lot of impossible things. 'Good,' he managed to say calmly. 'Consider yourself employed. Can you start today?'

'Yes.'

'And you must still use my first name.'

Ben appeared in the doorway, face crumpled from sleeping on something uneven, eyes heavy with sleep. 'Mum? I heard you crying. What's wrong?'

'Nothing. I'm fine.'

'Then why were you crying? If Dad's upset you again, tell me.'

'No, it's good news, for once. Silly, isn't it, to cry because you're happy. Come and sit down. There's a cup of tea left in the pot. While you're drinking it, I'll tell you about the wonderful job Mayne has just offered me.'

He was old enough to shoot the man a suspicious glance.

'It's a proper job, Ben,' she said quickly. 'I'm going to be his assistant, helping him with clearing out the house.'

'Not just clearing it, but organising some of the other small jobs, helping me decide what items are worth keeping, doing paperwork sometimes as needed.'

Ben's face cleared. 'Oh, I see. That sounds jolly interesting. Is that why you stayed home from work today, Mum?'

'No. I was sent home. They said I wasn't needed any more. *And* that Mr Walker tried to diddle me out of a day's pay, pretending it was a fine. Don't ever trust Cecil Walker, Mr Esher. Not in anything.'

'I can't stand the fellow.'

'That Mr Walker didn't deserve you anyway, Mum. I know how hard you always worked, how he kept you at the mill for longer hours sometimes without paying extra.' Ben gave Mayne a very adult, measuring look. 'I hope *you* will treat my mother with respect and fairness, Mr Esher.'

'You have my word on that,' Mayne promised.

What a good thing she had her children living with her and was sharing a bedroom with her daughters, Judith thought as she finished her cup of tea.

As long as Mayne continued to live back at the Dower House, the gossips would have difficulty stirring up trouble.

When Dorothy had recovered from her bout of weeping, she decided the best way to overcome her grief for the ruin of her plans was to start preparations for a new life.

She'd need to check that her cousin had meant what she said about them living together if anything happened to Reginald, so would have to write to Gloria. After she'd done that, she'd walk into town and post the letter straight away.

Best not to stay around the house more than she needed to or Reginald would come looking for her. She knew he'd try to persuade her to stay, but she wasn't going to give in. She sucked in a deep breath. She was *not* going to cry about this any more.

She glanced out of the window, to see what the weather was like. The sky was cloudy today. She might need to take her umbrella when she walked into town.

Two figures were walking along the side of the big house and she stayed to see who it was. Maynard and . . . who was the other one? Oh yes, it was Mrs Crossley. Poor woman. She'd had a hard time in her marriage.

Then the two of them stopped and it was unmistakable that Mrs Crossley was weeping.

To Dorothy's horror, she saw Maynard pull the woman into his arms. Was he just comforting her or was there more to it?

She watched carefully. There was no mistaking how her son felt, the tender way his arms curved round Mrs Crossley, the expression on his face. He wasn't just sorry for the woman. He *cared* about her.

Oh no! Taking a mistress at this stage would ruin not only his life but his business. People were very unforgiving about such things, especially when the woman was married.

Fancy an Esher getting entangled with a mill worker! What had the world come to?

Had Mrs Crossley left her husband because Maynard had come back? Who knew what women like that were prepared to do these days? And yet, she'd seemed so nice and decent when she and her children had stayed for a meal.

As the two figures went into the big house, Dorothy realised what this meant for herself and an angry sob escaped her control. She couldn't leave now. She had to stay here and stop her son making a fool of himself.

Which would mean making up her quarrel with Reginald.

The best way to protect Maynard from scandal would be to find him another woman, persuade him to marry, for the sake of the family name, if for no other reason.

Could she do that? She had to try to make him see sense.

17

Sergeant Deemer picked up the phone and was pleased to hear the voice of a fellow sergeant from nearby Oldham.

'Have you heard the bad news, Gilbert my lad?'

'No, what now?'

'Inspector Upham had a seizure yesterday. He isn't expected to live and, even if he does, he'll be helpless.'

'Poor man. He's been working too hard.' Then Deemer realised why this news was so bad. 'Oh, sod it! That means Halkett will be taking over till they appoint someone else. And they might even appoint him.'

'Yes. Precisely. I thought you'd like to be forewarned. Glad Halkett won't be my boss. I don't envy you. He's not the easiest person to deal with, is he?'

'No. And I have a ticklish situation here at the moment with a DP. Our new lawyer, Mr Bloody Gilliot, is determined to get rid of him.'

'Gilliot?' He lowered his voice. 'He's Halkett's cousin, didn't you know?'

'Are you sure?'

'Certain. Where I used to work, Halkett brought him in to play the heavy once or twice when he wasn't getting his own way on a case. I was glad to move to another district.'

'Just what I need.'

'Why is Gilliot causing trouble for this DP fellow? Is he giving you problems?'

'On the contrary. But from what Gilliot said to me, he hates Jews and wants me to send this DP back to where he came from simply because he's Jewish.'

Deemer went on to give a few details, then said slowly, 'I don't see what I can do to stop the pair of them deporting the DP now, not if Halkett's going to be in charge of our area. You know what he's like.'

'Hmm. There's one fairly sure way out of it. We had a similar case here, but unfortunately your DP hasn't been in town long enough to do the same thing.'

'Tell me what it is he'd have to do.'

When his friend had finished, Sergeant Deemer sat on by the phone, having a good think. It wasn't going to be easy, but he was on good terms with Miss Peters and *she* liked Borkowski. He'd consult her, perhaps enlist her help if she thought it a good idea. She could often get things done when everyone else failed.

He waited till his constable came back from his afternoon round and left Farrow in charge of the station.

Desperate situations needed desperate measures.

Deemer could see Miss Peters sitting in the bay window of her front room, watching the world go by. He'd noticed she wasn't quite as active as she used to be, but she still did wonderfully well for a woman in her seventies. Well, he thought she was in her seventies. He wasn't sure.

As he turned into her gate, she saw him and stood up, walking out of the room. He didn't knock, but waited for her to open the front door, breathing in deeply, enjoying the scent of a particularly pretty rose bush just under the living room window.

She flung open the door, beaming at him. 'How lovely to

see you! I was in need of some company. I've done all my chores for the day and was just wondering what to do next. Do you have time to share a pot of tea, Sergeant?'

'Yes, please, Miss Peters. I have as much time as is needed, because I've come to ask your advice.'

'Happy to help you in any way I can. Let's go and sit in the kitchen.'

She looked across the table at him and smiled. 'It's lovely, isn't it, not to have the worry of the war on our shoulders, to be able to switch on the radio and not hear about air raids and death?'

'I agree. I've heard a lot of people say that. There's still war in the Far East, think on, but at least Britain has taken over Lebanon and Syria now, so the Middle East is getting sorted out. We may have problems and hardships, but our lads aren't being sent out to be killed or imprisoned in Europe.'

She sipped her tea. 'I had some good news this week, Sergeant. My youngest great-nephew has been found alive in a minor concentration camp in Poland. He'll need careful nursing back to full health because he's skeletally thin, but he was categorised as 'missing presumed dead' so we'd given up hope. We're all thrilled about that.'

'I'm pleased for you.'

'Thank you. Now, that's enough about me. You're looking worried. How can I help?'

'It's that Mr Gilliot . . . ' Deemer reminded her of the trouble the lawyer had tried to cause for Jan and explained that unfortunately he was now likely to have the power to cause more trouble. He was sorry to see the smile fade from her face.

She thumped the table in frustration when he'd finished. 'I have no patience with such prejudice. What did we fight the war for? I won't allow that nice young man to be sacrificed to our new lawyer's nastiness. Gilliot is not a worthy successor to Mr Lloyd. I shall take my business away from him. I've heard there's another young lawyer coming back to Rivenshaw as soon as he's demobbed. If he looks at all promising, I shall move my business to him. If not, I'll go to someone in Manchester.'

She sat frowning into space and the sergeant waited patiently for her to continue.

'I must say I'm not up on the legal situation about Jan staying,' she admitted at last, 'and since we can't ask Gilliot for legal advice, I shall have to find out from someone else.'

'Well . . . ' Deemer hesitated, not certain how she'd take what he was going to say, then explained what his friend in Oldham had told him.

'Ah! If that's right, it may be just the thing for them both.'

'You think so?'

'Oh, yes. He and Helen get on very well. They've been like old friends almost from the start. He's a hard worker, and men of her age are going to be in short supply after all the deaths during the war, so they'd both benefit from getting married.'

'You think she'll marry him, then?'

'Probably she will. The two of them already look comfortable with one another. Thank you for warning me. I shall go next door later and sow a few seeds, or even broach the matter bluntly. I was feeling a little bored today, but as usual, something has turned up to keep me occupied.'

He sat on chatting, glad of a lull before what he was sure would be a storm. Halkett was famous for upsetting those who were under him.

The sergeant felt in a better mood as he walked back to the police station. He had found an ally, and as the old lady had reminded him, for all the shortages and rationing, it was wonderful to have the war in Europe over.

He was sure the war with Japan would soon end as well. If they could deal with Nazis and fascists, they could deal with the Oriental menace.

He wondered what life would be like in the next few years. Different from before the war, of course, but the British people would gradually pull things back into shape and get the country on its feet again. He had absolute faith in that.

Miss Peters decided now was as good a time to take action as any, so after she'd locked the front door behind Sergeant Deemer she went to visit her neighbour via the back gate to the garden. She felt her old friend Ethel Bretherton would want her to step in and give Helen a nudge.

She followed the sounds of hammering round to the far side of the house and found Jan up a ladder, covering one of the blown-out windows with planks. 'Good afternoon, Jan. Where did you find the wood?' she called by way of a greeting.

'Good afternoon, Miss Peters. I pulled the planks off this window carefully and put them on again properly, overlapping them so that the rain runs down, like the roof tiles. That left me needing one extra piece of wood and as there are some old planks in the shed, I used one of those.'

He leaned against the window frame, young and strong, smiling down at her. Oh, she envied young people their lithe bodies sometimes.

'I think this will keep the water out till we can get some glass again. I'll do the other windows one by one.' He looked up at the sky, which was covered in dark grey clouds. 'Do you need something? I'd like to finish this before it rains.'

'No, you carry on with it, young man. I came to speak to Helen.' She liked Jan in many ways. He'd had a hard life and sometimes his eyes looked old and sad, as if his mind was full of painful memories, but he wasn't bitter about it all. And he must be very clever indeed to have escaped pursuit for all those years. He was a survivor, which was not a bad trait for facing life. And a hard worker. And both of these qualities were very important.

She turned as she heard a sound behind her. 'Helen! You look better every day, my dear.'

'I feel guilty. I was having a rest and fell asleep. I keep doing that. I'd meant to finish some more sewing.'

'Don't feel guilty. Your body needs time to recover.' She pointed upwards. 'I see Jan's making a good job of this. I like that young man of yours.'

Maybe Helen still wasn't fully awake because she said without thinking, 'So do I.'

Then she blushed, which Veronica Peters thought an excellent sign. 'I'm glad to hear it.'

She took a sudden decision to be frank with Helen, then tackle Jan later if necessary. 'Do you have a few minutes to talk?' She lowered her voice. 'Something's happened that might cause trouble for Jan.'

'Oh, no. Come inside. Do you want him to join us?'

'I'd rather speak to you alone first.'

When Miss Peters had finished repeating what the sergeant had told her, Helen looked at her in dismay. 'So you think they'll try to send Jan back now, not wait the sixty days they've promised, not even review his case?'

'Yes. Some people seem to be born spiteful and Gilliot is one of them. Our good sergeant doesn't speak well of this Halkett fellow, either, and unfortunately he's likely to take over as inspector for the time being. And he's not only related to Gilliot, but cut from the same cloth by all accounts.'

'What can we do? Will Jan have to flee again?' Helen was surprised at how much the thought of losing him hurt.

'He can't keep fleeing. And there is a way for him to stay,

however . . . If he was married to an Englishwoman, he'd have an excellent chance of getting permission to settle here.'

'Ah.' She guessed immediately what Miss Peters was getting at.

'It's more than time the poor chap found himself a home, don't you think? He's been wandering round Europe, dodging danger for years. I doubt a fine-looking young man like him will have much trouble finding himself a wife, if he's given time, and then he can begin to lead a normal life. But will he be given time?'

Helen could feel her cheeks getting hotter.

Miss Peters laid one hand on her arm. 'Or has he found a young woman already?'

She didn't pretend. 'We . . . like one another, but we're only just getting to know one another. It's too soon to talk about anything more permanent.'

'Normally I'd agree with you, Helen dear, but desperate times need desperate measures. What if the only way he could stay was by marrying an Englishwoman straight away?'

Silence, then, 'He's quite a proud man. Talks of making money *then* marrying. I'm not sure he'd do it.'

'And you? What do you think of Jan? Would you be prepared to marry him?'

Helen didn't know what to say to that. She'd hardly admitted her feelings to herself, but she was starting to care for him.

'Do you really need longer to find out how you feel about him? I had a young man once and I swear I knew at our first meeting that we were meant for one another.'

'What happened to him?'

'He died of pneumonia. A beastly way to die. I was by his side and I hope to meet him again in heaven. That belief, the knowledge that once I was truly loved, has helped me get through life.'

'That's so sad.'

'Better to have loved than never to have cared for anyone. I wasn't pretty, so didn't attract any other men, but my Paul didn't care about my looks because I could make him laugh. Well, he wasn't good-looking himself. But oh, he was such fun!'

She took Helen's hand. 'Don't let anything stop you if you think you have a chance of happiness with Jan. If they send him back to Poland, you may never see him again. Indeed, he may well be worked to death there if what we hear is true.'

'I've heard that, too.'

'And here's another thing to bear in mind: your generation of young women will contain a lot of spinsters because so many men of marriageable age have been killed. It was the same after the Great War.'

'I know. I've thought of that myself.'

'Then carpe diem, my dear. You have a very nice young man to hand and he needs your help.'

'I do like Jan,' she said slowly. 'Very much.'

'Then think about it very seriously. Only don't take too long. Gilliot is turning out to be a nasty fellow. I happen to know his senior clerk, who is talking of retiring now the war's over, because he doesn't like the way this fellow treats him – or deals with the poorer customers.'

'Oh.' Helen took a deep breath. Did she dare? Of course she did. 'How would we do it?'

'Get a special licence and marry as quickly as possible. We've already told people you met him in 1935, when you were both too young to think of love, and corresponded with one another till the war stopped that. After all, his grandfather did visit this part of England then.'

'Yes.' She smiled suddenly. 'Are you telling me to lie, Miss Peters?'

'Only in a good cause.' She patted Helen's hand. 'Talk to Jan. Suggest it to him.'

'Yes. I will.'

When Miss Peters had left, Helen went to stand in the garden and watch Jan working.

He caught sight of her and a sudden smile lit his face as he called down to her. 'This window should be watertight now.'

'Good. I'll start making our tea.'

Helen didn't lie to herself. She wanted to do this.

But would a proud man agree to such an arrangement?

It took Helen a while to pluck up the courage to propose to Jan. After Miss Peters left, she couldn't stop thinking about it, trying to work out the best way to do it. She wanted to marry him! *Oh, yes. She definitely did.* She had no doubt about that.

Did she dare ask him? She wasn't a timid person, but this was going to be hard to do. Women didn't usually do the proposing. What if he said no?

Would he do that? She didn't think so but she was fairly sure he wouldn't be the first to speak.

When Jan came into the house to join her, he went straight to wash his hands at the kitchen sink as usual.

Helen couldn't help studying him in a new way, her heart beating faster with nervousness. But it was the realisation of how much she wanted him to stay, how much she cared about him already, that gave her the final jolt of courage to make the effort.

As he began drying his hands on the old kitchen towel, she sought for the right words to start with, finding it even harder than she'd expected to begin.

Jan came across and took her hand, making her jump in surprise. 'Never mind the tea, Helen. Miss Peters stopped on the way out to tell me you had something important to ask me. She said she approved of it but *you* seem upset. Is something wrong? Have I done something to upset you?'

'Let's sit down and . . . and talk.'

He pulled a chair away from the table and waited for her to sit before taking the chair next to hers.

'Didn't Miss Peters say anything else to you?' Helen began hesitantly.

'No, nothing.'

She could feel herself blushing, but when she looked sideways at him, she saw how patiently he was waiting, how gentle was the way he was looking at her, and that gave her the courage to start. She began by telling him about the area inspector dying and someone called Halkett taking over, a man related to the lawyer who had wanted Jan sent back to his own country straight away.

His expression became grim and yet deeply sad too. 'Ah. Does this mean Miss Peters thinks I should run away again? Only I don't want to leave. Oh, my dear Helen, I am so very weary of running and hiding. But most of all, I'd hate to leave you.'

'I don't want you to go and you needn't leave, unless you prefer to. Miss Peters has suggested another solution. Not only does she favour it but I— well, I— um, like the idea too.' She couldn't go on, just couldn't say the words.

After a few moments, he said softly, 'But it isn't easy for you to tell me what this idea is.'

'No. It's not easy for a woman to . . . to— '

He took her hand, his forehead wrinkled in thought, so she waited, giving him time to think. Maybe he'd guess.

'I have heard things on my travels and since I came to England, too. I have heard of people marrying to make sure one of them could stay in a country. Is that it?'

She didn't pull her hand away. 'Yes. You're very quick to work it out.'

'I have learned to think quickly to stay alive. But *you* don't have to sacrifice yourself for me, Helen, if that's what's troubling you.'

She wasn't letting him believe it'd be a sacrifice. 'Jan, I don't want you to leave. I like being with you, having you here.' Her face must be scarlet, it felt so hot with embarrassment.

He stilled, his mouth half-open as if surprise had stopped the words mid-breath. 'I hadn't dared hope . . . I hadn't dared believe such happiness could be possible for me . . . to marry you, stay here with you.'

'I'm older than you. And my arm will probably always have a weakness. And I'm not pretty or—'

He put one fingertip gently across her lips. 'Shhh! If you *want* to marry me, I will be the happiest man in England. Haven't you guessed that I love you, Helen? It began that first day, when you looked so tired. I wanted to protect you, help you.'

'You did?' She leaned forward instinctively.

'Oh, yes.' He took her face in both his hands, smiling slightly as he came close enough to kiss her.

It was so warm and tender, like no other kiss she'd ever experienced. It said everything, that kiss did, and she didn't want it ever to stop.

When he moved his head away, he caught hold of her right hand and raised it to his lips. 'You're sure of this?'

'Yes. Very sure now that I've seen you really do want us to get married.'

'Then Helen, my dear, dear Helen, I have never been so happy in my whole life.' He pulled her up from the chair, into a hug, rocking to and fro, then simply standing with his arms round her.

She felt moisture on her cheek and saw him try to wipe away a tear without her seeing.

'I think I should tell you I was engaged before, Jan. My fiancé was killed in France, but not before we'd . . . loved one another.' She was blushing again; she could feel it. 'Wilfred was a fine man, didn't deserve to die, so I'm not sorry we made love.'

'No. Why should you be?'

'I've felt so alone and sad without him. I think people need to love as well as to be loved. Only you have to find the right person, or it doesn't work. I believe, I really do, that you and I will be all right together, better than all right, good.'

'I've not had anyone to love since my grandfather. During the war I didn't even have friends. I've had much kindness from strangers, met many fine people, and some wicked ones too, but I never *belonged*, always had to move on.'

Happiness was shining in his eyes. 'What must we do to get married, Helen? And how soon can we do it?'

'I don't know.' She laughed, feeling suddenly young and joyous. 'I've never got married before.'

'We must go and see Miss Peters and tell her that we are happy to take her advice. Very happy. Then we can ask her how to make the arrangements. She's a very wise woman. She will know.'

He took Helen's hand and led the way through the little garden gate, stopping halfway to kiss her again.

The door was flung open before they reached it. 'Well?' Miss Peters demanded.

'We're going to get married,' Helen said. 'I'm so happy.' To prove it, she burst into tears.

This made Miss Peters blow her nose vigorously in sympathy and Jan blink his eyes hard again.

'What must we do?' he asked when they'd gone inside

and everyone had calmed down. 'How do we arrange it, Miss Peters?'

'You'll need to get a special licence so that you can marry quickly. You can't get one in Rivenshaw, so you'll have to go into Manchester. I know where to go. If you like, I can come with you. We can all take the bus there tomorrow. We shouldn't delay a minute. You never know what those people will do.'

'And the church in Rivenshaw? Do we have to book that for a wedding?' Helen asked.

'I don't think we should give Saunders a chance to tell anyone. If he realised Gilliot disapproved of Jan, he'd refuse. We'll simply turn up at his church once we have the special licence and ask him to marry you.'

18

Mayne got up on the Thursday morning feeling depressed about the trouble the big house was causing in the family. He was first in the kitchen, so made his own breakfast.

He lingered over a second cup of tea, hoping his mother would come down so that he could try to make peace with her and talk her out of leaving. But there was no sign of her.

The postman came just as he was about to set off for the big house. He picked up the letters from the hall floor and sorted through them: two for his father, one for his mother and two for himself. He took his own letters and put the others on the hall table.

His first letter was from Victor, with sad news.

My wife died a few days after I got back. Everyone said Susan had waited for me to return and they'd expected her to die sooner. Why didn't they tell me she was so ill? I'd have got compassionate leave and come home to say a proper farewell.

Things are difficult here and I'd like to join you as soon as I can. I don't want to stay in this house without Susan. It was her presence that made it bearable. I never did like the place, which was a wedding present from her family, forcing us to live nearby.

They disapproved of any changes I tried to make and created such a fuss that Susan begged me not to do anything else. Even as it stands, old-fashioned with dark wallpaper, I can rent the house out ten times over, given the current housing shortage. Later on I'll sell it. I shall never live here again.

I have another problem, which makes it necessary to leave quickly: Susan's parents have offered to take Betty off my hands and raise her, only it's more a demand than an offer. I won't agree to that. I've missed enough of my daughter's life already because of the war, and anyway, I want her to have a less rigid upbringing than they gave Susan.

Fortunately the child doesn't seem to have inherited her mother's poor health. She's very quiet, though. Their influence, I believe. I'd like her to run about and shout as other children do.

So, my friend, I don't care how roughly Betty and I have to live, as long as I can have her with me. There are bound to be women in Rivenshaw who can be hired to care for a child of seven, and run a house. Or there may be someone who can offer us lodgings. Anything to get away from here.

You can phone me at home at the above number to let me know it's all right to join you. Betty and I will slip away from here a day or two after you call without letting anyone know what we're doing.

Your friend
Victor

That was a cry for help he'd never expected. He was sorry to hear about Susan's death, but not surprised. He'd only met her a couple of times, but had seen how fragile she was and guessed she wouldn't make old bones.

Mayne decided to phone his friend immediately. From what Victor had said of his in-laws, they were ruthless when they wanted something. He and his daughter could camp out in the big house until they'd sorted out a more permanent place to live.

The other letter was from Daniel O'Brien, another member of their quartet of would-be builders. As well as being a good friend, Daniel had been an architect before the war, making him a valuable partner in this enterprise. Mayne was sure he would hear from Francis, the other member of their quartet, any day now.

He scanned Daniel's letter quickly.

I've celebrated the end of the war in style and now I'm ready for work. I don't want to go back to my old firm because they're planning to go back to designing shops and warehouses. As we've discussed many times, I want to create decent homes for people who deserve them after the long, hard years of war.

One problem I didn't expect is my wife, soon to be ex-wife. Ada's gone off with an American and after a stay of six weeks in some place in Nevada called Las Vegas, she will apparently be able to obtain a perfectly legal divorce. Her American fellow will pay for this – and I should think so too.

At least I won't have to get a divorce in the British way and spend a night in a hotel with a strange woman to prove 'adultery'. What an ass the law is sometimes!

Ada's packed up the house and says she's divided our joint possessions fifty-fifty. I've not been able to check that, as they're in storage, but I trust her. She's even found a buyer for the house, but the family wants to move in immediately.

She can be horribly efficient when she wants something.

That American never stood a chance once she'd decided on a future with him.

The good side of this is that I'll have some money to invest in our project without borrowing it. But I'm angry at her, I must admit. I shall never marry again.

I'll probably come to Rivenshaw next week. If you've nowhere to put me up, I'll find lodgings. I loathe the pitying glances and remarks I'm meeting here, so please keep quiet about what's happened to me. I'll make a fresh start in Rivenshaw.

I just need to say goodbye to a few family members and let them know what's happened.

Your friend as always
Daniel

Mayne let out a shout of joy just as his mother came into the kitchen.

She pressed one hand to her chest and he realised he'd startled her.

'Sorry. I had some good news.'

She inclined her head slightly, her face expressionless.

'Mum, I wanted to ask you to reconsider. Please don't leave Dad.'

She looked at him coldly, her expression blank, as if he were a stranger. 'I have reconsidered and I'm staying, but it's for your father's sake not yours. I'm not happy about you getting hold of that horrible house, and I won't pretend I am.'

'I'm glad you're staying, for whatever reason.'

'Are you?' She turned her back and opened a cupboard. 'If you cared about how I felt, you'd sell that house. Mark my words, it'll drag you down.'

He didn't even try to reply to that, didn't feel he knew her any more. She didn't ask about his letters, as she usually would have done, and her icy gaze didn't encourage him to share his news. 'I'll get off to work, then.'

She didn't say goodbye or ask when he'd be back, either. Well, if she thought emotional pressure would make a difference to what he intended to do, she was wrong.

He went back into his own quarters and slid the bolt he'd put on the connecting door. If he was going to put his friends up at the big house, he'd better go and check out the accommodation. They wouldn't mind roughing it, he was sure. He wasn't going to ask any favours of his mother.

There was Victor's child to think of, though. Betty had to be properly provided for, with someone to look after her.

He'd ask Judith's advice about that. She was a sensible woman. And as she was now working for him – a thought that pleased him greatly – he'd get her to help him sort out the accommodation as one of her first duties.

Judith helped Kitty and Gillian get ready for school, then walked down the drive to Parson's Mead with them, waving till they were out of sight.

She was deep in thought as she started walking back and jumped in shock as Mayne came hurrying out of the gate of the Dower House and nearly bumped into her. They stopped dead, just avoiding a collision, and laughed at the same time.

'Talk about two people with their minds on other things,' Judith said.

'Yes, sorry. Something's cropped up, something good. I need to talk to you about it. We'll go up to the big house and chat over a friendly cup of tea. The atmosphere is icy at the Dower House. My mother is very much against me taking over the big house. She even threatened to leave Dad if he passed it on to me.'

'She won't really leave your father, will she?'

'She says she's decided to stay, but didn't tell me why. I'm glad, though. Dad needs her, because he's so impractical. But *I* shan't be asking her help from now on.'

In spite of the rapidly darkening sky, they stopped speaking as a blackbird let out a warning call from some bushes, then Mayne whispered, 'I think it's nesting there. Look, you can just see a darker mass to the left.'

As they set off again, it began to rain, a sudden downpour with drops so heavy they bounced off the ground.

'We'd better take shelter. Come on.' Mayne took her hand and tugged her into an old summer house that was half-hidden by trees. The roof was leaking at one side, but the other side was dry enough.

'I thought I'd have time to get back to the house before it rained, so didn't bring an umbrella.' Judith took off her light coat and gave it a good shaking to get most of the moisture off while he did the same with his jacket.

The rain continued to pound down so Mayne dragged a bench across, dusting the cobwebs off it with his hand. 'We might as well sit down. I need to ask your advice.'

He told her about his two friends and their need for accommodation. 'Do you think we can fit them in at the big house? How many other bedrooms can be made habitable quickly, do you think? And what are we going to do with a seven-year-old child?'

'Your friend will have to send her to school till the end of the summer term. I'm sure Gillian will keep an eye on her, if necessary.'

'Victor talks of finding a house and housekeeper, but houses are in short supply. And even if he could find a housekeeper, I doubt any woman would consider living in the big house in its present state.'

She hesitated, looking at him doubtfully.

'Go on, say it.'

'Well, I could keep an eye on another child after school, as long as Betty isn't too demanding of attention. She could even eat with me and the children. I won't have time to look after your friend's needs, though, if I'm doing other work for you. And I don't know what will happen when Doug is released. I may have to . . . leave suddenly.'

He patted her hand. 'We'll worry about that when it happens. Are you sure about Betty?'

'Yes. Another thing. If you really are going to pay me so well, I'll be sending our washing out to the laundry and they can do the same. Simmons' do a good job. So that's another thing solved.'

'That's a generous offer. Are you sure you'll be able to manage Betty's meals? We can perhaps get someone in to help with cooking and housework once the place is cleared out.'

'I thought I'd be doing that.'

'Sometimes. But mostly you'll be my assistant, keeping track of paperwork, doing all sorts of small office tasks. Unless you'd prefer a job as a housekeeper.'

She stared at him in delight. 'No! I'd much prefer to be your assistant. I'm sure I can do it. I'm good at organising.'

'I'm glad you prefer that.'

'Wait till we've worked together before you say that.'

'I trust my own judgement where people are concerned. I learned how to assess and manage all sorts of people in the Army, where I had to organise several big projects with very tight schedules.'

Mayne spoke with such quiet confidence she believed him. It felt wonderful to have him speak so confidently about her capabilities. She didn't get many compliments.

He stood up. 'The rain seems to be easing. Yes, look, it's a mere pitter-patter now. Are you game to make a run for the big house before it pours down again? There are still a lot of dark clouds.'

'Of course I can run.' She set off, easily keeping up with him.

They arrived at the house together, pushing the doors open, panting and laughing.

A voice called from one side, 'Is that you, Mum?'

Judith turned to smile at her son. 'Yes, it's me, Ben. I met Mayne at the end of the drive and we sheltered from the rain in an old summer house till the rain eased off. Then we ran for it. Did you get yourself some breakfast?'

'Yes. I'll be glad to go to school on Monday, though. I'm missing so much and I don't want to fall behind. Anyway, it's boring with nothing to do.'

'Let's put the kettle on.' She put an arm round his shoulders and they walked together towards the kitchen. 'You can go back to school on Monday but you still need to take things easy for a day or two. I'll send a note to your teacher.'

'Can I help you do something today? I've finished my library book and I'm a bit fed up of reading anyway.'

'Perhaps.' She turned to Mayne. 'If it's all right with you, I'll get Ben to help me with your friends' bedrooms. As I clear them out, he can make lists of everything that can be salvaged, sold or got rid of. He writes a clear hand.'

'That sounds like jobs for three people, because you'll need to lift furniture about, I should think. Let's all work together, eh? It'll be quicker and I do need to find out exactly what I have here.'

Mayne took charge from then on, and soon had Ben hanging on his every word. She hoped her son would learn from him how a decent man behaved.

Most of all, she hoped Doug wouldn't be let out of prison for a good long while and that someone would warn her if they did release him.

She dismissed her husband from her thoughts, not wanting to spoil what was turning into a very happy and productive morning, in spite of the rainy weather.

Reginald Esher sat fretting as to whether he should go and see Mr Woollard on his own or take Maynard with him. All in all, he decided having his son there would be a help when dealing with a man famous for his bullying tactics.

When he mentioned this to Dorothy, she got a sour expression on her face, so he said in a firm voice, 'I'm not changing my mind about handing Esherwood over to our son.' He'd decided that the best way to deal with her reaction was to repeat this statement at regular intervals.

He waited and when she didn't volunteer a reply, he asked, 'So what do you think? Should I take Maynard with me to see Woollard?'

'You can do whatever you want. *My* opinions are clearly of no value in this house.'

'Very well. We'll go and see the fellow after lunch. The sky's starting to clear, so the rain should have eased off by then. And after that, we can go and see Gilliot about making arrangements.'

'You'd better find out whether they're free after lunch. Gilliot and Woollard are both busy men.'

'Good idea. I'll phone their offices.'

After making the phone calls and getting a positive response, Reginald got his coat and an umbrella, intending to see Maynard about the appointment he'd arranged with Woollard.

Dorothy came with him into the hall, straightening his jacket collar automatically. 'I'd better warn you about the woman who's living at the big house. Maynard is interested in her.'

'I beg your pardon?'

'That Judith Crossley person, the one whose husband beats her. He's interested in her.'

'Nonsense! Maynard's just helping her and her children.

And they deserve our help. Those two oldest are very intelligent young people and I daresay the young one – can't remember her name – will also get a scholarship of some sort to the grammar school when she's old enough.'

'If you use your eyes today for once, Reginald Esher, you'll see that I'm right.' Dorothy flounced off back to the kitchen.

He shook his head sadly. She was coming out with some strange ideas lately. He was quite sure she was wrong about this. Maynard wouldn't let the family down by getting tangled up with a married woman. Poor Dorothy. At the moment she was so unhappy, she seemed determined to look on the worst side of everything.

He took his time walking along the drive. The grounds of Esherwood looked freshly washed, and smelled of summer and burgeoning plants. It had been ages since he'd been allowed into the gardens of his own home. The Army seemed to have done a lot of damage, but flowers still managed to bloom. It was rather like England, really: damaged but still ready to blossom again.

He wasn't sure where his son would be working. Should he go in the front way or the back? Another shower sent him running in through the front door, which was nearest. Ah! He followed the sound of his son's voice up the stairs.

There was laughter and a woman's voice. He stopped moving for a moment. Was Dorothy right about Maynard and Mrs Crossley? He hoped not. He liked the woman and she'd had a lot to bear, but he didn't want any immorality happening at Esherwood.

To his relief, he found them at opposite ends of the room, and her son working with them. There! Dorothy was seeing problems where there were none. It was probably his wife's age. Women could turn rather strange for a while as they grew older. His mother had been the same.

It was the lad who saw him first. 'Mum! Mr Esher is here.'
All three swung round.

'Dad! Have you come to inspect the premises? That's what
we're doing: checking every detail of every room.' Mayne
gestured widely. 'Judith's been telling me which items she
thinks we can sell. She's had experience buying and selling
things at the market, you see.'

Reginald stared at the piles they'd made. 'I can't think any
of this rubbish is worth much.'

Judith held up a checked blanket, ragged at one corner.
'Because of the war, women have learned to use and reuse
things till they fall to pieces, Mr Esher. This is sound except
for the tear at the corner. It'll make a child's coat, perhaps
a small child's skirt as well, if pieces are patched together.
It's good quality wool and not too coarsely woven. It'll bring
about five shillings and it'll sell quickly because second-hand
clothing doesn't cost any clothing coupons.'

'Goodness.'

Mayne soon realised that his father had other things on
his mind. He was sorry not to continue this conversation,
because he'd been enjoying Judith's tales of the markets. She
knew more than he ever would about buying and selling
second-hand items of all sorts, because she'd had to eke out
her family finances by buying and selling, with growing
children to clothe.

She admitted to having an eye for a bargain, and had
occasionally bought other items cheaply at the market,
mended them and sold them to neighbours for a few pennies
or, if she was lucky, a few shillings more. Occasionally items
had seemed more valuable, so she offered them to a man
who had run an antiques shop before the war and would
do so again one day. What a clever woman she was!

He turned away from Judith regretfully. 'I presume you
came to find me, Dad. How can I help you?'

'I've got an appointment with Mr Woollard this afternoon, to tell him I'm not going to sell the house to him. I think it's only courteous to do that in person. I'd appreciate you coming with me, because he can be rather fierce when he doesn't get his own way. I've also arranged to go to the lawyer afterwards and get things started to transfer Esherwood to you. I've checked that they'll both be free.'

'I'm happy to go with you.' Mayne definitely didn't want Woollard bullying his father. 'Will you and Ben be all right carrying on with this on your own, Judith?'

'We'll be fine.'

Mayne watched Judith lay one hand on her son's shoulder, a familiar loving gesture that gave him a sudden pang of envy. His own mother had never touched or cuddled him casually, even when he was small.

He noticed his father watching this interaction too, as if studying an experiment.

Ben smiled shyly across the room at the two men. Mayne smiled back at him. 'Look after your mother.'

'I will, Mr Esher.'

As they walked into town, Reginald said, 'Nice lad, that. Polite.'

'Yes. All Judith's children have excellent manners.'

'Your mother thinks you're interested in Mrs Crossley.'

'I would never get involved with a married woman.'

'That's what I told her. She wants you married, though, is longing for grandchildren.'

'In my own good time.'

'Well, you need to meet someone you fancy, don't you? I was always glad you didn't marry that silly young woman, though.'

'Caroline?'

'Yes, her. Can't understand what your mother sees in her.'

They'd arrived by then, so the conversation didn't continue, which was perhaps as well. Mayne knew he'd have to take even greater care not to compromise Judith from now on if his mother was watching them so closely.

Mr Woollard's secretary showed them straight through to his office. When she'd left, Woollard shook hands, seeming slightly more affable on his own territory.

He gestured to chairs grouped near the fireplace and took the initiative. 'I don't think you're going to sell your house to me.'

Reginald gaped at him. 'How did you guess that?'

Woollard tapped the side of his nose. 'I watch people.'

'I'm sorry to disappoint you.' Reginald made as if to stand up again.

'What are you going to do with it, then?'

Reginald sank back, looking at his son, and Woollard immediately turned his attention to Mayne. 'It's you who's going to do something, I suppose? What? Or is that a secret?'

'For the moment I'm not talking to anyone about what we intend to do.'

'We?'

Hell, the man was sharp. 'Yes. I'm going into business with a couple of colleagues from the forces.'

'Are you now. Not like your father, are you?'

'He and I have different interests in life. But don't underestimate my father. When his attention is attracted, he can be very shrewd.' He stood up. 'I'm sorry to disappoint Mrs Woollard.'

'I'll find the wife somewhere else to live. There are a lot of large old houses being sold. I shall watch what you're doing with interest. Yours is the only place near town and yet with quite a lot of land. You could build a lot of houses there.'

Mayne hoped he hadn't betrayed how close this guess

was. As he and his father walked out, he wondered if he'd made an enemy or not. Woollard hadn't given away his own feelings at all. The man could certainly play his cards close to his chest. But he hadn't seemed annoyed about not getting the house, either.

It would pay to be careful what they said to people till they got going. He'd warn the others when they arrived.

'Maynard!'

He realised his father had been trying to get his attention. 'Sorry. What did you say, Dad?'

'We need to see the new lawyer chappie before we go home.'

'I don't like Gilliot.'

'We don't have to like him to do business with him.'

When he was in charge of Esherwood, Mayne decided, he'd definitely take his legal business elsewhere. It wasn't just a question of liking someone but of trusting them, as well.

The lawyer listened carefully to their request.

'If you would prepare the paperwork quickly, Mr Gilliot, we'd be grateful. We'll come in and sign things as soon as you give us word,' Mayne said.

'You'll need to pay off the debts before your father can transfer the property.'

He knew his father owed money. Was it more than he'd thought? Mayne saw his father avoiding his gaze, staring down fixedly at his clasped hands, and his heart sank. 'How much exactly do you owe, Dad?'

'I'm not sure. More than I can repay, I'm afraid.'

'Who do you owe money to?'

'Shopkeepers mostly. The bookshops are the important ones. I need another reference book. Mr Gilliot has been, um, dealing with them for me, finding out the total. We were thinking of finding something from the big house to sell.'

Mayne turned to the lawyer, who summed up what was owed, a surprising amount. How the hell could his father have run up debts as big as that? And why had Woollard not mentioned them if he'd been buying up the debts?

'We'll pay Mr Woollard off first, I think,' he said.

Mr Gilliot merely smiled and inclined his head.

Mayne did some quick sums in his head as they walked back. He'd have to sell a few items to pay off the debts.

'I forget money when I'm after books,' his father muttered.

Which was as near an apology as he was likely to offer. Mayne decided to make the new situation very clear. 'I won't pay any debts you incur from now on. You and Mother will have to live within your means.'

His father sighed. 'Everything always comes down to money. So boring.'

'I'll speak to Woollard about the money we owe him. And later on I'll see if there's anything at the big house I can sell to help fund the business.'

'Are there some paintings there still? I mentioned the others to Gilliot when we sold the one that used to hang in the hall at the Dower House, and he thought they sounded valuable. Surely some of them survived the occupation of the house?'

Since Mayne was certain his father still wouldn't take much care with money, he told a direct lie. 'Only one or two, unfortunately. I'll see if we can sell them to pay off these debts.'

'That's all right, then. Can you deal with that?'

'Yes, of course.' But he wouldn't do anything until the estate had been handed over, which meant paying off Woollard first. Dare he risk his own money on that?

19

Judith heard someone knocking on the outer kitchen door at Esherwood on the Friday morning and glanced out of the window to check who it was before unlocking it. She was taking no chances.

Constable Farrow was standing there, looking uncomfortable.

What now? was her immediate thought.

Jan came into the kitchen from the hall. He'd been about to go home after his night of keeping watch, but had lingered to talk to Ben. As the constable knocked for a second time, Jan looked towards the door. 'Shall I stay with you, Judith?'

'Yes, please. I don't like Constable Farrow. I can't see him without thinking something bad is going to happen.'

Squaring her shoulders, she opened the door, not inviting Farrow in. 'How can I help you, Constable?'

'Mr Compton-Grey, the magistrate, will be holding a preliminary hearing this afternoon, looking into the charges against your husband of assaulting a doctor at the hospital. He's sent me to tell you to attend because of you being Crossley's wife. Three o'clock sharp, he says.'

The constable turned away, clearly not expecting an answer, assuming she'd turn up. And unfortunately, she knew she'd have to go.

Her heart sank as she closed the door again. She had

expected to be called as a witness to the attack on her son, but there had been no mention of that, only the attack on the doctor. She didn't consider herself Crossley's wife now, and this wasn't a divorce hearing, so why was she required to attend? No use asking the constable. He wouldn't know. Or tell her if he did know.

Jan had been watching her shrewdly. 'Can they make you go back to living with this man who hurts you?'

'No. But if they release Doug, I'll have trouble staying free because he'll try to drag me back by force.' She tried to smile but knew she'd failed. 'Go home now, Jan. You need your rest.'

'I shall not be resting today. I'm going into Manchester with Miss Peters and Helen.'

He didn't explain why and she was too concerned with her own problems to ask him.

Jan and Helen called for Miss Peters at quarter to nine. As they waited at the bus stop, a big car stopped and a man poked his head out of the window. 'Miss Peters, by Jove! You're a sight for sore eyes. Now I know I'm really home.'

'Archie! I wondered when you'd return.' She moved to the car window and after a quick exchange of information, beckoned to Helen and Jan. 'My friend has offered us a lift into Manchester. Isn't that lucky?'

They piled in and she sat in the front, exchanging reminiscences with the driver, who appeared to be the son of a long-time friend.

Archie dropped them in Manchester, quite near the cathedral.

They obtained the special licence more quickly than any of them had expected. Because of the war, it had been made much easier to get a special licence. There were several other couples on the same mission and apparently one of the two clerks was ill, so a tired-looking woman was coping with the paperwork on her own, pushing the applications through quickly.

'Phew!' said Miss Peters as they left the building. 'We were lucky there. That poor woman has hardly had time to breathe today, let alone check your details, Jan. Seven shillings and sixpence seems a bargain to me.'

'And to me,' said Jan. 'I will repay you as soon as I can.'

'Tush, no! It's my wedding present to you both. No, don't argue!'

She looked at her old-fashioned fob watch. 'We have time to take a quick look at the cathedral because there isn't another bus back till one o'clock. Manchester Cathedral was beautiful, Jan, but it was bombed in December 1940. I've heard they're starting to rebuild it, though.'

Jan looked sad as they stood outside the shell of the building, thrusting his hands deep in his pockets and hunching his shoulders. 'I have seen too many ruined churches. Most of them had once been beautiful buildings, like this one; some much older, I think. And what good did it do to destroy them? What good did all this killing do to either side?'

Miss Peters patted his arm. 'We all wonder that sometimes, but we couldn't have let Hitler take over Europe. It cheers me to see that they've started work on rebuilding the cathedral, though. It's going to be a beautiful building again, even though it'll probably take years to finish. We mustn't linger too long in the unhappiness left by the war, mustn't dwell on our own or our country's losses. We must rebuild what we've lost and create new treasures for future generations.'

'*You* give me more hope than anything or anyone I've met,' he said simply. 'You and Helen.'

She seemed a little embarrassed. 'Oh, well . . . good. Now, let me buy you both luncheon then we'll catch that bus home. You can tell us how things are going at Esherwood, Jan. They're going to rebuild there too, aren't they?'

He smiled and gave her a sudden quick hug, which made her flush a little. But she didn't protest. When he offered both ladies an arm, they all linked up as they walked.

And that felt good.

As the afternoon passed and the time for the magistrate's hearing drew closer, Judith became more and more nervous.

Mayne came back for lunch, took one look at her and asked, 'What's the matter?'

When she told him, he swore under his breath. 'Oh, hell. I remember the Compton-Greys. Very snooty family. They live just outside town and keep their distance from most of the world. Many people consider this chap the worst of them all. He still believes in keeping women inside the home and obedient to their husbands. Which is probably why his own wife left him. After she did that, I heard he grew even more severe with the married women who come up before him. It's a pity your bruise has faded.'

After a pause he asked, 'Do you want me to come with you?'

'I don't think that would help. It would look bad.'

'I suppose so. But remember, you've got a home and a job here, whatever the magistrate says. Tell them you're the housekeeper and nanny at Esherwood. It'll sound better than being my assistant. We're certainly going to need your help with little Betty when Victor arrives.'

'I may have to leave town if they release Doug and he grows too . . . troublesome.'

'I won't let him attack you. That at least I can do for you.'

She shook her head. 'You can't watch over me every minute of the day. You have your own life to lead. And you can't watch the children, either. I'm sure Doug will try to use them to force me to go back to him.'

'I can arrange for others to help me protect you.'

'That's a comforting thought.' She glanced at the kitchen clock. 'I'd better get ready now. Wish me luck!'

Mayne went back to ring an antiques dealer he knew in Manchester. He was in luck. The man was in and seeking new stock.

'Why don't you come and look at a couple of items? I haven't got my car up and running yet and they're too big to bring into Manchester by train.'

After a few more questions, the dealer gave a provisional estimate of value, which was, thank goodness, slightly more than Mayne had expected.

He still had to see Woollard, but the man couldn't refuse to let him pay the debts, could he?

Dressed in her best clothes, Judith arrived at the police station with five minutes to spare. She couldn't bear to go inside until she had to. The less time she spent near Doug the better, as far as she was concerned.

With one minute to go, by the clock outside the nearby jeweller's, she pushed the door of the police station open and went inside.

Sergeant Deemer was waiting behind the desk. 'Ah, Mrs Crossley.'

'Maskell,' she corrected gently.

'Mr Compton-Grey won't allow that, and if you take my advice, you won't insist. We don't want to put him in a bad mood with you.'

At her nod of agreement, he moved from behind the counter. 'You'd better come into the hearing room. We've been holding the hearings here since the courthouse was taken over for the ARP headquarters during the war, and we've not been able to move back there yet.'

As he led the way, he whispered, 'Don't let Compton-Grey bully you about other things, though.'

She nodded, wondering what the sergeant thought she could do against a magistrate. She wished suddenly that she could run out of the police station and not stop running till she'd left Doug behind for ever.

A thin man with sparse grey hair and old-fashioned pince-nez looked up as she entered and frowned at her.

'This is Mrs Crossley, sir,' the sergeant said.

'She's late.'

'With respect, sir, she came into the station at one minute before three by our clock.'

'Then your clock is slow.' The magistrate studied her with a sour expression. 'Your face doesn't look bruised to me.'

'The bruise has mostly faded now, sir, and I've covered it with face powder.'

Again the sergeant stepped in. It was a relief to know that he was prepared to speak out for her.

'I saw the bruising myself, sir. Her husband must have hit her good and hard. The bruise went from here to here.' He demonstrated on his own face. 'Her son was injured too. The doctors insisted he spend a night in hospital after his father had knocked him unconscious. They'll have records if you need proof of that. Only thirteen, the son is.'

'Are there witnesses to it? Are you sure Crossley did it?'

'Several witnesses, sir. I'm quite certain it was him.'

'Oh. I thought this was just her word against his.'

'No, sir. I can send for the other witnesses, if you wish. But I am one of them.'

'We'll see how things go. Fetch Crossley in now.'

Deemer signalled to Constable Farrow, who left the room and came back two minutes later with Doug.

He's smartened himself up, Judith thought. How has he

managed that when he's been shut up here? Those friends of his, I suppose.

Doug looked across at her, not smiling, not scowling, just staring in the way he had when he was contemplating hitting her but hadn't reached flash point yet. She didn't let herself betray her fear, but she couldn't help feeling sick at the thought of being attacked again.

The door opened and Miss Peters came in. 'Good morning, Mr Compton-Grey. I'm sorry I'm late. How is your dear mother? I haven't seen her for a while. I really must call on her now she's back in the district.'

'Miss Peters, may I ask why you are here?'

'You're holding a hearing into the recent incident at the hospital, and will want to know what put Mrs Crossley's son there in the first place, is that not so?' Her eyes turned briefly towards Doug and scorn was evident in even that quick glance.

The magistrate tried again. 'We are, but I don't think—'

'Since I witnessed the whole incident where the boy was injured, I thought I might be of some use to you.'

For a moment, it was obvious the magistrate would like to send her away, but she moved confidently forward to sit next to Judith and he pressed his lips together for a moment before continuing.

What he said worried Judith. He didn't mention the attack in the hospital and seemed to have formed his own views of what lay behind the incident in which Crossley had hurt his son.

Fortunately for Judith, Miss Peters contradicted the magistrate several times as he outlined the situation.

'Madam, please let me continue.'

'Miss. I'm not married, as you well know.'

His thin chest swelled with anger.

'I was only preventing you from jumping to the wrong

conclusions, Gavin. I mean Mr Compton-Grey. I have very good eyesight still, and I was close enough to see and hear everything that happened on the Mead. I wouldn't be happy to see errors recorded. And you still have to mention the incident at the hospital.'

'We need to consider what *made* the man attack his son like that. I am of the opinion that the poor fellow had been driven to desperation, that his wife had alienated him from his own children and that had upset him so that—'

Doug spoke for the first time. 'You're right, sir. She'd drive a saint to desperation, that one would. Always answering back. She even sent the children to grammar school against my wishes.'

'What? She disobeyed you about something so important? Why, that's shocking!'

A voice spoke from the doorway. 'No, it isn't. What's shocking about sending a child who has won the Esherwood Bequest to Rivenshaw Grammar School, may I ask?'

Mr Esher came in to join them.

'Were you a witness to the incident we are dealing with, Mr Esher?' the magistrate asked.

'No, sir. But I was outside this room, having come to the police station about another matter, and I heard what was being discussed. I intervened in this matter of Kitty Crossley's education when her father tried to stop her taking up the scholarship. Our country is going to need its best minds training properly if it's to recover from the war and become prosperous and happy once more. Don't you agree?'

Judith found the courage to speak out. 'And it isn't true that I turned the children against their father, sir. *He* alienated their affections. They saw him attack me many times, and as they grew older he hit them too. They were as eager as I was to escape when he came back from the war, because they're terrified of him.'

'If you had been obedient and done your wifely duty, he might not have grown so angry in the first place.'

'He was always angry when he got drunk, sir. I could do nothing to stop him drinking and spending the food money on booze.'

'She's lying!' Doug yelled. 'Most men in Lower Parklea go down to the pub with their mates. I didn't get drunk, just had a drink or two, and it's not my fault she couldn't manage her housekeeping money.'

Sergeant Deeming said loudly and firmly, 'It's on record, sir, that Crossley's been arrested several times for being drunk and disorderly. It happened before you became magistrate here, but we kept the records safe when we moved out of the courthouse. I can get them out of the cellar later, if you wish.'

Compton-Grey frowned. 'Ah. Well then, Crossley, I shall put a requirement that you stay away from public houses into my final decision.'

Doug opened his mouth to protest but the magistrate continued speaking.

'Sergeant, I think we should give Crossley a final warning this time for resisting arrest, don't you? His wife had upset him.'

'I thought this hearing was about his attack on a doctor at the hospital, sir, not about his marriage. And about resisting arrest.'

'I'm sure the doctor will understand the poor man's frustration at being denied access to his son. I'll speak to him myself.'

There was dead silence in the room. 'I doubt the doctor will agree with you, sir. He was very concerned that Crossley should pay the price for attacking a doctor in a public hospital.'

'As I just said, I'll speak to the doctor myself.'

'And I don't like to see my men attacked sir, whatever the excuse. To condone resisting arrest sets a bad example to others.'

'I'm afraid I must disagree. It seems to me to be the best decision in this case.' He turned his attention back to Judith, speaking to her as if she were a halfwit. 'As for you, Mrs Crossley, you are to go back to your husband and do your wifely duty, as you promised in church. If it upsets him so much to see his children being educated above their station, then they must leave the grammar school and—'

'Over my dead body,' Mr Esher shouted. 'And since several prominent citizens, including your own aunt, are on the committee for the Esherwood Trust, I don't think this idea of yours will go down well in the town.'

'Mrs Crossley is not appearing before the court today as anything but a witness,' Miss Peters said, 'so I cannot understand why you have any reason for telling her what to do. Moreover, I don't think any court has the power to force a woman to go back to being beaten. I shall check that with my lawyer.'

The magistrate stood up hastily. 'I have delivered my verdict and will remind you all that we are still under the emergency regulations set up for this whole area during the war, so I do have extra powers and shall exercise them as I see fit.'

'Well, I won't go back to him,' Judith said. 'I'd rather go to prison than live with him again.'

The magistrate looked down his nose at her. 'I can send you there if you cause trouble. But whether *you* go back to your husband immediately or not, your children will be returned to their father at once. He is the head of the family. Sergeant, see to that.'

He looked across the room but Deemer didn't reply.

'Sergeant?' Mr Compton-Grey repeated sharply.

'If you insist, sir. Under protest, which I wish to be recorded.'

'You'll do as you're told or lose your job!'

'If he does, I shall go to the lord lieutenant. This hearing has been a travesty,' Miss Peters said.

The magistrate ignored her and walked quickly out of the room.

As the door closed behind him, Doug began to walk across the room towards Judith, a gloating expression on his face.

20

'Hold on a moment, Crossley,' the sergeant said. 'We have to do the paperwork before we can release you from custody.'

'Hang the paperwork. That magistrate said I'm to get my wife back.' Doug reached out to grab Judith.

She stepped quickly backwards, but he was between her and the door. Fear skittered through her. Was it all going to start again?

But Deemer grabbed Doug's arm and dragged him away, jerking his head to her in an unmistakable message to make her escape.

She rushed to the door as soon as Doug was taken away from it.

Miss Peters followed her outside. 'Wait!'

She hesitated.

'Take the children to my house. I'll hide you all. Now, run as you've never run before!'

Judith set off, feet pounding on the pavement, taking the quickest route she could think of through the back alleys.

Miss Peters went inside to confer with the sergeant. 'Do you have a moment, Sergeant Deemer?'

'Keep an eye on him.' The sergeant left Crossley in Farrow's care and came across to her.

'Surely there's something you can do to stop that man going after his wife?' she whispered.

He replied in an equally low voice, 'I'm doing it, giving her the chance to get away, but in the end I shall have to carry out the magistrate's instructions, even though this one's a fool and I disagree with what he's doing. I'm sure the emergency powers are being abused here. They were about war matters, not marital problems. But who's to question what a magistrate says?'

'I'll speak to the doctor.'

'So will Compton-Grey.'

She sighed. 'I'll see if I can find any grounds to stop him doing this to the children. I'd go and consult my lawyer, but Gilliot is another bad 'un where women and justice are concerned.'

'There's a new lawyer just setting up in town.'

'I heard one was coming but I didn't know he'd arrived.'

'Came yesterday. Name of Melford.' He gestured across the town square. 'He's renting the first floor of number seven.'

'I'll give him a try, then. In fact, I'll do it now.' She hurried across the paved central square.

Deeming watched her for a moment. 'If there were more like her,' he muttered, 'the world would be a far better place. I hope this new lawyer has more sense than Gilliot.'

Then he turned with a sigh to release as slowly as possible a man he detested and then hope fervently that Crossley wouldn't catch up with his wife.

When Judith arrived home, panting and flushed, Mayne came rushing down into the kitchen to meet her. 'I saw you running up the drive. What's wrong?'

'The magistrate has ordered the children to be returned to their father's care and told me to go back to my husband as well. I'm not letting Doug have the children and I'm never living with him again, if I can help it. Miss Peters says we can hide in her house.'

'You'll be seen going there.' He paused for a moment's thought. 'I'll hide you here and take you across to her house after dark.'

'They'll search this house first because they know we're living here.'

'They don't know about the secret chamber and from what you say, Sergeant Deemer won't try very hard to search the place anyway. Go and grab some of your possessions quickly. Ben's round at the old stables. I'll fetch him. The girls came in from school a short time ago and went up to their bedroom. Hurry! Ben and I will get the secret room in the attic open then I'll fetch you and the girls. After that I'll nip into town and consult a lawyer on your behalf.'

'Not Mr Gilliot?'

'No. This is a new man. I heard he arrived yesterday.'

'I can't afford a lawyer.'

'I'll pay.'

'Only if you'll let me pay you back when I can.'

'Never mind about that now. Start packing.'

She ran up the stairs and with her daughters' help, piled some of their clothes and possessions into the sheets off the beds, so that by the time Mayne and Ben came to fetch them, she had enough for them to manage on for a time.

Her savings bank book was now hidden under a false bottom in her handbag. She could only hope her meagre savings would be enough to get them started elsewhere. And even then, how long they would manage to stay safe was more than she could guess.

Once they were at Miss Peters' house, she'd bend her mind to how best to get away from Rivenshaw. She didn't want to leave, not when she'd found a job she liked and somewhere to live. If she'd been the weeping type, she'd have cried her eyes out.

She didn't know anyone in another town, so was having trouble working out where to go. Somewhere in the south perhaps? And how on earth was she going to get their ration books back without anyone finding out?

There were nothing but problems whichever way she turned.

She rued the day she had married Doug Crossley. He'd been a stranger to Rivenshaw and she'd felt sorry for him. He'd been fun in those days, though a bit rough around the edges, but not violent like he was now. And he'd said he loved her. That had meant a lot to her then, she'd been so lonely.

But his so-called love had soon worn off, and he'd started treating her like a personal slave, then thumping her.

The only good things to come out of her marriage were her children. It always surprised her that he had fathered such clever children.

As she crossed the square, Miss Peters was delayed by an acquaintance who wanted to tell her some good news. It was some time before she could get away without giving offence.

When she arrived at the new lawyer's rooms, she was amused to see the chaos inside. Boxes were half unpacked, heavy legal books piled along one wall and a shabby assortment of old furniture had been dumped haphazardly in the outer room.

'Is anyone there?'

A man came to the inner doorway, a rather splendid young fellow, she noted – she was not too old to appreciate that sort of thing – with wavy brown hair lightly sprinkled with grey and a cheerful expression on his face.

'I'm afraid I'm not really open for business yet,' he said. 'Unless it's urgent and you don't mind the mess.'

'It's extremely urgent and I don't care about the mess. I'm Miss Peters, by the way.'

'I'm Stuart Melford. I believe I've heard my grandmother speak about you.'

'Jane. Yes. Is she any better?'

'I'm afraid not. Come inside and I'll dust off a chair. I've had to turn out my grandmother's attics to find furniture, given the current shortages, but this chair is soundly built, if somewhat scuffed, and at least the leather hasn't perished.'

She took the chair and watched him dust another for himself with his handkerchief.

He stuffed it in his pocket and picked up a pad and pencil from a desk full of clutter. 'How may I help you?'

'I'm not here for myself. We have a bad situation in this town for one family and I'm taking an interest in them. I—'

There were footsteps in the outer office and Mayne peered into their room. 'Oh, sorry. I didn't think you were taking clients yet, Stuart.' He looked at Miss Peters. 'Have you come about the Crossleys, too?'

'Yes. I gather you know Mr Melford already.'

'We ran into one another here and there in London.'

The men exchanged glances that said they'd done more than merely run into one another. Probably something to do with the hush-hush work young Esher had been involved in, she thought. 'Why don't you join us, Mr Esher? I was just about to ask Mr Melford's opinion of Mrs Crossley's legal situation, not to mention the so-called emergency powers that idiot of a magistrate is using to carry on his personal vendetta against women. Wait till I see his mother! I shall give her a piece of my mind about her son. She always did spoil him.'

When they left the lawyer's rooms half an hour later, she

was disappointed. Mr Melford had been full of ifs and buts when offering his opinion of the situation. However, he had said he'd make enquiries about what exactly the extended powers of a magistrate covered, especially now that the war was over. She hoped that would help this situation.

As she and Mayne walked back to Parson's Mead together, she asked, 'Are you certain Judith and the children are safe? No one can find them?'

'They're safe for the moment, but they can't stay in that secret room for too long. It has no facilities and is very cramped with four of them in it, plus a few artworks. I'll bring them across to you after dark and we'll make sure Crossley doesn't see them coming. Except . . . don't you think the magistrate will insist the police search your house as well?'

She walked in silence for a while, then sighed. 'Yes. They'll probably be sent to search Esherwood first, since she and the children have been living there, but I wouldn't be surprised to see them at my house tomorrow, since I stood up for them at the hearing.'

'Do you have somewhere they won't be found?'

She sighed. 'Not really, unless we can keep watch for someone coming and get them out of the house.'

After a few more steps, she stopped, snapping her fingers as inspiration came to her. 'I know! I'll ask Helen to take them instead of me. I'm sure she will. Jan will help, too. He's been hunted more than once and knows what it's like.'

As they set off again, she looked sideways at Mayne and decided to trust him. 'He and Helen are getting married tomorrow. Don't tell anyone. Do you think you could come along and be a witness with me?'

'Of course. Is it a marriage of convenience or do they care about one another?'

'Bit of both. She lost her fiancé two or three years ago.

He's a nice lad, who's had a bad time during the war. How he kept out of the hands of the enemy for all those years, I don't know. He's Jewish, you know, but has abandoned any religion after what he's seen. Fortunately he's highly intelligent. A stupid husband wouldn't do for a girl like Helen.'

'There are others who managed to escape the Nazis as well, Miss Peters, some of them with the help of German civilians, because not everyone supported Hitler. Some of the escapees were very helpful to our government when we were planning certain aspects of the final stages of the war.'

She nodded. 'I've come to the conclusion after living through two world wars that some people have a more finely tuned sense of self-preservation than others. There will be a lot of stories to be told during the coming years. You should get Jan to tell you more about his adventures one day, and to write it down. The parts I've heard are good enough to make a film of and I haven't heard the half of it.'

They parted company as Mayne was stopped by Sergeant Deemer, accompanied by the constable.

Since Miss Peters was sure Mayne could handle the sergeant, she went straight home, wanting to ask Helen's help for Judith and her family. Before she did that, she went upstairs to look out of her bedroom window, to see if the sergeant was going home with Mayne.

Yes, all three of them were walking across Parson's Mead. Then something else caught her eye and she clicked her tongue in exasperation as she saw a figure following them, half-hidden behind some raspberry canes. Crossley.

Once Mayne and the sergeant had reached the upper end of Parson's Mead and turned into the drive to the big house, Crossley walked openly towards the Dower House.

She'd better go next door quickly. She'd ask Jan to slip across to Esherwood and tell Mayne he and the sergeant were being shadowed.

As she passed the kitchen window next door, she saw a cosy domestic scene, with two young people chatting quietly as they prepared their tea.

She envied couples that closeness.

No, she mustn't get maudlin. She'd had a good life, if not the one she'd have chosen. For many years she'd had the privilege of helping others, so her life hadn't been wasted, even though she hadn't married. There were worse ways to spend your time and money.

And this second war was over now. That in itself made everyone feel better about the world. Britain had paid a high price, was still paying it, but they'd won, hadn't they? She was proud of her country. Now the British people and government had to navigate the difficulties of settling into peace. People would no doubt get irritable about ongoing shortages and rationing, but you couldn't set the world to rights overnight.

And surely the authorities would have more sense than to lead people into another war in the years to come? Everyone had thought the Great War had ended that sort of massive conflict. And then it had started all over again.

Ach, she mustn't start thinking about that. She must trust that people had learned their lesson. This hadn't been a pyrrhic victory. It had been worthwhile. But it had been a costly victory and everyone had paid for it.

She rapped on the door and became brisk again as she enlisted the two young people's help. It was, as she'd expected, willingly given.

When Jan had gone to warn Mayne about Crossley following him, she smiled at Helen. 'You're getting a good man there.'

'I know. Thank you for nudging us to marry.'

'I'm an excellent matchmaker, if I do say so myself. You two will be all right. You look like a married couple already when you're together.'

Helen blushed. 'Do we really? I've felt comfortable with him from the first day I met him.'

'Do you want me to wait with you till Jan gets back?' She answered her own question without giving Helen time to respond. 'No, I'd better not. If they're looking for Judith and the children at Esherwood, they'll probably come to see me next. They must find me at home on my own, not with you, if we're to hide that poor family here.'

Helen walked to the door with her and gave her a sudden hug. 'You're the kindest person I know.'

Veronica Peters had tears in her eyes all the way home at that simple gesture. People didn't often hug her. Most didn't dare. The main thing she had to protect herself against the world was her formidable reputation . . . and her money.

But it was nice to be hugged too, now and then.

Mayne took Sergeant Deemer and the constable into the house via the kitchen. 'Now. How do you want to do this, Sergeant?'

'I'm sorry to intrude, sir, but the magistrate wants us to search the whole of Esherwood, since this is where Mrs Crossley and the children have been living.'

'Why is the fellow making such a fuss? It's not as if Miss Maskell has done anything wrong.'

'He's particularly concerned that she might take the children away from their father, and has asked me to speak to her. She'll be in contempt of court if she doesn't give the children back.'

His expression was wooden, his words were very correct, but Mayne could tell that he was angry at this.

'You're welcome to search Esherwood. They've been living here, as you know, but I've been out so I can't say whether they're here at this moment or not.'

'Very good of you to be so helpful, sir.'

Mayne showed them the bedrooms that Judith and her children had used. They bore all the signs of a hasty departure. 'Goodness! They must have left in a hurry.'

The sergeant allowed himself a quick wink, then turned back to the constable. 'They'll be as far away as they can manage by now, I should think. They may even have had someone with a motor car to help them on their way. Still, we'd better search the upstairs. I'll do that. You keep watch at the foot of the stairs, Farrow, to make sure they don't sneak out.'

'What about the servants' stairs, sir? They could get out that way.'

'Dear me, yes. How are we going to manage that?'

'If you stand at the back of the hall with the door to the servants' quarters open, you'll see anyone coming down by both the back and the front stairs,' Mayne offered.

The constable gave him a suspicious glance. 'Perhaps you could help us, sir?'

'No. I don't agree with what you're doing. I won't refuse you entrance, but I won't help you, either.'

He stared right back at Farrow. He wasn't going to let this oafish young man trap Judith and return her to that brute.

The constable scowled at Mayne before taking up the suggested position.

The sergeant made a noisy search of the upstairs, then came puffing down to join his constable. 'No sign of anyone up there.'

'Do you want me to do a quick second check, Sarge? I might see something you've missed.'

Deemer fixed him with a stern look. 'Are you suggesting I don't know my duty, that I didn't look carefully?'

'No, sir. Of course not.'

'You'd better not. I looked in every room on the first and second floors, and saw no sign of them, then I went up to the attics.' He turned to Mayne. 'Thank you for your cooperation, sir. We'll get back to the station now.'

He set off at his usual steady pace.

As they passed the Dower House, Farrow stopped. 'What if they're hiding here, sir?'

'I doubt they will be, but if you want to knock on the door, you're welcome.'

He watched with great pleasure as Mrs Esher told the constable in no uncertain terms that they had no fugitives here, thank you very much, and she had real work to do even if he didn't.

As they reached Miss Peters' house, Farrow looked at him uncertainly.

'I suppose you'd better ask if they've tried to take refuge here,' Deemer said. 'I'll go on to the station and see you there.'

Farrow's voice rose an octave. 'Me ask the old lady on my own?'

'Why not?' Deemer set off without another word.

When Miss Peters opened the door, Farrow explained that they were looking for the fugitives. 'Have you, um, seen them since the hearing, Miss Peters?'

'Certainly not. I haven't set eyes on Miss Maskell since I left the police station, and I haven't seen the children at all today.'

'Could I just have a quick look round?' Farrow asked.

She drew herself up to the height of his shoulder. *'Is my word not good enough for you? They are not here, Constable.'*

'Sorry, miss. If you say so, miss.' He backed away from the door and hurried down the street.

She didn't smile till she closed the door behind her, but her smile soon faded.

That evening Helen said goodbye to Jan, as he left for his nightly guard duties at Esherwood, then went to the front room window to watch him walk along the street. He was radiating energy and determination. Like her, he was very concerned to help keep Judith and her children safe.

As she went inside, she decided to sleep in her clothes, because unless things went very wrong, and she didn't think that would happen if Jan was involved, he and Mayne would be bringing Judith and the children across later. She doubted she'd be able to sleep anyway.

She and Jan had prepared makeshift beds for their guests in the attic, which was drier than the bedrooms whose damaged windows had been inadequately protected from the weather.

Jan disappeared from view and she was about to close the front door when she heard footsteps on the pavement. She frowned. So few people walked along this street at night.

Whoever it was didn't appear outside her house, but she heard the catch on the gate of Miss Peters' house make its distinctive chinking sound as it was opened, even though the person seemed to be trying to be quiet.

She lingered behind the nearly-closed door to listen. The person didn't knock on Miss Peters' front door or come out of the garden again. This could only be an intruder. One person sprang instantly to mind: Crossley.

Shutting her front door with great care, so as not to make a noise, Helen locked it and ran through the house, picking up a heavy knife-sharpening steel on the way in case there was trouble. She slipped quietly out of the back door, locking it behind her.

As she crossed the garden, she stayed on the grass not the gravel paths so that the intruder wouldn't hear her coming. When she reached the fence, she paused again to listen. There were faint sounds coming from the rear of Miss Peters' house. What was he doing?

Her best guess was that he was fiddling with her neighbour's back door, presumably intending to break in.

She was in no physical state to tackle an intruder and if it was Crossley, he was a big man, stronger than most, even with his injured hand. But still, if he broke in, she'd have to try to help.

A window upstairs opened and Miss Peters' voice floated down. 'Who's there?'

The noises stopped. By now Helen's eyes were more accustomed to the darkness and she could see the outline of the man, who was standing very still.

Miss Peters rapped something on her windowsill with a loud clunk. 'I know you're there. I'm just letting you know that I have my father's revolver loaded and in my hand as I speak. I always keep it to hand. It's old but well maintained and still works perfectly. He taught me to use it during the last war and I'm quite a good shot, good enough to hit any part of a person's body I choose. *Any part.* A man has some particularly sensitive areas that he wouldn't want damaging. I'd aim for those parts of the body if I was faced with an intruder.'

Helen heard a gasp and the faintest of muttered curses, then the man began to edge away from the back door. She wished the sky hadn't clouded over, as she still couldn't be certain who it was. She waited in the shadows till she heard the front gate clink, then went quietly back into her own house. What a redoubtable woman her neighbour was!

She couldn't go to the police station and report the intruder because there wasn't anyone on duty at night. And now that householders had no need to stand fire watch, in case of enemy attack, there'd be no one around in the town centre. She wished there was someone living in the house next to hers, wished she knew the other neighbours.

She must have dozed eventually, but jerked awake as she

heard footsteps in the street. Several people but again, trying not to make a noise. Had the intruder come back with reinforcements?

But these people entered her garden and walked past the front door. She ran through to the kitchen, hoping it was Jan.

Someone rapped softly on the kitchen door three times, then a pause and twice more, the agreed signal. She opened the back door, relieved.

Judith came in first, followed by her children, each carrying a lumpy bundle wrapped in a sheet. Jan and Mayne followed them.

'Are you sure you don't mind us coming here, Miss Bretherton?' Judith asked. 'I don't want to bring trouble on you.'

'I'm happy to offer you shelter. As long as you stay away from the windows, they won't know you're here.'

'I'll thump Dad if he tries to hurt my mother again,' Ben said.

How awful that a boy should feel like that about his father, Helen thought. She turned to Judith. 'For the moment I think we should all get some sleep. Jan and I have prepared beds in the attic. And please, call me Helen.'

'No lights, even on the stairs,' Mayne said hastily. 'We don't want to show any signs of life. Better that your guests stumble than are caught. We hope only to trouble you for a day or two, Helen. I'll think of somewhere else for them to go after that.'

He seemed more concerned about Judith than a mere acquaintance would normally be, and he kept watching her, not the children. It made Helen wonder if he was attracted to Judith. If so, how sad that she was already married to that horrible man.

She moved forward and led the way up to the attics.

When she and Mayne came down, leaving her visitors upstairs, Helen asked the question that had been worrying her. 'How did you make sure no one saw you come here?'

'We relied on Jan and Al for that. They kept watch, one in front and one behind us. And we moved only a short distance at a time. Believe me, no one would have got past Jan. I never knew anyone disappear so completely into the night or move so silently.'

'Miss Peters had an intruder earlier. I think it must have been Crossley. She shouted down to him that she had a gun.' She couldn't help giggling. 'When she said she'd aim at his private parts, he left straight away.'

'Good for her.'

'We saw him near the Dower House,' Jan said. 'We hid in the bushes as he walked up the drive. I left Al to keep an eye on him. I don't think he or anyone else will have seen us come into your house. I am very good at sensing the presence of someone watching me.'

'It's your house now, as well,' she corrected.

Mayne smiled at them. 'Congratulations on your engagement. Miss Peters suggested I act as the second witness to the marriage tomorrow. No, it's today now, isn't it? It's past midnight. Is that all right with you?'

'It's fine by me,' Helen assured him.

'I thank you for it,' Jan said.

As she locked the door behind the two men, Helen remembered the younger girl's terrified expression when they arrived, and the way her big brother put his arm round her shoulders for a quick hug, whenever their movements allowed.

They were such a nice family. They didn't deserve a father like that.

She hoped she and Jan would have children with his intelligence and courage. For a few minutes she lost herself in a dream of a happy future.

She had a lot to hope for now, and it had happened so quickly. How wonderful it would be to have a husband, to make plans together, not to be lonely.

21

Al greeted Mayne and Jan when they got back with a cheerful, 'All's quiet on the Esherwood front. I watched Crossley creep round the big house, but he didn't try to break in, so I didn't tackle him. He made so much noise I had no trouble keeping an eye on him. Kind of him to give you time to get them away, wasn't it?'

'Very kind.'

'When he left, I followed him back down the drive and he went off along the odd-numbers side of Parson's Mead. He doesn't know how to walk quietly, that's for sure. Are they all settled in with Miss Bretherton now?'

Mayne nodded. 'Yes. I bet the children are asleep already. They looked exhausted. I want to say how well you two did. We make a good team. If things go as I plan with the business, I hope to be able to offer you proper jobs in a few weeks.'

They both brightened.

'I'm prepared to do anything, but could you tell us a bit more about the jobs?' Al asked. 'It might keep Mum from nagging me.'

'Keep it to yourself, but I'm going into building, starting by renovating this place and turning it into flats. You've seen what a mess the occupiers left it in. I've heard that was common in requisitioned houses, and apparently we got off fairly lightly at Esherwood. Some big country houses that were requisitioned were beyond repair; some even burned down because of careless smokers.'

'Stupid buggers,' Al said. 'My captain wouldn't have stood for that sort of behaviour.'

'Given the shortage of housing, I think flats will sell well.'

'Yeah. And I reckon there'll be a good future in house building. There's bound to be a lot of it needed now the war's over.'

Jan hadn't commented, so Mayne looked at him questioningly.

'I will be happy to have a job and I will work very hard at whatever you need, Mayne. But building would please me very much. I've seen too much destruction.'

Mayne watched the two men exchange grins of pleasure. It seemed particularly unfair that men like Al, who'd fought for their country, could come home and find themselves without work. And yet Al remained cheerful. The post-war world seemed to be divided into the moaners and the positive types. He knew which he preferred.

His thoughts turned to their most pressing problem. 'I wonder what Crossley's going to do next.'

'Nothing,' Al said. 'Mum lives next door and she says he's already turned his house into a pigsty, though Judith left it immaculate. He told Mum he's not looking for work yet, not till he runs out of demob money.' He turned to Jan. They'll have paid him for his eight weeks' Resettlement Leave, which everyone got, with a day's extra pay for each month he served in the forces. I'm saving my money, not spending it. That'll give me a nice nest egg.'

'Crossley seems to be a lazy devil,' Mayne said.

'Yeah. He could perfectly well do his old job at the warehouse, even with the injured hand, and keep the money to have something to fall back on. Mum reckons his wife's better off without him.'

'I agree. But will he let Judith go? And how long can we keep her and the children hidden from the authorities?'

'Who knows? I'll help all I can.' Al put out one hand to stop him leaving. 'One other thing, Mr Esher. You asked me to keep an eye on the Dower House as well as the big house, since I do the front. I thought you should know that your mother had a visitor while you were helping Mrs Crossley and the children this afternoon. It was that Caroline something-or-other you used to go out with. I don't know her married name.'

'McNulty. And you say she called at the Dower House?'

'Yes, and stayed a good hour.'

'Damn! What is my mother thinking of?'

Al shrugged. 'She seemed very happy to see the woman. Where's Mr McNulty?'

'Caroline's a widow now. And unlike my mother, I'm not happy to have that woman visiting. Look, if she ever turns up here when you're around, make sure you don't leave the two of us alone.'

'Like that, is she?'

'Can be sometimes. She seems to think a man's physical needs are the way to his heart.'

'She was dolled up to the eyebrows today. Dark red lipstick and hair pinned into those puffy lumps on top of her head. I don't like women who look like that,' Al grimaced. 'Some women worry more about their appearance than about other people's feelings and needs.'

Mayne couldn't help smiling. 'That sounds like the voice of experience.'

'It is. But I shan't be caught again by a woman like that. And I'll watch your back too, Mr Esher, if I can.'

'I keep telling you: call me Mayne.'

'I did start doing that, but Mum told me off. She says it isn't right when you're my employer.'

'It's my name, my choice. I worked with a lot of men in the war, Al. We didn't stand on ceremony and I seem to have lost the habit of being mistered. Besides, I intend to start something that will grow. I need a tight group of men to take the first steps and be the core of the company afterwards. Play your cards right and you'll be set for life, if I succeed in what I've planned.'

'I'll be in on that . . . Mayne.' Al nodded as if sealing a promise, then changed tone. 'Well, if Jan is going out on patrol again, I'll grab a quick cup of tea, then follow his example. You get off to bed. We'll watch your back.'

Mayne was too annoyed to sleep yet, so wandered round the old house. He hardly noticed his surroundings, he was wondering what the hell Caroline was playing at. Surely he'd made it clear to her that he was no longer interested in her?

And what was his mother doing, inviting her round? Plotting something to keep him away from Judith? It was Judith's marriage that would keep him away, not his mother's silly plotting, and definitely not Caroline.

Something about her seemed harder than it used to be. Maybe she too had been affected by the war, in spite of trying to keep out of it. It would have done her good to be forced to do a job and work with women of all sorts. Hell, you'd think she'd have wanted to help the war effort, rather than hide herself away in Scotland. She must have been bored to tears. Serve her right.

Or was it her marriage that had hardened her heart? She hadn't spoken of her husband with love, and given how rich he'd been, McNulty mustn't have left her much, either, or she'd not be back in Rivenshaw.

Mayne decided to sleep in the library tonight, didn't want to go back to the Dower House.

He would move into the big house openly once his friend Victor arrived. Not till then, for the sake of Judith's good name. If she was able to come back to live at Esherwood, that was; if they could keep Crossley away from her and the kids, that was; and keep that stupid magistrate from interfering in such an arbitrary manner.

In the meantime, he wasn't getting tangled up in his mother's matchmaking again, and he'd tell her so as bluntly as was necessary to stop her. She'd introduced him to Caroline in the first place and he was well aware that she cared more about family pedigrees than whether people were decent and loving or not.

If he ever got married, he'd look for a very different sort of woman from Caroline. He wasn't the arrogant young fool he'd been before the war.

A picture of Judith flashed into his mind and he sighed. He didn't want her to leave Rivenshaw, yet he had no right to care about what happened to her. She was married. Even if she divorced Doug, and heaven knew she could prove cruelty under the easier divorce rules of 1937, she'd still have to wait years before she would be allowed to remarry.

Anyway, she might not want to marry again. It wouldn't be at all surprising if Doug had given her a hatred of the institution.

The following morning, Doug went to the police station mid-morning and thumped on the counter. 'My damned wife hasn't brought the children back to me like the magistrate said she had to. I want to lay a complaint against her.'

Sergeant Deemer scowled at him and decided to risk taking a little initiative of his own. 'Have you made arrangements for them?'

'Eh?'

'Somewhere for them to live. Someone to look after them.'

'I don't need to do that. *She* will come back as soon as they're with me.'

'Where are you living . . . sir? Do you have beds and bedding for the children?'

'Where the hell do you think I'm living? At my old address.'

'Watch your language, Crossley. And the address is?' Deemer pretended he didn't know and took it down, writing as slowly as he could to annoy the other man. 'I'll come and check the house, if you don't mind.'

'What? It's none of your business what my house is like.'

'But it is. If I'm to get the children back to you, I need to be sure you have somewhere suitable for them to live. No time like the present, eh? Unless you want to wait a day or two to get them back. I could come tomorrow, if you preferred.'

'No, I don't want to wait.'

Deemer lifted the flap of the counter and waved to Farrow to take over.

'I need her back now. It's *her* job to run the house,' Crossley grumbled as he walked along sulkily beside the sergeant.

'You shouldn't drive her away by thumping her, then.'

'She asks for it.'

'I don't think anyone asks to be thumped.'

'Oh, you're on her side, you are.'

'I'm on the side of treating people fairly, that's all. And not bashing young lads till they're unconscious.'

When they got to Crossley's street, a couple of women came out of their houses to see what was going on.

'I wonder if you'd help me,' Deemer said to one he recognised by sight. 'I'm checking Mr Crossley's house before I bring the children back to live with their father. Would you come in and witness what it's like? It'll only take you a minute.'

'That nosey bitch isn't coming into my house!' Crossley said at once.

'Then I'm not, either.' Deemer risked winking at the neighbour and her lips curved in a brief half-smile as she took his meaning. 'Your name, madam?'

'Mrs Needham.'

'Pleased to meet you.' He turned back to Crossley. 'Well? Do we do this or not?'

'Oh, all right. Come in, damn you.'

'Mind your language in front of ladies, Mr Crossley,' she snapped.

He ignored that, apart from scowling at her, and led the way in. 'I know it's a mess but Judith will soon clear things up when they all come back.'

'I heard she wasn't coming back,' Mrs Needham said. 'And I wouldn't do so if I was her, the way you knock her about.'

'She shouldn't cheek me, then.'

'I'd keep a poker under the bed, Sergeant, if anyone tried to thump me,' Mrs Needham said. 'He'd never sleep soundly again.'

He grinned. He reckoned he'd chosen a good ally here.

Inside, the house stank of sweaty clothes, tobacco and other unpleasant odours. The kitchen sink was piled high with dirty dishes and on the table were the remains of fish and chips, covered in vomit.

Crossley cursed and screwed up the newspaper the chips had come in, looking round for somewhere to throw it and not finding anywhere.

Mrs Needham looked at the sergeant, her face wrinkled with revulsion. 'Doesn't even know where to throw the rubbish, does he?'

'I damned well do.' Crossley opened the back door, stormed out and threw the mess into the dustbin.

'That bin will stink nicely now,' she commented when he came back.

Deemer judged it time to intervene before Crossley exploded with rage. 'We'll just take a peep upstairs, sir. See where the children will be sleeping.'

'I haven't been into their bedrooms yet. They're how *she* left them.'

There were a couple of ragged blankets on the double bed in the front room, no sheets or pillowcases, just the black and white striped ticking of the mattress. Mrs Crossley must have taken the other bedding with her, Deemer decided.

In the children's rooms the sheets and blankets had also been removed and the drawers emptied. The beds were old and sagging, the flock mattresses lumpy.

'I'd not bring a pig to live in this house till it's cleared up,' Mrs Needham said scornfully when they went downstairs. 'Those mattresses need replacing.'

'Well, I'm not bringing those children back to this.' Deemer scowled at Crossley. 'Come and fetch me when the place is cleaned up and once I've checked it out, I'll go and look for your children.'

'You're on *her* side. The magistrate said—'

'The magistrate won't send them back to this pigsty. I shall go and make a note of this visit in the occurrence book at the station. If you could pop in sometime today to sign it and say that it's the truth, Mrs Needham, I'd be grateful.'

'I'll happily do that. They're nice kids and don't deserve treating so badly.' She scowled at Crossley and walked to the door, where she lingered, openly listening to the conversation.

'You'd better come to the station too, Mr Crossley. You can sign the entry and comment if you like.'

'I'm not coming. You can go to hell – and take that nosey cow with you. I'll get the children back myself. They'll be up at Esherwood.'

'The constable and I have already looked there. No sign of them and their rooms have been cleared of bedding and clothes.' Deemer moved closer, step by slow step, and Crossley edged back until he was pressed against the wall. He cradled his injured hand against himself, as if in protection against being beaten.

The sergeant spoke slowly and loudly. 'If you lay one finger on your ex-wife or your children, I'll haul you in on a charge of assault quicker than you can say Jack Robinson. My dad used to hit my mum. I couldn't do anything about that, but I'll do something about you, if I get even half a chance. You've had your official warning now. Next time I can charge you . . . and I will.'

Mrs Needham applauded loudly and left the house.

Deemer gave Crossley a long, hard look as if to emphasise what he'd said, then followed her out, nodding pleasantly to her as he passed. She was already talking to two other women across the street. He had no doubt this piece of gossip would spread quickly.

If it came to Compton-Grey's ears, Deemer would have his defence ready in his entry in the occurrence book.

But there was something in Crossley's eyes when he spoke of his wife that worried the sergeant. He didn't like it. No, he didn't like it at all.

Twice in his long career, he'd seen murder committed by men with that look in their eyes. He'd always regretted not realising how bad they were, not stopping them in time.

He'd do his best to protect Mrs Crossley and her children, his very best.

Later that morning Miss Peters came to collect Helen and Jan for the wedding. 'You two look very smart, I must say. Your Aunt Ethel would be happy to see you wearing button-holes of the white roses from her favourite bush.'

Jan handed another one to her. 'Do you think Mayne would like one, too?'

'I'm sure he would.'

Helen stepped forward with a safety pin to fix the corsage to Miss Peters' coat lapel. 'Let's wait for him at the front of the house.'

'Just a minute. You're sure you wouldn't rather go to the registry office? It might be easier.'

'Only as a last resort, Miss Peters. It wouldn't feel right if I didn't get married in church. And anyway, we'd have to wait till Monday to get married at the registry office. I don't want to wait.' She smiled at her intended and he touched her cheek lightly in a loving gesture.

That made Miss Peters sigh happily.

Mayne came striding down the street almost immediately. He too said he was delighted to wear a buttonhole in honour of the occasion. These seemed to make it obvious to everyone they passed that a wedding was about to take place, and people called out best wishes.

They were fortunate enough to catch Mr Saunders in his church, fiddling with something on the altar.

He turned at the sound of their footsteps. 'Miss Peters. How may I help you?'

He's got even fatter in the past year, she thought. He must be buying black market food. Most people are thinner these days. 'It's not me who needs your services, it's these two young people, vicar. They've obtained a special licence and wish to be married today. Mr Esherwood and I are here to act as witnesses.'

Mr Saunders stared at her in surprise, then looked at Helen. As his gaze moved on to Jan, his expression became sour. 'Show me the licence.'

Jan held it out.

He read it then studied Jan again. 'Mr Gilliot has mentioned you, Borkowski. I gather you're Jewish?'

'I was born Jewish, but I don't practise that faith now.'

'You've been baptised into the Church of England?'
'No.'

Miss Peters exchanged annoyed glances with Mayne. 'What has that to do with anything?'

'I cannot marry someone who is not a Christian in my church.'

'He's as much a Christian as any of us.'

'I beg to differ. One has to maintain standards if religion is to mean anything. And you, young woman, should think carefully before you tie yourself to a Jew.'

There was silence, then Helen said quietly, 'Better a man like him than a Fascist bigot like you, vicar. You'd have got on well with Hitler, you would.' She left Saunders spluttering in indignation and led the way out, head held high.

'What do we do now?' Jan asked when they were outside.

'We find someone else to marry you,' Miss Peters said. 'That man is not worthy to be a minister of the church.'

'There's a young Methodist minister in Lower Parklea,' Mayne said. 'My father knows him because they share an interest in history. We could go and ask him to marry you.'

'Yes, let's,' Helen said at once. 'I don't want that horrible Saunders man to do it anyway, now that I've met him.'

They walked through the streets, continuing to attract interest. More people called out good wishes. A few, however, scowled at Jan and one called out, 'Shame on you, Helen Bretherton! Letting your family down like that.'

Miss Peters made a mental note of the ones betraying prejudice, vowing not to have anything more to do with them from now on. She'd change her butcher for a start.

She'd seen the new young minister and liked the looks of him. He'd been an Army chaplain and had lost an arm in the war. He'd only been in Rivenshaw for a few months, but people spoke well of him.

She should have taken her young friends to his chapel in

the first place and not bothered with that nasty old man. The parish church might be prettier than the others in town, but Saunders spoiled it, creating a sour atmosphere.

If this new man was a better Christian, she'd go to his chapel on Sundays from now on. And that would be noted.

Helen kept tight hold of Jan's arm as they walked. 'I'm sorry this is happening. I know we could get married in a registry office, but I'd much prefer to be married in church.'

'I'm sorry you're meeting prejudice against me so soon. I'd hoped things would be better than this in England. Do you truly not mind that I was born Jewish?'

'Of course I don't mind. You're a kind and honest man, that's what I care about. And it was only a few people who called out, wasn't it? More people wished us well.'

'A few people can make things unpleasant, though. And the foolish thing is, I'm not really Jewish now. I'm not anything. I can't even believe in a God after the horrors I've seen.'

'Maybe one day you'll find some kind of faith again, but if necessary, could you please lie and say you do believe in God, because we do need to get married if you're to stay in England?'

'For you, I can do almost anything. Jump over the moon, even.'

They'd entered a poorer part of town and now stopped in front of a small chapel set back at one side of a street of terraced houses.

A square wooden sign outside said: *PARKLEA METHODIST CHAPEL, ALL WELCOME.* As if to prove it, the door stood open, propped back by a copper vase of flowers, small but beautifully arranged.

Miss Peters led the way inside, but there was no sign of the minister, so she called out, 'Is anyone there?'

A young man with one empty sleeve pinned across his

jacket came out of a door to one side. 'Can I help you? I'm Tristan Gregory, minister of this chapel.'

Helen pulled Jan forward, determined to speak for herself this time. 'My fiancé and I have a special licence and wish to be married today.'

He blinked in surprise. 'Well, you've come to the right place, then. Far better to be married in God's house than in a registry office, don't you think?'

'Oh, yes. It's what I want.' She gestured to their companions. 'We've brought two witnesses.'

He studied the others. 'I've had you pointed out to me, Miss Peters, but I've not had the honour of meeting you properly before.' He offered her his left hand, then turned to Mayne. 'And you are Maynard Esher, if I'm not mistaken. I've seen your photo in your parents' house when your father was kind enough to invite me to tea and show me some of his books.'

He turned back to Helen and Jan. 'It's not that I doubt your word, but I need to check the licence.' He scanned it quickly. 'Yes, that's in order. I'm happy to perform the ceremony, but could you wait just a few minutes? Perhaps you could sit down and pray for your future together while I change into something more appropriate? This is my oldest jacket, which I wear for gardening and doing odd jobs.' He brushed at a smear of mud. 'A wedding deserves better than this, don't you think?'

His smile was radiant with that special something a few outstanding men of God achieved, Helen thought, as he nodded and walked away. *Love* was the nearest she could come to it, but there was so much more in Mr Gregory's smile.

'That is a good man,' Jan said quietly. 'I'm glad he will be the one to marry us, not the other.'

As they sat waiting in the front pews, Helen prayed fervently for their marriage to succeed and for Jan to settle happily in Britain.

She heard footsteps behind them and twisted her head round to see two women come in and hesitate at the back of the church.

Mr Gregory rejoined the wedding party, dressed neatly in clerical black now. He looked at the two women and explained, 'Mrs Border and Mrs Taylor help me keep the chapel clean and tidy. I don't know what I'd do without them.'

He raised his voice. 'If you ladies can wait to start cleaning, we're about to have the pleasure of a wedding. Do you wish to stay?'

'Oh, yes. I do love a wedding,' one said. 'Always makes me cry, the hope in people's faces. Good luck to you both.'

They sat down at the rear.

Mr Gregory turned back to Helen and Jan. 'Are you ready, my friends? Please come and stand before me to make your vows, with your witnesses on either side.'

Helen repeated the words of the marriage service solemnly after him. Only when they came to the ring did she realise she'd completely forgotten about that.

Miss Peters coughed to gain their attention. 'I guessed you'd forget a ring, so I brought this. It was to have been mine.'

'We can't take it from you!' Helen said.

'I can think of no better use for it.' She held out a ring made from two narrow golden bands joined together, crossing one another twice, and the ceremony continued.

Helen felt tears of joy trickle down her face as the minister pronounced them man and wife.

'You may kiss the bride.'

Jan kissed first one cheek, then the other, ending with a soft, sweet kiss on her lips.

Those two don't need to speak their love aloud; their eyes say it for them, Miss Peters thought.

'You'll need to sign the register now,' Mr Gregory said gently.

When they'd finished doing that in his untidy little office, they rejoined the others.

The two ladies who'd been sitting at the back were standing next to Miss Peters. One looked slightly flushed as if she'd been hurrying. She held out a little parcel wrapped in news-paper to Helen.

'We wish you well and wanted you to have a wedding present. It's only two eggcups that I'd been admiring in the junk shop at the end of the street, but they're good china and very pretty, even if there isn't a whole set.'

'How kind of you!' Helen took them and unwrapped them. They were, indeed, pretty.

'We shall always treasure them,' Jan said. 'Thank you very much.'

Outside Helen hesitated. 'Ought we to register Jan's new status at the police station, do you think, Miss Peters?'

'Monday will be time enough. And I'm coming with you when you do; so is your new lawyer, Mr Melford.'

'Do we have a lawyer? How did that happen?' Helen asked in surprise.

'I thought it best.'

'You're looking after us again.'

'Yes. Do you mind?'

'I love it. Can we make you an honorary aunt?'

The older lady flushed and her eyes grew bright with unshed tears. 'That would give me great pleasure.'

Helen was glad to postpone what she was sure would be a difficult interview at the police station, especially if the magistrate was around.

She walked back to Miss Peters' house in a daze of happiness, holding her new husband's arm.

Her husband! How she loved that word.

'I need your help carrying a few things,' Miss Peters said as she led them inside through the front door of her house.

'I've opened a bottle of port wine and some raspberry cordial for the children, and I've made biscuits with sugar and currants I've been saving for a special occasion.'

She gestured to the kitchen table, where a plate was covered with a tea towel and crystal wine glasses stood on a silver tray. 'I suggest we take everything next door, bring Judith and the children down from the attic and drink your health. You'll excuse my biscuits if they're not as perfectly rounded as they should be. I never could get them even. But they always taste good. It was my mother's recipe.'

'That was a lovely wedding,' Mayne said as they walked through the back gate to Helen's house, carrying the refreshments. 'I'm honoured to have been a witness and I wish you both every happiness.'

It was a delightful little celebration, too, an oasis of joy in difficult times. Even Judith seemed to relax visibly after they'd drawn the curtains so that no one could peep in at them.

22

Mayne slept at the Dower House that night since he had nightwatchmen now patrolling the grounds. He'd stocked up with food to get his own breakfasts now without going into the main house. He ate early, wanting to get started at the big house.

He hesitated as he was about to leave, feeling it was only polite to pop in to say good morning to his parents before he left each day. He didn't look forward to the encounter.

His mother was only just starting to prepare their breakfast and greeted him with, 'I expect you to attend church with us today, Maynard.'

'Sorry, but I won't attend a church where Saunders is the minister.'

She gaped at him. 'How can you say that? It's the only Church of England place of worship in the town.'

He drew a deep breath, trying to contain his annoyance at her peremptory tone. What did she think he was? A boy, still, to be told what to do? 'Mother, I despise the man and I won't follow his lead in anything.'

'I'm still your mother and you should listen to me. The Eshers have always gone to that church.'

'I thought we'd agreed that I'd manage my own life.'

'Where *will* you be worshipping, then?'

'Nowhere.'

'But—'

His father banged his cup down into the saucer. 'Leave the boy alone, Dorothy.'

She seemed to struggle with herself, then made an angry sound and thumped her spoon down. 'I'll expect you to lunch, then, Maynard.'

He couldn't say no again. 'Thank you.' But he didn't intend to make Sunday lunch a regular occurrence after he'd moved to the big house. He'd be working seven days a week once he got going. He intended to succeed.

The telephone rang just then and his father went out into the entrance hall to answer it, coming back a minute later. 'It's for you, Maynard.'

'Thank you.'

He picked up the phone, happy to hear Victor's voice.

'I'll have to put off coming to join you for a few days, Mayne. Betty has a heavy cold and the doctor wants to keep her in bed.'

'I'm sorry to hear that. I hope she gets better quickly.'

'She usually does. She seems a healthy little thing. But I'm not taking any risks.'

Mayne felt he had to explain to his parents what his call had been about, since he hoped to use their phone till he could get a connection put in at the big house.

After that, he went to take over guard duty from Al and one of his friends who was replacing Jan for a couple of days on the nightly watch, to allow the bridegroom a honeymoon of sorts.

Mayne didn't intend to relax his vigilance, because there had been sounds of people in the grounds a couple of times recently during the night, though they'd gone away when challenged.

'Could you come back around noon and keep an eye on things, Al?' he asked. 'Only my mother is insisting on me going there for lunch and she's making a big fuss about it. You can start later this evening to make up for it.'

'Sure thing.'

As he took over at the big house, he smiled at Al's American accent.

It was a good thing he was there, because twice he found people from the town wandering round the grounds and had to ask them to leave.

They didn't look the sort to go out for a Sunday stroll, and one had already picked up some firewood. So he asked the man to put it back and mentioned that he had armed guards patrolling at night.

The words, 'Mean bugger!' echoed back to him as they walked away.

He was beginning to wonder how many guards he was going to need to protect his property.

He wondered how Judith and her children were getting on in Helen's attics. It'd be hard on such lively children to be penned up like that.

Al didn't arrive at Esherwood till quarter past twelve. 'Sorry! My mother wanted me to stay for lunch too. We had a bit of an argy-bargy about that.'

'I'm sorry. I shouldn't have asked you. You have your own life to lead.'

'Doesn't matter. I'm out to earn money so I'm happy to do overtime whenever you need me. Did you have any trouble?'

Mayne mentioned the trespassers he'd asked to leave, then left Al to it. He strolled down to the Dower House, enjoying the warmth of sunshine on his face after the last couple of dull days.

He went in through his own quarters and stopped dead, furious to see that his mother had been in 'tidying', which meant snooping into what he was doing. He'd left the inner door barred, so that meant she had a key to the outer door.

He unbolted the dividing door and went straight in, stopping short in the sitting room doorway when he saw Caroline chatting to his father. There was no sign of his mother, but he could hear someone moving about in the dining room.

'Ah, there you are, Maynard.'

His father seemed in a genial mood, but Mayne wasn't paying attention to him. He was looking at Caroline, who couldn't keep the look of smug triumph off her face.

'I'll just go and say hello to Mother.' He went into the dining room.

'It won't work,' he said bluntly.

'What do you mean?'

'Setting me up with Caroline. She cheated on me once, and I'd never trust her again. Besides, I've grown out of foolish women like her.'

'Oh, don't be silly. Give her a chance. We've all had time to grow up during the war years.'

He could see that something more drastic was needed. 'Let me put it plainly, then, Mother. Any time you invite *her* to a family gathering, I shall walk out, as I'm about to do today. And since you've been into my rooms again and seem unable to allow me any privacy, I'll be moving up to the big house permanently straight away.'

'Don't you dare speak to me like that! You're still my son and owe me respect.'

He didn't argue, just turned to go.

'I *insist* you stay to lunch, Maynard.'

'I meant what I said.' He left the room, hesitated, then went to the doorway of the sitting room. 'I have urgent business at the big house, so can't stay to lunch.' He didn't look at Caroline as he said this.

In the housekeeper's quarters, he bolted the inner door

again and began to pack up his things. Luckily, he didn't have much, though he'd need Al's help with the big trunk.

When he'd got everything together, he fetched a wheelbarrow and loaded it with the smaller items, smiling wryly at his elegant carrier as he began to push it up the drive.

'Wait a minute!'

He turned to wait as his father caught up with him.

'You've upset your mother.'

'I'm sorry about that, but she's upset me. I won't have anything to do with *that woman* again.'

'Caroline?'

'Who else could I be talking about?'

'Hmm. You could have stayed to lunch, though. Doesn't hurt to be polite.'

'If I had stayed, Mother would be planning other meetings for me. I had to make my stance plain to her.'

'I suppose you're right. Dorothy does rather get a bee into her bonnet when she wants something. That young woman's pretty, but she's not very intelligent, is she?'

His father smiled. 'Well, I'm glad you didn't marry her, because I don't want stupid grandchildren. But your mother's right about one thing: it is time you married.'

'I know. And I'd like to settle down. But I have to find a wife first.'

'Your mother still thinks you've got your eye on Mrs Crossley.'

'I told you before, I don't tangle with married women.'

'That's what I told her. You always did have a strong sense of honour, even as a lad.'

'Thank you for your faith in me.'

'I'm not as absent-minded as some people think. And if Gilliot hasn't got those papers ready to sign by Tuesday, I'll make my feeling about the delay plain to him. The sooner it's signed, sealed and delivered, the sooner your mother will stop trying to persuade me not to hand over the estate. Any sign of the chappie who might buy the paintings?'

'He's coming round tomorrow morning first thing.'

'Good. Let's get it all sorted out as soon as we can.' He looked at his old-fashioned pocket watch. 'I'd better get back now and try to calm Dorothy. I wonder if that young woman will stay for long. I've a particularly interesting bit of research I want to get back to.'

As he walked away, he stopped to call over his shoulder, 'Don't forget, Maynard: we need to go and sign the papers on Tuesday morning.'

'I'll make sure I'm free. I'll need to set someone to keep watch here, though. We've disturbed several would-be looters today.'

His father shook his head regretfully, then brightened. 'I'll tell your mother that's why you're moving up to the big house.'

'Tell her the truth or she'll be trying to fix me up with Caroline again.'

'I have to live with her. I'd rather soften the blow. After all, you told Caroline how you feel when you met her the first time.'

'And she still came today.'

'But she'll understand why you left so abruptly. See you on Tuesday morning.'

Mayne watched his father amble away. He couldn't remember ever seeing him hurry. Damn his mother! He hadn't bothered to buy much to eat today.

Whatever his father said, when she heard he was moving into the big house, she was sure to think the worst, even though Judith and her family were no longer there.

He realised he'd stopped walking and began moving again towards the house. He mustn't keep thinking of Judith, should keep his mind on business.

He had better start locking up his papers at the big house whenever he left his desk. That would be inconvenient, but he couldn't afford to have his mother nosing through the papers and perhaps telling others what she'd found.

One of the things – one of the many things – he was worried about was people trying to prevent his project getting council approval. It took a lot of paperwork and cutting through red tape to get anything done these days.

Since Mayne was heading for the back entrance, he made a detour into what was left of the kitchen gardens to see what he could forage to add to his meals today. He was pleased to find some slender young spears of asparagus half-hidden in a corner, spinach and spring onions, too. There were the feathery green tops of carrots, but they weren't big enough to pick yet, and yes, a couple of crowns of rhubarb had escaped being trampled on! He could pick two or three stems, but he didn't have much sugar.

Still, it was wonderful that some fruit and vegetables had managed to keep growing. The plants seemed to be flourishing now that they weren't being trampled on. That felt like an omen.

He wished Judith and her family were still at the big house. They could have shared the vegetables and fruit. Still, he could send something to them by Jan.

Al came to the door when he heard the wheelbarrow rattling over the cobbles.

Mayne found himself blurting out the truth. 'I find it impossible to live with my mother. She goes through my things and she invited Caroline to lunch today.'

'I heard Caroline boasting about her invitation to lunch.'

'She would.'

Al shrugged. 'Rivenshaw's a small town and you used to

be engaged to her, so people are talking and watching to see what happens.'

'Well, if they pair my name with hers again in your presence, tell them it's not so.' Mayne tried to calm down, but he grew angry every time he thought of his mother's attempts to manipulate his life. 'I need to find myself a proper bedroom, away from Judith and the children's rooms, in case they come back. I don't want things to look . . . wrong.'

'How about using one of the rooms downstairs? You can put one of those hospital beds in it.'

'Good idea. I used to camp out in them before you and Jan started working for me. I'll make one of them a bit more comfortable now and use it permanently.'

'Do you want some help?'

'Yes, please, Al. But we'll keep an eye on the grounds as we work. I don't intend to lose one piece of timber, not even one brick, if I can help it. Oh, and I'll need you to come back and help me with a trunk I've put some stuff in. It was too heavy to manage on my own.'

'Can do. Things will be easier for you when your friends arrive.'

'Except Victor can't come now till next week. His daughter's ill. I hope Daniel isn't delayed as well. I need a chaperone for a while, I think. I'd not put anything past Caroline.'

Al let out a low whistle, then grinned. 'If you get desperate, I'll come and bunk up here. I'd hate to see a good man captured by a woman like her.'

'Will you do that straight away, start sleeping here from today?'

'Is she that bad?'

'Yes.'

'Okey-dokey. I'll help you fix a room to sleep in and look for one for myself.'

'Why don't we both sleep in the library? It's big enough for a dozen beds.'

'You *are* spooked by her.'

'I'm wary. I know what she's like when she wants something.'

Ben kept fidgeting, not happy to spend his time in the attic and only go out into the garden at night. 'I'm fed up of reading and playing board games,' he complained.

'Then you'll have to be fed up,' Judith snapped. 'Or do you want to live with your father?'

'I want to go back to Esherwood. It was interesting there. We had things to do.'

She sighed. 'I want to go back, too, but I'm thinking we'll have to move right away from Rivenshaw.'

'No!' Gillian looked at her indignantly. 'It's not fair, having to leave because of Dad. Why can't *he* move away?'

Kitty nudged her. 'Don't pester Mum. She can't help Dad being like that. She's trying to save us. Imagine what it'd be like to live with him again. You may be too young to remember how he used to hit us, but I remember it clearly.'

Gillian flung herself down on the mattress she and Kitty had been sharing, for lack of proper beds. 'I remember too, but Ben's right. It is boring being stuck up here all day.'

'When we see what the magistrate and police do tomorrow, we'll make plans,' Judith repeated for the umpteenth time. 'Until we know, we have to be ready to leave at the drop of a hat.'

There were footsteps on the attic stairs and Helen called out, 'All right if I come in?'

'Of course. It's your house.' Judith tried to summon up a smile.

'I thought you might be hungry so I've put some food together in the kitchen and drawn all the curtains. You could come down to eat. It'd make a change for you.'

'We can't take your food.'

'We'll manage for a while. It's only boiled potatoes with herbs Jan found, and bread with Oxo to dip into. I can't do any proper cooking till my arm's better.' She flexed the fingers of her hand. 'It's improved a lot, thank goodness. I was really pleased when Jan helped me change the bandage.'

'When one of the other lads hurt his arm, the doctor told him to exercise it to build up the muscles,' Ben said.

'I think it's time I did that too. I can start gently and see how I go.' She smiled at the girls. 'Let's go down, eh. I'm hungry, even if you aren't.'

The girls led the way and the two women followed.

Ben had learned enough manners to stand back and let the ladies go first. When he was on his own, he hesitated then went across to the window to stare longingly out at Parson's Mead. He tried to keep out of sight, but couldn't resist lingering for a moment to look out at the Mead. He hated being penned up all day.

He hated his father, too. None of this was fair. He knew his mother was worried sick about their future.

Someone grabbed his arm and dragged him back from the window.

Doug was sure his wife and children were hiding at Miss Peters' house, since the police kept insisting they'd moved out of Esherwood. Even Constable Farrow said they'd checked the big house and found no signs of anyone staying there.

He trusted Farrow to tell him the truth, unlike that sod of a sergeant. He and the constable weren't exactly friends, but Farrow was the cousin of one of Doug's mates and the two of them had drunk together at the pub a time or two at the beginning of the war.

He thought it over as he lay sleepless in bed just before dawn on Sunday morning, then tossed the blankets aside and got up. 'I'm bloody well going to make sure they're not there,' he muttered, dragging on his trousers and kicking aside the squashed cardboard suitcase they'd given him to carry his demob clothes back in.

He glared at it. The stupid thing had crumpled the first time he'd bumped into something. And he wouldn't have done that if he hadn't seen someone in the distance at the railway station who looked familiar, like someone he'd once known. Thank goodness the fellow hadn't seen him.

In fact, he'd been lucky during the war not to meet people from that time of his life. Now he was back in Rivenshaw there was no chance of that.

Downstairs he scowled at the pantry. Not much left to eat. He'd have to go shopping again, which meant queuing like a woman. His anger at Judith, whose fault all this was, grew stronger by the day. When he got her back, he'd teach her to mess him about, by hell he would. And no one was going to stop him this time, because he'd make sure the bruises didn't show.

Breakfast could wait till later. He slipped quietly out of the house, taking care not to disturb his nosey bitch of a neighbour.

As he walked through the streets in the grey light of pre-dawn, he met no one. Lucky, that. He was heading for the clump of bushes partway up Parson's Mead. He reckoned he'd be able to hide there and use it as a lookout. It'd be the perfect place to keep an eye on Miss Peters' house.

When he got there, he nodded approval of his hiding place till he tried sitting down. The ground was damp. He got up and wandered round the allotments till he found a rough wooden stool outside one of the huts. Taking it, he put it in behind the bushes and sat down again. Might as well make himself comfortable.

It was a full hour before there was any sign of people

moving in the houses near the park. Well, it felt like an hour. His father's old pocket watch wasn't working so he had to guess the time.

The old lady got up first. A light went on in one of the bedrooms. He didn't take his eyes off it, but it was the only light in the house and when the curtains were drawn back, only Miss Peters was revealed to the world, not his family.

She stared out so purposefully, he worried she might spot him, so he stayed perfectly still. After a moment or two, she disappeared from view, the light was switched off in the bedroom and he saw nothing more. She was probably down in the kitchen at the back getting breakfast.

His stomach rumbled. Judith ought to damned well be at home making his meals.

He wasn't risking the old lady taking her gun to him, so didn't attempt to get into her garden again. If he kept careful watch, he reckoned he'd see some sign of Judith and the kids *if* they were at her house. Well, where else could they be?

It was a while before people stirred in the other houses. These rich sods didn't have to be at work as early as people like him. He wasn't going back to work till his demob money was nearly used up. He'd pretended his hand was worse than it really was so no one would try to force him back, though the damned thing had been bleeding again after he'd bumped it.

The injury wouldn't stop him getting his old job back, though. You didn't need to be good at fiddly things to hump crates about. He was managing all right now without those two fingers.

He yawned and since there was no one in sight, stood up, stretching.

A movement at the attic window of the house next to the

old hag's place caught his eye and he sucked in a breath in surprise.

There was nothing wrong with his long-distance eyesight, and he knew his own son when he saw him.

Ben stayed by the window for a few moments, then jerked out of sight as if someone had pulled him. Doug laughed and sat down quickly. Too late! He'd found out where they were hiding.

What he had to work out now was how best to catch them. No use giving them warning and letting them run away. No, he'd have to get the police to come along, and maybe one or two of his friends as well, to make sure Judith and the kids didn't escape.

'What do you think you're doing, Ben Crossley, standing at the window like that?' Judith scolded. 'Anyone passing by would be able to see you. These are proper dormer windows, not skylights.'

'No one went past. I kept my eyes open.'

'What if someone had been walking across Parson's Mead? There are places where you can be out of sight from people on the street and still see what's happening. I've sat there myself when I wanted to have a think.'

'Sorry, Mum.'

He looked so despondent she gave him a big hug. 'Never mind. There was no one around. Just don't do it again. Come and get your breakfast. There isn't much, but it's the best Helen can do.'

'I don't care. As long as we stay free of *him*.'

She felt exactly the same. She utterly despised Doug. It hadn't taken him even one hour to start thumping her.

When Al passed by Helen's house, on the way home from his night's work, he brought a sack with a few bits and pieces in it from the gardens of the big house. He found Judith on her own in the kitchen. 'Mayne sent these. There are all sorts of things struggling to grow in the old kitchen garden.'

'People are so kind.'

'How are you getting on?'

Judith looked at him sadly. 'All right. I worry about getting Jan into trouble, though. He still hasn't got permission to stay. We'll probably have to leave Rivenshaw soon. I just want to try every way I can to keep Doug away from us before I take that final step and run away. That magistrate has a lot to answer for if he prevents my children getting a decent education.'

'You've got some good friends in town. Don't be in a hurry to leave. We'll think of something. Ma said you could come to us for a night or two if you were stuck for somewhere to hide. I'm going to be sleeping at the big house from now on, so you can have my old room. It's only got a single bed, though, so some of you would have to sleep on the floor. But kids can sleep anywhere.'

'That's kind of her. Your mother's always been a good neighbour to me.'

Judith watched him go, but knew he couldn't perform miracles. Mr Compton-Grey had far too much power. When were things going to get back to normal and ordinary people be left to run their lives as they pleased, instead of being ordered to do this and not do that?

No, she shouldn't think like that. It was the way the country had been organised, the rationing and other measures, that had kept the civilian population fed and enabled the armed forces to fight their way to victory.

Even Doug, she supposed, had given something. He had two fingers missing, after all.

23

As the week began, Sergeant Deemer heard some good news, for a change. He hoped it was true, but you couldn't be sure till it was confirmed officially, so he said nothing.

He whistled cheerfully as he began the day, but as the morning passed without any more information coming through, he began to worry. Had it all been a rumour? He hoped not.

His day grew suddenly worse when Crossley sauntered into the police station, looking smug. What had that sod been up to now?

Farrow peered out of the back room. Deemer wished he was alone. You could do a lot more without an observer, even stretch the law a teeny bit, or delay its application, though he'd only do that sort of thing as a desperate last measure, to give someone real justice. But he knew Farrow wasn't on the side of either Judith Maskell or Jan Borkowski and his heart sank when they both heard the opening words from Crossley.

'I've found out where she's taken the kids, so I need you to help me get them back, Sergeant, as the magistrate ordered.' He banged one fist on the counter. 'You let them get away once. Don't do it again, or I'll put in a complaint about you.'

Deemer got out his pad made from scrap paper stapled together. 'If you'll give me the details . . . sir.'

'You're not slowing me down this time with details. Write it up afterwards. I want them back now and it's your duty to help before they get away.'

Unfortunately, he was right, Deemer thought, not allowing himself even to sigh. 'I can't do anything till you give me the information.'

'They're hiding in the house next door to Miss Peters, the one where that bloody foreigner has pushed his way in. Well, he's gone too far this time. They'll deport him for sure when they hear he's been helping people break the law. But first, *I want those kids back in their own home!*' He thumped the counter again to emphasise his words.

'I'll go with you to get them, Sergeant,' Farrow volunteered, looking eager. 'They won't get past me.'

Crossley laughed. 'We'll need more than you two, me having been injured in the service of my country.' He waved his hand with its filthy bandage at them. 'So I've brought a friend to help. He's waiting outside. And I've sent another friend to fetch that magistrate fellow. *He* will see I'm not cheated out of my rights.'

Damnation! Deemer put his pencil down. If Compton-Grey joined in the hunt, all he could do was make sure that poor woman and her children didn't get bashed as they were brought in. 'Let's go, Constable.'

Before they could get out of the door, Mr Compton-Grey thrust it open so hard it banged against the wall. 'I hear we're about to make an arrest, Sergeant.'

'An arrest, sir?'

'Yes. The foreigner. He's been helping Mrs Crossley break the law. He won't get a permit to stay here now, and I'm glad about that. They're letting too many foreigners into the country as it is, especially ones of his persuasion.'

'I'd like to deal with Mrs— um, Maskell and the children first, if you don't mind.'

'I suppose so. And her name is Crossley.'

Deemer didn't contradict him, but walked out of the police station, deliberately moving slowly, followed by a small procession.

Helen, feeling well enough now to do her own shopping, saw them. The way the group was heading led straight to Parson's Mead, so she abandoned the queue, thrusting her basket at the woman next to her and running home by the short cuts through the various back alleys. She entered her garden by the back gate and burst into the house, yelling for everyone to get out quickly before the police arrived.

Judith was in the kitchen as the children came rushing down from the attics. Helen shooed them all next door, but to her dismay Judith darted back upstairs, yelling that she had to get her handbag.

She was down almost immediately, but as she got to the hall, Sergeant Deemer knocked on the front door. She ran through the house to the back, only to find Constable Farrow blocking her exit.

'I think my sergeant is knocking at the front door, Mrs Crossley. Perhaps you should open it to him. And Mr Bork—um, sir. Could you please stay in the house?'

'It's not for me to open someone else's front door,' Judith said. 'And I'm using my maiden name now, which is Maskell. I've left my husband, as you well know.'

'I don't think you're allowed to change your name.'

She continued to argue to give the children time. 'I won't answer to my old name.'

He looked past her to Jan. 'Please do not leave the house, sir.'

'I have made no attempt to leave it,' he said quietly. 'Helen, dear, shall I open the front door?'

'I think it'd be better if we did that together, don't you?'

She led the way, opening it but not inviting the callers in. 'Yes?'

'I think you know why we're here,' the sergeant said quietly. 'Is Mrs Crossley there?'

'She's here, Sergeant,' Farrow shouted.

In the kitchen they found Judith, standing with arms folded, clutching her handbag.

Crossley tried to get to her, but the sergeant roared at him to stand back then asked her, 'Where are the children?'

'I don't know. They ran out. They're afraid of their father hitting them again.'

'I see.' He turned to Helen. 'If they come back, tell them to stay here. And you, Mr Borkowski, please do not leave this house till you hear from me. It will make matters far worse for you, if you do.'

Jan nodded, his face expressionless. 'I will stay here.'

'You should take him into custody,' Doug said. 'If you don't, he'll run off like the rat he is.'

Jan addressed the sergeant, 'I do not break my word.'

'I believe you, sir. Now, Miss Maskell . . . '

When they'd taken Judith away, Jan pulled Helen into his arms. 'I'm afraid,' he said quietly.

'I won't let them send you away.'

'If they decide I have to leave the country, we won't have a choice. But facing them is the only way I'll have a chance of staying, so I will do that.'

'*We* will do that together.'

As the train rattled along the branch line from Manchester to Rivenshaw, two men in the compartment got into conversation, each recognising a certain military bearing in the other.

'Is your friend not joining us?' one asked.

'He's not a friend, just an old fellow I was talking to at the station.'

'Oh, I see. Going far?'

'Little place called Rivenshaw.'

'So am I. Irwin Woollard.' He held out his hand and they shook firmly.

'Jim. Do you live in Rivenshaw?'

'No. I'm going to visit a relative. Haven't been to the town since I was a lad. I was hoping you could tell me something about it.'

Jim laughed. 'I'd been hoping the same. I've never been there before. I'm looking for a fellow I'm told is living there, but you won't know about him if you're not from Rivenshaw.'

Irwin studied Jim, head on one side. 'You weren't in the Army, I think.'

'Royal Marines. I was a commando.'

'Your lot fought bravely on the beaches at Normandy.'

'Yeah.' The young man's expression grew tight and Irwin guessed he must have lost someone there.

'I was in special operations. We helped plan a few sorties that chaps like you carried out.'

'It took all sorts to end it.'

They were both silent for a minute or two, lost in memories of friends departed, battles fought.

'Well, it all worked out in the end. We won,' Jim said.

The train began to slow down and Irwin peered out of the window. 'I think we're here. Yes. There's the sign.' He hauled two cases down from the luggage rack. 'I've got to make sure they unload my trunk from the luggage compartment, so excuse me nipping off. Maybe we'll meet again.'

'I'll keep an eye on your cases.'

'Thanks.'

As they got off the train, they saw the old man again. He nodded to Jim and walked across to a bench outside the station entrance, sitting down as if waiting for someone, shading his eyes with his hand as he scanned the town centre.

Irwin waved the taxi driver across and helped him load the luggage. 'Know where Mr Woollard lives?'

The man lost his smile. 'Everyone in town knows that, sir. Church House.'

'Take me there, then.'

Jim went across to the old man. 'No luck with him. He doesn't know the town, either. I'll have to ask around. You and I should split up, I think. Might find out what we need more quickly that way.' He looked round the square. 'There's a library over there. They'll likely have a reading room. Meet you there in a couple of hours?'

'All right.'

'I'll see if I can leave my suitcase somewhere.' He got into conversation with the porter, left his small suitcase at the station and went for a stroll.

Mayne was standing looking out across the ruined kitchen garden when Ben ran out of the bushes. He came towards the house, yelling at the top of his voice, 'Mr Esher! Mr Esher! Come quickly. They've got Mum.'

'Who's got her, Ben?'

'The police and that magistrate. Miss Peters said to fetch you – the girls are with her.' Tears were pouring down his face. 'They're going to make us go back to Dad. I know they are.'

'We'll see about that. Where's your mother now?'

'They were taking her to the police station.'

'Hell and damnation! Good thing I've got the car operational.'

With Ben's help he opened the garage doors and got the car out, then left the boy ready to hide in the attics, if necessary, and drove into town.

There was no way Mayne would allow those children of Judith's to be forced to live with that violent bully again.

As Sergeant Deemer led the way inside the police station, they heard a voice to one side and the sound of a telephone being hung up. The part-time typist poked her head out of the tiny office.

'I didn't realise you were back or I'd not have put the phone down, Sergeant. That was area headquarters. They want you to call them back urgently.'

'Thank you, Miss Rollins.' He looked at the magistrate. 'Would you mind if I make this call before we look into this matter, Mr Compton-Grey? If they say it's urgent, I ought not to delay in responding.'

The magistrate waved one hand in permission. 'Go ahead. The constable can keep an eye on this woman. Or we could start questioning her.'

'I'm sorry, sir, but there are rules about how people are to be questioned. I'm the senior officer here, so I have to be present. We can start as soon as I've finished my call.'

'Ah, yes. Of course. We have to follow the correct procedures.'

Miracles would never cease. For once the magistrate agreed with him. Deemer turned to Judith, who was looking dishevelled and unhappy. 'Perhaps you'd like to sit in Miss Rollins' office, Miss Maskell?'

'She can sit next to me,' Doug said at once. 'And I keep telling you, her name's Crossley.'

'I'm afraid she can't sit next to you, sir, since you're the complainant. That would be against the rules as well.' The words 'rules' and 'procedure' continued to work magic with the magistrate and this won Deemer another nod of agreement. 'Please sit over there, Mr Crossley.'

Doug stayed by the counter, looking as if he was going to argue.

'Do as the sergeant says, man,' Mr Compton-Grey said irritably. 'Are you deaf?'

Doug flung himself down on the wooden bench, scowling at them all impartially. His friend had waited outside. 'The children will get away if we don't do something quickly,' he protested.

'They won't be able to get far on their own. Now sit down and let the sergeant make this important phone call. It's you who's holding things up.'

With a sigh of relief, Deemer went into his office, closing the door, because he wasn't having Crossley or even that damned magistrate listening in.

'Hello? Deemer here, returning the AC's call. Yes, I'll hold on.'

Miss Peters watched the group of men take Judith down the street, then she went back into her house, where Gillian and Kitty had taken refuge. 'Right, girls. I haven't got a good hiding place for you, so we're going up to the big house now, while they're all occupied. You did say you know how to get into the secret room there?'

Both girls nodded.

'Then we'll go out the back way and hide you there till I can find out what's happening to your mother. She'll be glad to know you're safe and it'll be better if they can't use you to threaten her.'

'What about Ben?'

'He'll be at Esherwood already, I should think. I'll just let Helen and Jan know what we're doing.' She came out a couple of minutes later and beckoned to the children. 'Come on! Jan's going to follow us to make sure we get there safely. You won't see him most of the time because he's very good at staying hidden.'

As they slipped into the grounds of the big house, they

saw a car coming down the drive, but its occupants didn't see them.

'That's young Esher,' Miss Peters said in tones of satisfaction. 'Ben must have told him and he'll be going to help your mother. Come on. Let's get you two hidden, then I'll go to the police station and see what I can do.'

They arrived at the big house in time to see Ben shouting at two rough-looking men who were trying to push their way inside. He was jabbing a chair at them to stop them getting past him. But it was only a matter of time before they got him out of the way and one of them managed to grab the chair leg and yank it out of his hands.

'Hoy!' yelled Miss Peters. 'What do you think you're doing?'

They swung round and one of them groaned when he saw who it was.

'I know you,' Miss Peters said. 'You're cousins and you live in Oxton Terrace. I'll remember your name in a minute. If you take one step into the kitchen I'll report you to the police for breaking and entering.'

They stepped back, exchanging wary glances, but though they were twice her size, they made no attempt to attack her.

She continued to speak loudly. 'The best thing you can do is get off the grounds, then no one can accuse you of trespassing. I'll forget I saw you, as long as you don't return.'

That seemed to settle it, and they ran off.

Jan stepped from behind a tree and mimed locking the door, waited for her nod, then vanished again even before she closed the door.

'Where's Mum?' Ben asked. 'What have they done to her?'

'They've taken her down to the police station. She'll be all right. Sergeant Deemer won't let anyone hurt her. Neither will Mr Esher. I think the best thing we can do is get you three into that hiding place till we see what happens. You don't want your father coming to get you, do you?'

The shudders of the three children were eloquent.

She supervised them, quickly finding something to eat, sending them to use the bathroom and then puffing her way up into the attics behind them. Ben pleaded with her to leave the door of the secret room open, but she was adamant about having it closed.

'And don't speak above a whisper, either,' she added. 'We want to keep you three safe.'

She'd taken other steps to help this family, but hadn't seen anything come of it yet. Even if her friends did step in, would they take action in time to keep Judith and the children safe? And would they find a way to keep Crossley at bay?

You could never be sure what would come of an official intervention.

Sighing, she went to sit in the kitchen of the big house.

As an afterthought she picked up a heavy poker. Just let anyone else try to force their way in.

Sergeant Deemer was on the phone for longer than anyone had expected. Farrow kept his eyes alternately on Crossley and the doorway of the room where Judith was sitting.

The magistrate began pacing impatiently up and down, looking at his pocket watch a couple of times.

When the door to the sergeant's office eventually opened, everyone turned to stare in that direction.

'Well?' Mr Compton-Grey demanded.

'I've been speaking to Acting Superintendent Halkett. It seems someone higher up is taking an interest in this case. We're to do nothing till we hear from him.'

Just then there was the sound of a car pulling up outside and its doors opening.

Mayne strode into the station, leaving the others outside. He looked round. 'Where is Miss Maskell? What have you done with her?'

'Her name's Crossley,' Doug shouted again.

'She prefers to be called by her maiden name now she's left you,' Mayne replied, his quiet voice in contrast to the other man's loud one.

Doug scowled at him. 'You can't just change your name like that.'

Mr Compton-Grey cleared his throat. 'Actually, you can. As long as it's not for unlawful purposes, you can call yourself anything you like. Which doesn't mean I approve of her doing it.'

'Well, she's going to stop that rubbish soon. And I bet it's unlawful for a married woman to have a fancy man like him,' Doug sneered. 'Look at him, didn't take him long to run here after her, did it? But I'll forgive her and make sure he doesn't come near her again, for the kids' sake.'

'I'm *not* her fancy man; I'm her employer.' Mayne still spoke calmly. 'I have a very high opinion of Miss Maskell and I wouldn't dream of treating her with anything less than respect.'

The magistrate looked at him sourly. 'She's Mrs Crossley because she's still this man's wife.'

'That's between them. What I'm concerned about is that if he forces her to go back to him, he'll beat her again, as he has done before.'

'A man has a legal right to chastise his wife,' the magistrate said.

'The law is wrong about that. And has he the right to knock out his son and put the boy's life in danger? Or to knock a doctor flying?'

There was silence, apart from Doug muttering something under his breath.

After the clock had ticked its way through another five minutes, Mayne looked across the room. 'Can you explain what we're waiting for, Sergeant?'

'I've been told to wait until I hear from Acting Superintendent Halkett before I take action. I'm to do nothing until then. In the meantime Miss Maskell is perfectly all right sitting with our station clerk,' he gestured to the small office, 'and I may as well get on with my daily tasks until I hear from my superiors. Perhaps you should go home, Mr Crossley, and we'll send for you when something is decided?'

'I'm staying.' Doug folded his arms.

Mr Compton-Grey pulled the big gold watch out again from his waistcoat pocket and made a tsk-tsk sound under his breath. 'I have someone coming to see me in a quarter of an hour. I shall have to leave you, but I'll return to keep an eye on things once my visitor has left.' He stared at the sergeant. 'I presume you're not intending to release Mrs Crossley?'

'No. She'll be safer here, sir.'

'Then you'd better send the constable to look for the children.'

'I've been told to do nothing about them either until further notice, sir. I have to obey orders.'

'I suppose so, but this is most inconvenient.' Mr Compton-Grey frowned. 'What about that foreigner? Should we fetch him in for questioning?'

'Mr Borkowski gave me his word he'd stay in Miss Bretherton's house and I trust him. I'm quite sure he won't run away.'

'I hope you're right. I expect he's resigned to being deported now he's seen we don't want his sort here.' The magistrate left the station.

'Perhaps you'd like to sit down and wait, Mr Esher,' the sergeant said.

'Yes. I'll do that. I'll just go and move my car.'

He parked it to one side of the square, where it'd not get in people's way. As he got out, he saw a man staring in through the open door into the police station and hesitating.

'Do you need something? Sergeant Deemer's inside and he can be very helpful.'

'It's all right. I've found the fellow I'm looking for.' Jim jerked one thumb towards the police station. 'That fellow sitting across there. You don't happen to know his name, do you?'

'Doug Crossley.'

'Ah. So that's what he's calling himself now.'

Mayne stared at him in puzzlement. 'As far as I know, that is his name, and has been for about fifteen years.'

'That may be what he calls himself now, but I know different.'

'Is there something you should tell us? The information may be useful to us as well.'

Jim hesitated, then shook his head. 'Not yet. I've got to see someone else first. Is there some kind of court hearing going on?'

Mayne explained. 'The sergeant is waiting for word from his superior. It's getting late, so he probably won't do anything else till tomorrow. You could check that with him. He's very helpful.'

'I don't want a certain gentleman to see me.'

'I'll go and ask for you.'

'Thanks.'

Sergeant Deemer seemed certain nothing would happen till the next day, and not until about ten o'clock, so Mayne went out to let the mystery man know.

'Thank you for your help, sir. Much appreciated.'

He walked off briskly towards the railway station, which was at the far side of the square, whistling cheerfully.

What was that all about? Mayne wondered. What did the stranger know about Crossley? He went inside to wait, wishing he could sit with Judith, returning Crossley's glare with an icy look.

24

Jim walked across the square to the library and peeped inside. He waved and waited outside the door.

He didn't bother to greet the man who came out. 'Let's go down that street. I'll go first. You follow. I don't want them to see us together yet. I looked through the doorway of the police station. You were right. It is him.'

'I was sure of it.'

'He looks a lot like you did twenty years ago.'

That won him a scowl and a sharp, 'Well, he might *look* like me, I get no choice about that, but he's never behaved like me.'

'Bit of luck, that resemblance, though. He was sitting looking towards a door at one side. Good thing I saw him in the railway station that time. When I asked some fellow here, he said his name was Doug Crossley.'

'So what are you going to do, lad?'

'It's getting late, and nothing's going to happen here till tomorrow, the sergeant told this fellow I met. Nice bloke. Very helpful.'

'And the hearing?' the old man prompted.

'I'm getting to it. Some bigwig seems to be taking an interest in the case so nothing's likely to happen till tomorrow. I'll find a lodging house and hang around the square, just in case. You've got time to go back to Manchester to fetch the others. Bring them here tomorrow morning. Nothing will happen till about ten o'clock, the sergeant says.'

'Good. I'll catch the next train back to Manchester. Have you got enough money for a night's lodging and in case you need to buy someone a round of drinks?'

''Course I have. I'm not a fool with money, like him.'

'Nay, you're not a fool about anything, our Jim.'

The young man watched him go, then strolled round the square. He was lucky enough to see the man he wanted come out of the police station, scowling as he glanced up at the railway station's clock.

Jim followed Crossley to a small pub with peeling paint-work, and turned down a side street, from where he could see his quarry waiting outside for opening time, together with two or three shabby-looking old men.

After a few minutes the landlady opened up and they all went inside. Jim waited a few minutes longer then followed suit. He bought a half of shandy and asked the landlady about lodgings. She was able to oblige him herself and give him a simple evening meal, which suited him down to the ground.

He stayed for a while, making the drink spin out, then went into a side room to eat his meal.

He came back and bought another shandy to give him a reason for staying there. He kept an eye on Crossley, who got through several pints, growing redder in the face and looking angrier with each one.

Jim watched in disgust, wishing he could hear what he was saying. But the pub was quite crowded now. He didn't like boozers like this one, had seen what could happen when drunks lost control.

Eventually the landlady called, 'Time, gentlemen, please,' and the pub began to clear. Jim helped her collect up the glasses, then went up to his bedroom, glad to get to bed.

Tomorrow promised to be a very interesting day.

After Crossley had left the police station, Sergeant Deemer sent Farrow out on patrol and took Judith into his office. 'I need to be sure you won't run away,' he said bluntly. 'Do I have to lock you up or will you give me your word not to leave town?'

She looked at him with tears in her eyes. 'If I stay, he'll get the kids and ill-treat them. And you know what that magistrate is like. *He* won't stop Doug.'

'I know, lass, but we all have to obey the law.'

There was a knock on the door and Mayne peeped in. 'I've been wondering what's going to happen to Miss Maskell.'

'We're trying to decide. I can't just let her go. I may not always agree with the law, but I can't break it openly. If she'd give me her word not to leave town, I'd let her go for the night, though I don't think she should stay up at Esherwood with you.'

The sergeant looked earnestly at Judith. 'I can't tell you any more, but I wonder if you could bring yourself to trust me when I say the best thing you can do is face the law tomorrow. There are certain things happening that may be to your advantage, but I can't explain what they are yet.'

He patted her shoulder. 'And I have to tell you, my dear, that you're not the sort to run away and hide. You've no experience of that sort of life, and the way things are regimented and rationed these days, you'd have no chance of making a life for those children if the police were looking for you.'

Still Judith hesitated.

Mayne looked at her. 'I agree with the sergeant. I don't think you have much choice.'

Her shoulders sagged. 'Where shall I go tonight then?'

'Back to Helen's, do you think?'

'I suppose so.' She turned to the sergeant. 'I give you my word I won't try to run away for the next twenty-four hours.'

'Fair enough.'

'What are you going to do about Jan?' Mayne asked. 'Only he's supposed to keep watch at Esherwood tonight and we're having a lot of trouble with would-be looters.'

'I'm going to see him when I escort Miss Maskell to the house where he's staying. I'll ask him for the same as I asked her: a promise not to run away. He said he wouldn't go, but I want to make it formal.'

Mayne smiled. 'I don't think you need to do that. He'll not leave Rivenshaw now.'

'Oh? Why not?'

After a moment's deliberation, Mayne told them. 'Jan's married Helen. I was one of the witnesses.'

A smile brightened the sergeant's face. 'That's the best news I've heard all week. He'll stand a good chance of getting permission to stay in Britain now.'

'I hope so. More important, I think they'll be happy together.'

'Is it a love match, then?' He sounded surprised.

'Oh, yes. If you watch them together, I think you'll agree.'

'I'll watch them when I escort Miss Maskell back. Are you ready to go, my dear?'

With a sigh Judith followed him outside. She knew this man didn't mean her any harm, but she didn't trust the magistrate.

Mayne decided it was better for her if he wasn't seen with

them, so said goodbye and took the short cut home along the back alleys.

At the big house Mayne found Miss Peters still sitting guard in the kitchen.

'Ah, there you are, Mayne. I've sent the children into the secret room. I didn't like to let them roam round the house in case someone saw them.'

'I think they can come out if they stay in their bedrooms. The hearing's been adjourned till tomorrow, we don't know why. It was hinted that some bigwig is taking an interest in the case.'

She beamed at him. 'Oh, good. I hoped he would.'

'Ah. Using your connections, are you?'

'What's the point of having 'em if you don't use 'em in times of trouble?' She put the poker back in its stand. 'Two men were trying to push their way in when I arrived, intending to loot the place, I should think. I sent them packing but they're in that group Crossley drinks with. You might keep a more careful watch than usual tonight.'

'I will.'

'Do you have enough food for the children?'

'Yes. I'll nip up and let them out of the secret room at least. It's very dark and stuffy.'

When he returned, he said, 'I've told them to stay in their bedrooms. They were so relieved to be let out, they promised not even to look out of the windows. Um, I wonder . . . could you stay here until I've nipped down to Lower Parklea and left a message for Al?' He grinned. 'I'd back you to rout anyone trying to get in.'

She picked up the poker again and brandished it. 'They won't get past me.'

'It'd be a brave man who'd try.' He caught her by surprise and gave her a quick hug. 'You're a marvel, Miss Peters.'

She didn't smile till he'd gone, didn't want to let him see how much she'd enjoyed being hugged. But she rather thought he'd guessed.

The night passed slowly. Judith didn't sleep much. She couldn't help worrying about her children even though Miss Peters had popped by when she returned from the big house, to say the three of them were all right. Mayne was spending the night inside Esherwood to make sure no one tried to break in, while Al and Jan were patrolling the grounds as usual.

But that wasn't the same as Judith seeing Kitty, Ben and Gillian herself.

She was guilty of staring out of the window of Helen's attic more than once. She'd forbidden the children to do that, but couldn't help checking whenever she heard a strange noise. It was a still night and quite warm, not even a breeze to stir the trees, and the moon was bright enough for her to see anyone passing the house or walking across Parson's Mead. Apart from a cat padding along the street, she saw nothing.

It was a relief to see the sky lightening in the east. She wished she had a clock to tell her the exact time. In the end, she crept downstairs and checked the one in the kitchen, then decided it was a waste of time going back to bed and put the kettle on.

Helen joined her a few minutes later. 'Couldn't you sleep?'

'No. Today is going to be so important.'

'For Jan and me, as well as for your family. You knew we'd got married, didn't you?'

'Yes, Mayne mentioned it. Congratulations. I hope you'll be happy together.'

'If they don't let him stay in England, I don't know what I'll do. Apart from the fact that I care for him, I still need help.' She wiped away a tear. 'That lawyer, Gilliot, is dead set against him, and he has a cousin who's the acting area commander. Compton-Grey doesn't like foreigners either. Or if we're blunt, those three particularly don't like Jews. I've never understood why anti-Semitism makes people so hateful.'

'Some people don't like Catholics, either.'

'Silly, isn't it?'

They were both silent for a few moments, brooding on their problems and the day to come, then Judith pulled herself together. 'It'll do no good to keep looking on the black side, will it? Let's have that cup of tea.'

'Good idea. What time do you have to go to the police station?'

'About ten o'clock, Sergeant Deemer said.'

'The sergeant told Jan to attend at that time as well. He'll be back soon from his night duty at Esherwood, so he won't have time to sleep for more than an hour or two. I gather Al's rounding up some friends to keep watch today because it'll be known in the town that Mr Esher will be away from the house, so they're worried they might get looters.'

'It's awful how some people are turning into thieves and racketeers, isn't it?' Judith said. 'We ought to all be pulling together to get over the war.'

At half-past nine, Sergeant Deemer received a phone call from Halkett, telling him not to start questioning people until he arrived.

'Is anyone coming with you, sir?'

'No. Of course not. Do you think I'm incapable of managing on my own?'

'Just wondering about chairs, sir, whether to bring extra ones in.'

'Stop fussing about unimportant details and make sure everyone we need to interview is there.'

Deemer's heart sank. This wasn't the call he'd been

expecting and he didn't think Halkett would be very sympathetic, either to Judith or to Jan. It'd be a crying shame if the police were ordered to drag those poor children back to their father. Or deport Jan.

Farrow came in looking eager and alert, clearly enjoying the excitement.

He would, Deemer thought sourly.

The people concerned started to arrive before ten o'clock. Jan and his wife were the first, looking so right together, so much in love, that Deemer would be surprised if anyone could look at them and claim this was merely a marriage of convenience.

Miss Maskell followed them in shortly afterwards. The poor woman had dark circles under her eyes and looked extremely anxious. Well, her whole life was at risk, wasn't it?

'Miss Peters had to see someone, but said to tell you she'd be here soon,' Judith said.

'All right. Please take a seat over there.'

Crossley was the next to arrive, newly shaven but with a crumpled shirt on that needed washing. He gave his wife a nasty smile, a smile that said he was confident of getting his own way.

That fellow didn't want a wife; he wanted a punching bag, Deemer thought sourly. He indicated a seat in the corner, but Crossley chose one closer to his wife.

'Please sit over here!' Deemer shouted. 'Do not disturb my seating arrangements. There are other people to come, you know.'

All hung in the balance for a moment, then Crossley whispered something to Judith and slouched across to the corner.

She winced, looking even more anxious.

Young Esher arrived next and took a seat near the door. Esher flicked one quick glance in Miss Maskell's direction as he came in, then avoided looking at her.

Very wise, too, Deemer thought and stared at the clock again. Coming up to ten.

There was the sound of a car outside, its noise quickly lost in the arrival of the third train of the day from Manchester.

Soon afterwards, a young policeman held the door open and Acting AC Halkett could be seen getting out of a car. He stopped to wait for Compton-Grey, who was walking across the square, and the two of them had a quiet conversation before they came in. Probably plotting how to get that poor woman beaten and that poor young man sent to die in a work camp, Deemer thought gloomily.

Compton-Grey led the way into the room they'd be using for the hearing and took his place at the big table.

Deemer heard Halkett say, 'I don't think you should start yet.'

But the magistrate scowled and said, 'I want to get it over quickly.'

Everyone else who entered the room sat where Deemer indicated. At least Crossley seemed more subdued in the presence of important people.

The magistrate rapped his gavel on the table and when he had everyone's attention, said, 'We shall open the hearing immediately.'

At the railway station, Miss Peters scanned the train anxiously for her cousin, but there was no sign of Judge Dennison Peters. She clicked her tongue in annoyance.

Three people did get off the train, but they were strangers.

She left the station feeling upset. It wasn't like her cousin Dennison to let her down. Well, she wasn't leaving Judith to face Compton-Grey on her own. She'd put in a formal complaint herself if the decision against either of her protégés was unfair.

But would a complaint from her do any good at this late stage?

To her surprise the three people who'd got off the train walked in the same direction as she did.

When she reached out to open the door of the police station, the older man said, 'Allow me, miss.'

As he held the door open, another car pulled into the square, a big official one. Was it her cousin? She gestured to the others to go inside and waited for the passenger to get out of the car.

'Dennison! You're late.'

'Sorry. The traffic was terrible.' He turned to his driver. 'Take a half-hour break. You've earned it.'

Then he turned to his cousin. 'Veronica, I still find it hard to believe what you told me.'

'Well, let's go inside and see what they're doing to my young friends. You'll soon see that I'm not exaggerating.'

Mr Compton-Grey looked over the top of his reading glasses at Judith. 'Have you sent your children back to their father, as ordered?'

'Not yet, sir. I wanted to beg you to recon—'

He held up one hand. 'I have given you a direct order. Where are the children at present?'

'They'll be up at the big house,' Doug said eagerly. 'Send that policeman to fetch them.'

'*Quiet!* When I wish for a comment from you, Crossley, I'll ask for it.' He turned back to Judith. 'If you are determined to leave your husband, I cannot stop you, but he is the head of the family and it is for him to make provision for his children.'

'But he'll beat them, sir, and he won't know how to look after them.'

'There is an easy solution to that. You can go back and do your wifely duty.'

'I daren't. He'll kill or cripple me, if I live with him again.'

'Nonsense! Don't exaggerate. Sergeant, get this woman to take you to where the children are being kept and see that she hands them over to her husband.'

He turned back to Doug. 'And you, Crossley, see that you moderate your violence *and* your drinking. No, you can stay here till they get back. The handover will be done under my supervision.'

Well, that was one good thing, Deemer thought as he beckoned to Judith. The longer Crossley was kept away from her, the better.

Mayne, who was sitting near the door, looked angrily at the magistrate.

As the sergeant passed him, he gave a quick shake of the head, trying to warn Mayne to keep quiet.

For a moment Judith couldn't move, then she followed Deemer out. She didn't know what to do now, how to protect her children.

She had failed them.

'I'm sorry,' Deemer whispered when they were in the reception area. 'There's nothing either of us can do. He'll put you in prison if you refuse to hand them over and you'll be no use to them there. At least if you're still free, you might have a chance to help them in an emergency.'

He stopped in surprise when he saw who was standing just outside the room: a very famous judge called Dennison Peters, a relative of their Miss Peters.

Judge Peters put one finger to his lips and gestured to them to sit to one side.

Before he joined Judith on the bench, Sergeant Deemer went across to the four people sitting waiting at the other side of the room. 'Could you come back this afternoon, please? Only I won't be able to attend to you for a good while.'

'We'll wait,' the older man said.

'It could be hours.'

'We'll still wait.'

The lady was wearing heavy veiling over her low-brimmed hat, and didn't even raise her head to look at him, let alone respond. The two young men, who must be brothers, or even twins, they looked so alike, stared stonily at him. They were all respectably dressed, but they had grim expressions on their faces as if there was something troubling them. What next?

He caught the judge's eye and sat down next to Judith.

'Who are those people?' she whispered. 'Those young men look familiar, though I can't quite place them.'

'Shh!' Deemer put a finger to his lips, gesturing towards the judge, who was standing near the half-open door next to Miss Peters, both of them listening intently. 'I think this is going to be interesting.'

Compton-Grey looked round the room, his gaze settling on Jan. 'Stand up, you!'

Jan got to his feet, face expressionless.

It was Helen who looked anxious. 'Tell him!' she whispered.

'Silence in court!' Compton-Grey ordered in a loud voice. 'Do you have a permit to be in Britain, Mr Borking?'

'My name is Borkowski.'

'More importantly, what is your nationality?'

'I was Polish.'

'There is no "was" about it. You *are* Polish and therefore must go back to your own country. What is your religion?'

'Methodist.'

Compton-Grey's voice rose. 'That's a damned lie! You're a Jew.'

Helen stood up. 'Sir, I have some important information.'

'There's nothing you can say or do. This fellow has admitted he has no permit to live here, and that he's Jewish. It's an open and shut case.'

'He's my husband and has a right to stay here.'

'Since when?'

'We were married in the Methodist chapel last week.'

The magistrate seemed to swell with anger. 'Then you fell for a ploy to enable him to stay in Britain. I'm not so gullible. He's married you only to stay here.'

'No. I love him and he loves me.'

He made a scornful sound. 'Rubbish. You've only just met him. Case dismissed. Constable, take that man in charge.'

'Just one moment.'

Everyone turned to look at the man who had pushed the door open and stepped into the back of the room. He was followed by Miss Peters, looking extremely pleased with herself.

Mayne recognised the newcomer and let out a low whistle of surprise, then looked hopefully towards the doorway, where Judith and Deemer were now standing.

The magistrate fell silent. It was obvious that he too recognised the tall, grey-haired gentleman.

'May I speak to you in private, Mr Compton-Grey?' The voice might be quiet but somehow the words penetrated clearly to every corner of this room and the one outside.

'You can use my office, sir,' Deemer said.

The magistrate scowled at the sergeant and opened his mouth to ask why he was still there, but something in the judge's expression made him shut it again.

'Thank you, Sergeant. Mr Compton-Grey, please join me?'

When they'd left the room, there was a hubbub. Doug, who had not recognised the newcomer, asked loudly who that old fellow was.

No one answered. People were talking in low whispers, waiting, wondering . . .

Outside, the old man sitting on the bench nudged the veiled woman. 'Now that one really is a good man, even if he is a judge. I've read about him time and again in the newspapers, but I never thought to see him in action.'

'I'm more interested in Doug,' the woman said sharply. 'As soon as they come back, I'm going after him, and no one is going to stop me.'

'Keep your voice down, Ma, or he'll hear you,' one of the young men said. 'No one can mistake that it's you when you shout like that.'

She smiled and lowered her voice, 'I've waited years for this. I can wait a bit longer if I have to.'

25

Inside Deemer's office, Dennison took a seat behind the desk and gestured to a chair. 'Please take a seat, Compton-Grey.'

He looked round and called, 'Sergeant! Could you join us?'

Deemer came in.

'We need another witness before we start. I can't ask Miss Peters to do it, because she's a relative of mine.'

'What about one of those people waiting to see me? I don't know who they are, but they're strangers, so can't be accused of being involved, and they look respectable, don't you think, sir?'

The judge peered out. 'Yes. Pick whoever you think best.'

Compton-Grey was looking more uneasy by the minute. The judge hadn't even looked his way since he'd sat down.

Deemer went out and asked the old man if he was prepared to act as a witness to something.

'I'd be delighted to help an officer of the law.' The stranger got up and followed Deemer, who closed the door behind them.

'Your name?' Judge Peters asked the newcomer.

'Robert Cross, your honour.'

'Give the sergeant your address before you leave.' He turned to Compton-Grey again. 'This won't take long. There have been several complaints about your decisions being biased. After listening to the two cases today, I'm in complete agreement with the complainants. I've never been present at such cursory hearings and I'm shocked that you were ever appointed as a magistrate. You made no attempt whatsoever to get at the truth, but let your own prejudices guide you. British justice is available to all persons and all creeds, I would remind you.'

Compton-Grey turned pale and opened his mouth to protest.

'No. Keep quiet, if you please. It's your turn to listen to a rapid judgement, only this time, it will be one based on facts. When I've finished, you will go back into that room and tell people that new evidence has come to light, but that you're feeling ill, so will leave me to deal with this case. It's still rather an unorthodox way of dealing with this situation, but from what my cousin tells me and what I've heard today, you are not fit to be a magistrate and the sooner you hand in your resignation, the better. You will do that, won't you? If you don't, I'll go after you with the full might of the law I have served for the last forty years.'

Compton-Grey's face was chalk white but he didn't protest. Although the judge had been nothing but polite, there was something very daunting about him, something steely that said he was not a man to defy.

'If that young man from Poland has married an Englishwoman, he has a right to stay in this country. It's as simple as that. Moreover, I am assured they're deeply in love.'

'I can attest to that, sir,' Deemer put in. 'I've seen them together several times.'

'I'm glad to hear that. Then we come to Miss Maskell's case. I gather that poor ex-wife of Crossley's has had a lot to bear over the years, the children too. He must be warned away from them and—'

Their witness cleared his throat. 'I have some information relevant to the case, sir, but I'd rather give it in their presence, if you don't mind. It, er, sheds new light on the whole situation.'

The judge studied him then nodded, as if he liked what he saw. 'Very well. We'll go back into the hearing room. Once Mr Compton-Grey has handed things over to me, you can share your information with us.'

'Thank you, sir.'

They all stood back to let the judge lead the way out.

Compton-Grey's announcement that he was stepping back from this case due to ill health caused a sensation in the crowded room, but his pallor lent credibility to his words. He bowed stiffly to Judge Peters and left the room, not meeting anyone's eyes on the way out.

At the sight of Judge Peters, Gilliot slid down in his seat, trying to remain inconspicuous, but the judge's thoughtful gaze settled on him for a moment and a frown crossed the older man's face.

'I will now take over, since one at least of these cases is easy to settle.'

'You're right, your honour,' Doug called out. 'She's my wife an' she has to come back to me an' do her duty.'

'Wait your turn, Crossley. I'm not talking about your case.'

He turned to Jan and Helen. 'Congratulations on your marriage, Mr and Mrs Borkowski. I hope you'll be very happy. There will be a lot of paperwork, but you've won the right to stay in this country, Mr Borkowski.'

Jan looked as if he'd been struck dumb, so Helen thanked the judge for him, then tugged her husband to sit down. He whispered something to her, then took her hand. His own hand was shaking as he held hers, and he kept swallowing hard and blinking, as if fighting back tears.

The judge turned to look at Judith. 'Please come forward, Miss Maskell. I must apologise to you for this fiasco of a hearing. Only in wartime could legal matters get into such a tangle.'

'What do you mean?' Doug demanded.

'*I said quiet, you!*'

'As Mr Compton-Grey told you all before he left, new evidence has come to light. Perhaps the gentleman providing some of that evidence will come to the front of the court.'

Mr Cross moved forward, accompanied by the veiled lady. The two young men remained in the doorway, barring the way out. As he reached Doug, the old man stopped.

For a moment Doug stared at him, then gasped as he recognised the stranger.

'I don't suppose you expected to see *me* here today, did you, Douglas? '

Doug was out of his seat in a flash, trying to push his way to the door.

Mayne took great pleasure in helping bar the way.

As the veiled woman moved towards them, Mayne made sure Crossley stayed where he was.

'You wouldn't have been expecting to see *me* today, either, would you, Douglas?' She pulled back the veil to show a badly burned and scarred face, to which she pointed. 'You didn't wait round long enough to see whether I survived what you'd done to me, did you?'

He cowered away from her, looking terrified.

'Perhaps you could tell us who you are, madam, and to what you are referring?' the judge prompted.

She turned and went to stand looking across the big table at him, very upright as if unafraid of the world. 'I'm that man's wife, your honour – Mary Cross. He ran away when our sons were babies, after beating me senseless and knocking me into the fire for answering him back. He didn't even bother to pull me out of the hot ashes. My life was despaired of but I recovered. These burns were his doing.' She pointed to her badly scarred face.

'And now I want justice. I want him tried for injuring me, then I want him locked away where he can't attack women and children again. And where he can't pretend to marry innocent women.' She turned to look at Judith. 'I'm sorry to do this to you, love, but he's never married you because he's still married to me.'

The old man moved to her side. 'I'm sorry to say that I'm Doug's father, your honour, and everything Mary has told you is true. We've never had a bad 'un like him in our family before, and I'm ashamed of him. Deeply ashamed.'

Even the judge looked shocked. 'He's a bigamist, you say? As well as a wife-beater? Do you have your marriage lines with you, Mrs, um, Crossley?'

'She's Mrs Cross. And his real name's Cross, too, same as it always was, same as mine,' the old man said bitterly. 'I wish it wasn't.'

She took some papers out of her handbag and passed them to the judge.

There was complete silence in the room while he studied them. It didn't take long.

'These seem to be in order. Of course, they'll have to be checked carefully and if you're right, the case will have to be tried in a higher court than this. But in the meantime, Sergeant, you may arrest Crossley – now known to be named Douglas Cross – and detain him until he can be taken to Manchester to await trial.'

Doug made a second break for freedom, hitting out wildly and shoving his way almost to the door this time. But there the two young men stopped him. And as they held him, their resemblance to him became obvious. All fight went out of him and he sagged in the firm hold of his twin sons.

The judge had to thump his gavel on the table several times to make people quieten down at these unexpected revelations.

He looked across the silent room. 'First of all, I wish to say that no shame attaches to Miss Maskell, who could not have known she was being tricked into a sham marriage. Or to her daughters and son, who are, I am told, fine children and highly intelligent.'

He looked at the other woman, who was holding her head high and hadn't veiled her face again. 'Madam, you have my sympathy for what you've suffered.'

'Sir, I'm sure you will see that justice prevails. That's all I ask.'

'You can count on it.'

As the meaning of what had happened sank in, the room seemed to spin round Judith and she clutched the arm of the person next to her. It was a moment or two before she could pull herself together and realise she was sitting beside Miss Peters.

'I can't believe it!'

'It surprised me, I must say. But it's good news, surely? You're free of him, and he'll be locked up for a good long time.'

Her voice was bitter. 'Good news in one sense, but it means my children will be called "bastards" from now on.'

'They must learn to hold their heads up and face the world. The shame is not theirs. Or yours. I shall continue to associate with them and you, and quite a few people in this town will, I'm sure, follow my example.' She looked up as Mayne came to stand beside them.

'I just wanted to say that you still have a job and a home

at Esherwood, Judith,' he said quietly. 'My partners and I are going to need your skills.'

He moved on and her eyes followed him involuntarily.

Miss Peters nudged her. 'Don't show your feelings for him, Judith. Leave that till a few months have passed, then allow him to court you in the usual way.'

'Is it so obvious how I feel?'

'It is to me. And before you ask, I'm sure he feels the same about you.'

Judith smiled, a rather watery smile, but the first sign of her recovery from shock. 'At least I'm no longer tied to Doug. That feels wonderful, as if a heavy weight has gone from my shoulders. I think I'd like to go home now, though. I have to see the children and tell them before anyone else gets to them.'

'I'll walk with you. And has it occurred to you that you can now have your house and furniture back? Even if you don't go back there to live, you have things you'll want to keep . . . or sell.'

She could see Judith start to think about that and was pleased to have given her a new task to consider.

When Judith and Miss Peters went outside, they found Mrs Cross and her family waiting for them.

'I wanted to say again how sorry I was to have to tell you so publicly, and I'm sorry for what he did to you,' the woman said. 'My lads have something to say to you, as well.'

One of the twins spoke up. 'You've got children, they said.'

'Yes. A boy and two girls.'

'They'll be our half-brother and sisters. We'd like to meet them. Me and Ted always wished we'd had brothers and sisters.'

Judith was so surprised by this, she couldn't speak for a few moments, then she said, 'Yes. Of course.'

The old man added quietly, 'And I'm their grandfather. I'd like to know them, too. Don't judge our family by Doug. He's always been a bad 'un. The rest of us are honest folk.'

She looked at them with tears in her eyes. 'I'll be happy to let them know their family once things have settled down.'

Mrs Cross held out a piece of paper and Judith took it automatically. 'These are our names and address. We all live together. It's easy for us to get here from Manchester by train. We can come and see you. And later you can come and see us.'

Judith swallowed hard. It seemed this terrible day had brought her a family again. They seemed very decent people. And her children had half-brothers and a grandfather who might care about them more than her own father did, too lost in his new so-called romance.

As the four of them walked away together, Judith said, 'I can't believe those nice people are related to Doug.'

'They seem very pleasant, I agree. Shame about her face.'

Judith shuddered. 'That could have been me.' Then she sighed and asked, 'How do I tell the children, Miss Peters?'

'Tell them the truth, simply and without embellishment. They'll be happy to be free of him. And I think they'll like having close relatives. That should distract them a little.'

Jan and Helen left them and went into her house. 'Those two are very happy,' Miss Peters said with deep satisfaction. 'I'll walk up to Esherwood with you, just to make sure things are all right. If you don't mind, that is?'

'I'd welcome your company.'

They met Al as they walked up the drive to Esherwood. 'Mayne told us how things went,' he said cheerfully. 'I couldn't believe my ears at what Crossley done to you.'

In the kitchen Mayne was waiting for them. It was Judith he spoke to. 'Are you all right?'

'Yes. Shocked, but getting it all sorted out in my head now. I have to see the children before I do anything else.'

'Of course. You'll be staying on here, continuing to work for me?'

'Yes. Thank you.'

'Good. I'll get back to work now.' He went off towards the dining room.

Miss Peters watched him go then smiled at her companion. 'He'll be courting you before the end of the year.'

'But he's an Esher and I'm . . . nobody now.'

'Rubbish. You're a capable woman and this is 1945. We've won a war against a tyrant and now we'll all be rebuilding our lives. Give things time to settle down, my dear. It'll be a ten-day wonder, then people will find someone else to gossip about. No one with any sense will blame you.'

'Do you think so?'

'Of course I do. Then later, when Mayne comes courting, I'd advise you to snap him up as quickly as is respectable. He was a nice lad and he's grown into a very charming young man. And I'm quite sure he loves you.'

She smiled at the blissful expression that brought to the younger woman's face.

Judith walked slowly up the stairs, dreading what she had to do. Hearing low voices coming from the girls' bedroom, she knocked on the door and went inside.

The three of them were there and stopped speaking to stare at her. She couldn't think how to begin.

'Are we safe?' Gillian asked at last.

'Yes. Your father is in prison. Sit down and I'll tell you about it.'

When she'd finished, Ben said angrily, 'Everyone will call us bastards, and I'm ashamed that *he* is my father.'

'Don't be. You did nothing wrong. There's another piece

of news, good news this time. You have another grandfather and Mr Cross is a very nice man. And you have twin half-brothers. They all want to meet you.'

That stopped them dead.

'Really?' Ben asked.

'And they're not like Dad?' Kitty wanted to know.

'They're very nice, perfectly respectable, not at all like your father. We'll invite them over to tea in a week or two.'

When she went to bed she expected to lie awake worrying, but she was worn out. She felt so safe now, so relieved to be free of Doug, that she soon slipped into a dreamless sleep.

EPILOGUE

Two weeks later

Judith took the scones out of the oven, then went out into the garden to cool her heated face. The girls were upstairs, getting ready, trying to look their best for the visit of the Cross family. Ben had gone to the station to meet them.

She stopped as she saw Mayne standing by the old stables, a notebook and pencil in his hand. She hadn't been alone with him since the day of the court hearing, had wondered why he'd been avoiding her.

He shoved the pad into his pocket and came towards her. 'Have you a moment, Judith?'

'Yes. Could we go for a stroll?' She didn't want to stand talking to him in full view of the girls' bedroom window.

She felt shy, didn't know what to say, and Mayne walked in silence, too.

'Let's go and sit in the summerhouse,' he said at last. 'If you have time to chat for a while, that is. I know you're expecting company.'

'They're not due for half an hour, but Ben couldn't sit still, so I let him leave early. I've got everything ready.'

'I'm sure you have. You're an excellent organiser. I've valued your work since that first day Esherwood was handed over to me. You even knew an antiques dealer who could sell some more of my very unlovely ancestors. We sold a couple more paintings yesterday, by the way.'

'I'm so glad. What did your mother say about that?'

'You've seen what she's like, doesn't approve of what I'm doing. I don't go into any details with her.'

'She seems a very unhappy woman.'

'My father isn't the type to make any woman happy, I'm afraid. He's utterly selfish, for all he can be charming at times.'

When they got to the summerhouse, they both smiled at the bench they'd sat on that rainy day.

'Shall we sit here again?' he asked. 'Just for a short time. There's something I'd like to say to you, something personal.'

'Oh?' She sat down, taking care to smooth her skirts, looking down, not daring to face him till she heard what he wanted.

He took her hand. 'I've been talking to Miss Peters, asking her advice. She says to wait, but if I had my way, I'd start courting you now, Judith.'

That made her stare at him. He was looking at her so lovingly that something inside her that had been tight and angry ever since the court hearing began to soften. 'Would you really?' She immediately got annoyed with herself. What an inane thing to say!

'I would indeed. You must have guessed that I'd begun to care for you.'

'I'd wondered, hoped. Only . . . after you heard that I'd been duped by Doug, that I had lived in sin—'

'*You* hadn't committed any sin!'

'Some people seem to think I have. They call my children bastards and me . . . worse. Ben's been in two fights already. It hurts me to see that. So . . . no one would blame you for backing off.'

'As if I would.' He raised her hand to his lips and kissed it gently. 'As if I want to. I haven't changed how I feel about you, dearest Judith. What about you? Do you care for me at all? Or has that man given you a distaste for marriage?'

She could feel herself flushing, but was determined not to be silly about this, not if he really meant what he had just said. Gathering all her courage together, she told the simple truth. 'I love you, Mayne. Very much indeed.'

His smile lit up the darkness inside her heart, made the world suddenly seem a brighter, more hopeful place.

'That's wonderful. May I kiss you, Judith?'

He didn't wait for her to speak but took her shy smile as a yes and pulled her into his arms, kissing her till she was breathless, then holding her close and resting his head against hers. 'I love you so much, Judith.'

'I love you too, Mayne. I tried not to. There are such differences between us. You're an Esher and I'm—'

'A wonderful, brave woman. The differences don't matter, Judith. I didn't fight a war to go back to the same narrow way of living.'

They sat close together for a while, then he sighed and pulled away. 'We mustn't show our love for a while, not till people have grown used to your new status. But in two or three months . . . As soon as Miss Peters says it's all right . . . We'll do the whole thing properly and I shall come a-courting.'

She raised her hand to caress his cheek. 'I'll wait impatiently for her permission. But she's right. She's such a wise woman. We have to tread carefully, for the children's sake. And for your sake, too.'

He looked at his wristwatch and sighed. 'We'd better go back. One more kiss. It'll have to last a while.'

Afterwards, she walked sedately back to the big house beside him, but in her heart she was dancing, joy singing through her.

It wouldn't be easy, but things were going to work out for the two of them, she was suddenly quite sure of it.

ABOUT THE AUTHOR

Anna Jacobs grew up in Lancashire and emigrated to Australia, but she returns each year to the UK to see her family and do research, something she loves. She is addicted to writing and she figures she'll have to live to be 120 at least to tell all the stories that keep popping up in her imagination and nagging her to write them down. She's also addicted to her own hero, to whom she's been happily married for many years.

CONTACT ANNA

Anna is always delighted to hear from readers and can be contacted via the internet.

Anna has her own web page, with details of her books, some behind-the-scenes information that is available nowhere else and the first chapters of her books to try out, as well as a picture gallery. You can also buy some of her ebooks from the 'shop' on the web page. Go to:
www.annajacobs.com

Anna can be contacted by email at
anna@annajacobs.com

You can also find Anna on Facebook at
www.facebook.com/AnnaJacobsBooks

If you'd like to receive an email newsletter about Anna and her books every month or two, you are cordially invited to join her announcements list. Just email her and ask to be added to the list, or follow the link from her web page.

Don't miss the next book in
Anna Jacobs' heart-warming
Rivenshaw
saga:

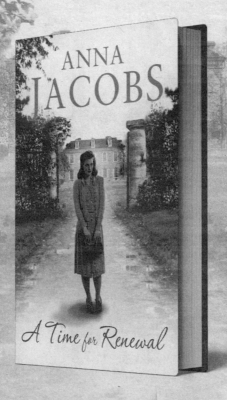

ANNA
JACOBS

A Time for Renewal

Out in hardcover in September 2015

Beautiful new editions of the Gibson family saga now available